SHADOW OF A DOUBT

SHADOW OF A DOUBT

A Mirabel Sinclair Mystery

JEFF REYNOLDS

Trollbreath Creations

First Printing, 2021

Shadow of a Doubt is a published work from the deep, dark vaults of Trollbreath Creations. Remember: if it's stinky, it must be Trollbreath.

ISBN: 978-1-7377016-0-6 (paperback)
ISBN: 978-1-7377016-1-3 (ebook)

Cover design by Bookfly Covers

Contents

*To Jennifer, who helped me realize dreams are
truths to be nurtured and pursued, made manifest.
In love, as in writing.*

I

Mr. Green

All I wanted to do was get some shut eye, but the phone rang. I considered ignoring it and going back to sleep. But I'd never learned how to ignore that sound, even when it barked at me in the middle of the night. It didn't help my mood I had to run downstairs to answer it, hoping to get to it before it woke Ingrid as well. Jacob would ignore it, but he was a ghost, and the dead don't answer phones.

"Hello," I said tersely. Exhaustion prevented me from hiding my anger at whoever had interrupted my chance to collar a nod.

"Lucky's dead," my boss said. His voice sounded tinny over the phone line static.

I blinked sleepiness from my lashes, his words waking me like a slap of cold water. "Lucky Gambini?"

I needn't have asked. I only knew one person he called Lucky. In my defense, I'd worked until well after ten o'clock processing the film from his last stakeout. All I had to show for a night's work—besides exhaustion and a chipped fingernail—was a stack of grainy photos that would be pornographic in thirty territories and the Republic of Texas. Not to mention the final nail in the coffin of a client's failed marriage.

"Yeah, that Lucky," he said drily.

"Sorry Mr. Templeton," I said. Well, shit. Bad enough I'd been churlish to him, but did I have to go and do it after his closest friend had died? I felt the flush of guilt staining my cheeks. Clearly more important things were happening in the world than my lack of sleep.

"Forget it, Mirabel," he said. "I need you to do me a favor."

"Sure, name it."

"I need you to meet with a client for me while I take care of things."

"Right now?" I'd repeatedly requested a case of my own for over a year, only to be turned down time and again. Now he served it up on a silver platter, but he couldn't have picked a stranger time. The clock on the wall read two thirty. The darkness outside the window confirmed the clock's grasp of the lateness of the hour.

"No, this afternoon at Patapsco reservoir. The north turn-out. Fifteen hundred hours."

I converted naval time to standard in my head, while trying not to be angry he hadn't needed to call until morning. Mr. Templeton was nothing if not oblivious to time. "Three o'clock, got it."

"Good. I wouldn't ask, Mira, but—"

"—It's no problem," I interrupted. I'd waited a long time for a chance to show him I could do more than develop his films and research his clients. That I could run a case on my own without needing help. My sleep-deprived brain decided this might be the op-portunity I'd been seeking. No way I'd pass it up or let him change his mind.

"Thanks," he said, and hung up without saying goodbye. I placed the receiver back in its cradle and turned to walk up the stairs to my bedroom, but Ingrid had already started down. She wore black pajama bottoms and a matching top, a blue, silky robe pulled loosely over her shoulders. Even half-asleep she looked gorgeous. Ingy had style and class, not to mention smarts and magical talent, and I couldn't look at her but love her. Not that I'd ever let her know.

"Sorry I woke you," I said.

"Phone woke me, not you; it's the person on the other end who should be apologizing. Let me guess; Templeton."

"How'd you know?"

"Who else would call you in the middle of the night? The rest of us like to sleep."

I snorted. "Yeah, it was Mr. Templeton. He's got a job for me."

"Now?" She waved at the window. "Mira, it's almost three in the morning."

"Not right now. Later today."

She tossed her hands up and walked over to the liquor cabinet. "I swear that man hasn't got a lick of sense in that swollen head of his. If it wasn't for the fedora, his brains would fall out." She opened the door and took out the bottle of bourbon. "So, what's the job?"

"Meeting a client about a case for the agency." I gave her the details, as much to seat them firmly in my own memory as share them.

She poured herself a glass as she listened, nodding. When she turned, she leaned back against the wall, crossing one arm over her waist and holding her liquor with the other hand. "I'm sorry to hear about his partner. That lets him off the hook for waking us. As for the meeting; it's at the reservoir? Well, that's a public spot but private enough. Means the guy wants to put you at ease but doesn't want to be overheard. Should be safe, but you take your gun, you hear? And a couple of those charms I spelled up for you last month."

I nodded. She sometimes seemed more protective of me than Mr. Templeton did. Which I didn't mind, although I wish it meant something more. Mr. Templeton did it because he didn't think I would ever be good enough to take a case on my own. He saw a young woman, not an adult who'd become a capable detective in her own right. Ingy did it because she was a friend, and that's what friends do for each other when you didn't have family to care for you. She'd wound up at the orphanage because her parents had died; I'd wound up there because mine had abandoned me. Didn't matter the reasons. We ended up best of friends, and that would do. I loved both of them far more than I'd ever be able to tell them, if in different ways.

"Is he finally letting you off your leash? I bet you can practically smell the opportunity."

She asked the same question I'd been myself asking, and damned if I didn't love her all the more for it. Always getting in my head. I didn't have an answer, either. But with Lucky occupying his time, I had an opening. A chance to finally prove I could do this work. To be more than a gopher, researcher, photo developer. Or the erstwhile pick pocket I'd been when he met me. To be a private investigator like he'd been training me. "I hope so."

"Hope so? No, you *make* it so. You're ready, damn it. You make sure he knows it." She emptied her glass and left it on the liquor cabinet. "I'm going back to bed. Get some rest if you can, you're going to need it."

"Thanks."

She touched my shoulder on her way past and left me standing alone in the parlor. I pondered the situation for a few more minutes. Never good enough. I wanted to *feel* good enough for the job. Good enough for Benjamin Francis Templeton. Good enough to impress Ingrid. I imagined myself in a fedora, my gun tucked in a shoulder holster, the night surrounding me as I bent to pick up a clue. The killer lurked in the dark somewhere, and I was hot on their trail.

"Stop day dreaming and get back to bed so you can do some night dreaming." I walked up to my bedroom, my long nightgown swishing against my legs. The wood floors chilled my feet, and I welcomed the warmth under the blankets. But I couldn't turn my brain off as I lay under the covers. I imagined the meeting in my head, thought on what I'd say. How I would respond to questions they might ask. I made and discarded a dozen plans; ran through my list of items I'd need to take. Then, to be thorough, I ran through client meetings I'd gone to with Mr. Templeton and examined the questions he'd asked for nuggets of advice I could bring with me. The different techniques he used to get information.

What I didn't do was fall asleep.

With a sigh of disappointment, I gave up on mister sandman. I slid out of bed and headed for the bathroom to clean up and get ready for the long day ahead.

***

The early wake-up call guaranteed I got there long before the meeting. The lack of sleep meant I'd weighed down my stomach with large quantities of coffee to stay awake.

I patted the side of my coat and confirmed the comforting weight of my revolver resting in its holster, tucked up against my side. "Why am I always early," I said.

There was no one to hear me; my car sat alone in the otherwise vacant turn around located next to the reservoir. I kicked at the rocks pebbling the parking area, and stuffed my hands in the pockets of my coat to keep from glancing at my wristwatch again. I had a slim pulp novel to keep boredom at bay, but anticipation had me too wound up to read. My fingers twitched as though reaching for a cigarette, but I'd been trying to quit and had none.

I turned my attention to the lake and saw fall the way it should be. Not the ugly falls of Baltimore, with muted browns and dingy yellows. The leaves in Baltimore didn't fall until almost December, some holding on until January. An industrial, slow, tired fall. Baltimore was a working port city of steam clippers and steel mills, tenuously tied to the other twenty-nine regions of the United Territories of Coventine by iron rails, concrete roads, and airship routes. It seemed to regret its autumnal season, as though the idea of shedding its summer trappings in a burst of glamorous color was a ridiculous concept better left to less productive cities.

This lake recalled the splendor of a proper autumn and coaxed its trees into vibrant displays. Brilliant reds and flashing yellows drew my eyes in an explosion of color. I nodded my head in appreciation of the dryads and naiads who ran the local chapters of flora and fauna.

I turned at the sound of an engine and watched as a black car pulled into the parking lot at the exact time Mr. Templeton had indicated, a precision I found enviable. Mr. Green's Caillouet looked shiny and nearly new, a muscular vehicle that dwarfed my Model D. Gravel crunched under its tires. It seemed fitting, given the size of the troll who slid from behind the steering wheel.

He walked like he knew how to handle himself. He wore a long black trench coat cinched at the waist. A bowler hat the size of a washtub rested on his head, and his eyes were covered by dark glasses. The spectacles and hat did little to hide his features. Not that there was anything wrong with being a troll, but most didn't flaunt it given the bigotry from white folks. His skin appeared green-tinged, with the odd hairy wart plastered to it. He jammed his right hand into a coat pocket, but I could see white lines of crisscrossing scars on the knuckles of his left hand, which held a lit cigar. That suggested he was used to using his fists to do his talking.

I realized my gun wouldn't do much good if I needed protection. I'd loaded the snub-nosed revolver with silver jacketed, cold iron slugs, the ends scratched with a holy glyph of warding, but trolls had amazing powers of healing. Getting shot would probably only anger him without doing any lasting harm. If I had to fight, I'd have been better served with lighter fluid and a zippo. Or a can of gasoline and some matches. Maybe a nice, sturdy torch.

He stopped next to me and stared out over the still, gray waters, puffing on his big cigar. The smoke curled in a wreath around his melon-sized head.

"Nice," he said, his voice a rough growl. "Nice spot. S'good, isn't it, Miz' Sinclair? Baltimore's drab, but this reminds me of being back in the old country."

"I suppose if you enjoy nature and such," I said, playing down the view I'd been admiring. "Beats watching dirty airships flying over a shabby harbor. So, what can I do you for? Why did you want to meet?"

"I wanted to meet your boss, Templeton. He sent a girl instead."

I tried not to get too angry at his comment, though by rights he'd just insulted me. I was twenty-six, not a girl. I'd been a police officer as well, if briefly. He'd done it to get under my skin, and it had. He looked relaxed, confident; his eyes fixed on the distant shoreline as he puffed on his cigar. No tension in his body, no shifting of his eyes beneath his dark shades. Nothing that prickled my worry other than his trollness.

"He had a lot to do and figured I could handle this."

"I hear Templeton can find things. He 'sposed to be a detective; summit like that. Right?" He flicked an ash off the end of the cigar, and swung around to face me. I noticed the bulge inside his coat near his left breast. An involuntary spasm passed through my body as my muscles tensed. Relax, take a breath. Ingy said he wanted to meet here because it's public, and Mr. Templeton wouldn't have sent me if he had any reason to worry. He'd probably read the signs and portents before calling me to assure my safety. Reassuring and galling at the same time.

"If they are lawfully owned and the proper spiritual assignations have been signed and attested to, then yes," I said. "We have some talents in that area." I leaned against the wooden fence bordering the reservoir, my arms crossed as I waited for his reply. I wanted to appear all casual intent, but my muscles tightened and a tingle of danger danced across my nerves.

"It's good pay."

I'd stuffed my small clasp in one of the pockets of my jacket, and I already knew without looking what it contained: two dollars in ones and a little loose change; my driver's license; an expired book of A&P stamps. Maybe a moth or two, which would fly out when I opened it like in those cartoons that played before the main feature at the Bijou. The agency struggled, like so many others during the Depression. There wasn't a single city or town in thirty territories where things had come up smelling of roses. We needed the work.

"What's the job?"

"Something was lost. I'm hiring you to find it." He took another drag, the end of his cigar lighting up his face, a gnarled vision in scarlet. He turned back towards the lake, waiting for my response.

I tried to remember the questions I'd planned to ask. The way Mr. Templeton would guide a contact so he could puzzle through a problem. Why would a troll hire a human agency? That one I could easily answer. They'd only hire humans if they were expecting to deal with other humans because people got twitchy around non-humans who packed heat. Then again, people got twitchy around anyone who didn't look like them, whether trolls or elves or humans of a different color. People were generally assholes. I needed more information.

"What was stolen?"

"What do you know about trolls, Sinclair?"

"What I read in the dailies, and some of the pulps when I'm bored. Big. Stupid. Piano movers." I knew better, but tit for tat. Maybe insulting him back would put him off his game, though I'd strayed beyond simple insults into racist doggerel, and felt immediately ashamed. This might not have been my wisest move. I gave up two feet of height and three or four hundred pounds of weight to him. But anyone working for the Templeton Agency would have been smaller than Mr. Green, so it was a moot point. I wanted to get a response, to unease him the way he'd so easily uneased me.

His eyes turned back to me once more and his brow furrowed under the brim of his giant hat. Other than that, he went back to studying the lake. I pressed on.

"I heard some trolls work with the blood boys and the mob these days. Whipping up a race war for the elves? Or are you breaking knee caps to collect gambling debts?"

He grinned. It didn't improve his appearance. He pulled something from his pocket. His baseball glove sized hand held a box, small and delicate, made of dark wood, mahogany perhaps, inlaid with gold filigree along the edges. The middle of the lid was speckled with gold leaf in the shape of a skeleton key. He passed one finger over the key shape, and the box dissolved, leaving behind a scroll in his hand. He held out for me to take.

I examined the scroll for hidden symbols or covert auras, running magic through my fingers, searching the tangled threads of power that connected everything. A simple spell; not considered *acceptable* magic, but quick and effective. The kind of magic I found easy. It would have taken longer to rely on Ingy's magical charms, good as they were. And oh, she was very good at her work. You don't go from the orphanage to being tutored by Lucinda Falkenreath if you weren't. I'd save those for another time, though. Truthfully, I cherished all her little gifts and often found myself reluctant to part with them.

No tingles came, nothing burst into flames. I reached out and took the worn, brown sheet from him. Unrolled, the material crackled under my fingers, smelling musty. The writing had faded, but I could see it once had been red. Perhaps blood red. The language was unreadable to me. Trollish, not one I'd been well versed in. I could pull out a word here and there if pressed; mostly words I'd learned from my friend, Lugnut. It said something about *shadow* and *stolen*, but I couldn't get much more from the text. Dead center in the middle of the scroll sat the image of a bird, large and white, floating on a pool of blue color. Little more than an outline with few details, but easy enough to decipher.

"What is that, a duck? Swan?"

"Goose." He dropped the remains of his cigar on the ground and crushed it under a massive, well-polished black shoe. A last wisp of smoke curled around the toe.

"What do you want with a goose?"

He shrugged. "Not me. The one who hired me is the one wanting."

"Why would your employer want a goose? Dinner?"

He removed his glasses and lifted the brim of his hat, giving me a better look at his face. His black eyes held mine, and I took a step back. But he held no hostility in his gaze. The expression seemed worried. Maybe even a little sad.

"That there is the most important magical artifact in existence. People have loved it, coveted it, fought over it. Hell, do you know how many wars were started by that thing? Even you fucking racists have written stories 'bout it." He reached into his inner jacket pocket and pulled out another cigar. A silver lighter appeared, and he puffed on the cigar until a cherry glow winked at the end.

I stared at the ancient scroll, the back of my head itching with ideas and conclusions, already guessing what he would say.

"That goose lays gold eggs," he said.

Jackpot, I thought to myself, and I rolled the scroll back up. "I'll call you soon as we make a decision and we'll draw up a contract."

The golden goose. What if we didn't take the job and someone else found it? Imagine what a person could do with unending amounts of money. They could buy anything they wanted. Or anyone. They could fund an army, and the research to create devastating new weapons They could crash the world economy by flooding the market with cheap gold and devaluing everyone's currency. Endless, unlimited power easily obtained.

But for me, the personal outweighed those unsettling thoughts. This case would be a chance to prove myself. A chance to put the agency on solid financial footing. A chance to finally show Mr. Templeton what I was capable of.

A chance to mean something to someone.

I tried to hand the scroll back, but he shook his head. "You hold onto it. If he don't take the job, I'll come get it. Maybe try'n talk Templeton into changing his mind. I hear he's the best. Maybe not such a face like you."

Heat rose in my cheeks as I blushed in embarrassment. "Look, I'm sorry about what I said. I'm not a racist."

"Yeah, sure you're not. Go on, get out of here, Sinclair."

I waited to say more, but he ignored me. I turned and walked to my car. Elated for the chance to take on a case that could make us solvent. Pissed at myself for acting the fool and trying to get a rise out of him when I knew better. Well, I had plenty of time ahead to fix my mistake and make it up to Mr. Green, because this case would be mine.

2

No One is Ready

"Hey there, doll," Petunia said from behind the receptionist's desk when I arrived at the office. The Templeton Agency held the lease to a fourth floor suite in an old brick office building off Light Street in Baltimore. It perched precariously over the harbor, as though it planned to slide into the water at any moment. Not bad views from the rear, which served as the reception area, although the walk up four steep flights could be grueling on hot summer days.

Petunia sat sideways to her desk, her legs crossed as she filed her nails. A blue polka dot dress covered her petite body to a point below her knees. Her hair had been perfectly coiffed as always, with long, blonde ringlets that fell across her shoulders setting off her green eyes. The typewriter clacked away behind her, the keys moving up and down on their own, the carriage return hammering home to feed the next line as though pressed by invisible hands.

"Is he in?" I asked, jerking my thumb at Mr. Templeton's door.

"Yeah, but he's with someone. She'll be out in a moment." She leaned forward and lowered her voice. "He's half a bottle deep and still going, you better catch him while he's able to stand up straight, toots."

I sighed and nodded, and Petunia gave me her best *he's having a tough day* smile. She turned back to finish her nails by blowing across them and waving her hands in the air like a demented ground control specialist guiding an airship into its hangar. The typewriter kept banging away as the inner door opened and a woman walked out.

She was tall and willowy, with a long, pale-green dress over her thin figure. Her eyes were big and green, set into a face that would have done well on the big screen, all Myrna Loy meets Hedy Lamarr. Skin as white as snow, and black hair running down over her shoulders flat and straight. Her hair covered her ears but I thought she might be elven, from the upright way she walked to the ethereal beauty of her face. She closed the inner office door behind her, nodded at Petunia who gave her a smile, ignored my presence entirely, and swept out of the office like a queen leaving her throne room. I wondered who she was. Another client? Another chance to bring in some bucks? Hopefully. I gave Mr. Templeton a respectable thirty seconds after her departure to compose himself, then knocked on his door.

"Come in," came his muffled reply.

I opened the door and stepped into the room, closing it behind me. I hung my black jacket on the coat rack next to his long, grey trench. Then I sat in a creaky chair, slouching, my arms dangling over the armrests. I couldn't suppress a sigh of relief now that I could unwind.

In front of the window rested an ancient desk made of dark wood. It slouched on squat legs, the front decorated with a carved relief of leaves and vines. The feet were shaped like bear paws, large and curled, the claws hidden beneath the pads. A metal desk lamp illuminated the surface, with stacks of papers on one side and a black rotary on the other. Next to the phone sat a large bottle of dark liquid, less than half full, and a small tumbler glass, almost empty. A yellow, metal file cabinet took up a corner, and several pictures hung in frames on the wall. He kept his office neat as a pin, though sparsely furnished.

Mr. Templeton eased back in his chair. He'd undone his white shirt at the collar, his black tie loosened beneath a square chin bedecked with five o'clock shadow. He kept it too warm in here, despite the autumn chill outside. A ceiling fan lazily stirred the closed air, and dark circles stained the pits of his shirt. He rubbed his blue eyes with one hand as he reached for the glass with the other, downing the rest of the bourbon before pouring himself another shot. He appeared exhausted, the lines in his cheeks and forehead deeper than I remembered. In front of him on the desk sat the morning edition of the Baltimore Sun.

"To your health," he said, raising the glass towards me. He took a long pull, nearly draining it. His cheeks were not flushed, which in my experience meant he was either sober, or had been drinking long enough today it wouldn't matter either way. "You met the contact?"

"Yeah. You didn't tell me he was a troll." He didn't respond except to grunt, so I continued. "I haven't run a background check on him yet."

"Curious thing, a troll hiring a human agency. What next? Pixies typing?" He gave a thin smile that failed to touch his eyes and glanced at the door. "I better keep it down, Petunia's the best secretary I've had, and I'd hate to lose her."

"You're damn straight, you big jerk," came Petunia's retort, muffled by the closed door. We glanced at each other before we burst into a brief round of laughter that trickled away, our voices stilled like pebbles disappearing under the surface of a lake. Mr. Templeton's somber mood infected me, and I found myself thinking of the handful of people I'd known who had died. The bustle of sound that leaked through the closed window reminded me the world continued to revolve. For some anyway.

He remained quiet, and I wondered if he thought of his partner, the loss of a friend. I couldn't find words to comfort him. Ben Templeton had been around the block more than once; far be it for me to give him a comforting shoulder, a woman twenty years younger and with a tenth of his experience. He stared into the glass he held, plumbing the depth of his liquor for answers to questions that had none, and he knew it. Questions I hadn't even thought to ask yet. I examined the wall behind his graying hair, the picture of him with his old pals from the third precinct.

"Looking at the picture?" He stared at me as he rocked back in his chair, leaning it on its rear legs, his blue eyes intent on my face, studying me, sizing me up.

"I was remembering what you used to tell me about him and all the trouble the two of you got into when you served together. All the times you thought you'd wind up dead." I'd heard the stories plenty of times, along with others. Twenty years serving on the police force left him with lots of stories to share. The one story he never shared was why he gave it all up.

"So was I," he replied, and slid the paper across the desk until it dangled on the edge of the scratched, wooden top. I grabbed it before it could fall. He'd turned to the obituaries, a neat crease folding it in half lengthwise.

"Still checking the death notices every day to make sure your alive?" One of his peculiarities. I didn't really understand it. Part and parcel of the man I worked for.

He nodded. "I'd hate to wake up and find myself dead, visiting with Chancy and Mr. Sticks. That would be a wicked pisser."

"Who?"

"The welcome committee waiting for us at the end of all things." He waved his hand in the air. "Never mind, it's not important."

A picture dominated the top left. The man in it smiling, handsome, though at this size his face was an impressionist's study in inky dots. His hat pulled down, hiding all but a wisp of light-colored hair, and his crooked lips painted a roguish grimace that didn't detract from his affable features.

"Lucky's obituary," I said, stating the obvious.

Ben nodded. "Vincent. We all called him Lucky on account of how many times he got shot at and lived to walk another beat."

I scanned the obit, letting my eyes pick out various phrases. *Lieutenant Vincent Gambini of the Third Precinct . . . died tragically . . . car accident.* The entry was short, although it garnered the top of the page and rated a picture since he had been a former police officer. He was pre-deceased by his mother and his sister; survived by his wife, Lucille Gambini, and his father, Henry. No children were listed, a small blessing in a tragic death.

"I never met him."

He shrugged and finished his drink, wiping his mouth with the back of his hand. "You wouldn't have. He was in the hospital recovering from another gunshot wound when I grabbed you on the docks picking pockets."

"Right," I said and grimaced. "I was quite the master criminal, getting busted at fourteen by the first flatfoot who caught me nicking."

"You're lucky I'd gone a little soft in the head by then and Sister Mary Margaret had a space for you. Not many eggs get a break like that. She loved you, you know." He paused; eyes distant. "She said you were her rock. That you had such potential."

I shrugged. "She thought Delores Estes had potential, too. Look where she ended up."

"Well, she said it a lot, but she was right about you if not Delores. Still, it could have been worse for poor Miss Estes."

"She got busted for armed robbery, murder of a bank guard, and was re-arrested while out on bail for trying to bribe a witness. She's doing ten to twenty in the Baltimore jail for women. Oh, and she's pregnant. And you think it could have been worse?"

"She's not dead, is she?"

"You have a point." I placed the paper back on the desk. "I'm sorry, Mr. Templeton." That seemed the right thing to say, if not nearly enough. Platitudes seemed meaningless when the scars ran deep, like applying topical ointment to a bullet wound. But I'd been taught to do the polite thing, even when it felt wrong. Sister Mary Margaret had drilled it into us orphans, and God help the ones who ignored her lessons.

He didn't meet my eyes, staring at the glass in his hands instead. "How many times do I need to tell you, you can call me Ben? You're not the scared little scrap of girl I met down on the wharf twelve years ago, Mira."

"You know I can't help it."

He sighed and bent over, pulled a second glass from his bottom drawer and added an inch of liquor to both, draining the bottle. He tossed the empty bottle into the open drawer before closing it. He pushed one glass across the desk towards me and lifted the other.

"To Lucky," he said, and waited for me to respond.

"To Lucky," I replied, and took a short pull. He never paid for the good stuff. It burned going down my throat, but I held back a cough as the bourbon slid into my gut. I couldn't stop my eyes from watering, though.

He placed his empty glass on the desk and leaned back. "I'm going to see his widow. Lucille. She's a good woman. Lucky always thought she was the luckiest break he ever had. You might have seen them; they're parishioners at Saint Brendan's. Were. You should come to church once in a while. You don't have to believe, but it's good for the soul. Father Gregory is one of the good ones."

Church. He kept bringing it up, and I kept avoiding it. The endless sermons about the evils of elves and trolls, gnomes, pixies, all the other races, how they lacked an immortal soul. The not-subtle implication blacks were another race, too, as well as the great nations of peoples who lived here before we came. Brown skin, differently shaped eyes, it didn't matter the physical categories. Anyone not human, not white, were included. Although yes, father Gregory didn't preach such racist tripe, nor had sister Mary Margaret or the nuns within Saint Brendan's orphanage. But I avoided them all on general principle. Ingy believed in a world spirit, and that appealed to me more.

I opted to change the subject. "Who was the dame?"

"Hmm?" he said, and glanced and the door as though trying to remember. "Oh, her. Hiems. A friend from my youth. Librarian. She was in town and stopped by to pay her respects about Lucky." He fiddled with the glass on the desk and stared at it as though he could find answers in a bottle of bourbon. "What did Mr. Green want to hire us for?"

"He's searching for the goose that laid the golden egg. Said he was sent to hire us to find it. I'm not sure what the real motive is, but there's a story there. I suspect I can peel it apart like an onion and it'll make us cry. I'm ready to get started."

He leaned back and watched a reflection of sunlight play across the ceiling. "There's a lot going on with Lucky's death. I'll have to give the case some thought. We could use the business, though."

I tried not to sound eager. "I can do it."

I sounded eager.

He shook his head. "No."

"Come on Mr. Templeton, I'm ready."

"No one is ever ready, Mira. Not really."

I sat up straight, leaning forward in the chair. Make it so. You're damned ready. Ingy's words provided courage. "I've studied hard. I was near the top of my class at the police academy and the first female to graduate." We both knew that hadn't panned out, but I pressed on. "I've got excellent research skills, and can dig up information no one else has access to. I've tagged along with you on a dozen cases in the past year, you trusted me to handle meeting a client, and even you say I'm a better shot than you ever were. Let me take this so you can focus on your friend."

"You're a better shot than me when it's stationary targets, not when someone else is shooting back. And the answer is still no."

"Why not?"

"Because I said."

"Come on, I'm ready."

"No, you're not!" He slammed his hand down on the desk.

I jerked in the chair, a flush growing in my cheeks. He'd never yelled at me before, not once. Not even when he'd arrested me on that day long ago. I shrank in my seat, feeling very small.

"You're not ready. You think this is all fun and games, a mystery to solve, some Nancy Drew shit. You've got no appreciation of how tough it is, the long hours you put in, the things you give up. The things you have to do. What you lose."

He reached into his pants pocket and pulled out something shiny, rubbing it with his fingers. His Saint Brendan's medallion, the worn-down picture of the saint standing in front of a lighthouse, a ship cradled under his arm with a cloak pulled around his robed body. He stood, watching his fingers play across the metal ridges, and then glanced at me.

"It's a hard job. You do stuff that's not pretty, stuff that's not easy to live with." He rested a hand on my shoulder for a moment. "Give it some time; with a little more experience, you'll be ready soon enough."

I nodded, not daring to mouth the reply that hung in my throat, not meeting his gaze. Sending me out to meet a client on my own provided the first glimmer I might be able to take on a case of my own soon, and he'd pulled the rug out from under me. Was it because of Mr. Green? Probably not, he knew I Lugnut and I were friends and I understood trolls. So, what? Not ready. You're not good enough. It hurt too much. Ingy would be disappointed, which made everything worse. I mutely accepted his decision even as I mocked myself for not fighting harder.

"Find out what you can about Mr. Green and this squab hunt of his, and check back with me before you take any further steps," he said. He pulled his trenchcoat off the rack and thrust his arms into the sleeves, cinching the belt at the waist. "I've got to go see a widow now." He grabbed his fedora and left the office, the door banging against the wall when he thrust it open.

I sat there for a long time after he left, staring at the picture on the wall behind his desk.

3

Where the Heart Is

The row home Ingy and I rented lay in the shadow of the recently closed National Brewery building that towered on the hill a block away. A giant Natty Boh sign topped the building, the dapper symbol of better days for the part of Baltimore called Highlandtown. His glowing, neon red eye guided me home and cast a hellish light over the dilapidated brewery. I didn't understand why someone didn't turn it off. Baltimore Gas and Electric should have shut it down as soon as the business closed shop, but the garish thing kept blazing high over the city, never sleeping, an eternal watcher. The red glow only made nearby homes look shabbier.

We were lucky to get this place. Not only were single women rarely allowed to live anywhere outside of rented rooms in boarding houses for girls, most white landlords in Baltimore wouldn't rent to blacks. Oh, they'd rent to me, a good Catholic white woman, especially with a former officer like Mr. Templeton as a reference. But I couldn't afford rent on my own, and Ingrid didn't pass most landlord's color test. She'd been my closest friend at the orphanage, and

I couldn't imagine having anyone else as a roommate. It was the two of us, or the boarding house, and those were segregated as well, so we'd be in different parts of the city. I couldn't stand that thought. Ingrid had agreed when I'd suggested it, which thrilled me.

Mrs. Bargeman seemed more tolerant than most, though, and gave Ingrid the nod of approval after Mr. Templeton's recommendation. "Well, as long as Ben Templeton vouches for the two of you girls, you can rent the place," she said, giving Ingrid a long look-see that suggested she had her doubts and had decided to be charitable. "I haven't forgotten all he did for this neighborhood when he was a police man. But you will act like young ladies, not wild hooligans, and you will remember the rules."

The rules were a list of thirty-two *Thou Shalt Nots* she provided us in triplicate when she handed over the keys. It felt more than a little demeaning, but we smiled and accepted her word as house law. She made us sign one copy then folded it in half, tucking it into the pocket of her apron. The other two copies were for us.

A young maple tree had grown out of an empty square spot in the sidewalk in front of our door, the only one of its kind on the block. Like most Baltimore trees this fall, its leaves were almost all a uniform dingy brown. But a single branch near the top sported bright red foliage for the first time since Ingrid and I had moved in. All the love, the watering, the little charms Ingy had hung from the branches, had done their work.

"Nice work, Emery," I said, patting its silvery bark as I passed. He needed a good pruning, but I didn't have the energy. I walked up our dingy granite steps and slipped inside.

Music drifted across the front parlor in front of me from the direction of the dining room. The music grew louder as I approached the basement door, strains of piano and clarinets, the thump of a standup bass, something bluesy. A vocalist joined the instruments.

I recognized Billie Holiday's throaty singing style, a song about moonlight and moonbeams and magic.

In the basement, Ingy lay on her back on the couch, one leg hung over the worn armrest, holding a book in her hands over her head. She'd washed her updo away, and her long, dark hair spilled around her head. She favored black clothing to go with her black tresses, tonight a long skirt and matching top. Several charms dangled from leather thongs around her neck, spilling across her chest and the pillow propping her head.

She took my breath away. For a second, I forgot all my worries. Only a second. But those seconds are the best seconds of your life and can stretch from the start of time until its very ending. You have to love and savor those moments.

She glanced at me before returning to the words in her book. "You meet the guy?"

I eased into an old chair at the side of the desk, kicking my shoes off. "Yeah, I met him. He was a troll."

Ingy grunted in response. "Bunch of jokers, with a few exceptions like Lugnut. So, what's going to happen now? Is Templeton going to take on the case? I'd think with all he's got to deal with right now, he'd hand it off to you. You're best suited for it and he's in no emotional shape to be objective."

"Mr. Templeton is thinking it over." I let my voice trail off, feeling the weight of my disappointment as I stared across the room at the painting of an elegant couple dancing in front of a fountain. We'd found it in one of the never-ending piles of debris that showed up on the streets after an eviction. Possessions the families didn't want or couldn't carry with them, left behind to be picked over and carried away by neighbors who had the better end of luck during the depression. The woman's face stared at me as the man held her in his arms with his back towards the viewer, and I thought her eyes seemed disappointed in me as well. *You could have tried harder*, her stare said.

"You asked again, didn't you," Ingy said, with that way she had of getting into my head. "And he said you weren't ready. Again."

I shrugged, even though she wasn't watching, wasting an opportunity to practice acting nonchalant. "I'm as ready as I'm going to be. I can do this."

"You should have fought harder."

"I did. He's holding me back."

Ingy turned away from the book and looked at me. "Holding you back? Is that what you think he's doing? Sometimes you don't understand people, Mira."

"Well what about you? You hide behind your books and snap at people who are telling you they had a miserable day." I felt bad saying it, but I was pretty sore at how I'd left things with Mr. Templeton and it loosened my tongue. I shouldn't have snapped at her.

"See, that's exactly what I mean. You make it all about me, and don't even notice it was about you. I know who I am. I understand me, and I understand why, and I'm okay with that. You don't understand Templeton, and you don't know who you are. Not yet."

"I know. I'm sorry, I didn't mean what I said. But right now, I feel like a sidekick. He's the Crimson Avenger, I'm Wing."

"Yeah, because you don't fight for what you want," Ingy said. When I turned away, she added, "Sorry, forget it, I'm suffering from sobriety and a lack of liquidity. Spell work hasn't paid much lately and the charms don't sell as good right now. Brothers can't be sparing a dime, you know. But if you want what you want, you have to grab it and hold onto it. Make him say yes. He'll give in, trust me."

Sound advice. One day I'd be strong enough to take it. I wriggled my toes and looked past my foot to the dingy green carpet beneath, my eyes drawn to an oval-shaped stain that often reminded me of Australia. "Kangaroos."

"Sharks," Ingrid replied, instantly taking up the game we'd invented when we discovered the carpet.

"Teeth."

"Bite."

"Flesh."

"Eat."

"Blood."

"Love," she finished.

The word game faded into silence. I sat glumly, knowing I had work to do, but unable to find the motivation for it. Ingrid dropped the book over her head onto the floor and swung her legs off the couch to stand. She stretched, the kinks in her back and neck popping like tiny revolver shots. "Are you going to the Undertow?"

She waited for my nearly imperceptible nod as I made up my mind on the spot. Maybe if I buried myself in research, I could still the voices that nagged me. Mr. Templeton would be expecting a full report on Mr. Green's background and the golden goose. Feeling sorry for myself wouldn't put food on the table. Visiting the Undertow would put me in a better frame of mind, too.

"Don't go too deep, don't spend too much time in there, and don't get fooled by a grindy or a spook, you know how those bastards like to play games with the queries. You stay too long in the Undertow, and it's going to smack you hard someday. You keep in mind what Lucinda told us when she drew the portal." She slouched through the doorway leading to the basement kitchen, voice fading as the door closed behind her. "And tell Jacob to stop taking my stuff when I'm not looking or I'll find a crucifix and spear his spectral ass with it when I exorcise him."

"Why don't you tell him?"

"You know damn well he never talks to me," her voice said from the other room. "You're the only one the little thief bothers to talk to."

I sat for a while, staring at the stain on the carpet. I tried to empty my mind of worries and concerns. Not good enough, never good enough. Over it over it interrupted. It reminded me of being a kid on the streets, all those years of feeling unwanted. The only person I could rely on had been myself. Later, I'd come to rely on Ingy and Mr. Templeton.

Mr. Templeton had done so much for me it seemed childish to complain. He had helped me get into the orphanage and off the streets. He had backed me when I applied to the academy even though women were considered unfit to wear the uniform. He stood with me when I graduated, helped me apply for a position with his old precinct. Most importantly, he had offered me a job when being a flatfoot turned into being an object for catcalls and gropes from the officers who thought a woman's place was in the kitchen, not on the streets of Baltimore walking a beat and running down criminals. Punching Halley in the mouth after he tried to kiss me had been satisfying, but I was the one who got busted down to a desk job and, ultimately, quit.

"I knew you couldn't handle the job," Halley had said, leering at me as I packed up my few items in a cardboard box and made my way to the door. "Stick to typing, sweet cheeks. Or better yet, find yourself a swell guy like me and settle down, leave the police work to those better suited to it. I could use three squares and your warm body next to me in bed every night."

My hands had been full or I would have punched him again. Instead, I gave him my sweetest smile, leaned in close as his grin grew, and then kneed him in the groin. His howls of pain and the laughter of some of the other men were all the satisfaction I would get from my brief career as a cop.

Mr. Templeton treated me like an adult, not a little girl. Like a person, not an object. Yet he held me back now, and it was hard not to resent him for it. Twenty-six, and I still reacted to him as though I were a kid.

I rose and walked to the utility room where the furnace stood. A curtained alcove stood to the right of the coal bin, and I pulled the drapes back to reveal a small closet. A copy of the stage bill for *Zou, Zou*, starring Josephine Baker, was pasted on the door. It was Ingrid's favorite film and favorite actress, a reminder of her short-lived stint in community theater. She loved the applause, but hated the throngs of fans who demanded attention when she wasn't on stage.

The tiny room was empty but for dust and a few scurrying insects. On the wall glimmered the pattern, a circular, maze-like shape that was dizzying, ever morphing and changing, like a ball of snakes that moved and shifted with each other, bodies always in motion. A gift from her mentor, Lucinda, on graduating from her tutelage. A membership to the Undertow to help her through the first year of life after she had passed all her tests. Ingy had willingly shared it with me. It had proven itself beyond any repayment I could make.

I stared at it, my mind relaxing as the pattern roiled and coiled. My eyes traced the swirls, following the intricacies of it through the turns and towards the center, though I doubted anyone could draw a path through its convolutions if they tried. Instead I let myself be pulled, stilling my thoughts, not trying to follow it but letting it guide me. My body responded to the magic contained within the glyph, my consciousness scurrying along the pathway before me until I felt a sharp tug on my abdomen, a yanking sensation as though I'd been hooked like a fish and was being reeled in. Then I was *elsewhere*.

4

The Undertow

Elsewhere was a dim hallway of cut stone lit by gaslights more appropriate to the previous century, not 1938. In the age of dirigibles and automobiles, the flickering lamps seemed out of place, but they were part of the charm of the Undertow. It clung to the old if it still worked, ignoring any advance that didn't create some necessary improvement. The Dewey decimal system: in. Electricity: out. Besides, who were they going to hire to do the wiring job down here?

I walked down the hallway until I reached a wooden door painted green and set into an opening in the stonework, not much taller than myself, the top a rounded arch. In the middle of the door in faded gold paint were the words *Undertow Collection*. I took the silver handle in my hand and turned it, pushing the door open to reveal the cavernous room behind, with its high ceiling and endless book shelves, like a cathedral turned into an old warehouse. I inhaled deeply, enjoying the rich scent of old muslin and dusty pages. Libraries were among my favorite things in the world, and this not only my favorite library but so much more.

Mr. Langmere sat behind the hulking desk to the right of the entryway, his stockinged feet propped up on its scratched wooden surface. The socks were red, and a gnarled toe poked through a hole in one. He kept the room unevenly lit by gas lights and candelabras, one of which he had moved next to him, the flickering candles providing light as he turned the page of a book he held in his hands.

"Mr. Langmere," I said.

He shifted on the wooden chair that supported him, lowered his book, and peered at me over the top of his silver spectacles. A few hairs on his wispy gray beard were tangled in the pages, and the book tugged on them.

"Miss Sinclair," he replied. His voice came as a hoarse whisper, though it managed to seem loud in this place. "It's been a while."

"Been keeping busy," I replied.

He lifted his feet off the desk, lowering them until they dangled from the chair, still far from reaching the floor. "Is there anything in particular I can help you find today?"

"I'm doing some research and need to use the file system."

He nodded and slid down to the floor, the top of his head barely rising above the edge of the desk, though tall for a gnome. He walked around and handed me a clipboard with a pen attached. The document contained hand written names with dates and times next to them. I signed my name where indicated, and—after glancing at my watch—wrote in 7:45 PM.

"Right," he said when I handed it back, reading it carefully as if he didn't know me well enough from all the visits I'd made in the past twelve months. Then again, for all I knew he had some ward built into the clipboard that traced my handwriting and compared it with my previous visits to make sure I was really who I was. You never knew with the Undertow. I didn't want to know. The mystery had always been part of the charm of the place.

"Mirabel Lee Sinclair," he read softly before tucking the clipboard under his arm and sliding his glasses higher on his nose. "If you'll follow me please."

He led me between two towering stacks of books though I knew the way as well as he. The hours I'd spent with my nose buried in the stacks of the Undertow seemed countless, but I'd never tired of the repository and always found something new to intrigue me, something wonderful to admire. I came here for work, but found here a peace I didn't know existed until I'd walked through those doors for the first time with Ingy as my guide. Suddenly, I had an explanation why Ingy knew so much about magic. When you could find any information you needed at your fingertips, research became a breeze.

In a dark corner was a small alcove, and in the alcove was a tall table made of wood, and on the table sat a typewriter, its metal painted green and the words *Oliver No. 9* written in gold lettering with black trim. It was old by any standard, with keys hexagonal in shape, the arms split into butterfly wings on either side of the platen. Instead of swinging up in an arc from the front towards the rear, the arms swung across from the left or right before returning to their place. A single gas light was mounted high above the table, and hanging below the light and above the typewriter was a blank chalkboard, its black surface covered with remnants of white dust.

"A reminder that you have six days left on Lucinda Falkenreath's gift account at which time payment is due for continued access," Mr. Langmere said, examining a document on his clipboard. "Given the current rate of inflation, the price will naturally rise slightly, though we are working to hold costs down as much as possible."

"How much?" I asked, aware my wallet remained as empty as it had been when I'd met Mr. Green. Certain Ingy's was equally depleted.

"The Tip Top account Miss Falkenreath bought will cost you $15 per annum, with a discount if you purchase additional years. Of course, that gives you access to our entire library of curiosities and print copies, as well as once a month use of the Typeprompter." He waved his hand at the typewriter.

"What's the cost of the other accounts?"

He frowned, flipping pages on his clipboard until he came to another one. "A lifetime High Roller Account is available, at $200, but that is obviously out of your price range. The First Rate gives you access to all materials and curios, and use of the Typeprompter once yearly for one hour for the price of $10 a year. The Extraordinary level provides print copy access only for $5 a year, including a limited selection of restricted volumes, and the Basic plan gives you access to unrestricted print volumes only for $2 per annum. Cash only of course, we don't take checks and we don't provide access on an IOU basis."

I hoped Mr. Templeton would accept the job Mr. Green offered us. We needed the bucks. "Thank you. I'll see what I can scrounge up in the next few days."

He tucked his clipboard under his arm and pulled a pocket watch out of his jacket. "It's now 7:50. The Typeprompter will answer your questions until 8:50 and the session will terminate. Best of luck to you, Miss Sinclair." He didn't wait for me to respond and turned, walking away briskly on his stockinged feet. They made a swishing sound against the floor, like a janitor running a broom.

I stepped up to the typewriter. A shelf underneath the table top contained blank paper. I took a sheet off the pile there and inserted it into the machine, cranking it around until the top of the sheet was in front of the platen. I typed *Mirabel Sinclair* and hit return.

Dusty words appeared on the chalkboard as though written by a ghostly hand. *Welcome Mirabel Sinclair.* It waited for my next prompt.

Query: I typed on the page, followed by *Green, troll, Baltimore, police data.*

The first words disappeared in a small cloud of dust after a pause, and the blackboard began drawing again. *Green, Crankshaft,* it wrote.

Species: Troll; Sex: Male; Age: 37. His physical details followed, weight and height and descriptive marks—such as the scars on his knuckles—telling me it was the same man I'd seen this morning at the reservoir. Next came a long list of criminal offenses running back nearly thirty years, when he would have been a child.

Mr. Green had been a very busy and very naughty fellow. His list of arrests ranged from petty theft and criminal mischief to assault with a deadly weapon and attempted murder. He'd spent seven years off and on in the Baltimore West correctional facility, housed with the rest of the violent non-human offenders—*including blacks,* I thought with disgust—had been last released in 1934, and remained on parole. Known affiliates included a who's who of Baltimore petty criminals. He'd also been tied to a couple of gnomes who made children's toys, though they had no criminal records. Updates over the last few years from his parole officer said he'd remained clean, working as a bouncer at a local nightclub. He'd been trying to turn his life around, go straight.

I pulled my battered notebook from an inside pocket of my coat, found my pen in another pocket, and jotted down some notes, including the address of the club where he worked. Mr. Green had no known address other than that, and the telephone number pointed to the same address. Either he lived at the club, or he preferred no one know where he lived. It didn't matter, I had a way to find him if needed.

I hit the carriage returned twice to get a clean line on the page and typed a new query. *Goose, Golden, arcane lore, and factual information.* I waited as the blackboard dutifully removed the information regarding Mr. Green. It paused again as it pondered my query. I tapped my finger on the desk, musing once more on the magic of the Typeprompter and how it functioned. Whatever the logic behind this device, I thanked the stars it functioned as advertised because it saved my legs a heck of a lot of walking.

It took longer than usual and I grew impatient, aware my time ticked away. I chewed my bottom lip and started tapping out the rhythm to various songs, doing what I could to distract myself. Finally, it wrote, small script that filled the chalkboard from top to bottom, the word ~continued~ below. Myths and stories, half-truths and rumors, anything related to the golden goose that had been relayed as part of a serious study, or was considered a report from a suspected eye witness of the artifact itself. I took notes quickly on anything that seemed interesting or relevant and then typed *continue.*

The board emptied and refilled, and I gave an audible groan at the volume of information I had to wade through. The goose had been talked about for centuries. Sorting fact from fiction would be an untenable task, even with my skills. The history of the goose and the resulting fairy tales surrounding it were lost in the murky recesses of history, made safe by the simplest and most powerful lock: the passage of time. I might as well have been asking for the height and weight of Merlin, or the color of Joan of Ark's eyes. Rumor and innuendo trumped fact. My hour was soon gone, several pages of my notebook filled with cramped writing.

The most pertinent details said the goose was an artifact, a magical construct of either elvish or gnomish creation. It had been stolen many times, and had been lost from official records for almost two centuries. There seemed no doubt of its authenticity, though, no reason to believe it only another fairy tale. Scholarly articles concerning it revolved around its resting place, but were inconclusive. Some suggested it wound up in the lair of the Great Wyrm of Vaudreching, although that particular dragon had been killed early in the Great War when it had seemed the world would fall under the might of steel and gunpowder and magic would die. Others suggested the goose had been hidden with the dead, lost to the end of time. There were more theories than drops of water. My fingers ached from writing.

The chalkboard went blank for a moment, and then spelled out ~*Thank you for your patronage, please come again*~.

Mr. Langmere had returned to the counter when I reached the front of the library. He glanced at me briefly before his attention wandered back to his book. "I hope you found what you were looking for, Miss Sinclair," he said, licking the tip of one finger and turning the page.

"Everything I'm going to get for now," I replied. "Thanks."

"Come again soon. Bring cash if you want to renew."

"Because you don't check checks or IOU's," I finished for him.

"Indeed." He turned another page.

I nodded without saying anything further and left the way I'd come, closing the green door behind me. When I turned back, the alcove it stood in had gone, only blank stone wall meeting my eyes. I briefly touched the stones, then walked down the hall to the place where I'd entered, finding the outline of our mark on the wall next to dozens of others. I traced the maze with my eyes again until I felt the twisting pull once more, and was *elsewhere*. This time my own basement.

Jacob's presence swept into the basement almost as soon as I pulled the curtain shut. The room chilled as he hovered behind me, the dull expression of dead eyes boring into my back. The hairs on the back of my neck prickled.

Jacob? If I concentrated, he could hear my thoughts as easily as if I spoke.

Hey there, Jacob replied.

"You know how Ingy feels about you stealing her stuff, don't you?"

He radiated a sense of amusement, but didn't reply.

"Yeah, well, she's not laughing. And I've got to live with her."

Try living with the dead, he said, still amused.

I almost chuckled. "I do, funny ghost. But you know how she feels. If you keep it up, you know what she'll ask."

His mood darkened, and he turned sullen.

"I know. You're my friend as well. We all need to get along if we're going to live in the same house."

Sure, he said gloomily.

"Thank you. I don't suppose you know anything about birds that lay gold eggs, do you?"

But he'd gone; the room warming. I couldn't feel his presence at all in our home, although that wasn't surprising. He kept a low profile when he wanted. He was buried six feet under, like all the dead. Their dirt invaded every crack and crevice; their bony dust covered every surface. If not for the living, the world would belong to them.

"Catch you later," I said, getting the reply I'd expected, which was none. I walked into the living room and sat down on the couch Ingrid had vacated. Any warmth from her body had faded. I flipped through my notes to the first page and re-read Green's criminal record.

"Who are you working for, Crankshaft? Who's footing the tab for this search?"

Something crashed overhead and Ingy yelled. I scrambled for the stairway, vaulting up the steps to the dining room. Another yell from the second floor. I ran through the parlor and up the next flight. I nearly crashed into Ingrid, who stood on the top landing.

"Bring me back my comb, you dumb ghost, or I'll beat your phantom ass," Ingy yelled into the empty hallway. She'd wrapped a towel around herself. That, her wet hair, and her anger told me enough of a story.

Beautiful. Angry and beautiful. A grin split my face.

She glared at the nothing before her, shot me a look with arched eyebrows that dared me to say something, and stomped into her room. She slammed the door shut and left me standing in the hall trying not to laugh as I watched her ghostly footprints drying on the wooden floorboards.

5

Lucky's Goodbye

I rolled over and glanced at the wristwatch which lay on my night-stand. The hands said six fifteen. I'd stayed up late, reviewing my notes and organizing the case file. The four hours of sleep I'd received as my reward couldn't slake the drowsiness that held me fast in bed for a few moments more. But today was Saturday, the day of Lucky's funeral, and Mr. Templeton expected me to join him.

I shuffled to the bathroom, peering at myself in the mirror through half-lidded eyes. The face reflected wasn't appropriate for a loose woman returning from a night at a speakeasy, let alone a private detective's assistant at a funeral. I ran some water into the tub and undressed, sliding in when it got deep enough.

I lay back and let the warm water hold me, replaying the meeting with Mr. Green and his job offer, the information I'd learned in the Undertow. I'd typed up my notes and placed them in a folder to give to Mr. Templeton, then spent a few days at the regular library re-searching the goose. I would pass the information along to him and let him tell me what to do next. He was the boss; he would have me do what I did best; dredge up information and clues. I frowned, not liking the thought I had no role beyond sidekick. I wished he would let me run with this case, but I knew there was no way in hell he would change his mind. He never changed his mind once he decided, for better or worse. I splashed the water in frustration and got a mouthful of soapy suds as a reward.

I picked out my best dress, a knee-length, dark-blue number. Formal enough for a funeral, but casual enough for a dinner party. I'd attended more of the former than the latter I realized, as I slid the zipper up. Over the last two years I'd been to three funeral services and zero parties. I pulled in a deep breath, adjusted myself in the mirror, applied the minimum makeup needed to look presentable, and fixed my hair up with some bobby pins.

The house echoed in silence, Ingy asleep. She would sleep until two, drink a lot of coffee and do whatever she could to make a buck. Hocking spells and charms weren't any easier than detective work in the current economy, but we made ends meet. I moved softly to not wake her, grabbed my coat off the wooden chair in the kitchen, slid my clasp into one of the pockets and my keys into the other.

The streets of Baltimore were quiet this early on a Saturday morning. I navigated my way across town, well ahead of schedule. Early for everything, the one who waited for that next something to happen while others showed up at the last minute or—much less forgivable in my eyes—late. Mr. Templeton fell into the second category. His sense of time included "time to wake up," "time to have a drink," and "time to go to sleep." Everything in between subject to the vagaries of his memories, and whether he had wound the ancient, black wristwatch he was never seen without.

I crossed Harbor City Boulevard, staying on Lombard. The row houses here were meaner, with peeling paint and broken windows. Some were boarded up, and a section of one block showed signs of fire, blackened bricks on both sides of a partially collapsed home.

There were people sitting on their stoops, a mix of humans and dwarves, a handful of trolls. Ripped and torn clothing; dirty faces.

Mr. Templeton had already arrived at the small cathedral of Saint Brendan's. I parked next to his dented black Fjord. His wheels were newer than mine, and far outstripped my trusty Model D in looks and speed, but I wouldn't call it a glamorous ride by any stretch. He waited for me by the front grill of his auto and waved me over impatiently.

"You're late," he said.

"I'm twenty minutes early."

He glanced at his wristwatch. "Oh. Forgot to reset this thing after it wound down last spring."

"You mean you've been late for the last six months?"

"I'm always where I'm meant to be when I'm supposed to be there."

"And usually late," I reminded him. I handed him the folder.

He browsed the contents, nodding. "Good work." His eyes scanned the list of known associates of Mr. Green, then he tucked everything back into the folder and tossed it into the open window of his car. He waved at the door. "Come on. Let's go pay our respects."

I picked out Lucky's wife, Lucille, the minute we stepped through the door of the church. She sat in the front row of Saint Brendan's, her black dress blending with the dark brown wood of the pews. Her red hair had been pulled into a messy bun in back, and a black pill hat spilled a veil over the front of her face. She looked pale, although I couldn't tell if she had fair skin or if her coloration came from her grief.

We sat near the back; Mr. Templeton as rigid as a plank of wood next to me. His face chiseled out of stone; shoulders squared off. I'd have thought he'd become a statue if we hadn't walked into the place together. He didn't shed a tear either. Not so much as a sniffle passed his nose during the service. Not knowing Lucky beyond stories, I felt no grief, but the soft sobs of his family tugged on my heart and left me with a profound sense of endings.

When the ceremony finished, Mr. Templeton excused himself and walked to the front. He shook the hand of a frail man with a mop of white hair who leaned on a cane, his rumpled blue suit hanging off his frame. Probably Lucky's father, Henry. He spent some time sitting next to Lucille, his hand resting on her arm. They spoke quietly, and though I could hear the murmur of their voices, I couldn't make out the conversation. When he started to stand, Lucille wrapped her arms around him and sobbed. Her cheeks were stained wet, her mascara running.

His face had flushed red when he returned. "Come on, let's get moving." He donned his fedora and led me out the front door. Then he surprised me by opening the passenger door of his car. "Get in. We're taking a drive."

He remained silent for some time. He eased his car through the narrow back streets of west Baltimore until we found our way to Route 1. The clouds had moved in, and spats of rain hit his windshield.

"Where are we going?"

"Lucille told me about Lucky's work. Did I mentioned he had quit the force and started his own agency?"

"You don't tell me much of anything, boss."

"I don't? No, I suppose I don't. Sorry." He shook his head. "He was doing some security and detective work for private firms around town. Small contracts mostly, nothing too posh. Trying to move into an untapped marketplace. Gnome manufacturing, troll iron works, a few pawn shops run by immigrants, that sort of thing."

I nodded to show I listened.

"Hand me a snipe." He lit the cigarette with the car lighter and opened the ashtray, full to overflowing. I cracked the window open and waited for some of his smoke to drift my way.

"Well, he took a case recently. Lucille gave me this." He left the cigarette dangling from his lips and reached inside his coat, pulling out a business card he passed to me. The edges were worn, the ink smudged. It read:

Beezallel, Bollo and Tim

Tinkers and Toy Makers

"Recognize the names?"

"They were listed as associates of Mr. Green. But what was Lucky working on?"

"That's what we're going to find out."

"But why?" I asked, frowning. "Shouldn't we focus on the goose?"

He remained silent again for a few minutes, and then asked, "You bring your piece?"

"No. I didn't think I would need it at a funeral."

He opened the glove box. The space was stuffed with crumpled up papers and empty cigarette packages. He leaned over, rummaged through the items, and pulled a small .22 from under the pile.

"Always be prepared. Didn't I teach you anything, Mira?" He placed the pistol in my hands and dug out a spare clip as well.

"Yeah, you taught me a lot, Mr. Templeton." I checked the magazine and the safety, and then pocketed the gun and the spare clip as he turned his attention back to the road. I hadn't dressed for action and would have preferred if I were wearing a pair of trousers, or at least one of my working skirts. At least I didn't own heels; flats would be easier to run in.

We turned onto Camp Meade road and wound our way past derelict warehouses and factories. The Colt 45 beer company rose on the left, a line of trucks and wagons going in and out. No one had any money, but somehow, they kept selling booze. Not long after we passed its brick facade, we turned onto one of the many narrow side streets branching off the main drive. Ben flicked his butt out the window as we slowed, his eyes scanning the empty buildings.

He wedged the car in a narrow alley strewn with all the modern amenities, from broken glass to drifting pieces of paper floating in idle circles on an errant breeze. The alley continued for another fifty or so feet before dumping out onto another street. Directly across the street from the exit point of the alley stood a white, wooden warehouse.

"Beezallel, Bollo and Tim's place," Mr. Templeton said, nodding towards the crumbling structure ahead of us. "I'll work my way around the back, you wait here."

"But," I began.

He cut me off. "No buts. You wait here and keep an eye on the car. I don't need you snooping around in there and getting hurt. You watch for anyone taking a powder and whistle if you see them, but you stay out of sight."

"What's this have to do with us?"

He frowned and gripped the steering wheel. The silence lingered for some time. "Lucky was my friend." He shrugged and said no more. Honestly, what else he could add? He'd left unsaid all the things he knew I should understand. I did, too, that's the thing of it. If it had been Ingy or Lugnut who had died? I would have done anything to make sure their work had been completed so they could rest.

We stepped out of the car and he stared at me until I jammed my hands in my pocket and leaned against the brick wall beside me, found a bit of trash on the ground to stare at. Nope, nothing interesting going on here at all, I'm just watching the ground get wet. Then he walked down the alley to the street, kitty cornered the angle towards the right as he crossed, and slid down another alley between the gnome's warehouse and the next building.

My nerves kicked a fuss, so I whistled up a stray breeze to keep myself distracted, something Petunia had taught me when we first met.

"You just put your lips together and blow, and the wind comes calling," she had said as we blew smoke rings on a park bench near Mr. Templeton's office while we watched the steam clippers coming and going along the harbor. We ate our lunches together, swapping stories of our childhoods. Petunia had wanted to be a hair dresser growing up, but her quarter pixie blood meant she wasn't allowed into the beauty schools. She could easily have passed for fully human, but she never lied, so she put it on her applications. None of the schools wrote her back.

"So, I took up typing instead," she said, gracing me with her infectious grin for the first time. "Glad I did, too, because it turns out I'm pretty darn good at it. What about you, kiddo? What'd you want to be when you grew up?"

"A thief first. Then a cop." I ate my sandwich. I didn't say anything more about it, and she kindly didn't ask. She understood.

I glanced at my watch, saw it had only been a couple of minutes. I tapped the toe of one shoe and crossed my arms over my chest as I waited in the gloom of the alley. Cars and trucks rumbled by on nearby roads, but this side street remained quiet.

After five minutes, I started pacing back and forth. I would have killed for a cigarette. They were toy makers. How dangerous could it be? I pictured myself walking over and peeking in a window. Mr. Templeton would be angry if I did anything but stand here. But the longer I stood, the more my guts twisted inside me, the more I wondered what was happening, the more I itched to be moving.

I'd just peek through the back windows. What harm can come of that? I'd get a better view of anyone bolting. Once I moved, the pain in my stomach faded and became nervous energy. I hastened to cross the street, and angled for the alley on the opposite side of where Mr. Templeton had entered. I slunk down the dirty space next to the gnome's workshop, staying close to the wall, a few stray drops of rain wetting my face. I worked around boxes and an overflowing trash bin, my feet splashing through puddles shimmering with the rainbow skim of oil and grease.

I circled a stack of crates and found a side door recessed into the wall of the building. There were no windows at all, only the grimy wood entrance with a scarred, metal handle. No problem. I'd just open it a crack and take a looksee. It seemed reasonable. I'd come all this way. Might as well go a little further.

I examined the lock, then fished a couple of bobby pins out of my hair. I held the handle, whispering to the air currents eddying around the back lot as I examined it for magical wards. Once I determined there were no magical or mechanical alarms attached to the mechanism, I slid my makeshift picks into place. I turned one to put pressure on the lock, then raked the lock pins with the other. I'd lived on the streets until the age of fourteen. Picking locks had been one of the first skills I'd learned, and it still came easily twelve years later.

The door opened with a slight creaking sound, and I listened long and carefully before entering. Crates and shelves blocked my view for more than a few feet to the left and right of the door. Dim voices echoed from across the warehouse. I walked in that direction, hoping to get a better view. I stayed close to the edge of the shelving that filled the open space.

Everywhere I turned were shelves and boxes, stacked high to the roof, which had to be fifty feet overhead. Some crates had their sides off, straw strewn around the floor next to them. There were piles of metal sheets, rolls of wires, huge bundles of paper, bins of screws and nails, cans of paint, lumber. The raw goods needed to manufacture toys or other items.

The voices grew louder, and I could make out snatches of conversation. I peeked around a stack of lumber. A broad, open area in the middle of the warehouse contained benches and tables, set up for working. Scraps of wood, metal and wire were scattered around some mechanical equipment; drill presses, table saws and the like. On the other side of the space were two very short men in coveralls and boots talking in high pitched voices to a tall man dressed in a suit and fedora.

"The product isn't ready."

"Whether or not they're ready, it's time you delivered," said the tall man. "The situation is growing complicated." He had a high-pitched voice not matching what I could see of his appearance. It had a musical lilt to it, as though he said everything in song, though I caught no trace of rhyme, no actual notes. More of an overtone, like the ringing in the ears when the world goes silent for a time.

"But we have yet to perform a test firing," one of the two gnomes said. "The results could be disastrous if we don't properly test the weapons."

Weapons? That's not what I would have expected from toy makers. I moved, jockeying for position so I could see the tall man's face. I managed to sneak in between a towering stack of crates which listed to one side and a shelf filled with paper and cardboard. I leaned out, supporting my weight on the crates so I could glance around the corner.

Tall man faced me now, but bent over to talk to the gnomes, the curly brown hair on the back of their heads blocking my view. I whispered to the air currents of the warehouse, and they stirred. A tiny eddy roamed through the open space, tousling the hair of the gnomes, brushing the edges of the tall man's clothing, and then re-turning to giggle in my ear. The wind said there was magic here, sur-rounding the figure in front of me. I couldn't tell what kind, nor did I dare do more for fear of raising their attention.

"When are we going to get paid?" the other gnome asked. "You promised us gold for this work."

"You'll have your money in good time. Just see you meet the production schedule, or we'll find someone else who will."

He stood up straight, giving me a clear shot at his visage. A long face, smooth cheeked, and golden eyes gleaming beneath sleek black hair that peeked out beneath his hat. His clothing looked finely made and clean, suggesting money. He seemed thin, and his presence gave off a strong, healthy vitality. Elvish perhaps? Then he wheeled and strode away from the gnomes with long, graceful steps. There was a brief flash of light as he opened a door, and then it closed behind him.

I turned to ease my way out of the building, but the crate shifted under my hand. I looked up, watching in horror as the pile leaned further with a basso groan. It tumbled forward, crashing into massive heap on the floor in front of me. The noise rolled on forever, though everything came to a rest after a few seconds of tumult.

"Shit," I said.

Both gnomes scurried in opposite directions. I picked one of them and followed, leaping over large pieces of wood that lay tumbled across each other. I don't know why I chased him since technically we were the ones trespassing, but it seemed the thing to do, so I did. Loud cursing from across the room suggested Mr. Templeton had taken up pursuit of the other gnome.

He twisted in and around shelving, crates, and barrels, disappearing from time to time. He knew the place far better than I did, and used it to his advantage.

I reached the side of the building, slowed, turned left then right. The gnome had vanished, but I heard a thump to my right. I ran in that direction. A huge crate stood in the aisle ahead of me, almost nine feet tall, blocking further progress.

I started back the way I had come, scanning the heaped piles of boxes. Maybe he'd hid in among them, or climbed into one. I'd reached the junction again when I heard a cracking noise behind me.

The crate burst open; the wooden door torn to splinters. A giant, metal figure stood inside, vaguely man shaped. Steam hissed from its ears, and two jade gemstones gleamed from a bucket shaped head, like glowing green eyes. On the forehead was written EMET. When it stepped, it clanked, and its heavy foot thudded against the floor. Small metal items fell off the shelves and tinkled onto the ground near it.

It took a second step, then another. I realized each ponderous step was deceptively slow, and it covered the ground between us rapidly. I backed down the corridor. When it reached the junction, it turned toward me. It bellowed a blast like a steam whistle, white vapor shooting from a vent where a mouth would lay. I covered my ears against the cacophony. When the noise stopped, it came towards me.

I ran.

I pulled the .22 from my pocket and stopped, spinning to take aim. I fired a round. The gun popped and a bullet ricocheted off the shoulder of the huge figure with a trail of sparks. Beyond a small scratch, it appeared unharmed. I ran some more.

I spotted an opening under one of the shelves to my left, and dove through, rolling into a smaller aisle. I rose and ran as shelving exploded behind me, the creature smashing through the metal frames. Something slammed into me from behind, knocking me to the ground. Some of the metalwork from the destroyed shelf framing tangled the feet of the iron monster, and it struggled to free itself as I pushed myself up again.

My ankle throbbed. I limped now as I hurried away. My breath came in rapid gulps, and I inched towards panicking. Damn it, damn it, damn it. I did not need this right now. How had a simple peek gone so horribly wrong? I turned another corner and saw the back door in the distance. The crashing of the monster grew closer.

When it blasted its whistle, I ran as hard as I could, ignoring the pain.

I hit the door with my shoulder, fingers fumbling for the knob. I yanked it open and threw myself out of the building as the metal man came rushing down the corridor. I stumbled down a short flight of metal stairs and started limp-running towards the alley on the opposite side of the building. Behind me, the wall caved outward, collapsed by the weight of the monster as it gained on me.

No time to get to the car, no place to hide. I turned and fired, two shots zinging off its jaw and nose, the screech of metal on metal. I stumbled again as I tried to aim for one of the eyes, hoping to blind it, but missed. I fell on my ass painfully, and pulled the trigger to the clicking of an empty chamber.

Then it came for me.

6

EMET

A gun thundered nearby. The bullet sparked as it hit the letter E on the forehead of the monster and obliterated the paint. A squashed metal cylinder pinged as it bounced off the pavement. My ears rang from the noise.

It took a step closer, and another, slowing now, and then collapsed to one knee, a hand thrusting out to catch itself. Hissing steam spewed from both ears as the body began to shudder. The creature fell apart, metal plates separating, individual gears and valves bouncing off the ground. It fell into a pile of steaming metal and lay still. Two huge green gems, dust covered and dingy, glared up at me from the heap of slag.

"Lucky shot," I said as Mr. Templeton walked over to me and offered me his hand. I took it. Oh, but I'd made a mess of this. I plastered a grin of relief onto my face as he pulled me up onto unsteady feet. I'd been the lucky one. Lucky he'd been here to bail me out, but I figured a joke would lighten things up. Keep him laughing, that always seemed to work.

"I told you to wait by the car," he said. His voice came out flat, emotionless, his face a rigid mask. The eyes were narrowed, and the crow's feet beside them were deep creases.

Oh, that face. I knew that face too well, and it told me how badly I'd messed this up. Words dried in my throat and stuck there. He'd warned me to stay with the car, and I'd made a complete mess of the situation. The nervous relief that filled me at his timely intervention evaporated. Good job, Mira. Messing up I could handle. Disappointing Mr. Templeton? That cut.

"No!" screamed a tiny voice. Mr. Templeton's hand snapped up, aiming. The gnome I'd been chasing crawled across the rubble of the wall and ran to the pile of metal hissing and steaming on the ground. The little man picked up the two green gems, cradling them in his arms before pocketing them. Tears ran down his face as he gazed upon the remains of the metal goliath.

"Which one are you, Beezallel or Bollo or Tim?" Mr. Templeton asked.

I bit my tongue and vowed to stay in the background, let Mr. Templeton ask the questions. I'd screwed up well enough as it was.

"You don't understand," the gnome said, sniffling. "This was my thesis."

"What?" said Mr. Templeton.

"My thesis. My graduation statement. My attempt at showing that the animation of inherently inanimate objects by magical stabilization is possible. I spent my whole life putting it together, forty years finding the right parts and the spells to bind it, and now it's all gone. All gone." He blinked back tears.

"Listen, I'm sorry about your . . . thing there," Mr. Templeton said.

"EMET," he said.

"Okay, sure, EMET," Mr. Templeton said. "I'm sorry about EMET. But it did try to kill my assistant."

The gnome took a dirty handkerchief out of his back pocket and blew his nose. Once he finished, he sat on a mound of broken parts and seemed to notice Mr. Templeton's gun pointing at him. He held his breath for a moment, and exhaled slowly. "I am sorry there was any attempt to hasten the terminus of her worldly existence. I designed EMET to protect our goods from potential thieves."

"Who are you working for you need that sort of magical defense?" asked Mr. Templeton.

"We work for ourselves," the gnome said, his voice rising as though insulted.

Mr. Templeton waved the barrel of the gun at the building. "Then who was the spook with the greasy hair in the fancy duds?"

"I don't know," the gnome said, his voice desultory as he toyed with the pieces of the golem scattered in front of him.

"What do you know about him?"

"Not much. I don't like him, you should know up front. I'd tell you his name if I knew it. He owes us significant money for our work."

"Is he working for someone else?"

The gnome picked up a small gear and scratched the back of his head with it, disturbing his already matted brown hair. "I don't know. I don't give it much consideration either as long as we're getting paid."

"Did he pay you to build the metal man?" Mr. Templeton asked, waving at the metal pile.

"No! I've already told you, this was my thesis assignment for the summation of my university career, which would allow me to finally receive my Grand Master degree." He rummaged through the remains, pulling out a spring, and two tiny ball bearings.

My vow to keep silent fled, and I blurted, "You're making weapons for him, aren't you?" Mr. Templeton turned to look at me. The heat of his eyes bored into my skin. I tried to ignore his anger.

The blame for this mess belonged to me. I needed to show him I could get something useful out of the mistakes I'd made. I'd over-heard more than he had or he would have gotten to the heart of the matter by now.

He nodded at me, acknowledging I'd gotten a step ahead. "Answer the lady's question."

The gnome peered at me with beady, black eyes, scowling. "You're all alike you know."

"Who's alike?" I asked.

He frowned and turned back to the parts in his hands, trying to fit them together. The metal clinked dully as he twisted the parts around. "Humans. All of you, with your lordly attitudes, your bigotry. You break into our place and expect me to answer questions."

My temper rose, and I clenched my fists. Who was he to tell me what I thought? He didn't know me, didn't know Mr. Templeton.

"We should call the cops," Mr. Templeton said. "Gnomes making weapons won't sit well with the police. I'll bet these jokers don't have a proper manufacturing permit for the work."

I thought the gnome blanched, but he said nothing more. I watched him as he toyed with the pieces of his destroyed creature. "Why don't you go ahead, Mr. Templeton. I'll keep an eye on this one." I pulled out the little .22 and replaced the empty clip with the spare.

I expected Mr. Templeton to lower his voice and growl at me to go make the call. Instead, he watched me for a few seconds, as though weighing whether or not he should. Then he gave one brisk nod, holstered his weapon, and turned his back to us. "Keep him on ice. I'll be back shortly."

A surge of pride went through me that he gave me this. Trusted me enough to watch a potential criminal. I stared down at the little man, keeping most of my weight on my good leg. I decided to ask another question. "Do you know anything about Lucky Gambini?"

"Who's that?" He sat cross-legged on the ground, gathering a small pile of bits and pieces in front of him. He tinkered with the parts, running the wire through a short length of tube, adding gears and cogs to one end. As he worked, he brushed his fingers over the metal, and pieces would stick to each other, or meld into one new part. I sensed the magic he employed, though I didn't understand it. The tangled web of machinery and metal, oil and gas, breaking and reforming their connections like a master mechanic in a welding shop.

I tried a different question. "Tell me about this person who hired you."

"The big shot elf? Why do you care who he is?" The gnome glared at me and held the tube out. The apparatus now resembled a weapon.

"Gun!" I threw myself to the right. A ball bearing exploded from the barrel of the apparatus and twanged off the ground near my legs.

I rolled over and caught a glimpse of the gnome disappearing around the corner of the building, moving fast. I aimed, but I didn't have a clean shot and kept my finger off the trigger. Damn it, damn it, damn it!

Mr. Templeton had only just reached the door. He raised his gun and fired once into the sky, ran to the corner, stopped when he got there. He tipped his hat back from his eyes, then turned and walked back, scowling, his jaw working as he ground his teeth. He didn't have to tell me the gnome had gotten away; it was written in the lines of his face.

He stood over me and I couldn't meet his eyes, but when he held out his hand, I took it and he pulled me up again. "I figured he might rabbit," he said. "I needed to see how you'd react if he did."

I winced. One easy task, and the criminal had escaped. I'd thought for a moment he'd finally begun to trust me. Now, any opportunity to lead the investigation had been lost, and my heart sank through my shoes. "I'm sorry, Mr. Templeton."

"For that? Don't be. Happened to me more times than I care to remember. But now you know what a desperate person will do. And I know you can avoid getting shot and call out a warning at the same time. Good reactions." He took a last look at the corner of the warehouse. "Let's go. You've come this far, might as well see it through. Let's find the other gnome or a phone, there are unresolved questions."

I walked behind him, trying to hide the limp. My eyes darted left and right, taking in everything. Remembering all the things he'd taught me. Details, details, the devil's always in the details. Don't rush, stay focused, fix the scene in your mind. Build a case from the ground up.

There were hundreds of places to hide, and a search would take hours. When we reached the area where the production line stood, Mr. Templeton noticed a door located in the far-left front corner of the building and nodded at it. We stole over and stood to the side of it.

Mr. Templeton tested the knob and found the door locked. He rubbed his medallion for a moment and mouthed a prayer. He glanced at me and whispered, "Stay behind me." After a brief pause, he put his shoulder to the door, hard. I enjoyed the satisfying crunch as the frame separated from the wall and it fell inward.

Parts and pieces strewn across various desks and tables, the office in a state of messy disarray. An old typewriter sat on one desk, the cover shrouded in dust. There were papers everywhere and a small wood stove in one corner, the door open and the fire lit. A huge pile of documents was going up in flames. Mr. Templeton swore and grabbed one of the fireplace pokers near the stove, pulling out flaming papers and stomping on them with his feet. He salvaged perhaps a quarter of the documents, ranging from singed to badly scorched. The rest went up in smoke.

"Start going through what's left. I've got a call to make."

He found the phone beneath a blueprint and dialed the police precinct. As he talked, I grabbed scattered pieces of paper and began reading through the notes. There were orders for toys, deliveries of materials, sketches for devices. They'd been what they seemed, at least at face value, a manufacturer of doodads and gewgaws. Invoices and receipts comprised the bulk of the paperwork, most of it unremarkable. It wasn't until I examined the blueprint he'd moved off the phone that I found our first significant clue.

"Mr. Templeton," I said, holding it up.

He paused his conversation and stared at the diagram, white lines on blue paper. "Jesus, Joseph and Mary," he whispered, his eyes widening. He put the speaker to his mouth again. "No, that wasn't directed at you. I'm looking at a blueprint here of what appears to be a Thompson gun." Pause. "Yes, machine gun." Another pause. "No, this isn't a military facility, it's a toy maker. Look, stop arguing, Bronchowski, and get some boys down here right away, you're going to want to see this."

He hung up and took the blueprint from my hands, spreading it on the counter. His fingertip traced the white outline of the weapon. "I'm no grease monkey, but from what I can tell it's made from stamped steel. Should be easy and cheap to mass produce. Let's see if we can find anything else in this mess."

We scoured the room for another fifteen minutes. We gathered any references to weapons and piled them on the counter. We'd hand those over to the police when they arrived and let them deal with the cleanup. But I could tell my boss wanted something more, something to tie the gnomes to Lucky. He perused documents, tossing them aside, swearing under his breath. The fire warmed the room, and sweat dimpled his brow. I tried to understand his eagerness to find remnants of Lucky's last case. Maybe he wanted to finish the work of the man, put to rest the remaining pieces of his life. Whatever drove him, I didn't think we would be getting paid for it, and money seemed to me to be the most pressing priority. But I kept my trap shut, already in deep in trouble, and scanned half-burned pieces of paper.

I found what he wanted lying half under the stove. The top of the document had scorched to nothing from the heat of the hot metal above it, but the rest remained legible, if crispy. The ledger page had neatly divided columns and rows, a long list of items on the left, and prices on the right. Near the bottom were two that drew my eye, especially the payments. *Misery* written with meticulous penmanship on the left, and *Two Golden Eggs* on the right. *Company* on the left, *Five Golden eggs* on the right.

"Holy hell," I said.

Mr. Templeton was at my side in a moment. "What did you find?"

I handed him the document and watched as his eyes read the page. When he reached the bottom and his eyes widened, a tiny surge of joy passed through me. I loved when I could draw surprise from him, a sort of recognition I'd done well.

"Holy hell is right," he said. "I've got no idea what misery or company are code for, but considering they tried to burn it, it can't be anything good." He flipped the document over and examined the other side, which appeared blank. Then he folded it carefully in half and slipped it into an inner pocket of his coat. "I don't think this will be missed by the police. They're going to be busy figuring out why the gnomes are making guns."

I pointed at the stack of paperwork awaiting the police. "It's all right there for them. Dates of manufacture and sales."

He shook his head. "Everything's in code, there's no telling who they are selling to. But they've got some good brains on the force, and a couple of witches on retainer. I'll let them figure it out."

I chewed on my lip and tipped my head sideways as I thought. I didn't want to upset him now that his mood had improved. Taking on a case always did this to him, changed his frame of mind, made him more positive and less prone to losing himself in somber reflection at the bottom of a bottle. But the ties binding our case to Lucky seemed frayed and likely to snap at a close examination. I wanted him to be prepared in case the connection fell apart. "This doesn't mean Lucky had something to do with the golden egg, does it? I mean, someone could be manufacturing them out of raw gold bars or something. Right?"

He nodded, but nothing in his face changed. "You may be right, and I'd already thought of that. But one thing I've learned in almost fifty years of life is there are no coincidences. A troll comes to us to find the goose that lays the golden egg, and when we investigate Lucky's last case, we find a reference to gold eggs. It smells hinky."

By then, the muffled wail of sirens echoed in the distance. "It's going to be a very long afternoon," he said.

***

The detectives questioned us for several hours before letting us leave. The police knew Ben Templeton well. Hell, several of them were old enough to remember his years on the force, when he and Lucky were partners. That's probably why we got off the hook for breaking and entering. But they questioned us closely and carefully about the gnomes, the weapons, our reasons for being here. It fell short of an interrogation, though. I took Mr. Templeton's lead and answered the questions with thoughtful intent. My calm, outward exterior hid a roiling interior, where frayed nerves kept me sitting on the edge of my seat.

"No, I'd never met them before," I said.

"Yes, I realized at the time what we were doing might look criminal," I said, "but we were following up Mr. Gambini's last case."

"We didn't know about the illegal weapons they were building until we got here," I said.

"You'll have to ask Mr. Templeton that," I said. That one I repeated often, and each time the boss nodded at me as if to say *that's right, put it on my shoulders, kid.* So, I dropped it right there where he could do the heavy lifting.

When Mr. Templeton slipped behind the wheel of his car, he tossed his fedora in the back seat and ran his hand through his thinning hair. "This is one hell of a mess. We've got gnomes making illegal weapons, some crackpot who is paying them, probably in golden eggs he doesn't have, and a list of weird items which could be a code for something else. And on top of that, I've got an assistant who doesn't listen."

The last comment came with a pointed glare, one I couldn't return. I'd gotten over the initial flush of regret at my actions, and had made up for it—at least a little—by finding the clues he needed to tie Lucky to the gnomes. That it also tied the golden goose to the gnomes seemed of secondary importance to Mr. Templeton. For me, though, it had been the first tangible proof the treasure hunt wouldn't be a search for the improbable and the mythical. The goose was real, a true magical artifact that, even now, criminals were seeking. Excitement coursed through me at the possibility of finding it first, the potential rewards and payoffs. Maybe we could even keep one of the golden eggs, make the agency solvent for a change, rent a better quality of office, replace our aging automobiles with new wheels. I pictured myself in a trench coat made of oxblood red leather, holding a silver-plated colt in my hand as I walked away from my new Caillouet, the breeze catching the tail of my coat—

"Are you listening to me, Mira?"

I started. "I'm sorry Mr. Templeton, what did you say?"

The look he gave me could have withered a dessert. "What do I tell you about paying attention?"

Heat rose in my cheeks. "Pay attention, or pay the ferryman."

He nodded. "I need you to contact Mr. Green and let him know we're taking the case."

That gave me a sense of relief. We'd have the funding we needed to keep in business, at least a few more weeks. "I will. What about Lucky's case, though?"

"I'm following Lucky's leads, too. We're going to do both. I need to find out how deep this weapons mess goes and how they tie together." He banged the steering wheel and swore softly. "Can you imagine what will happen if those weapons get out on the streets? Jesus, Joseph and Mary. We'll have a damn war on our hands in Baltimore. The cops will be outgunned by automatic weapons." He took his pack of smokes off the dash and jiggered it until a single cigarette stood out, placed the butt of it between his lips, and lit it. "And I wouldn't blame folks one bit, either. Not the way they've been treated. But it'll be they who will pay, not the people they're angry at. Certainly not the people who gave them the guns."

He started the car and we drove for a while. But when he turned away from the direction of the church, I had to ask. "Where are we going?"

He lit a fresh cigarette and exhaled, letting the smoke roll out the windows. "Lucky's office. Where you will do everything I tell you to and nothing more, is that clear? You want to be a detective, you need to learn to listen."

"Yes, sir," I said. A bright spark of joy flared inside me. I turned away from him to look out the window, trying to hide it. Another chance to prove I could do the work. Another shot at redemption.

7

The Evidence of Failure

The car tooled along, and I happily let Mr. Templeton smoke and think, drinking in the scent of Baltimore, my city. The odor of the H&S bakery drifted through the window, along with the reek of oil from the car shops. Those mixed with the tang of the ocean and the fog of exhaust fumes from the traffic. Everything that made Baltimore unique could be found in its aromas, something I'd learned as a kid running around the docks and alleys. I focused on the city instead of the damn fantasies I kept having about the work. He'd been right of course. Nancy Drew shit. I'd gotten too wrapped up in stupid stories, pulp novels, and day dreams. It was about Lucky now. Focus on the important things. Friends and family. You do this for them. To keep them safe. Failing that, to bring them some justice.

I broke the silence as he lit his second cigarette. "Where is Lucky's office?"

"He had a small place he rented in Roland Park. We'll check there first, then swing by his house to see if there's anything else he kept there."

We took the turn for Cold Spring Avenue, and he eased the car off the road and into a gas station, the signs on the store windows advertising ice cold cokes for a nickel. He pulled up to the pumps, brought the car to a stop, and handed me a five spot. "Go get me a coke and a roll of tape. If they have it, pick up a hammer."

"What for?" I asked.

"If his office is locked, we may need to do a little persuading on the door handle."

"That explains the hammer," I said, "but what about the tape?"

"Oh that." He jerked his thumb towards the back of the car. "I've got to patch up a couple of tears in the rear seat of this jalopy. Not going to be getting a new one any time soon, I'll have to make the best of it."

I walked into the store and around the aisles until I found the hardware section. I grabbed a roll of masking tape and a hammer, and then grabbed two bottles of pop from the refrigerator aisle. He could spring for mine as well. I paid for everything, taking my change from the old woman who staffed the register, and left.

The attendant replaced the gas nozzle and screwed Mr. Templeton's gas cap back on as I walked over to the car. I slid into the passenger seat. The boss passed the payment through the window and the young man walked off, a greasy rag dangling from the back pocket of his coveralls. I showed him the tape and the hammer.

"Good enough, that'll do. Let's get moving."

He took some side streets. I thought we double backed at least once, and his eyes kept flicking to the rear-view mirror. I peeked a looksee myself, but didn't notice anyone behind us. After several twists and turns, and one shortcut down an alley barely wider than his car's side mirrors, he seemed to relax, and we soon arrived at a block of modest, cheap looking office buildings. He circled the block and, when he seemed satisfied, he parked along the side of the road, easing in next to the curb.

Lucky's office was in a six-story brick building, nondescript except for the archway with columns in front of the door that stood out from the plainer structures on either side of it and gave it a look of grandeur those buildings lacked, like an aging southern belle. Not expensive digs, though. It looked a little run down and worse for wear, the bricks dirty, the grass on the strip of lawn between it and the road going brown in places. The windows on the first floor were barred. We slipped through the rotating glass doorway and found ourselves in a spare lobby with an empty guard desk and a couple of elevators on the opposite side of the open area.

We found the name *V. Gambini* on a small plaque between the two elevator doors, his room listed as 412. We waited for the elevator, and I glanced around the lobby until it dinged and opened. I tried not to fidget with nervousness as we rode up. I stuffed my hands in my coat pockets, felt for the cold weight of the .22, and silently counted until the doors opened again.

The hallway before us was as spare as the lobby, with a worn, red carpet stretched between two light-brown walls with several doors on either side. About halfway down the padded length we found Lucky's door, his name painted in gold stenciling on the frosted glass window. The door stood open, and a quick glance at the jamb revealed it had been forced, the wood broken where the lock had pushed through the softer material, splinters of it on the floor. Both of us pulled our guns at the same time. I stepped to the left of the door and he to the right, and he nodded at me before he pushed the door open and entered first. I followed closely, turning right when he turned left.

No one waited for us. Mr. Templeton reached past me and flipped a switch, turning on the overhead light and illuminating a mess. The walls of the single room that comprised Lucky's office were lined with shelving. Books were scattered across the floor, along with papers and assorted bric-a-brac.

"Still think Lucky's death and the golden bird aren't related?"

I shook my head. "I can't say that I do."

"Neither do I."

"I didn't think you had."

He tipped his fedora back. "Up until now I hadn't been sure. The obit said a car accident, but Bronchowski gave me the details. Driving while intoxicated. Only Vincent didn't drink. I found it hard to believe he'd get behind a wheel if he'd been drunk. His mother was killed by a drunk driver. It turned him into a teetotaler."

"Why didn't you say so sooner?"

His eyes were distant, haunted by some memory. "People change. People have a bad day. People make a single, stupid choice and throw everything away. Until today, I didn't have any hard evidence against those things. His car crashed, he smelled of liquor, and they found empty bottles of whisky on the floor of his car. Open and shut case, no need to dig more. One bad day." He sighed and nodded at the room. "Now, I'm sure. Go through the stuff on the floor, see what you can turn up. I'll check the desk."

I squatted, sifting through the hastily scattered debris. I started with the paperwork, letters and files that must have come from the big file cabinet sitting near the window, whose drawers were open and empty. There were folders labeled with case numbers and dates, the most recent one with the tag 03-09-1938_TGTLTGE. A couple of informational tracts from The Godly Teacher, Saint Brendan's Catholic relief charity, stuck out of it. I knew the charity from my time spent at the Mary Magdalene School for Wayward Children.

Mr. Templeton sat down in the rolling leather seat behind the desk and examined the drawers. They were dusty inside, and when I stood and stepped closer, I could see the outline of the objects each once held. The right top drawer had held pens and paper or file folders. The next drawer revealed the outline of Lucky's revolver, and a square shape behind it that could have been a box of cartridges. Both were missing.

"Do you have your powder kit?" the boss asked. When I nodded, he held out his hand and I pulled the makeup compact from an inside pocket and handed it over along with the dusting brush. Ben applied a small amount of powder to the tips of the bristles, and ran it against the drawer handles, watching as the fingerprints became visible. I could see they were repeated all over the desk.

"I'm guessing these are Lucky's," Mr. Templeton said as he sat back, the old chair creaking under his weight.

"And the people who ransacked the room?"

The boss pointed at a single mark on the edge of the desk. A faint impression, almost no lines, a uniform smudge that spread out three inches long and an inch wide, shaped like a finger. "There's the culprit. Looks like an air sylph. It's not something that'll show up in the fingerprint files down at the precinct."

"An air elemental? Who the hell uses air elementals to ransack a building?"

Mr. Templeton rubbed his chin. "Someone who doesn't want to be seen breaking and entering," he said. He rose and walked over to the open file cabinets, began searching through the remaining contents. "Someone with some real magic on their side."

Real magic on their side. I'd have to talk to Ingrid about real magic. Maybe she would have some ideas. I stepped around the books on the floor, scanning for any evidence. A slip of paper sticking out from the corner of one large volume caught my eye, and I leaned over to examine it. As I thumbed backwards through the pages, I recognized it. A children's volume of fairy tales. The piece of paper marked the start of a story. I turned my head sideways to read the title.

"Did you find something?" Mr. Templeton asked, walking over to me.

I nodded. "The Goose that Laid the Golden Egg."

"Grab the book and all the paperwork on the floor. Let's get out of here and go back to the office. We'll go through them together, and I'll swing by Lucky's place tonight to see what I can find there."

I gathered up Lucky's folders and paperwork. "How are we going to stop a sylph?"

"Don't worry, I can handle it." He handed back my powder and brush and headed into the hallway. I scooped up the detritus from the floor and followed him to the elevator, back down to the first floor, and across the lobby of the building.

As Mr. Templeton pushed through the revolving door, one of the glass panes shattered and a sharp crack split the air. Pinpricks of splinters scratched the side of my face. Mr. Templeton turned and threw himself to one side as I dropped to the floor, still stuck inside the entry, the documents scattering around me as I fumbled for the gun under my coat.

"Damn it, I had a feeling we were being followed," he said, drawing his pistol. "Should have trusted my instincts."

Another pane of glass shattered, followed closely by another crack. A shower of glittering fragments filled the air. The gun came free, and I looked for the attacker.

There were two of them in a black sedan, the passenger aiming his handgun out of the window and firing. I pulled my trigger, hammering off two quick shots through the broken doorway. Gunpowder smoke burned my nose and my ears rang. I thought one bullet might have cracked the rear window, but from this distance, I couldn't tell.

The engine started, and the car pulled away. I stood, limping as fast as I could towards the road. I angled towards Mr. Templeton's car, ducking behind the fender as another bullet whined past my ears. *By the time you duck, you're already dead,* the boss had once told me, but it was instinct, so I ducked anyways. I caught only a glimpse of the passenger, his bearded and slicked back hair, dark glasses over his eyes. Could have been human, could have been a dwarf, even gnome; I couldn't tell from this distance. The car accelerated. I rose and fired, emptying the pistol. I doubt I hit anything, but it soothed my wounded pride.

"Come on, boss," I yelled, yanking on the door to his car. Only then did I realize both tires on the passenger side were flat, the whitewalls gashed by a knife. I wiped away a trickle of blood seeping down my neck and watched the sedan recede, until it turned a corner with the screech of distant tires.

Mr. Templeton sat with his back against the building, holding his gun in his lap with his right arm, his left tucked under his coat. His fedora lay on the ground to his right, and his breath came in wheezes. I walked back and crouched next to him, my brow wrinkling in concern.

"Are you alright, boss?"

"Sure. I'll be fine. Got the wind knocked out of me. Stash those papers in the car, then find a phone and call it in. I need to catch my breath."

I scooped up the papers in the doorway and carried the pile over to the car. I opened the door to place them in the back seat, then thought better of it and laid them on the floor, tucking them under the front seat until they were out of view. Satisfied, I closed the door.

There was a phone booth down the street on the corner. I walked over and dialed the operator. My hands shook when I picked up the receiver. Nervous energy, body still wired to respond to a threat. Damn, I'd been in a real shoot out. It hadn't at all been like I'd imagined. Far scarier, in fact.

"Operator," said a shrill voice. "Who may I connect you with?"

"Can you connect me to the nearest police station? It's an emergency."

"One moment please." A long pause followed, and the sound of clicking. I drummed my fingers against the side of the booth and muttered under my breath, urging them to hurry.

"Police dispatch; please state the nature of the emergency."

My heart slowed, and my breathing eased. My hands shook a little, and my legs weakened. I leaned against the pole the pay phone was attached to as I spoke. By the time I finished talking to the dispatcher, my heart rate seemed normal, but I felt exhausted, the rush fading from me as swiftly as it had pumped me into action. I pressed my head against the cool wood and steadied myself. Once my legs were less rubbery, I pushed away and headed back.

Mr. Templeton no longer sat upright. He'd slumped over, a red blot marring the front of his shirt, to the right of his heart. His hands were open, his Saint Brendan's medallion resting in the palm of one. His gun lay on the ground.

I ran to his side, and dropped to the ground next to him, tearing my dress, skinning my knees. I shook his shoulder, but he didn't respond, so I cupped his hands around his medallion and held them with my own as I spoke to him. "Come on, Mr. Templeton, wake up, don't fall asleep. Don't do this; please; you're going to fine. Please boss, come on, stay with me, they'll be here soon." I watched the street, the wail of sirens starting, but still far away. Faster, please come faster. Why was it taking so long?

"Come on, Mr. Templeton, please. You can't do this to me. I need you to help me with the answers. They'll have a lot of questions, Mr. Templeton. You're better at talking to them than I am. They know you."

Tears ran down my cheek. My legs folded and I sat on the cold concrete beside him. I pulled him against me, cradling his head to my chest. I fought back sobs. The sirens were too far away. They echoed off the buildings, repeating themselves. They seemed to be everywhere but here, where they were needed. Were they punishing me? Mocking me? Reminding me how I'd been too slow, how I'd failed him? His hand sticky with blood, blood on the ground, blood soaking into the hem of my stained and torn dress. Too much blood. Lucky's blood, Mr. Templeton's blood. Whose blood next?

"Don't go. Don't go. Don't go." Please don't go, Mr. Templeton. Please wake up.

Don't leave me. Please, don't leave.

Don't leave.

No.

8

The Hospital

I sat on a loading dock, my knees pulled up to my chest. The lip of the roof covered me, but rain pelted down beyond the toes of my shoes, and stray winds wafted flecks of moisture against my face and hands. My clothing grew damp, and I shivered from cold and wetness. I held his medallion in my hand, noticing a faint, green verdigris over its surface. I brushed my fingers across the markings, tried to rub it clean. The green remained, annoying, a reminder of something nagging my thoughts. I stuffed it back in my pocket. I didn't want those thoughts.

I couldn't stop those thoughts.

Petunia stayed with him. She arrived moments after the ambulance, her face twisted in a grimace of pain, fighting to hold back tears. No one had called her. She knew what had happened and where we would be in the same way she knew when a client was arriving at the office, or exactly what the time was though she had no watch or clock for reference. Whatever magical insight she had, it told her Ben Templeton had been shot, and she needed to get to the

69

hospital. That he lay dying in some emergency room. So, she came, and she found me, standing next to his gurney, trying desperately to hold it all together. I tried to turn away from her as the nurses rushed him into a separate emergency room, but she grabbed me and hugged me tightly until my sobs were the only thing I could hear over the ringing in my ears. I didn't know if it were Ben's injuries that made me cry harder, or the fact she hugged me despite the fact it had been my fault.

I'd been too slow to react. I couldn't stop them.

I'd failed him.

When I broke free of her grip, I'd said, "I need to use the bathroom," and Petunia had only nodded. She pulled a handkerchief from her pocket and wiped my cheeks.

I found a small restroom nearby, and I locked the door. I'd been holding his medallion, praying, all the way to the hospital. In the bathroom, I tucked it into my pocket. I didn't want to pray. In no world could a God take Benjamin Francis Templeton from us and leave his killers free to roam the street. In no world would that be fair, so this world had no God I could beg justice of. I knelt over the toilet, my body heaving up what little I'd taken in that morning, until I emptied, my stomach clenched in a knot of pain as I dry retched for a while longer. Then I rested my head on the cool porcelain surface and let my tears dry.

I hated hospitals. Hated the sickness and the death, the aroma of cleaners and incense that overlay the scent of decay. I hated their white walls and gurneys, the doctors with their white coats and somber faces, the staff witches with their white veils and red-crossed smocks. I hated the bright, white lights that hurt my eyes and gave me a headache, and the warmed-over cafeteria food that filled a stomach without fulfilling a need. Take one bite and call me in the morning, everything will be the same, everyone dead.

I couldn't remember staggering from the bathroom floor and

making my way out a side door and around the building where I found my uncomfortable seat. Only when Petunia wrapped a large coat around me did I become aware of how much time had passed and how cold I'd become. Mr. Templeton's trench coat, damp on the outside but warm beneath the lining, as though containing the heat of the man. Petunia held me close as I watched a leaf swirl along the edge of the pavement, caught up in a stream of water rolling along until it tumbled down an embankment and joined the river that flowed beside the hospital.

"The doctor said . . ." She paused and I knew. No magical insight needed; she wore the pain nakedly upon her face.

"He's gone." My voice cracked as I said it. Cracked like the world, like a fragile egg bursting open. To say it made it real. Sitting here alone, I could pretend this day had never happened. The shell pierced, but inside I found . . . what? Nothing. I had nothing left to give. There were no more tears. Just a hollow where I used to have a heart. Emptiness.

Petunia nodded, and pulled me close again, crying against my shoulder. I held her close and let her feel what she needed. I'd gone beyond, gone numb, had spent my grief already. I wrapped my arms around her body and squeezed tight, though the action seemed useless. How could I soothe another when I'd become so empty myself? How could I begin to lift the spirit of this woman who worshipped the man she worked for when I was responsible for his death? I could no more comfort her than I could comfort myself.

Not good enough. Never good enough. No, Ingy, I wasn't ready. I'd been lying to myself all this time. Ben Templeton had been right to hold me back.

When Petunia sat up straight, I wiped away her tears. "I didn't know pixies cried."

"I'm only quarter pixie," she sniffled, a small laugh punctuating the remark. Then her smile fell again. "I miss him. I miss him so much."

"Don't. Don't start again. Your eyes are already swollen and red."

Petunia half laughed, half sobbed. "Oh goodness, my mascara is running." She dabbed at her eyes with a tissue wadded up in her hand. "You're so strong, Mira. He saw that in you, he did. He always told me when you weren't around."

Not strong enough. I knew something had been up by the way he drove, watching over his shoulder. I should have been ready. I'd been too slow and weak, and it got him killed. I didn't say any of that. She didn't need any more on her plate, had herself to care for now. In time, she would realize what I had done. The magnitude of my incompetence. That would be when she would stop saying the nice things and realize Ben Templeton had deserved better watching his back. She'd leave me, and I'd be alone again. They'd all leave me. All I'd ever been good for was being abandoned by those I had loved.

I hated those thoughts, though I felt powerless to stop them. I tried to pull myself together. "I don't know what I'm supposed to do now."

"We need to go inside." She pulled gently on my elbow, helping me stand. "The detectives want to take a statement. I told them not to rush you, you'd come when you're ready." Petunia patted my arm, and then broke out into a fresh round of tears.

I wrapped my arm around Petunia's frail shoulders and, leaning on each other, we found our way to an entrance and walked back to the ER, leaving a trail of soggy footprints on the floor. We rounded a corner and found the chief of police standing there, along with a few policemen in crisp, blue uniforms. He looked tired, his shoulders slumped, his eyes puffy and red like he'd been on an all-night bender. He held his fedora in his hand, and his fingers twisted it, distorting the shape. Ben Templeton; so respected and admired his death rated the head of the Baltimore police department, not a common detective.

He stepped towards us and placed a meaty hand on my shoulder. "Mira, are you okay? No, don't bother answering. I've been doing this so long, it's natural to ask even though I know the answer. I always know the answer, but I have to ask, you know? Everyone expects me to ask. I'm sorry, I'm going on. Everyone loved Ben, everyone. He was good people."

I shrugged, took a shuddering breath to stifle a scream lodged in my throat. Don't be nice to me. I don't deserve nice. "Thanks," I said, choking on the word. I didn't have the strength for more. What I wanted to do was leave, not be here in this room with these men answering questions about why he'd been killed and how it had come to be.

"I know this isn't the best of times, but we have to take a statement. You know how this works. I'm sorry."

"Don't be, I get it. It's procedure. Go ahead, let's get this done."

"Why don't you sit down and we'll get this over with. Bronchowski here has a few questions for you." He indicated a thin man with a thinner moustache in Baltimore blue, holding a pad of paper in and a pen.

So, I sat, and I didn't tremble at all, though my stomach had rung itself into knots you'd need a sword to untangle. I didn't sweat. I didn't cry. I answered questions. I kept each answer short and to the point, the way Ben Templeton taught me. Just the facts. I gave no more detail than needed to explain what had happened. I never mentioned the troll or the goose, the case we were taking on. I had no reason too; this was about Mr. Templeton and Lucky Gambini. These men, these cops, his colleagues and friends, they would understand. They would instantly grasp why my boss felt he had to follow up on Lucky's activities prior to his death, despite it being ruled an accident. They would have done the same if the shoes were swapped.

I had no proof Mr. Templeton was killed as part of the hunt for the goose, although it certainly rang true. There are no coincidences. But if the police had any reason to suspect it, they'd only get in my way, reduce my ability to move freely. No matter how much pain I felt, a part of me understood I needed to be free to pursue leads. It would be me who found Ben Templeton's killers first, not the cops.

I wanted the first shot at putting them in their graves.

I might fail. I probably would fail based on my accomplishments the last few days. But I'd damn sure leave a lasting impression on someone.

Guilt clenched my gut, as though Ben Templeton frowned at me in disapproval from heaven above. I glanced at the ceiling and let my eyes plead forgiveness. Weren't you doing the same thing for Lucky? Yes, you had been. Now I will. You taught me *too* well.

"Alright, do you have enough?" the chief asked. An hour had passed, and the old man seemed as exhausted as I felt. When Bronchowski nodded, the chief sighed, shifting his weight forward and letting his belly pull him more or less upright.

"Go on home, Mira. We've got things under control here and we know how to reach you if we need." He leaned over and gave me an awkward hug, patting my shoulders. He had comforted hundreds of grieving widows and family members, and I knew he learned the art of it. How to be comforting. He cared. But not when the body was Ben Templeton's. His own feelings were involved, and he appeared as lost as the rest of us. Then he lumbered from the room, two officers in blue drifting along behind him, following him downstream.

Bronchowski paused on his way out the door. He nodded, swallowed hard. "I knew him, too. Good man. Vincent's death hit him pretty hard." He turned away, but before he left, he gave me one last look, eyebrows furrowed. "You be careful. I can't stop you from doing what I think you're going to do. What he would do. But you call me if you need anything."

Not so smart then. Bronchowski knew I hadn't told everything. But he let it pass and his warning had been mild. He had an idea what I planned. For Ben Templeton, he'd allow it.

I didn't move all through the shift changes and as night fell. I stayed in that uncomfortable seat until Petunia found me again and told me we should get some rest. Directions, good. Orders. I needed those. I rose and we walked together to her car. The rain had stopped, though the clouds were low and threatening, the lights of Baltimore reflecting off their underbellies like an orange glow of a fire roiling overhead, churning and eating everything in its path.

I rolled down the window and let the scent of the city seep into my lungs while Petunia slid behind the wheel and drove out of the parking lot.

"I'll take care of everything. All the arrangements." Petunia's voice caught in her throat, and it landed like a punch to my stomach as I thought about him lying six feet deep beneath the cold, black soil. I pulled his warm coat tighter, and I slid my hands into the pockets. One hand found his medallion where I'd tucked it away. The other touched the cold metal of his car keys.

"Turn around," I said, pulling the key chain from my pocket with a rattle.

"You should get some rest, Mira."

"I need to move his car. We left it at the," and here I trailed off, not wanting to say those words out loud. The murder scene. "We left it behind when the ambulance came."

"I don't think," she began, but I cut her off.

"Please, Petunia, I need to move it before it gets damaged by someone. It's not right to leave it there."

Petunia gave me a sidelong glance, and then sighed, turning right down a side street and doubling back towards the center of the city. "Where am I going?'

"Head north on the York turnpike and turn left onto Cold Spring. It's not too far from the turn, you won't miss it."

My body felt light and empty, and my stomach reminded me it needed to be fed even while my heart couldn't bear the thought of food. Petunia's headlights illuminated the concrete roadway, and the world dimmed to the yellow glow that the car followed as it lurched forward.

Petunia found his Fjord with little difficulty, passing it and pulling over a few dozen feet further along. She kept her car idling.

"You're going straight home, right?"

"Yes, I promise."

I stepped out of the car and closed the door. Petunia leaned across the passenger seat and frowned at me out the rolled down window. "You be careful. I'll know if you're not."

I nodded and watched as Petunia placed her jalopy in gear and swung out onto the empty street. She turned a wide circle and headed back towards the pike. Did she know what I really planned? Maybe. Probably. Her special way of seeing things meant she'd know what I would be doing the next few hours. But she drove off anyway, bless her. Sometimes you need to be alone with all you're feeling. She let me have that.

I walked to the black Fjord sitting in front of the empty office building. I kept my eyes on the dented fenders, daring myself to ignore the front steps, the spot where Ben Templeton had fallen. The scene of the crime.

I unlocked the car and sat behind the wheel. The interior cold, lifeless. I wanted a cigarette, my fingers twitching towards the glove box before I pulled them back. How could it be possible I'd been with him only the past morning? Was this even the same day? Would I open the glove box and find a note from him there telling me I should always come prepared? I bit my lip to hold back a keening wail that wanted to escape my throat. Held it at bay as Ben

Templeton's life washed over me. The car held memories of him. A faint scent of cigarette smoke. His cologne. A trace of leather polish mixed with gun powder. A detective's life.

When I'd mastered the need to scream, I bent over sideways and felt around under the seat until my hand touched the book and the pile of documents I'd stashed there a lifetime ago. I pulled them out and tucked them under my arm, relief passing through me. The end of the worst day ever, but one thing had gone right. One single thing I hadn't fucked up entirely. I exited the car again, locked it. I glanced at the two flat tires next to the curb. I'd call someone tomorrow and have them tow it, fix the tires for me. Clean out the scent of the man who'd been my mentor. My guide. My friend.

I began the long walk home.

9

Hollowed Out

Petunia had called Ingy and told her what had happened. Not the details; Petunia was too upset to share them. Ingy didn't know I'd been with him when he'd been killed. I wouldn't tell her either; she had enough on her plate.

I resented Petunia for spilling the beans only slightly. Had expected it actually, knowing the woman I worked with well enough. Petunia wanted to make sure I was okay, and that was the best and worst thing about her. When she should be caring for herself, she took care of others. Her grief had to be every bit as powerful as mine, but she worried about me instead of her own needs. Maybe for her, that's how it worked. Maybe that was her way of dealing with powerful emotions, with the pain of loss. In time though, she would grind herself down to lift up others and we'd lose her. When I found the capacity to feel again, I'd sit down and have a talk with her.

Ingrid held the door open for me as I came in. The clouds had broken up during my walk. A few bright stars glimmered through the sodium haze of the slumbering city. She didn't reach for me, didn't embrace me. Her way was not Petunia's way. She closed the door and locked it when I'd crossed the threshold.

I stopped moving. I stared at the far wall. What do I do now? I didn't know. The impetus had been to get the documents and get home. One step, two steps, keep walking until I arrived. Get home to Ingy. Now, I'd completed the task I'd set myself. I stood like a sailing ship on a becalmed sea. I had no course now.

She took the folders and book from me and put them away. Then she stepped behind me and helped me take the coat off. She hung it for me, removing the .22 from the pocket and unloading the clip. She checked to make sure the chamber was empty, slid both into a drawer. I stood numb, empty, my bloodshot eyes as dry as a desert.

"There's a hot bath waiting for you upstairs," she said. "You go up, strip, and get in. Leave your clothing outside the door so I can take them and see if I can get them mended. You don't have many nice dresses. Your nightgown is on the edge of the sink. Put it on, then go to your room. I will meet you there."

Directions, focus; exactly what I needed. I would have thanked her if my tongue worked. But it had swollen, stuck to the dusty roof of my mouth. I nodded mutely and climbed the steps. I expected with each riser I'd feel Jacob coming to talk, but he remained hidden. Strange that, a ghost who hid during the night and only seemed to be around during the day. For now, I needed the space. I would have died again if he'd come to comfort me, as I'd died on the steps to Lucky's office. Jacob wouldn't let me be an empty vessel like Ingy would. He'd need to draw me out, and I didn't think I could handle that.

The water welcomed me. I heard Ingrid gather my things outside the bathroom door. I floated on a sea of warmth and comfort. But, when I closed my eyes, I saw his blood, and it ran in rivers over the concrete sidewalk and down the street, flowing into the gutters, down to the Jones Falls, into the harbor, the ocean turning red. I took the sponge and scrubbed myself. I wished it were rougher, hard enough to scrape my skin raw, scrape it off, reveal the muscles below, the bones, the rotted black marrow of my useless frame.

I stayed there long past the point the water grew cold. Not until I shivered did I get out, knowing Ingy wouldn't come in no matter how long it had been. I toweled off and put on the nightgown. I did nothing with my hair. It didn't seem important. I paced around the room. What was I supposed to do next? Right, the bedroom, where Ingrid waited with eyes that would surely be disappointed. I walked barefoot over cold floorboards and into my room.

Her face. Beautiful. Impassive. No emotion passed her gaze. She looked like a picture in a celebrity magazine, a movie star doing her damnedest to be cool and collected. I wanted her. So much, so very hard. But who would want me? Not the parents who abandoned me; certainly not the man who'd taken me under his wing, and who now lay dead in the hospital morgue. Chip away all the pieces of me, and what would you find beneath? Nothing anyone would want.

"Come here," she said. She held a brush in her hand, and when I stepped in front of her she took my shoulders and turned me, like a nun turning a recalcitrant young girl. I waited for the tug and pull of the brush, the hard yanks signifying her displeasure at having to administer attention to such a wretched human being. Make it hurt, make it hurt, please. Make me feel something, pain at least, anything.

She brushed my hair gently, with great care. I almost sighed at the first tender stroke. One hand held my damp locks, straightening them as the other drew the brush slowly through. Once, she stopped and took a small towel off her shoulder, squeezed it to wring moisture from some strands that were too damp. Would she wring moisture from my eyes, too? Would I cry now? I didn't feel like crying. I hated that I couldn't cry any more. I'd broken myself. My emotions had been scooped out and stolen from me. Would this new me even be Mira?

Ingy guided me into bed. I thought she would leave as I turned onto my side away from her. Cold gripped me, and I shivered under the blankets. Instead, she slid in behind me, still dressed, pulling the blankets over herself. She curled up against me with one arm crossing over me. I did lose control then. The touch of her rent a great heaving sob from me, a howl of grief and pain and loneliness and endless desire for a woman who would only ever be a friend, and who would despise me if I told her how much I desired her. And shame burned through me to mix with all the other emotions. That I could want her now, when Ben Templeton's body lay cooling on a slab. Pathetic. But still no tears. No more tears.

She pulled my damp hair off my neck. She radiated warmth against my back, and I soon stopped shivering. Her breath tickled my ear as she whispered, "Now sleep."

I . . .

***

The scent of food woke me. I rolled over to find myself alone in bed. I wondered how long Ingy had remained with me. Probably not long. Why would she? She had more important things to do than waste her day keeping an unconscious woman company. I couldn't tell how long I'd slept, although the light coming in around the curtains suggested late afternoon and well on towards sunset. I felt rested, though I hadn't done anything to earn it. Ingy probably had used a charm on me to put me to sleep. Well, she was allowed. If anyone else had tried that little trick, I'd've punch them in the teeth.

Heat grew inside me. The numbing wash of sadness had faded, the pain of grief gone. Now? Now came anger, like a hand pulling my guts into knots and punching through my chest. When had my grief turned to anger? Sometime while I slept, I suppose. While the sun coursed across the sky, it melted the pit inside me, the cold bubble of grief and pain, and forged the molten remnants into slag steel. It burned hot inside me, waiting to be unleashed.

Voices murmured downstairs. Ingrid talking to someone. On the phone? No, I could hear someone replying. Male, deep voice. I knew the voice, even if I couldn't make out the words. Of course he came. If I thought I could avoid people, I'd be nothing but a damned fool. He came because of me, and I owed it to him to respect that. I'd have to make an appearance sooner or later. Might as well be sooner.

I tossed the blankets off and grabbed my robe from the chair by the window. I shrugged into it on my way down the hall. By then, the voices had stopped. They'd heard the creak of the floorboards. Ingrid came into view first as I descended, standing between the parlor and the dining room. She held a glass half filled with dark liquid in one hand, a bottle in the other. Her face as expressionless as last night, as though leaving to me to lead on the emotional front. Good old Ingrid; she could stuff emotional pain right down into her cracks, plaster them over, and no one who didn't know her would ever be the wiser. I wanted her type of strength.

I'm so sorry, Jacob said, his sadness a hammer blow to my body. The room temperature plummeted.

"Jacob, stop it," Ingrid said. She shivered.

Behind her . . . "Mira," Lugnut said. His voice didn't hide emotions, it crackled with worry and empathy. His eyes were red and he'd clearly been crying. Seeing him almost broke down the walls I'd begun to construct, doused the flames of rising anger and sent me straight back to cold grief. The sad frown, the concern in his eyes. He didn't wait for me to close the distance, but stomped across the room and swept me into his arms. Lord, but his hug felt good, so very good. I didn't know until then how badly I needed one good hug from a troll. I tried to say his name, but all that came out was a choking gasp for air. He released me, carefully lowering me to floor.

"Sorry," he said, grimacing. "I sometimes forget you're a bit on the frail side."

"Compared to you, yes, but I'll take it as a compliment. How have you been, tough guy?"

He tipped his head and his frown deepened. He took my hands in his. "Mira, I'm so sorry about Mr. Templeton." His voice cracked when he said the name.

I tried to pull away, my eyes turning towards the floor, but he wouldn't release me. "It's fine, Lugnut."

Wrong thing to say. I didn't know what else *to* say. But he took note of my denial.

"Fine?" His frown deepened further and his face wrinkled over his nose as his eyes narrow. "No, it's not fine, not by a long country mile. He was a good man. Respected. Decent. And you shouldn't have to grieve alone . . ." His words trailed off and ended with a help-less shrug. I understood. There are no words for that.

What to tell him? I'd put grief aside? Hardly. I'd burned it to ash, that's what I'd done. Right down to my core. I'd replaced it with malice, a growing desire snapping at my thoughts. I wanted to see the bastards who murdered Ben Templeton put into their graves. But without him, I didn't know how to make that happen. Rested now, I understood what I hadn't last night. The agency had died with the man who built it. And it seemed wrong to desire such a thing. You don't tell others you want someone dead, even if they'd under-stand. "Okay, not fine. I'm not fine, none of this is fine. But I can't spend the next week or month or year crying over it. He'd want us to keep going, keep moving. Only I don't know what I'm moving on to."

We know, Jacob said. *I know; better than most*

He did, too. I didn't want his sympathy, though. The last thing I needed was a ghost trying to help me feel better when his own existence contained incorporeality and painful memories. "It's okay, Jacob. You have your own worries to think about. I'll be okay."

"Mira." Ingy's voice came sharp as a whip slashing the air. She'd put down the bottle and glass, crossed her arms over her chest. "It's fine to feel what you feel. And it's fine to tell us the things you need to. But for fuck's sake, be honest; we aren't going to judge you. Every single person in this room, living or dead, has lost someone or something that mattered."

She left the conversation wide open for me, as if she knew what I wanted to say. I could fill the void with anger, or pain, or anything I wanted. Damn her. "What am I supposed to feel, Ingy? What? Sadness? An ache in my gut that won't go away? Anger? Burning me up from the inside until I boil? Tell me what I'm supposed to feel." My voice rose as I spoke. I held my right hand curled into a fist and jammed it against my stomach as though I'd punched myself in the gut, and pressed my head with my left. "What am I supposed to feel? In my gut here? Or up here where all those feelings go?" I patted the side of my head, harder and harder, trying to slap some feeling into myself. "What should I feel, Ingy?"

She stepped toward me, took my hand, stopped it. "All of it. You feel all of it. And when you master it, when you control it, you channel it."

"Channel it where?"

"Right at the bastards who killed Templeton. Find them, take them down. If you have to, you kill them."

Had this been any other day in our lives, it would have startled me to hear her speak of murder so bluntly. Ingy always knew were my mind seemed to be, but murder? Well, hadn't I been having the same thoughts only moments before? I couldn't even gasp in surprise. Instead, a giggle passed my lips, edged in hysterics. I shoved my fist against my mouth to stifle them. "There's no agency any more. I'm not a detective. I don't have any in with the cops like he did, no license, none of his contacts. I'm the sidekick. The Templeton Agency is dead." I shook my head, emphasizing the no.

Her hands reached for my face, stilling my head, forcing me to meet her eyes. She spoke slowly, emphasizing each word. "You are the Templeton Agency now."

"If that's the case, Petunia and I better start looking for jobs." I didn't mean it, or maybe I did. I couldn't judge my own truths any more. If I were honest, the feel of her hands against my skin was, for the briefest moment, the only thing in the world that mattered. Everything else, gone, flashed away. Her lightest touch unbound me. Shamed again, too, because it didn't change that my boss remained as dead as he had been last night.

Ingy, though, took the comment seriously. "No, you're going to lick your wounds, take a couple of days off. Then you find them."

Take a couple of days off. She meant get prepared for Ben Templeton's funeral. I'd prepared for plenty of funerals in the past. I didn't know how I would be able to prepare for this one. How to say goodbye to the man who took me off the streets, gave me purpose?

No, I wouldn't say goodbye. Not until I'd finished the work. Only then would I have earned the privilege. That seemed right. Ingrid knew exactly what I'd needed to hear. She gave me focus again.

"He trained you to do this work," she continued. "You're ready. And I'll help."

"You're going to work for me?" I smiled crookedly at the thought.

"The hell you say. Consider me a witch for hire, nothing more. You couldn't afford me full time anyways."

Lugnut placed one massive hand on my shoulder. "Me, too. You could use a bit more muscle on your side."

"Hey, I can take care of myself, big guy."

He grinned, and it wasn't a sweet grin full of happy memories. It wasn't all that different from Mr. Green's grin, in fact. "I know you can, little witch. But I'd feel better if you'd let me come along while you're investigating. If trolls are involved, I can help grease the wheels a little. At least they won't be calling me piano mover."

Guilt slapped me as I remembered the way I'd talked to Mr. Green. I'd wanted to make him react, see if I could push him a little. Goad him into spilling more information so we could decide if we wanted to take his case. But the things I'd said were racist and petty, and I didn't believe a word of them. Why'd I say it, then? Maybe I couldn't claim to be better than the assholes I despised, the church attending masses who ate up all the nonsense about keeping the races segregated. Their insistent belief non-whites were non-human as well, their blood tainted by generations of mixing with the other races. Vile bullshit. Ben Templeton would have been ashamed of me if he'd known.

"I'm sorry," I blurted. Said it to Ingy, too. I owed a whole world of apologies.

"You get used to it. Hey, you hungry? I cooked up a cassoulet. You don't have much in that kitchen of yours, so I went down to the market on the corner and picked up some items."

I sniffed the food again. My appetite, missing in action when I'd woken, made a tepid appearance and demanded some attention. I couldn't eat much, but I needed something. "Smells wonderful. Lead me to the table."

10

Six Feet Under

On a somber Wednesday in early November, we laid Ben Templeton to rest. His final resting place would be the cemetery next to Saint Brendan's, not far from where an old oak tree cast its limbs outward. Leaves fell in a soft cascade littering the swath of grass and earth below. The world smelled earthy, the scent of loam and crushed grass, dying leaves. His pall bearers were six Baltimore city policemen, including Bronchowski, dressed in their dark blue uniforms. The chief came in full uniform as well and stood with the crowd. They looked swell. Ben Templeton would have been proud to have seen them. Once upon a time, it would have been him carrying a casket in such a uniform. That the police honored him, an ex-cop, with a formal ceremony said a lot about the man.

Petunia stood there, somehow looking radiant in black even as she sobbed at the front of the large crowd, her hand held by her boyfriend, Melvin. A dwarf named Grubby, who ran Mr. Templeton's favorite diner and had been friends with him, stood on the other side of her in a threadbare black suit that had seen better days, his tangled matt of dark hair brushed back and slathered with something resembling motor oil. There were other people as well, folks I barely knew or didn't know. Many of them had faces covered with cowls or hats pulled down and stayed well away from the police. That they came to pay their respects despite their concern about the law said even more about him.

I sat in the back row of the church during the mass, flanked by friends. Ingrid sat to my left, wearing her best black dress and a string of fake pearls. It confused me to see her dressed up, and I kept looking at her, as though I didn't know who she was and questioned her reasons for sitting next to me. The woman I'd fallen in love with, a secret I would carry to my own grave if I had to. It contributed to the surreal feeling, a sense this was all a dream I would awaken from at any moment. I'd walk into the office later this morning and Ben Templeton would be there with a bottle of whiskey and five o'clock shadow reading the obituaries. Lugnut sat on my right, shifting in his seat as though uncomfortable, though he wasn't out of place in this crowd. Not only were there dwarves besides Grubby, there were a couple of other trolls as well, and one very old elf who held a hand-kerchief over his mouth during frequent bouts of a racking cough. Ben Templeton had been a man who treated people with respect. All people.

People took their turns approaching the casket while we waited for it to be time to walk to the grave and for father Gregory to give his eulogy. Some spoke quietly for a while. Others paused for a moment, signing the cross, then walked on, or rested their hand on the edge of the brown wooden box for a few ticks of some invisible alarm clock measuring the length of time for paying proper respect before chiming the viewer to withdraw. A few performed simple magical charms; spells of peace, passing, remembrance.

I didn't go near the casket, the wooden bed where he would rest eternal. I hadn't earned the right to see him at peace. He deserved the comfort of those who had taken care of him, helped him, not the woman who'd let him die. I feared the anger I held inside me would be too fragile to survive seeing his face. It would crumble to dust leaving me with little left to work with but pain. Pain wouldn't motivate me to do what I needed to do. Sorrow would hinder me, put me on my ass instead of on the trail of killers. So, I sat in the back and I watched and my face remained dry, just as his had during Lucky's funeral. There would be no widow for me to go sit with after, either. No father or mother to provide comfort to. As far as I knew, Petunia and I were the closest thing to family the man had left. And Petunia had Melvin; she didn't need me.

I rose with Ingy when it came time to march to the grave site. We waited for the bearers to pass by, for the mourners to exit, and we followed far to the rear of the rest of the crowd.

Father Gregory walked around the edge of the grave, the dirt covered in gold colored fabric, to provide the eulogy. He stood at the foot of the coffin as the spectators gathered around. His short, black hair had grayed along the sides, and he peered at the mourners through silver spectacles framing puffy brown eyes, his robes stirring around his body. A gold cross bearing the likeliness of the crucified Jesus hung from a silver chain around his neck, and when he spoke in his cracking, high pitched voice, I found my eyes drawn to the light that flashed from its surface. He held the bible open in front of him, his face long and somber.

"Our brother lies here today, and we are here to pay him honor, in the name of Jesus Christ our lord. While Benjamin Francis Templeton was not the most devout of God's followers, I can see he was loved and cherished by many and will be deeply missed. By myself as well." He talked for a while, but the rest of his words didn't register. I thought only of the man and what he meant to me. That's what funerals are for.

When the priest finished, Petunia stepped forward, wiping her tears with a white handkerchief. She paused for a few breaths, and glanced around.

"I'm not much for speaking in front of crowds. But I wanted to say how much I loved Ben Templeton. He was a good boss, and a good friend. He always treated everyone good, the way he wanted to be treated. It didn't matter what you were or where you came from. He was kind in his own way, even if he drank too much, and sometimes got drunk before breakfast." A few people laughed. She did as well, more than half sob, then went on. "And he didn't have to . . . have to give me a job, but he did . . . he hired me when no one else would give me a chance . . . he was like a father . . ."

She broke down in tears, her racking sobs drowning out fresh sniffles from the onlookers. Melvin stepped over and wrapped his arm around her shoulders, guided her back to the throng standing in the cold. Everyone watched two attendants as they lowered the casket into the grave. Off to the side, a dwarf began playing a set of bagpipes. Seven officers raised rifles, and in unison fired three sets of shots.

When the formalities were over and the attendants had stepped away again, the mourners marched pass, Petunia in the lead, and said a few quiet words or tossed flowers into the hole. The crowd thinned until only a few of us stood there. The attendants left us alone with the deceased. I thought that decent of them.

Petunia and Ingy flanked me, Melvin on the other side of Petunia, as we stood over the open earth, looking down at his simple coffin. Lugnut stood behind us, looking over our heads.

"Do you think there's a place we go to after we die?" Petunia asked. "I mean, is he someplace where we could maybe see him one day, tell him thanks." Her mascara ran down her face, and I pulled a tissue from the trench coat I wore. Ben Templeton's coat. It had seemed the thing to do, at once a memorial to him as well as a reminder of the work I had yet to complete. I rubbed the wet smears from below Petunia's eyes and tried to smile, but my attempt at comfort felt poor.

"If there is, he's probably got a bottle in one hand and a glass in the other," Ingy said.

That brought a small chuckle to those of us who remained. I had no words, though, because a lump lodged in my chest and I had to hold it back or I'd be done for. It took all my will to choke it down. To bury it like I would his casket. I rolled up the long sleeves of his coat, then took a shovel from the large mound of dirt that lay next to the hole. The caretakers had removed the fabric that had covered it during the service. I scooped a shovel full and dumped it into the hole. Ingy and Lugnut joined me. Petunia and Melvin took turns as well when one of us paused. We got it half full and left the remaining pile for the grounds keepers to finish up with. They'd fill it, flatten it, lay sod over it, and put up the simple headstone Petunia and I picked out for him. The church had sprung for it, father Gregory proving beyond generous. *Cineri gloria sera venit*, it said in Latin. Fame comes too late to the dead.

Though the day was cold, I sweated by the time we finished. I wiped the moisture from my brow and tossed the shovel aside. There didn't seem to be any more to do. I couldn't say goodbye. Not this way. Not with his killer out there running around free. That would be my goodbye to him. My thank you for his care for me, as disappointing as I must have been for him. This hole in the ground didn't have any connection with me or the man whose name marked the headstone.

We walked back to my car—Mr. Templeton's car, which I'd decided to use in place of my Model D—parked along one of the narrow dirt lanes threading their way between the gravestones and statues and mausoleums. The shadow of the cathedral fell across us as we drove towards the exit. I glanced at the towers which made the dilapidated row homes around the cathedral seem so small and shabby. But Saint Brendan's, and father Gregory, tried to help the community. As much as I despised the leanings of the Church, this parish knew what its real purpose should be and welcomed all who needed help. All immigrants, all races, no matter what the problem. I couldn't find fault, though I doubted very much I'd ever return to this spot again. Nothing remained here for me but the cold ending of a gray day.

We started planning as soon as we got back to Highlandtown. Grubby held a memorial service with food at his diner. Knowing the cops, it would be more like a drunken wake. I couldn't bear that. All those people, all of them remembering a good man, sharing their condolences, singing and laughing. I had nothing to laugh about. No songs I could sing. I'd rather get right to work while I still had the fire inside. Ingy understood and agreed immediately. Lugnut took more persuading. Petunia, surprisingly, fell right in with Ingy. I'd thought she'd have been harder to convince.

"You gotta do what you do, Mira," she had said. She sat between Melvin and I in the front seat of the car and patted my arm as I drove. "I don't know if it's right to be finding the people who killed him. But if it helps you, then it can't be a bad thing." I wonder what kind of world we'd live in if everyone had a Petunia on their side. Had to be better than the one we'd been given.

All the files were at the house, tucked away where Ingrid had stowed them. The folder with my notes, as well as the documents we found at Lucky's office. We spread them over the dining room table and everyone went through them, looking for anything we might have missed. I took the notes Lucky had written and strained my eyes to make heads or tails of anything. His writing was messier than the boss' had been, and Ben Templeton had been known for a chicken scratch which only Petunia could seem to decipher. But after a long evening broken only by dinner cooked up by Lugnut, as the night grew towards the witching hour, we'd gotten no further than when we'd started. Petunia and Melvin said their goodnights and headed home. I couldn't begrudge them getting some rest. It had been a long day and hard on her.

Lugnut volunteered to stay longer, though, and I made up the couch in the parlor for him if we got too tired to continue.

"If we agree Lucky was murdered, and we know Templeton was murdered, then can we assume they were both killed by the same people?" Lugnut asked. He sat on the floor, his back to the wall, holding a glass of gin. "It's not much a stretch I'm thinking."

I flinched at the boss' name. In conjunction with the word murder, it felt like being slapped. But neither Lugnut nor Ingy noticed my reaction, or were kind enough not to mention it. "I'm going to make that leap. It's the only thing we have to go on right now."

Yes, it seemed reasonable. I had no proof they were related, but, as Ben Templeton had said, there are no coincidences. Two different firms hired to investigate the golden goose; two different men murdered. Different facts for each murder, but everything else fit, including the timing of their deaths, not long after each had been approached. "The question is, who had a motive for murder?"

Ingrid drummed her fingers on the table, tiny sparks dancing from the tips with each thump. "Maybe someone who is opposed to whomever hired them?"

I nodded slowly, chewing on the thought. Made sense when you looked at it the right way. If more than one group wanted the goose—more than one group would, for certain—then they would naturally be at odds. They'd want to stop the others by any means necessary. If they couldn't easily get to one another, they'd target any intermediaries working for their opponents to try and slow them down. "Still leaves us with a problem."

"What?" Lugnut asked, filling the hole I'd left for the question.

"I don't know who's providing the moolah to finance our little search." I knew what I meant when I said it. What it implied we needed to do. Now I needed to talk Ingy and Lugnut into what I had planned.

"What about Mr. Green?" Ingy asked, as if I'd prompted her.

"Messenger," I said. "He never said who'd hired him."

Lugnut stood and stretched his back, hands on his hips. "Maybe we ought to go ask this fellow."

Bless his heart. I didn't have to try and convince them of what I'd already decided. My best angle would be to find Mr. Green and try to work the information out of him. I'd get him to sign the contract. Assuming he still would. But we had the scroll he needed. Maybe I could leverage that. A little light blackmail. No return of the scroll until we found the goose, or until we failed. Failure meaning, of course, my own death. I had no illusions about the possibilities. Small price to pay, though, for all I owed Ben Templeton.

"You keep going through these documents and see if you can uncover anything. I'm going down to the club to pay Mr. Green a visit." I rose from the table and turned to go change into something more appropriate, but Lugnut took my arm and gently turned me around.

"What?" I asked.

"We're going with you," he said, pointing at his chest and then Ingy. "We came along on this little adventure so we can help. You need to let us."

His concern and empathy covered me like a warm blanket. Ingrid, though, appeared angry, her face drawn tightly, eyes narrowed. "There's no way I will let you face the world when you're so damned naïve about how it works."

"I understand how it works," I said. The rage inside me bubbled and I had to squeeze my body tighter to keep it under control. "It's a club, it's no fancy whoop."

"The Tom Tom Club, right?" she asked. I nodded. "In Little Italy? Where whites generally don't go unless they are *slumming*?"

She spit out the last word and I flinched. No, I hadn't really thought of it that way. I knew where the Tom Tom Club was located, but it hadn't occurred to me it would be a club catering to other races and minorities, and a white person would stick out like sore thumb. Damn it. Didn't they know I didn't want them to come? Couldn't stand the thought of putting them in danger? But the club might not even let me in. My options were either try it alone and fail, or take two people I love with me and hope it didn't all come crashing down around us.

Ingrid seemed to understand where best to apply pressure. "You're not going to get in without us there. I've been there, I know how to work the door man. You need me."

"She needs us," Lugnut chimed in.

Ingrid shot him a look with raised eyebrows, then shrugged. "Us."

Misery loves company. "Alright, alright. All of us." I couldn't decide if their eagerness to help pleased me, or if my fear of losing either of them would undo me.

Both, probably.

I I

Tom Tom Club

A swanky crowd filled the harbor area. Most whites stayed close to the water, frequenting segregated gin joints and jazz clubs. No blacks, no dwarves, no trolls allowed. But little Italy opened its doors to a mixed crowd, all the people who couldn't or wouldn't pass for white and wanted to get their drinks and dancing. They filled the sidewalks, humans mixing with dapper dwarves, natty gnomes, posh goblins, even a rakish elf or two. I drove slowly to avoid well-dressed individuals crossing the road, the rolled-down windows letting in a wash of music from nearby clubs. It took longer than expected to drive through the mess and find a place to park.

When I stepped out of the car, the two of them followed. Lugnut twisted and stretched to loosen himself from the cramped confines of the car, and Ingy tossed her spent cigarette to the ground and crushed it out.

Trolls didn't run any nightclubs in this part of town, but they often worked as bouncers, like Mr. Green. The Tom Tom club was one such place, and a neon sign proclaimed its name and proudly lit the exterior. Formerly a warehouse, its current owner was a well-connected dwarf who ran a string of laundromats and shipping firms and kept things on the up and up. The line to enter stretched a half block long, and I winced at the noise of the live band playing swing music that throbbed through the brick walls. I could see flashes of light behind arched windows high overhead.

Ingy walked behind as Lugnut and I approached the roped off entryway. A troll in a black suit manned the door, letting patrons in by ones or twos. He had a squashed nose, like a two-bit boxer, and one snaggled tooth stuck out on the right side of his mouth.

"Him?" Lugnut asked.

"No, that's not Mr. Green," I said. "Maybe we should go around back and sneak in,"

"To hell with it," Lugnut said. "Follow my lead." He took the front steps in large strides as he put his fedora on. He stood half a head taller than the bouncer, who gave him the kind of stink eye reserved for bad smelling fish.

"Back in the line," the doorman growled.

"No can do, I've got two rich young tomatoes here looking for a good time and there ain't nothing that's going to stop them." Lugnut thrust his thumb at me and Ingrid. I tried to grin, but I was too nervous to say anything. I pulled my wrap around my neck.

Ingrid had no such fears apparently. She swayed up the steps and stopped beside Lugnut. She'd left the pillbox hat back at the house, and the black mourning dress worked swell for a night on the town. "Why is he stopping us, Mickey," she said, leaning on Lugnut's arm and doing her best imitation of a spoiled woman. All those years of acting had clearly paid off. She reminded me Nina Mae McKinney in *Gang Smashers*. "Isn't he gonna let us through? My date's gonna be real sore to be kept waiting, and I need a drink."

I held my breath. I wondered how dedicated he felt to his job, if he had strict orders about whom to let into the joint. Words alone might not get us through the doorway. I considered the back door again. That might be our only option.

Lugnut took a step closer and straightened his back, towering over the bouncer. "Boss isn't going to like you keeping Miss Lucia and Miss Penny waiting." His hand slid forward, blocked from the sight of the rest of the crowd by his body, a greenback folded between his thick fingers.

The bouncer's eyes swung back to hold Lugnut's for a few moments, and then he took the money and tucked it into a pocket, smooth and quick. He unlatched the red rope from its brass stand. "Go on, go on, beat it before I get in trouble. Get that little slummer of yours off the street before someone sees her."

We walked through the door, and the two of us laced our arms through Lugnut's on either side. "Thanks, sugar," Ingy said, blowing the troll a kiss.

Once we were inside and out of sight, I let go of Lugnut and took a long, deep breath. "Damn, that couldn't have gone any better," I said. "I'll pay you back soon as I can."

Lugnut laughed. "You better, because that was my last twenty bucks. It's easier to get inside when you grease the wheels a little. You need to spend more time at gin joints. Everyone wants to make a few extra bucks. Now let's find this Green fellow and get out of here."

The music swept over us as we entered the main dance floor, drums and horns pounding like a writhing force that wanted to shove us onto the wall. The good life of Baltimore put itself on display, the exuberant and colorful joy of it, which it didn't show the world often. Fast people with their slick cars and pretty clothes, the ones lucky enough to have enough money to get out for a night. There were hundreds of them drinking and dancing, everyone mingling with laughter and smiles. A mirror ball rotated over the middle of the floor, flashing sparkles of light around the room.

For a brief moment I could imagine a better world, where everyone got along no matter the shape of their ears or the color of their skin. It took a quasi-illegal juke joint to put them in a room and get folks like me to show a little respect. Then the bright flashes of strobes blinded me as the club's picture taker shot a frame of us walking in, spoiling the moment. I squinted against the glare.

Lugnut leaned towards me, his mouth moving.

"What?" I said, straining to hear him over the music.

"We should split up and look for him."

I nodded my assent and gave them a quick description, trying to remember the shape of his face, some of the warts he had and where they were located. Then Lugnut moved to the right, working his way through the tables. Ingrid went up the middle towards the dance floor and the swinging band. That gave me the left, and I headed for the bar, where a knot of men crowded against the wood and brass to order glasses of booze for themselves and the ladies at their sides. I lost sight of Ingrid and Lugnut, too short to see over the crowds between us. I shouldered through the tight throng of bodies and worked my way down to the end of the bar.

It didn't take as long as I feared. I spotted Green sitting alone in the corner where the bar met the wall. His cigar lit up his features each time he took a long drag, and I remembered the crags and crevasses of his face. His bowler rested on the top of the bar next to a tall glass filled with dark liquid. I worked my way through the crowd, fending off bodies until I reached his side.

"Green. Green!" I shouted to get his attention over the loud music as the band ramped up into a fast number featuring the tom tom drums that were its namesake.

He swung his gaze at me and blinked a few times. "Sinclair. What's doing?" I couldn't make out the words, but the rumble of his voice cut through the background noise, and I could tell what he said from the shape his lips made.

"We're accepting the contract!"

"What?"

He couldn't hear the higher pitch of my voice over the screaming brass section. "Templeton Agency! Sent! Me!" Not a lie. Not really. Ben Templeton hadn't sent me, but I represented the agency. Never mind Petunia and I were all that remained of the agency. There'd only been the three of us anyway.

He shook his head to indicate he still couldn't hear me. "Hold on," he mouthed. He finished whatever was in the glass in front of him. He grabbed his hat and waved his hand to show me I should follow him. He didn't head through the crowded room. He hugged the wall and turned left down a narrow corridor. I glanced behind me as I followed him into the hallway, and saw Lugnut watching me from across the room. I waved to show him I wanted him to follow, then hurried to catch up with Mr. Green.

There were small, semi-private rooms along the hall, and he led me into one of them. Curtains gave the room a modicum of privacy from passing eyes, but when he moved to close it, I shook my head. "Leave it open, I've got some friends coming along."

He gave a grunt, then slid into a seat behind the round table in the center of the small room. "More faces I bet. You like to slum it down here, don't you?"

I said nothing, certainly not admitting I didn't usually frequent the clubs around the harbor. I never had the dough for such luxuries. I watched the doorway for their arrival. Ingrid entered first and slid into the chair to my left. Then Lugnut, who stood leaning against the doorway, crossing his arms over his chest. There was an extra chair available, but Lugnut remained on his feet.

Green checked them over, and then turned his eyes back to me. "Templeton hires untouchables, does he? Must cost less."

I took a pause to check my anger, letting my breath out slowly. He hadn't heard about Mr. Templeton's death, which made things easier. But he wanted to push my buttons, like I'd pushed his at our first meeting. I let the anger unwind, checked my breathing, made sure I wasn't tensed. Only then did I speak. "These are my friends. Ingrid shares a house with me. That's Lugnut, who runs a garage out near Towson."

Mr. Green nodded at Lugnut and gave a smile. "I know the place. Some say you do pretty good work for a piano mover."

Lugnut nodded in return, but his jaw tightened. "Good to hear my reputation proceeds me. If you've got a car, bring it on out, I'll get it running silky smooth for you. My rates are competitive. But don't call me a piano mover."

Green laughed. "Competitive he says." He turned back to me and jerked his thumb towards Lugnut. "I like this guy. Fair enough, I apologize. No more insults." He pulled a cigar from the inside breast pocket of his suit jacket. The silver lighter came out and he soon had it lit. "So, what are you doing here, Sinclair? Taking your friends out for a little night on the town and couldn't get into any white places? Did you bring them along to show me a good little Miss Anne's gots soulless friends?"

I let out the breath I'd been holding and put on my serious business face. "Two reasons. First, I wanted to apologize for the way I acted when we met. I shouldn't have said the things I did. It was stupid and immature, trying to act tough. It won't happen again."

He waved his hand through the air, stirring his cigar smoke in whirls. "No need. I knew you was trying to get a rise out of me, like I did when I called you a girl. Fair, you gave good as you got. 'Sides, you think I haven't heard it all by now? Takes more'n words to get under my skin."

I gave him the next bit I'd prepared. This rested on his either not reading the papers, or not caring who took the job. "Second, we're accepting the case."

"Good, good," said Mr. Green. He eased back in the chair,

stretching his legs out in front of him. "Your agency came highly rec-ommended."

"Why a human agency?" Lugnut asked, framing my next question as though I'd prompted him. "There are other firms to handle prob-lems for trolls. It makes more sense to me you'd hire a guy like, say, Axelrod Cerulean, then a human."

Mr. Green didn't look at him, but he tensed slightly, his mouth narrowing. "Got my reasons," he said.

"We don't take a job until we know who we're working for," I said, crossing my arms. A lot of defiance for a broke firm with a dead boss, but I wanted to find out. We needed to know. Knowing who hired us would lead to who wanted to stop them, give us a direction to investigate. Hang the fucking goose, I needed those killers.

Mr. Green shrugged and waved at Lugnut to pull the curtain. Then he leaned forward, resting his elbows on the table.

"Look, I got no beef with you or the cops. I've gone straight. I don't need to be a made man these days." He tipped his head as though indicating the club. "I get good pay, all the drinks I want, and I stay out of trouble. Even the dolls around here will tell you I keep my hands to myself and my work is clean. Mr. Oakpike gave me a chance. I did my time; I don't want to go back."

"None of which is an answer," I said. The cigar smoke had me craving a snipe, but now didn't seem the time to discard my hard-earned freedom.

"I got bills to pay," he said, pausing to take another drag. "You know. History. I take a few jobs on the side to pay off those debts."

History. We all have it. I had a history of petty theft and criminal mischief. What kind of history would Mr. Green have? A history of violence. He'd been arrested and incarcerated, but what if not all the crimes he'd done had yet been revealed? What would Mr. Green's associates do to him? I put the pieces together in my head, and a very different image of history emerged from the puzzle.

"You took the job because of your past," I said. Not a question, but a plain fact. "You need the extra money to pay off some old partners."

He tapped his cigar, and the ash fell on the floor. "Not so dumb as you act, Sinclair. S'good, really. Less I have to explain."

"But who suggested you hire us?" I asked.

He seemed to ponder that for a time, staring off into the distance over my head as though contemplating whether or not to answer. Then he turned his eyes to Lugnut, as though seeking his approval.

Lugnut nodded. "You can trust her. She's a good person. Not like most, whatever it was she said before."

Mr. Green turned and leaned closer to me. I mirrored his action, until our heads almost touched. "Young woman, very pretty. Bit of an accent; kinda reminded me of relatives I've got from Boston. But she's working as an intermediary."

"What's her name, and who is she working for?" I asked. Frustrated, too. We clawed our way up a food chain. Bouncer, to intermediary, to . . . who?

He lowered his voice further until I almost couldn't hear him despite our closeness. "I don't know exactly, but I overheard her on the phone talking to someone, and she used a strange word. Rowan. I don't know who she was talking to, what a rowan is, and it weren't my place to ask too many questions. She said she needs the goose to trade for something important. The girl's just a courier."

Rowan could have referred to the tree, but it could also be a name. Maybe a code name. I'd research it when I had some time. I tried a different approach. "She told you to hire the Templeton agency?"

He sighed and ran his free hand through his hair. "Look, Sinclair, what does it matter? She said hire a human agency, said the work might require lots of contact with the cops, and figured it'd go easier for a face. She recommended Templeton. Cops don't get along with us soulless bastards, you know that. Cerulean, he's good, but he ain't got the in a guy like your boss does. I checked. Templeton comes up smelling pretty fresh for a Charlie."

"What about Lucky Gambini?" I asked. Not because I expected answers, but because the mention of Ben Templeton had almost undone me. I had to change the topic fast or lose what cold water running through my veins remained.

He shrugged and leaned back again in his chair. "Don't know him. He anyone?"

His face looked impressively blank. I couldn't tell if he had lied or really didn't know Lucky. "Another private dick. He's dead. Probably murdered."

Green rubbed his eyes. "Look, I'm sorry the man is dead. My condolences to his kin. I hope they find whoever put him in a pine box."

"He'd been hired to find the goose, too, but wound up dying in a car accident," I said.

Mr. Green barked a laugh. "Accident. That's a good one. Accidents like that only happen when someone wants them to happen."

"Do you know something about his crash?" I asked.

He shook his head. "I don't know nothing. And if anyone asks, I didn't tell you nothing about who hired me, neither. Do you want the job or not? You got a contract for me to sign?"

He continued to smoke his cigar and didn't look at me again, his gaze steady on the wall a couple of feet behind my left shoulder. I wanted to press for more information about Lucky, but I didn't think he would give more than he had. I couldn't tell if he were withholding or really didn't know who sent him to hire us. Whatever he knew, I didn't feel he would be sharing it with us. I couldn't find a reason to hold back. I reached into my coat and pulled out the forms. "You got a pen?"

He did, in his inner breast pocket. I filled in his name on the blank lines, signed it where indicated, and gave the pen back to him. He signed. By the time he'd tucked the pen away, the magic had bound the Templeton Agency to his case. Which was good, because with the agency's owner dead and buried, there existed no more agency. But the magic bound me now every bit as much as it would have bound Ben Templeton. I could feel the thread connecting us.

I'd tucked the contract away when a loud whistle drew our eyes to the curtain. The band stuttered to a stop in a squeal of noise, the horns cutting off mid-note. Voices rose, men yelled, a few women screamed. The drum cymbals crashed. Above it all we heard, "Police, this is a raid," and the trample of feet.

"I thought this joint was legal," I said, standing.

"Sure. Don't matter, the cops still raid us from time to time. It's how they get a fat payoff for letting us stay open. This isn't no white club, where the cops are polite and friendly."

"That's not right," I said.

"No, you wouldn't think so," Mr. Green said. "The rest of us are used to the normality of this shit."

Ingrid grabbed my arm. "Mira, if they find you here," and trailed off. She waved her arm around the room. Two trolls, two women, one black, one white. No, it wouldn't be good if they did. Mr. Green might not mind a few nights in jail, but he didn't deserve it. Neither did Lugnut or Ingy.

"Is there another way out of here?" I asked.

He reached for the back wall of the room. His fingers moved over one of the panels, and it slid to the side, revealing a dark opening. "Go on, go," he said, jerking his thumb at the entry. "Won't smell nice, but you and your friends won't be seen."

"Thank you," I said. I extended my hand and refused to leave until he took it.

He finally shook, then gave another smile. "They catch us holding hands, they're going to break my arms. Get the hell out of here, Sinclair." He reached into his coat and pulled an envelope out of his breast pocket, tossing it to me. "She said there's about two fifty in there, but I haven't counted it. Consider it the down payment for services rendered. We'll settle up when you bring the goose." He leaned back in the chair and smoked as though the ruckus from the club didn't exist. He exhaled and started humming, something like *Brother Can You Spare a Dime.*

We went, the door sliding shut behind us, plunging us into darkness. Ingrid and I crouched to avoid bashing our heads against the ceiling. I kept my arms in front of me, feeling my way along the dark tunnel. Lugnut came behind, and cursing softly as he crawled on all fours.

"We'll be out soon," I said. I hoped. I started to ask Ingrid to give us her flames so we could see, when the floor dropped out and I pitched forward, sliding down a steep slope. The cries of Ingrid and Lugnut behind me told me they'd found the drop-off as well, but I was too busy trying to save my skin to worry about them as I accelerated into the dark depths below.

I hit the bottom of the tunnel hard, knocking my breath from my lungs. Stunned, I lay there, unable to move though I knew what would come next. Ingrid slammed into me first, yelping with her own pain as I gasped for air. I tried to crawl away, as I choked out a warning. "Lugnut."

Ingrid rolled against me, pushing, and we scrambled across the floor. Then Lugnut tumbled out of the opening and crashed to the floor behind us with a wet thwack.

"Ouch," he said, and lay there for a few seconds. "This reminds me why I try to avoid gin joints and swing music."

"It would be a hell of a lot worse if we'd gotten caught up in the police sweep," Ingy said. She crawled over to where I sprawled on my back. "Are you ok, Mira?"

I nodded, wincing as a flash of pain passed through what was left of my brains. "I'll live." I didn't add we were only down here and in trouble because of me. If I hadn't decided to see Mr. Green, they wouldn't have followed me. I wouldn't have had to run down a tunnel to keep folks from getting beat by the cops because a white girl had wandered into a mixed-race club. I became acutely aware of how stupid I'd been, how I took for granted these friendships despite our differences of backgrounds. It humbled me. I put them in danger. I trusted the system would protect me. They didn't have that luxury.

We were in a tunnel. Tall and wide, with cut stones fit closely. The floor sloped slightly towards center and a trickle of water flowed down the middle.

Lugnut glanced both directions and gave a sigh. "Figures the escape route would be through Baltimore's marvel of modern engineering, the sewer system. Which way?"

"Hold up your lighter." When he did, I bent over, watching the water for a moment. "This way."

"Why that way?"

"Because it's the direction the water is flowing. Shit flows downstream."

He grunted. "Alright smart ass. I'll lead." He stepped out, and we swung in behind, following the fluttering fairy light he held in front of his stooped body.

12

Rum Running in the Sewer

We walked a short distance before we reached a much larger tunnel, tall enough for Lugnut to stand up straight. The small trickle of water under our feet joined a larger stream. Above us, a narrow cylinder rose through the ceiling. Pinpricks of light shone through tiny holes in a manhole cover.

Lugnut hoisted me into the narrow shaft and I pushed against the metal cover with no success. "I can't lift it," I said. "You're going to have to climb up here and see if you can lever it open."

The wet slap of footsteps echoed along the tunnel. "Damn it, what now," Lugnut said, lowering me. The tunnel curved ahead of us, and we could see shadows on the wall, stretched out and distorted images of creatures approaching. A sense of fear and panic clenched at my heart. The first one rounded the corner as I pulled my revolver.

"Clipper City crew," Lugnut whispered. "Sorry little rum running bastards."

There were more than a dozen of them, all goblins, each wearing ragged suits; torn shirts and pants, a few with raggedy suit jackets and ties. They had sallow skin, like a human with jaundice, and black pupils rimmed red. No one wore a fedora, and everyone had slicked back their hair with pomade. A few of them carried guttering, smoky torches, and the wavering flames lit the tunnel, casting a ghoulish light upon the small crowd of figures. Others in the group carried wooden cases filled with bottles, which clinked as they walked. They came to a stop a dozen feet away from where we stood.

"Look what we have here," said the one in the lead, holding a dagger loosely in his right hand, his left brushing a lock of shiny black hair away from his eyes. "Seems we got ourselves a bit of company, Ralph."

A second goblin pushed forward, turning his head to spit on the ground. He scratched behind his ear and cocked his head. "Coppers?"

The first stepped closer and squinted. "Nah, ain't no police here. A couple of lost tourists I think, come to see our beautiful city. A slumming white girl with her friends, taking in the sight of our marvels, the beauty of a grand old dame who lifted her skirt for them and shown them a little something they shouldn't be seeing."

A smaller one, his eyes darting around, muscled between them. "What we do, Jacko? What we do with them? They've seen us."

"We don't want any trouble," Lugnut said, holding his hands up and spreading them. "We got lost and we're just looking for a way out."

The one called Jacko lifted his knife, and his grin widened until it filled his jaw. "Oh, won't be no trouble at all, troll. We remember what your people did to us back in twenty-seven, don't think we haven't."

"I wasn't part of the gang," Lugnut said, his fingers curling into fists.

"You're always part of a gang, even when you're not," Jacko said. "That's the thing, ain't it? Don't matter what someone does, they're always going to be lumped with everyone else who looks just like them."

The little one hissed, and stomped his feet. "Can we kill them, Jacko? Please? I'm so hungry, and they look so tasty."

Jacko squinted at him, and patted him on the head. "Alright kid, alright, settle down. You're scaring the tourists." He seemed to ponder for a moment, scratching his chin with his free hand and staring up at the roof of the tunnel. "But they have seen us, and they could report us to the . . . what's the term . . . oh, right. Prosper authorities. And since we haven't paid up with the local constabulary in a while, we might find ourselves in a heap of trouble. Such a predicament as I've never had to think about in some time."

The smaller one watched Jacko, then snatched the knife from his hand. "Fuck you, you ass. Kill them!" He ran towards us, and the rest followed a moment later, screaming and cursing as they drew their own knives and cudgels.

I unloaded, my first shot taking the small one in the shoulder and spinning him around. He collapsed in a heap, clutching his shoulder, but the ones behind didn't pause, stepping on him to get to us. I shot again and again until the chamber emptied. Two more fell, but it wasn't enough. With a scream the rest were upon us.

For a moment, I thought Lugnut would sweep them out of the way. His massive fist swung round and plastered one against the wall with a sickening crunch. The next one grabbed Lugnut's arm, and a second his leg, and I clubbed at the attackers with the butt of my gun, the hot barrel burning my hand, knocking one down before the rest were upon me as well.

We fell under a sea of bodies. A knife rose high in the air at the end of a goblin's arm, the blade dark with rust and blood stains. Then a bang rattled the walls, and light flooded the tunnel, followed by a crashing sound. Something hard and heavy smacked into something soft and squishy.

Ingy stood in the middle of the fight, a thick piece of wood in her hands. The length of it glowed white hot, and waves of heat radiated from it. She was wreathed in blue flame from the top of her dark hair down to her black boots, her eyes two black lumps of coal set inside her face. As she swung her weapon, goblins flew across the tunnel, smashing into walls and falling into limp heaps. Words leaked from her mouth, the harsh gutter of magic, words that made my hair stand on end. She'd always been better at it then I, had applied herself more rigorously to learning magic. I could see the threads, strum them, but she wove a new tapestry with a well-placed phrase. Until then, though, I didn't know how much she'd learned. She rose dark and terrifying and beautiful and beautiful and oh so damned beautiful. My heart hurt just to look at her.

A dagger flew through the dark, and Ingy batted it down like a baseball player taking a fastball for a line drive. Jacko stood frozen in front of her for a few heartbeats. He glanced around for support only to realize he was suddenly alone. A few groaning friends lay nearby, but the rest retreated down the tunnel, bottles clacking as they ran with their cases of hooch. He blinked several times rapidly, then turned and fled after them. The sounds of splashing footsteps diminished as Jacko rounded the corner and disappeared.

The fire around Ingy faded and guttered out. "Come on, let's get out of here." She took my hand and hoisted me off the wet ground. Lugnut squeezed up the ladder and thrust the manhole cover aside, and the three of us returned to the fresh night air of Baltimore above.

***

We sat in the house, nursing our wounds. My head hurt, and four aspirin hadn't touched the pounding that bashed against the back of my eyeballs. I'd bathed, and bandaged my head, as soon as we got back, but the pain seemed to be eternal, a twisting maze of agony circling around and around inside my skull. The gun burn on my hand hurt as well, but it was incidental damage compared to the way my temples throbbed. My ankle hurt worse than before, swollen now in sympathy with the rest of my aches.

Lugnut looked like a victim of a car accident, covered in bandages. He had been bitten and scratched on his neck and arms, and one of the toughs had slashed him across his forehead, a nasty gash that had me worrying about infection. He changed his dressing for the third time, tossing the bloody scrap of cloth into the trash can next to his chair. He'd heal far more quickly than I would, though. Small blessing.

Ingy had gotten out unharmed, though she appeared exhausted, with bags under her eyes, her skin ashy. Still beautiful. She sat on the floor, her legs crossed, playing with a dagger she'd brought back.

"They're a gang of hooch makers, running cover for the speakeasies," Lugnut said. "The bosses let them smuggle bathtub gin and heroin under the streets and, in return, they keep away prying eyes. It's no surprise the escape tunnel went down into the sewers; no cop would be stupid enough to go down there."

I shrugged. "We didn't have much of a choice, did we?" I didn't mention my faults in guiding us to that result, my bravado that led us into the situation in the first place. It had been a week of one Mirabel Sinclair disaster after another. My inadequacies exhausted me.

Ingy glared at me for a few moments before turning her attention to Lugnut. "You're damned lucky the knife wasn't poisoned like some of the others. If the goblins slash you with one of those, we'd be burying you."

Lugnut sighed. "I'm immune to poison, but you'd probably like that."

She gave a thin smile. "Not really. I'd have to help carry you."

He chuckled. "Yeah, I'd be a pain in the rump to haul to my grave."

Ingrid didn't reply. She yawned and stood. The piece of wood she'd wielded as a weapon turned out to be a baseball bat. I had no idea where it came from, but suspected she'd charmed it as a hermetic token, and could call it when needed. She carried the bat into the kitchen where she wiped it down with a wet wash cloth until the wood gleamed again. Then she placed it in the closet under the stairs.

"I'm going to take a bath and go to bed," she said, not waiting for a reply.

I watched her disappear upstairs. She was smart as hell. Her magic far and away better than mine. Beautiful, too. Everything I wasn't in fact. Without her, Lugnut and I would have been killed tonight. I had that to rest on my conscience, and it didn't rest well, but scratched and nipped at my brain like a cat begging to get out.

Lugnut lay his head down on the arm of the couch, his eyes already closed. I rose and got him a pillow and a blanket from the closet, and spread the soft cotton over his body. He stirred long enough for me to tuck the pillow under his head.

"Thanks, little witch."

"Least I could do."

"Yeah." He settled down on protesting springs, and I went upstairs to my bedroom.

I stripped off my dirty dress and tossed it into the hamper. Once I had my nightgown on, I shivered in the cold of the room. Bed waited for me, and I sighed as I pulled the covers up to my chin. My eyes closed of their own accord, but sleep eluded me. My mind drifted back again and again to the day's events, and mocked me for a fool.

The chill deepened when Jacob entered the room. He could always sense what Ingy or I were doing, though he never barged in on us when we were disrobing. He might be a ghost, but he had manners. He hovered at the foot of the bed, sending me thoughts of worry and concern.

"Nothing to get under your skin about, Jacob. I had a rough day."

Lend you an ear?

I thought for a moment. Here I was, a poor excuse for a detective, beaten and bloodied, being asked by the ghost of a dead man to bare my soul and let all my worries be carried away on his strong, spectral shoulders. A psychologist would have a field day with this one. "I made some mistakes is all. Lots of mistakes. Like people do, you know?"

He knew all about making mistakes, and told me so. I realized the irony of it before he finished.

"Of course you know about mistakes," I said, "or you wouldn't be a ghost. Sorry."

No apologies needed.

He didn't sound sullen or angry. Resigned would be the closest I could come to describing it. "Thanks," I said. "I've got enough apologizing to do already."

This, too, shall pass, as do all people.

"I hope so," I murmured. "The first part, not the second." The aspirin kicked in, and the pain lessened enough for me to drift into slumber. Jacob stood watch at the foot of my bed, a long-dead guard who cared enough about a living woman to watch over her. It was comforting, and I wondered what I did to deserve friends like these.

Not a damn thing, as far as I could tell.

13

Weaving Clues

I didn't sleep nearly long enough. Exhaustion weighed on me when I staggered downstairs in the early morning hours. Ingrid remained asleep in her room, and Lugnut snored softly on the sofa in the parlor. Jacob had gone who knows where. I hoped he slept, too. That seemed fair and right. The world remained anything but.

I sat at the dining room table, the documents from Lucky's office spilled its surface. My hands propped up my head, fingertips rubbing my temple to ease the painful headache. As though I could rub away the memory of the last twenty-four hours, the last week. Smooth out the ripples of my mistakes; fill the hole in my heart with plaster and putty. Cover it all up with a shiny new coat of bullshit.

It didn't work. Ben Templeton slumped like a sack of potatoes, his blood spilling onto the ground. Lugnut fell under a rush of goblins wielding rusty knives. Ingy, her eyes coal black, raised her bat. I squeezed my eyes shut and rubbed them with the back of my hands until flashes of light spoiled the matinee of my worst hits. Then I grabbed at the documents in front of me and rifled through them, ignoring the ones that fell on the floor for the time being. I read them quickly, needing something, to push the memories away. My hands shook as I tossed each one aside.

I didn't know what I looked for. I knew it had to be here, believed it with every ounce of my heart and soul. In hindsight, that was wishful thinking of course. That I would find anything of note would be a small miracle. Someone or something had ripped apart Lucky's office trying to find exactly what we'd been seeking, and it seemed every bit as likely they had and had taken it when they left. But I needed something other than the stench of failure and death that surrounded me. A single word was all I had. Rowan. It meant nothing to me.

Magic has always been part rigorous study, part intuition. Prior to the eighteenth century, intuition had been the path most practitioners took. You didn't study magic, you felt it, reached out with your mind and body, grasped the threads of it and wove it together, only half understanding what you were doing. When Danton and Chester had written the first book of magic for lay practitioners and codified the language, the path to power had radically changed. Inevitably, schools of magic sprang up, and it became more of a science and less of an art. A not quite respectable science of course, replete with its fair share of charlatans and hucksters. Ingrid had the unusual combination of both art and science, and far better at the science part than myself.

For me, intuition remained my bread and butter, and what few tricks others had shared with me. Ingrid for one, and Petunia as well. Mr. Templeton of course. But I'd had no practice in theory and application, no older witch to mentor me. Maybe that's why things worked the way they did for me. Maybe that's why I felt the tug of something as I read the documents, the hidden strings knotting my manic need to the object of my desire, imbuing it with energy. Maybe what I wanted hadn't even been there until I decided it needed to be. I pulled those strings as I tossed documents aside, unconsciously tugging on the threads that wove all things together. My skin tingled, and the world flashed off and on again, as though all the light in the universe disappeared and returned.

The folder labeled TGTLTGE rested beneath my fingers, and I opened it. Pamphlets about The Godly Teacher charity had been tucked inside. The first couple of documents were religious tracts, mixed with receipts for donations. Lucky had been generous over the last few years, giving sizable sums. That money would have found its way back to the community in a variety of programs, from soup kitchens to housing assistance. A good man, just like his former partner had been. Baltimore should have treated these two men far better than they'd received.

I examined a pamphlet. When I opened it, a piece of paper fell out onto my lap. I unfolded it carefully. It looked like a handwritten page from a notebook, one edge ragged where it had been torn unevenly from the binding. Lucky's penmanship left a lot to be desired, the words small and cramped together. But the heading could be easily read: The Goose That Laid the Golden Egg. My heart beating too fast, I opened other pamphlets to find more pages. A dozen all told. Each of them with Lucky's chicken scratch; each about the case.

The folder initials didn't stand for The Godly Teacher charity; it stood for The Goose That Laid The Golden Egg. Lucky had hidden them in plain sight. The pages had dates on the left, notations for each on the right. Some no more than a single brief word, and some with several long paragraphs.

My heart leapt. We'd overlooked this file a dozen times, assuming it contained nothing of use. I flipped through the notes. Three weeks of Lucky's investigation reduced to twelve pages. The last notation was dated the day of Lucky's car accident. I squinted, trying to make out the tiny script. He'd been hired by a woman, paid cash up front.

Same woman who had the troll hire us? It had to be. She hadn't given her name, but she worked for someone else. There wasn't a contract in the pile of papers we'd recovered, so whomever tore the office apart must have snatched it. She'd given him a scroll, one with clues to the location of the goose. I presumed it was the same or a similar one based on Lucky's notes, which included a description of the goose glyph.

A week before his death, his notes began to make reference to shadowy figures following him, black sedans tailing his car. Some of them seemed to be dwarves, others he thought might be elves, though it was harder to tell elves apart from humans. One note jumped out at me. *Made the license plate of the sedan that followed me to my office. LG possible party of interest.* Perhaps that explained why he hid the pages of his notebook. He'd grown worried he'd been made and the criminals at the center of the conspiracy were tailing him. I'd never know his reasoning, but it seemed probable.

Lucky referenced the same letters early on when discussing possible people to approach who might know more about magical artifacts. Gnomes ranked high on the list, and he'd scratched off several names down to Beezallel, Bollo and Tim. Their names were underlined, exclamation points following, as though Lucky had learned something from them. But, if he had, it wasn't in the notes.

On the day of his death, his last note displayed the initials again. *Positive now they are working for LG. BT suggests I contact the police as soon as I've visited Jack Nory to see if he knows who is at the center of the case so I can give them a name. Rock Ledge park, take the path around the pond, enter the woods near the standing stone, follow slope upward.*

Who was LG? Lucky Gambini? That didn't seem likely. Why would he put his own initials into his notes and refer to himself in the third person as the person he sought? What about BT? Could that be Ben Templeton? It could be, but I wouldn't know for sure. No address for Nory. Nothing but those strange directions. Had

Lucky set up a meeting with this man, Jack Nory? The name tripped any number of bells in my head, though I couldn't place a finger on the reason why. But Rock Ledge park was on the route Lucky would have taken when he had his accident. It couldn't be a coincidence he'd been on his way to see this man and had been killed.

I grabbed my coat off the chair where I'd tossed it. When I put it on, I felt a lump in the pocket. I pulled out the crumpled envelope Mr. Green had handed me as we fled the club. When I opened it, I found a thin stack of green backs, all twenties and tens I rifled through them and counted out two hundred dollars, then shoved the rest back into the envelope and into my coat. I tossed the coat back onto the chair and limped down the stairs into the basement.

The Undertow waited for me, embraced me, as I sank into the image in the closet, my body pulled and twisted, spit out on the other side. The cold hallway waited for me. I shivered through my clothing, wishing I'd brought the coat. But discomfort gave me another something to focus on instead of what had happened. I didn't ignore the cold, I embraced it, let it drive me to distraction as my teeth chattered.

Mr. Langmere sat behind his desk as always. I wondered if he ever slept.

"Good morning, Miss Sinclair," he said as he held a copy of the Baltimore Sun in front of him. "Did you want to renew your account?"

I fished the cash out of my pocket and slapped it down on the counter. "High roller."

His eyes widened slightly, the only reaction I'd ever gotten out of him in all my visits to the Undertow. But he took the money and it disappeared into a drawer in the huge desk, so quickly I couldn't tell which one of the many he had placed it into.

"Welcome to the High Roller club, Miss Sinclair. You may use the Typeprompter once per week at your new rate for one hour. I'm here if you have any questions at all."

I walked to the alcove with the typewriter, ignoring the many tomes and books that lined the shelves. I didn't need them; the Typeprompter would give me what I needed. The keys were waiting in silent anticipation. I typed out a series of questions in rapid strokes, the clicks and clacks filling the room.

The newspapers were bursting with detailed theories about the gnomes and their weapons. There were suspicions it was all a plan for someone to arm insurgents, create small uprisings, and get the government to declare martial law, forcing the rest of the country to accept equality for all at the end of a barrel. The usual Christian charity about helping the poor and unfortunate drowned under a sea of long letters to the editors calling for the destruction of the ghettos and the forcible removal of all *soulless sub-humans*. Send them back home some said, failing to note the irony: we had all lived together for centuries and few had a homeland any longer. Their land had been taken by others who had conquered them.

I fought the temptation to write my own letter to the editor and tell people what assholes they were being. *Fade into the background*, Mr. Templeton always said. Observe, watch, learn, and build a case. Don't get emotionally involved.

"I am emotionally involved," I murmured, a sharp stab of pain passing through my chest. I blunted it, grabbed onto the chill of the subterranean library, focused on that.

The magical channels were open, and I began my search, typing *magic, rowan*. I'd expected to find information about the use of rowan trees in spell work. Instead, I found endless stories. Tales of a coven of witches who lived for centuries, mostly in the Northeast territories. They might have been descendants of Rowan Canny, an Irish witch who, the stories said, had been burned at the stake in 1697, and walked the streets of Limerick again every night the following winter, seducing young lovers into her bed and killing them before dawn. Bodies were found skinned and laid out on bloody pentagrams, crucified upside down on the steeple of the local parish, even propped up in the pews with their heads in their laps as though attending some macabre mass of the dead. The tales were the type of childhood horror stories parents used to keep little children in bed.

When Rowan grew bored torturing those who had wished her dead, she supposedly boarded a boat and traveled to the new territories. The boat sailed into New Amsterdam harbor covered in blood, the crew skinned alive to the last man, each of them hung to the yard arm. She then met a handsome French trapper near Boston, who took her north into the woods of New England. He returned many years later alone, his mind splintered like ice that breaks apart and rushes downstream with the current after a spring thaw.

Early nineteenth century stories centered on Maine. Tales of a coven of witches who snatched babies away at night, sacrificing them to dark powers. Stories of innocent people burned at the stake for witchcraft while the real culprits continued to prey on the good Christian people of the territory. Myths of orgies of women and non-humans around bonfires in secret clearings in the forest. The typical religious lie conflating sexuality with evil, the story they'd told themselves since Adam and Eve. A story to take power from women and minorities and give it to the Priests, who were all male, all white, all human. The original sin, repackaged for consumer consumption. Sex, lies and victrolas.

I ran out of stories. The trail went cold, and by the twentieth century everyone thought it another ghost story. Witches and magic existed, sure. Evil murdering witches who skinned their victims alive and crucified them? Who stole babies away to eat during their dark masses in the forest? Not so much. People lit the world with electricity and sodium arc lights, and drove away the darkness feeding the need for good versus evil. It was all shades of gray now.

When the chalkboard cleared, I typed *Jack Nory*. Words filled the wall again, chalk dust raining down like tiny flakes of snow. Jack Nory's story was as dark as Rowan's, and as soaked with blood. But his wasn't myth. A mass murderer from Boston who'd been sent to the hangman in 1925. Dozens of people killed, hundreds more suspected but their remains never found. He tortured his victims with a straight edged blade, the kind men used to shave with. Cut them into tiny pieces, presumably while they were still alive. Men, women, children; he didn't discriminate in his evil. Only one victim had been found whole and unblemished, her neck broken so badly her head was twisted around one hundred and eighty degrees, her body otherwise unmarred. She'd been his wife. Nory had claimed he wasn't her murderer, and he'd never have taken her life. He said she'd put him on a path to redemption. He said it had been his brother, also named Jack. He was still saying it when the trapdoor fell open below his feet.

This was the man Lucky had been set to meet? A convicted mass murderer, hung over a decade ago? No wonder the name rang a bell, it had probably been headline news in the paper when it happened. But it had happened far enough away and long enough ago I didn't recall any of the details. Some subconscious part of me remembered, a dark recess in the back of my head from when I'd still been a street urchin, hanging around downtown, nicking watches and jewelry off the well to do. I had to discount it being the same person. Maybe he had the misfortune to share the name with the one who had been executed. Lord knew Jack was a common enough first name. He'd do well to keep out of the limelight given its association with a mass murderer.

I returned home, scanning my notes, fixing the information in my memory. I had a direction now. I had focus. I slipped on my trenchcoat, slid my gun into a pocket, and headed out the door.

Ready. Aim. Fire.

14

Jack Nory

I tightened the belt of my trench coat, and stared off through the damp forest. My feet stood on the gravel path running around the edge of Rock Ledge pond, and the boots I'd chosen were dry enough, but a wide swath of tall grass stood between me and the trees, and a morning rain had soaked everything. Water dripped from branches, and a mist rose from the ground to meet the drizzle that fell, sputtering from gray clouds overhead. I'd left Ingy and Lugnut asleep at the house. I could do this one on my own, no need to disturb them or put them in further danger.

The standing stone had been easy to find. Twice as tall as the knee-high grass, a rough finger pointing towards the clouds above. Carvings marked its surface, worn smooth by time and weather. The rough image of a man, stick figure, above an eye. The petroglyphs were centuries old, perhaps a thousand years. They spoke of the nations of peoples who had been here before settlers came, and had welcomed them with open arms. Whites, blacks, dwarves, elves; they'd opened their land to everyone.

The many nations of peoples were gone now. Their open arms had been well received at first when the settlers were new, in need of support to survive their first harsh winters. Later, their welcome had been repaid with death at the end of the barrel of a gun, the seizing of their lands, the massacre of their women and children. Thousands had been killed in the name of expansion of new nations. Our great manifest destiny. Some had been enslaved by the Borealian Empyrean, and their descendants toiled there even today.

The rest had disappeared. They'd vanished into the dark shadows beneath the vast, eastern forest. No one knew where they'd gone. Some suggested they were still there, shifted out of resonance with our world, occupying the same time and space but neither of us able to interact with the other. All anyone knew—all I knew—were they were gone now.

Stones like this one marked the boundary of their lands far to the west for endless miles. Stones every bit as ancient, too. As they lost their homes in the east, they joined others and built a refuge. Hundreds of millions of acres west of the Mississippi remained undeveloped, and would for as long as those stones stood. A place where industry and progress never arrived, forever left wild by the magic of those who protected the land before we came to change it, develop it, strip it of its resources. You could visit there for short periods as long as you left the place pristine. A little hunting or fishing, a simple campfire, living off the land, sleeping outside. The land accepted these things. Those who tried to build homes, dig mines, carve out roads, cut down forests? Those folks disappeared and were never seen again, leaving no trace. The homes would be gone, the roads returned to nature, the mines filled in, the trees unmarred.

The power of this stone coursed through the air. It thrummed with energy, invisible but palpable. I could feel its thread, tangled with an older magic of green, growing things. I closed my eyes and could see the web, like a great loom spread around me. Everything flashed again, and the web grew visible. I plucked a single strand from the ball of the yarn that gave the world form. I held it between two fingers, the magic available for my calling. But I'd only touched the edges of this magic in the past. It felt as old as the universe, primal. My mind raced out and the skein of Everything grew, engulfed the world. Layers upon layers, thicker and deeper until it seemed I would be buried in strings, my heart pounding. I opened my eyes and shook my head, drew a shuddering breath. Ingy didn't trust this type of magic and had warned me about it time and again. And yet, it called to me. So simple, I could do it in my sleep.

I stepped from the path and walked through the grass, my feet growing wet as I strode into the forest. The woods of Maryland weren't old. The territory had been logged out at the end of the previous century, and most forests consisted of younger trees, closely spaced as they competed for the sun. Thick underbrush made passage through them difficult in places. Remnants of old logging roads were visible, and a person could follow them from town to town without ever stepping onto a paved road.

Here, though, lay a small piece of ancient forest. Rock Ledge park remained unblemished because of the power of its single stone. Most of the trees were untouched by saw or axe. The logging companies passed up the opportunity due to economics, terrain, even the lack of navigable streams to carry logs to their sawmills. Or so they said. The stone made them find reasons to leave these trees be. They were huge, their canopies blotting out the sun, wide spaces between their thick boles. Below the massive boles and thick, dark canopy, little undergrowth flourished, although a pad of decaying leaves and moss covered the ground like a carpet.

I wanted a smoke, but it would wait until I got back to the car. I'd bought a pack on the way here. Quitting no longer seemed to matter. As much a silly tribute to the memory of a lost mentor as my own weakness. Stupid, but there it was.

The ground rose steeply past the boundary of the trees. My breath came in white puffs as I worked my way up slope, gripping low branches when my shoes slipped on the damp forest floor. The occasional bird call or chattering squirrel punctuated the soft dripping of water off the trees. The temperature grew colder.

At the top of the rise, the ground flattened and dropped into a shallow depression. On the opposite side, a rocky outcropping had split down the middle by a gash, and the ground curved down again. I didn't know which way to go now. I walked into the center of the bowl and squatted, my right hand touching the ground. I whistled softly, calling a breeze, letting the wind guide me to him. If he even existed. For all I knew, I was chasing a ghost story.

"What you doing that for, love?" he said.

He stood in the rocky cleft, leaning against the stones, one leg crossed over the other. He wore all black, the clothing and shoes speckled with mud, a bowler cap tipped over one side of his face so the eye on that side was shrouded in shadow. The other eye glinted like a sapphire. A single yellow blossom protruded from a button hole on his coat. He held a long dagger in one hand, and used the tip to dig dirt out from under the fingernails of his other. Even considering the poor quality of newspaper photos, he looked the spitting image of the man they sent to hang over ten years ago in Boston.

"Jack Nory?"

He stopped digging under his nails and pointed the tip of the dagger at me. "Now who be asking that?"

I stood slowly, spreading my hands out, palm up. "I'm here to talk about Lucky Gambini."

He scratched his head with the hilt of the dagger, pushing the hat up away from his eyes. "Don't know no Lucky Gambini," he said. He pointed the dagger at me again. "Comes to it, I don't know you either, girl."

"He was a private detective investigating a lost treasure," I said.

I slid my hands into my coat pockets and hunched my shoulders as though I were cold. I did feel cold, actually, but I really wanted to wrap my right hand around the hilt of my revolver in case I needed it. "He was on his way out here to talk to you about it when he died in a crash."

He tilted his head back and looked up at the canopy over his head. "What's that you say, Mr. Sticks? Weren't no accident?"

I glanced up, but saw nothing except the trees. "Who are you talking to?"

"Yes, she's a wee bit of a naive one, isn't she, my friend," he said, and then he turned his eyes to me again. "So, girl, what's that old black bastard, Jack, got to do with some detective? Quick now and give an answer, before I send you off to meet my friends, Sticks and Chancy." The dagger flashed down and he held it at his side. He straightened, radiating tension as though he were poised to spring at me.

I yanked the gun out and aimed it at him. Aimed it where he'd been. He wasn't there anymore. A hollow laugh echoed through the woods, disembodied. I turned in a quick circle, but he'd disappeared.

"Oh, so you'll shoot me now," his voice said. It came from everywhere and nowhere. "And here I thought we was getting along so fine."

I tried to calm myself, take slow, deep breaths. Tried to still the racing of my heart. "I don't want to hurt you."

"The only one who'll be getting hurt today is you girl, if'n you don't put that gun away."

My arm had locked in place, and it took a considerable amount of will to force it down. I checked the safety before I eased my gun into my coat pocket. "It's away," I said, the words quivering slightly as they came out. But I kept my fingers wrapped around the handle.

"You come here and threaten old Jack with a pistol," he said, standing by the rocks again. A grin split his face, revealing brown and black teeth. I could almost smell the rot from here.

"So, you *are* Jack Nory," I said.

He nodded his head, and then gave a little bow. "Right you are, love. Black Jack Nory at your pleasure. Now, talk quick girl. My blade hasn't taken a life in a good long while, and it's almost time to be getting back to me business again."

"But they measured you for a hemp scarf ten years ago in Boston," I said. Cold shivers ran down my arms, raising goosebumps.

He laughed, and it rang through the forest the way a glacier pushes through a valley, slowly driving aside everything before it. All the birds and squirrels went silent. Even the dripping water seemed to pause, as though waiting to take a breath. "Yes, they put old Jack in the noose, girl. And they'll kill me again one day, and again another. But I've got as many lives as mankind's got ways of taking them, and more I suspect. They kill my brother Jack, and his brother Jack comes right back. Jack be nimble, Jack be quick, Jack's sharp razor makes a snick. Jack be here and Jack be there, Jack the ripper everywhere."

"What about your wife?" I asked. I gambled, trying to find some weakness in this terrifying man, poke a hole in his murderous façade.

It worked, too. His smile faded and his eyes grew distant. "She weren't Jack's wife. She was Jack's brother, Jack's, wife. And I took her away from Jack, because his time had ended. He'd gone soft around the edges. Image that, a black soul like Jack settling down. It beggars belief. But I didn't give her the knife, I left her clean and whole so Jack could see what Jack had done."

He looked up at the sky again. "Why?" he asked, and waited. "But I want to cut her." He paced in a circle, waving the knife in the air. "She comes here unbidden, asks Jack all these questions." He stopped, his back to me, and then he plunged the dagger into the branch of a nearby tree. "Fine, Jack will do as you say. But if she comes back here, her blood is mine."

"Who are you talking to?" I asked.

He turned and sneered at me. He left the dagger in the tree and walked closer, until he stood only a few feet away. "Didn't Benjamin Francis Templeton teach you nothing, girl?"

One single name, and my heart stopped. I opened my mouth, tried to say something. But all I had to give was breath without form, no words on my tongue, my throat constricting. I shut my mouth again and shook my head, as the memory of his death replayed in the cinema of my thoughts. Not ready for the likes of Jack Nory. He'd been right to warn me.

He mocked me by opening and closing his mouth, teeth clacking, his eyes wide. "There's a girl, pulled her leg. Got nothing to say now, do you. You try to hurt Jack with talk of a wife and can't take the heat when it's cast back."

I forced words through my mouth, my teeth clenched. "How do you know Ben Templeton."

He grinned again. "Chancy and Sticks told me, love. They know everyone who comes to the end of things. Old Jack is closer to the end than anyone else, and cans talk to them whenever he wants. I suspect you'll meet them in time, and maybe Jack will help you along to that place." He glanced up again, the smiling slipping away. "And sometimes the bastards talk when Jack doesn't want to hear." He shook his head, and now he scowled, so darkly I took an involuntary step back. "Fuck you, Sticks, I said I'd leave her be. I don't need your insults to mind my place."

I'd let go of my gun and balled up my fingers into fists in my pockets. I squeezed them until my fingernails dug into the palms of my hands, staring at the ground between us. I wouldn't let this bastard get to me. I had a job to do, so I focused on the cold, the wet, the smell of damp leaves and soil. "Lucky died on his way to see you.

He was looking for the goose that laid the golden egg when someone killed him."

Jack's eyes found mine again. "Treasure hunting, are you? Or are you looking for a murderer? That'll get you far, and get you nothing good in the end."

Fuck this bastard, he wouldn't beat me by scaring me. I didn't fear death if it gave me a chance to meet Ben Templeton's killers. "You either know where it is, or you've wasted my time." I turned and began walking through the trees.

Jack stood in front of me, leaning against one of the trees. He scrubbed a toe through the wet leaves, stirring them. "I didn't say I'd be disinclined to help you along, girl. But what's in it for old Jack?"

What would a murderer want? A chance to kill came to mind. Anyone. Me. I didn't fear death, but I had too much left to do to get murdered just yet. "I've got nothing that would appeal to the likes of you."

His mouth dropped open in an impish grin again. "Oh, so now she know's me, does she? Thinks I'm an open book she can read, like the ones she used to love?" I must have blanched, because he chuckled as he watched my face. "I knows lots of things, girl. It's one of Jack's special little secrets. Although somes calls it a curse, too. Knowing too much isn't a blessing from God."

"Name your price," I said.

He removed his hat and dropped to a knee, spreading his arms wide. "I ain't but a simple killer, Mirabel Lee Sinclair. Look around and see; all I've gots is this forest, these trees. The old stone keeps me imprisoned here, and there's naught for Jack to do but eat runty squirrels and chase deer. I knows you can feel the threads. I tasted your power on the winds you whistled up. You find my thread, and you cut it. You free me."

Free Jack Nory. I didn't know who had trapped him here, but they'd done the world a favor. Here he couldn't do much harm, unless someone wandered through the woods and found him. Released, he'd return to the towns and cities, and another murderous spree would begin. It might end with him in the noose once more, but that didn't bring Jack fear. That brought Jack a release, and a chance to start over again fresh. But if I didn't free him, maybe the murderer of Ben Templeton would go free, and I'd have to live with the fact I couldn't finish his work and grant him the release he deserved. He'd forever be a ghost in my mind, pattering around my memories and reminding me of my failures.

I let my mind wander. I could feel the skein again, see the threads connecting all things to everything. Jack's thread was painful in its clarity, twisted in knots. Black and ancient, winding on forever into the dim past. But near this end, near his body, there was a great loop in the line wound around the threads of the forest, tangled with those of the rocks and trees. I reached out with my thought, plucked his cord like the string of a harp, and heard the silent strum.

Jack hissed. His face turned up once more, but his eyes were closed. "I felt that, girl. I felt your touch on old Jack's life. Release me now if you want my help."

"Cut your hand, Jack," I said.

"What?"

"I need your blood."

He drew the dagger and ran the blade across the palm of his hand. He didn't seem to apply any pressure. He kept those blades as sharp as the winter wind and it drew blood instantly, welling in dark spots on his dirty skin. He held his hand out, turning the palm down, letting it drip, drip, onto the loam beneath him, blending with the drip of water from the trees.

I had a pen in my pocket with the small notebook I carried. I pressed the tip of my hand against it, hard, until it stung. When I pulled my hand out, a tiny spot of blood dotted my fingertip. I reached out, fighting the nausea rising in my throat. I took his hand,

and he squeezed mine, hard enough I gasped. My other hand stroked Mr. Templeton's medallion in my pocket.

Yes, I would make a deal with the devil himself.

"Swear to me, Jack Nory, that you'll tell the truth and will do no murder until I've completed the task which I've set myself upon."

"I swear this to you," he said.

"I swear by my blood and your blood and by the old gods and the new god, you will be free," I said. I found his thread again and I jerked it, straightening it until I found the closest knot.

He shook as he held my hand and his breath came in ragged gasps. "Now give me what I want."

I cut his chord as neat as you please, and then I tied it to my desire, the thread I followed to find the killers of a murdered friend. When I'd done the deed, I yanked my hand away and stepped back. I drew my gun and aimed it at him, holding it with both hands to steady the shaking. "Talk, old man."

He ran a bloody hand through greasy hair, pushing it away from his face. His grin returned and he placed his hat back on his head, then spun in a circle, throwing his arms out wide to the world. "I feel it, love. Old Jack is free."

"Old Jack has five seconds to tell me what I came here for, or old Jack will be replaced by new Jack," I said. I pulled back the hammer of my revolver.

He tipped his head at me. "You drive a hard bargain, girl. But so did Templeton. Go you up to Maine, to the town of Damascus Mills. Find that witch, Rowan, and her seasons. They'll give you what you seek. No goose, no. They'll lead you to his killer. That's what you really want."

A drop of water fell into my eyes and I blinked. In that instant of a moment, Jack Nory disappeared, although he left behind the echo of his laugh ringing from the trees around me.

15

Heading North

I had plenty of time to think on the drive back. Thinking did me no good at all. But, stuck in a slow car with a long drive, I couldn't stop myself. I chain smoked to try and distract myself, calm my nerves. All it did was make me cough.

What had I done? I went to meet with a man I didn't know, and ended up bargaining with a demon who'd been a stain on humanity's face since we first began stabbing each other to death in defiance of the law. How could anyone have lived as long as that man, let alone survived the noose? But I stood with him, talked with him, and gave him a taste of what he wanted.

On top of Jack Nory, I'd put my friends in danger. Stupid, stupid, stupid. I hadn't taken seriously what might happen at the club, a white woman hanging out with a black woman and trolls. I'd accepted their offers to come along, and we'd nearly gotten arrested for our troubles, then almost killed while escaping. I didn't consider their needs when I followed mine. That couldn't happen again. I didn't deserve their friendship and loyalty, and they didn't deserve to have their lives threatened. Things were hard enough as they were without Mirabel Sinclair making it tougher for them.

The boss had been right. I hadn't known what I'd be willing to give up for this work. What I would end up losing. A piece of my soul, that's what. My first real case, and already I bargained with evil to do what I thought was good, and it ate away at me inside. What would another hundred cases do to me? What had it done to him? I slammed the steering wheel with my palms and screamed inside my car, for the little good it did me. No good here, just a woman playing at being a detective and getting it all wrong with every step she took. Not worthy of my friends. Certainly not worthy of Ingrid's love. Well, I could stop fretting about my secret desire for her. A woman like me didn't deserve a woman like her, even if she felt the same.

But I'd only given Jack a taste, and that at least provided me a tiny ounce of relief. A hint of what would come. I'd had no qualms about tricking him either. He felt my will and desire, and it came through the thread to him as freedom. His mistake. I'd bound him to the case and my successful conclusion of it. Until I found and dealt with Ben Templeton's killers, he'd remain as chained to the old patch of forest as he had before. I wouldn't have a bloody Jack Nory rampage on my conscience, because I had no doubts I wouldn't finish this case. It would end with me dead in a box like my boss, and the world would go on revolving. I only hoped to learn enough and share it with the authorities so they'd bring the right people to justice. As if justice is ever done right. Not in this world it's not.

Jacob greeted me at the door when I arrived, shortly after sunset. "Hey J man," I said. Jacob always liked the radio serial, *G-Men*, and I figured the nick name might sit well with him. Put him in too good a mood to notice my somber spirit.

Ingrid went out, and Lugnut went back to the garage to take care of business for a while

I tried to think of a reason those things would be bad. Couldn't come up with a one. In fact, not being here made things easier for me. "Well good, they probably needed a break from all the detecting. Can't say I blame them, either."

He shared all sympathies, but let me know he was proud of what we were doing.

"You're too good for the likes of us, Jacob." I plastered a fake smile on my face. "I'm going to head up to bed. It's been a long day."

Where have you been all day

The question came with happy tones. Which suggested he wasn't concerned, just making conversation. "At the library, trying to run down some more information. Work, work, work, it never ends." I yawned to show him I was tired, though truthfully, I hadn't felt more awake then I did right now. "Talk to you in the morning?"

Alright

No one here. I had a short while to take advantage of the fact. I'd already made up my mind on the drive, and the absence of Ingrid and Lugnut allowed me to do what needed to be done without interference. I'd go alone. Up to Maine, find the witch, get the truth out of her. Give Ben Templeton the justice he deserved, or die trying. Ingy and Lugnut would stay here. I turned it around a few times, buried the guilty hitch it caused my heart, and sold it to myself at a discount. I'd sneak out of Baltimore like a thief in the night. If I talked to them about it, they would insist on coming and I loved them too much to say no. Whatever happened up there, I'd be the only one in danger. Their deaths would scar my soul, and it already hurt too much to even consider the possibility.

I pulled the cheap, cardboard suitcase from under my bed, and began filling it with clothing from my dresser. A few pairs of pants and shirts, a couple of pairs of unmentionables, extra shoes. All the extra ammo I had for the revolver. Hair brush, a couple of sturdy ribbons to tie my hair back, a toothbrush.

I added the wind-up clock from my bedside table, and the picture of Sister Mary Margaret. I didn't have a picture of Mr. Templeton, or I would have taken it instead. She would do. I stared at the picture, her eyes looking back at me, judging me, condemning me.

"I didn't do anything Mr. Templeton wouldn't have done," I said defensively. "It was a necessary evil."

She didn't reply, but her stern face told me everything she would have said. It told me good girls didn't make deals with the devil. Didn't free a murderer to avenge a murder. Didn't carry a gun and resort to violence to get what she wanted. Good girls held their rosaries and said their prayers and confessed their sins.

"I'm not a good girl," I told her, and closed the lid.

Jacob entered the room seconds later, and I silently cursed. I should have known he'd realize I wasn't getting into bed, would want to know if I were okay. The temperature dropped and he came through the door, his ghostly eyes seeing the suitcase on the bed, the drawers opened and emptied, the picture gone from the dresser.

What's going on?

"I'm taking a short trip," I said, trying to sound nonchalant. Easy breezy, that was the key. Keep it simple and don't upset the ghost. "Got a lead I need to follow up on. Nothing dangerous. I'll be gone a few nights, that's all, but I'll be back before you can say Jack Spratt."

Jack Spratt

"Funny," I said. "But you know what I meant."

Where are you going? Does Ingy know?

He asked too many damn questions. I'd thought I'd need to worry about Ingrid, but I should have been focused on Jacob. Maybe I could weave an intricate tale of taking my clothing to the dry cleaners, and the gun to the shop for repairs, and the picture to get the frame re-gilded. Sure, he'd buy that. If he were three. Stick to facts, Mira, you're better with those.

"I'm going to Maine," I said. Blunt, firm, not allowing for any argument.

I could feel his worry, the air temperature dropping more.

"It's what I have to do, Jacob," I said. I began checking the room to make sure I hadn't forgotten anything. His spectral presence floated around me, the cold tendrils of his fingers brushing my arms as he tried to get my attention, get me to listen to him.

Can't we help you somehow?

"No, I need to do this alone." I thought of how Ingrid would feel when she returned and found me gone. That got me nowhere. She'd be rightly mad, and I couldn't deal with those thoughts as I packed to leave. "It's better if I go now while everyone is busy."

If you run off, I'll tell Ingy where you went. She'll follow you.

"That's not fair."

Sure, go ahead, tell a ghost what's fair in life.

We were getting nowhere. I had to hit the road before I changed my mind and I could only see one solution. I picked up the suitcase and placed it on the chair by the window, and then shrugged out of my coat. I tossed it on top of the suitcase. "Fine. I'll tell them in the morning and we'll make plans then. I'm going to bed."

He waited for a few moments as I plucked at the buttons of my shirt, then drifted out of the room, his sense of decorum strong enough that, even though he suspected I might be pretending, he wouldn't stay. But I could feel his scrutiny through the thin wood separating us even after he'd left. I quietly pulled my coat back on, but sat on the bed so the springs would squeak. I pulled Ben's Saint Brendan's medallion from a pocket and ran my thumb across the green-pocked surface, feeling every ridge and indentation. Every mark left by him, a reminder of him, that he'd existed, wasn't some fading dream. Here in my hands lay one of the results of his life, proof of the man, and I squeezed it tightly. I did this for him. If I stopped now, the work would never be finished.

The chair sat close enough I could reach the suitcase. I popped the lid, found my compact, and sprinkled some powder in a ring on the floor. I stepped into the middle, careful not to disturb the lines, and held the medallion with both hands, closing my eyes. Well, I'd already made a deal with the devil. This hardly seemed the same level of evil choices, but somehow what I planned to do now hurt far more. I'm not sure Jacob would ever forgive me.

"Sorry, Jacob," I whispered. I let my mind drift down through the dark tunnel beneath my waking thoughts, down into the chasm of memory and forever, down into the tiny white jewel buried deep beneath the world of the alive. I'd never tried to reach the dead before, but I understood the theory, and I reached for the gem. I could see the threads again, the interconnections of the living and the gone, lines spooled around me like an endless woven tapestry. I almost tried to find Ben Templeton's thread, but I shook my head and concentrated on what I needed right now. I reached out and stroked the strings, testing each one until I found the one I sought, connected to the gem. Jacob's string. I plucked it free, breaking it into two parts, tying them to the string of our home. Then I followed the path up and up, through the thick, tangled skein of the world's dreaming.

When my eyes opened, sweat dappled my brow, the room uncomfortable warm. I could sense Jacob's presence outside the door, his bewilderment. I picked up the suitcase and stepped into the hallway, glancing at the dim mist of my friend as he floated frozen in front of the room.

"You'll understand when you think about it," I said, touching the spot where his cheek would be. "No one else will die because of me. Not you, not Lugnut." Here, my voice hitched. "Not Ingy. I have to do this alone."

Then I left the house. I drove north from Baltimore as night took hold, aiming towards the far northern regions of the country, where city lights never touched and real darkness slumbered beneath the veneer of a civilized world that had no right to claim such a title. I found the ball of my anger and tied it to the steel of my desire, pushed all my grief aside, and I rode my rage north towards New England.

***

I spread the map I'd picked up at a gas station the evening before across the hood of the Fjord. I tried to find Damascus Mills, placing rocks on the corners to hold it down in the tricky breeze, which held the scent of winter. The area was littered with town names I didn't recognize, like Skowhegan and Millinocket. My finger ran up and down the map in straight lines, reading every name twice, until I reached the northern border where Maine butted against the Borealian Empyrean.

"Damn it." I'd already been on the road for a day and a half. I'd napped in the car the first night, somewhere north of New Amsterdam, the great city itself. I'd arrived in Maine late yesterday, gassed up, and spent the night at the first motor lodge I'd come across. Here, so close to the quarry, I couldn't find the way. I folded the map and tossed it back in the car. I walked to the office and entered, the bell above the door tinkling. After a few seconds, the old gentleman who had waited on me the evening before stepped through a back doorway and bellied up to the counter.

"Ayuh," he said. "Can I help you, miss?" He peered at me through round glasses and scratched his ear.

"I'm going to be checking out now."

"Alright. That'll be two dollars in cash."

I handed him a ten. He rang up the register and began counting out my change.

"There you go," he said as he handed the money to me. "I hope you're going to get a chance to enjoy Maine. The weather's been pretty darn nice for fall. T'ain't been too cold at least."

Outside the window, a thin crust of dirty snow covered some of the grassy areas. I wondered what he thought would be cold. "Well, I'm heading north, so I'll get to enjoy some of it unless it gets any colder." Already too damn cold. "Do you happen to know where Damascus Mills is?"

His pleasant smile dimmed. "What'd you want to be going all the way up thayah, for?"

"I have some friends I'm visiting who moved up there a few years ago." The lie told, and less difficult than casting a spell on Jacob, or leaving behind Ingrid. A lie in the service of running down a lead I wouldn't considered a lie at all. Well, there went another piece of myself. So easy to slip into bad behaviors and find ways to justify them. What would Ingy say about me now? Probably she'd say I'd finally started to figure out how the world worked. She might even approve, assuming she wasn't so pissed she'd turn me into a rat out of spite.

"Don't nobody visit up there. There's much nicer things along the coast, you know. I could show you on the map some sights to visit."

Tourist places, probably run by his relatives and friends. "Thanks, but just directions to Damascus Mills."

He rambled on, ignoring my question. "People up there come from away and you cahn't trust folks from away. No offense intended of course, miss. Best to be along the ocean. Got a nice breeze. Good for the health."

"Please."

At last it seemed to register to him I wasn't going to be dissuaded from my intent. "Well, you don't got to take my advice. 'Course you should. You follow this here road up to Old Orchard, up through Portland and Rockland. Just follow a little further east for a bit, and look for the signs for route twenty four north. There'd be several forks along there, just stick to twenty four. It's up the road a piece. Bit of a rough road I hear, only I don't get up that way so I wouldn't know."

"Thank you," I said, heading for their door.

"Well, I don't know as if you'll thank me once you get there, but you're welcome."

The coastal road turned out to be a pretty drive, weaving in and around small coves, passing through old fishing villages dotted with sail boats. Lobster traps were piled high on the docks, the wooden slats weathered gray with water and age, pieces of seaweed dangling from the edges. There were small enclaves of bigger homes, right against the rocky shoreline, places where rich folks probably stayed. *Folks from away*, I thought, as I viewed the grand estates through screens of trees. The maples and elms and oaks were bare, covering their rough root toes with blankets of colorful leaves. Only the pine trees remained green and vibrant, branches waving in the fickle wind. Winter was their time to shine without the competition of their slumbering brethren. Baltimore would have been jealous if it had a mind to care, but I suspected Baltimore looked down its nose at Maine the way a once-rich lumber baron fallen on hard times would look down their nose at another poor person.

I followed the roads deeper into the dark Maine woods.

16

Hiems and the Jacks

I'd slept in the car my second night in Maine. I'd found a rutted, narrow road beyond a small town I'd passed. I parked in among the trees, out of sight of the main road. Sleep had been fitful, the strange night noises of the woods waking me every few minutes. I'd never been so cold in all my life, even when I'd been living on the streets. I'd wrapped my coat around me as tightly as I could manage.

I missed Ingy like hell, too.

Guilt. It nestled deep in my bones, mixing with the cold. I should have talked to her. I wished she were here now to set me straight. This had been a stupid damned decision. Nothing to do know, though, but follow through. I'd come this far, hadn't I? But the decision to leave without a word ate at me, and the lack of her presence left another void in my life that couldn't be filled.

Once inland and away from the coastal road, the sleepy fishing villages with their picturesque harbors were replaced by little towns, often no more than a single store littered with old signs, or a post office that seemed more like an abandoned home than a place to buy stamps. The few houses that weren't simple wooden homes were two-or-three story Victorians that had seen better days, their age marked by sagging porches and peeling paint. I passed an apple orchard as I drove through a long succession of rolling hills, the fields separated by lines of trees and loose rock fences there since settlers first came. Now the fences were forgotten markers overtaken by brush and weeds, the early snowfall half covering all of it. The roads were dirt, filled with potholes not always patched. The car bounced as I crawled north.

At last, I passed a large sign marking the edge of Damascus Mills—population six hundred and fifty, a "Fine Place to Live and Work"—well before noon. It took a few more miles of woods and fields before I came to the town itself, a collection of small homes, a general store, a bank with a name I'd never heard of, and a few side streets. Nicer than some of the smaller towns, but a place without much future. A place children would leave when they grew up.

Now what do I do? I didn't know where to begin looking for Rowan and her seasons, assuming they resided in the area. I felt nervous about asking as well. Would they think I was a lunatic *from away*? They'd probably have me committed for chasing old ghost stories.

Ahead, near the center of town, stood a white building with twin columns flanking the doorway. *Damascus Mills Library* read the black lettering above the door. My favorite place in the world, a library. It put me at ease, my muscles relaxing. A library I could work with. I pulled into the curb in front of the building.

I left the cold November air of Maine for what I hoped would be the relative warmth of the library. There were no other patrons besides myself. A young woman stood behind the curving desk, her stamp thumping against a book as she checked it back into circulation. The desk framed the front of a circular room in the center of the library, beneath a central dome arched high above. The inside of the dome had been painted with figures of people reading books, and scenes from the books playing out behind them. Shelves of books lined the wall behind her, and a cart stood in front of them, more books piled on top. It was charming, comforting. I inhaled the scent of books.

I tried to locate the card catalog. I could hunt for books relating to the witches, perhaps disappearances or strange events. Maybe I would get lucky and find information about them buying or building their property in old town records. But no, those were probably held at town hall. Newspapers then. Local would be better.

"May I help you?" asked the librarian, closing the book she had stamped and placing it to one side. Her long, dark hair hung down her back almost to her waist. Her eyes were twin emeralds in a sea of pale skin. Her simple, checkered dress seemed tawdry and plain in comparison with her features. She was nothing like anyone else I'd seen for the last few days, but I recognized her when she lifted her face. Recognized those big, green eyes, and Hollywood starlet looks.

"May I help you, Miss?" the librarian repeated.

"You were at Ben Templeton's office," I said.

Her face went rigid, the eyes widening slightly. She balled her fingers into fists, and for a second, I thought she would either run, or attack me. She did neither, but lifted a portion of the right side of the desk to let herself out and walked past me. She flipped the sign over the door from *Open* to *Closed* and turned the lock.

By the time she turned back to me, I had my right hand in my pocket holding the handle of my revolver. A whistle hung behind my pursed lips, ready to be called if needed. But her face had softened, and she gave a tentative smile as she took a few steps towards me.

"I didn't realize you were the same woman I saw in his office that day," she said.

I nodded. "You didn't seem to notice me."

She sighed and brushed her long hair away from her face. "I had a lot of things on my mind. I suppose it was rude to rush through his office and not acknowledge you, but I was preoccupied."

I relaxed the grip on my gun and slipped my hand out of my pocket. If she wanted to play nice, we'd play nice. But this *old friend* of Mr. Templeton's had become suspect number one in my investigation. The ball of anger and rage roiled in my gut, and I knew I wouldn't hesitate to kill her if she gave me half a reason. What would Ingy say about all this? She'd understand. That provided little comfort, though. Maybe she would. Maybe not. My heart throbbed at the thought of Ingy never forgiving me for leaving like I'd done. Or Lugnut. Jacob. Petunia. But Mira had made plenty of mistakes already. Chalk it up to my nature.

"You are Mira Sinclair, his protégé. Yes?"

"Yes."

"He spoke very highly of you," she said. "I think half our conversation was about you and what he was teaching you. He seemed to think you'd be a better detective than he was, one day." She paused, as though waiting for me to reply, but I held my tongue at first. It found it deeply pleasing to learn he'd been talking about me in such a glowing way, but my emotions churned and any reply got stuck on the way from my brain to my throat.

I gave her a brief nod once my tongue loosened. "And you're Hiems, right?"

"Yes," she said. No last name offered. "We got word a couple of days ago of his death. I am so sorry. Ben was a good man."

"Mr. Templeton," I said, reflexively correcting her as I often did myself. I chided myself for the response, and forged ahead. "What were you doing in Baltimore? And where were you when Mr. Templeton was murdered?"

She kept her hands at her sides. Kept her movements small. I thought she might be trying to appear nonthreatening. "It might be best of you speak to grammy Rowan about that," she said. "She can fill you in on all the particulars of my trip."

Rowan. I ignored the name, pregnant with possibilities, for the moment. "You can't speak for yourself?"

Her face tightened again, and her eyes narrowed. Her pale skin flushed just a little. Her poker face wasn't as good as I'd first thought. "I can speak for myself," she said, "but only grammy Rowan can give you the whole story. I came down to Baltimore to see Ben and extend our condolences over the death of his friend, Mr. Gambini."

I wondered if she knew her excuse damned her more than vindicated. It made her a suspect in both murders. "How could you have known he was dead, let alone get to Baltimore so quickly, if it had been no more than twenty-four hours?"

"Grammy Rowan knew before it happened, one of her special dreams. She sent me to be with Ben in his time of need. She would have gone herself, but it's a long trip and she no longer can travel." She walked around me in a wide circle, lifting her hands slightly so I could watch them. She stepped behind the desk again and planted her palms face down on the dark, wood surface. "You don't believe me, do you." Not a question, but a statement, punctuated by a smile.

"No," I said. "Why should I?"

"Did you see who murdered him? You were there, weren't you?" She watched my face, reading the lines that passed through my features. "Yes, you were there. You still bear the memory of it like a chain weighing you down."

I'd stopped listening to her. The memory of Mr. Templeton's death played out in front of me now. The smell of gunpowder in my nostrils. The ringing of my ears from the gunshots. The black sedan pulling away from the curb, a face looking back at me as I hammered off shots, hitting nothing. Hair slicked back, sunglasses, a thick beard. Male; human, maybe dwarf. Not a woman. Not this woman. But she could have hired them, perhaps. "You may not have pulled the trigger, but it proves nothing."

"How about this," she said. She reached under the counter, and I almost drew my gun, but relaxed when she lifted a purse. She set the black leather purse on the desk and opened it, pulled out a long slip of paper and lay it down. "My train ticket back to Portland."

I stepped over and examined it, my eyes scanning the printed text. She'd left Baltimore at 10:15 AM on Saturday, hours before Mr. Templeton had been murdered. Here, at least, was an alibi, even if it didn't absolve her. I didn't trust her, didn't trust anyone at this point. Didn't even trust myself to make a good judgement about the information I'd received. "Doesn't prove anything."

She took the ticket and put it back in her purse. "I'll take you to grammy Rowan and you can talk to her. She'll confirm what I'm saying and you can make up your mind about the truth."

Indecision gnawed at me. The cold didn't help. I'd been cold since I arrived in Maine, and shivered even in the warmth of the library. But I'd come here to find Rowan, and now she'd been offered to me on a platter. Ingy would have told me I'd be a damned fool not to take it. I nodded. "Alright, we'll go see Rowan. But we'll take my car, not yours."

"I don't have a car," she said. "Let me finish this stack of returns, and I'll lock up."

I nodded my agreement at the plan. While she stamped returns and carried them into a small office, I walked around the library, reading the spines of books. The collection looked small, but so did the library. Certainly, far smaller than the ones in Baltimore, which were tiny compared to the Undertow's collection. But the building had been well maintained, and the books lovingly cared for, that was easy enough to see. My feet led me into the fiction section, where they had stocked the classics. Cervantes, Shakespeare, tucked in with more modern novels by Filcher, Fitzgerald. Not as many of the latter as the former, but enough to show she kept up with trends. Even a few mysteries, some Conan-Doyle along with Wentworth. She had the entire series of novels by gnomish author Halliday Gerinshtuple, which told the comic adventures of Marish the nanny who served in the home of some minor ogre nobles. I'd read them all when I was ten, along with the Alice in Wonderland books.

"Miss Sinclair?" Hiems called out.

Her voice startled me, and I twitched my hand away from one of the books I'd been examining as though I'd been caught nicking it. I returned to the front desk where she stood waiting for me. "You ready?"

"Of course," she said. She led me out the door and waited for me to pass. She locked the door behind us, then followed me down to the car.

I tossed her my keys. "You drive?"

She caught them deftly, her eyes never leaving me. Neat trick, that. "I do. Not well, but when needed. Why would you let me drive your car?"

I had no reason to dissemble about the decision. "I don't trust you. I'd rather have my hands free in case you try something."

"Well then, just as you say," she said, and she opened the driver's side door. She slipped into the seat and waited for me to join her before sliding the key into the ignition and starting the engine.

Mr. Templeton's Fjord sounded rough, the cold weather not doing it any favors. She slipped it into reverse and eased out of the parking spot. She stalled it trying to shift into first, grimaced, then ground through the gears once she'd started the car again. We lurched into motion.

"Sorry," she said. "It's been a while."

Her lack of skill with a motor vehicle ruled her out as the driver of the murderer's black sedan. They'd roared away, not missing a gear, and screamed around the next corner without having to tap their brakes. She drove like a little old lady, her fingers clenched around the steering wheel. Her eyes darted left and right, and we were going ten miles under the speed limit. When I pulled my revolver out of my coat pocket and held it on my lap, she gave it only the briefest glance before her eyes turned back to the road. Her face tightened.

I cracked the window and lit a snipe. She glanced at me, frowning, but remained quiet as I blew the smoke out the window. We rolled out of town and into the woods again, following the road as it curved through the pine forests.

"How many of you are there?" I asked as she drove.

"How many of what?"

"Seasons," I said.

"There are always four seasons," she said.

"How does Rowan pick her seasons?"

"It would be better if you speak to her. Grammy Rowan can decide what you need to know. We're almost to the turn off."

We topped a short rise, and Hiems jammed the brakes. The car skidded on the crest of the hill, slewing sideways before coming to a stop in the middle of the dirt road. My gun tumbled out of my lap and onto the floor. I swore as I slapped my hands against the dashboard to keep from slamming my head into it.

A lumber truck blocked the way ahead, stretched from one side of the road to the other, its dirty blue cab in the ditch. My side of the car had turned towards the truck, but I didn't see anyone moving around it. I reached down and retrieved the pistol.

A shot rang out. I slid down into my seat instinctively. "Down, Hiems!"

She ignored me, opening the door and sliding out of the seat, disappearing from view. Another crack, the whine of a bullet screeching across the metal hood of the Fjord. I slid across the seat bench and fell out onto the ground beside the car. Hiems crouched nearby as we kept the bulk of the car between us and the shooter.

I rose to a squat and lifted my head, glancing through the door window towards the truck. I caught the flash of a gun muzzle between the truck cab and the load of logs a split second before the door window shattered, raining shards of glass across the road and myself.

"Probably more than one," I said, waiting until Hiems nodded. "When I start firing, I want you to break towards the rear of the car and run into the woods. I'll cover you."

I leaned forward until I could see past the front of the car and waited, holding the gun with both hands. I saw movement in the gaps between the cab of the truck and the bed of logs, and another movement off to the left in the trees, the opposite side of the road from where I wanted Hiems to make her break. That meant at least two, and I wouldn't be surprised if there were more hiding nearby.

"Who the hell are these people?"

"The Jacks," Hiems replied.

"Who?"

"They're lumberjacks, but they call themselves the Jacks. They drive trucks and hire themselves out for robberies, knee cappings, and other lucrative activities."

A bullet ripped a hole in the air near my head, causing me to duck and wince. "Why the fuck is every bad guy named Jack? Get ready."

I rose and leaned over the hood, aiming for the junction between the front of the big truck and the logs. I hammered home the trigger, firing off rounds in a quick burst as Hiems ran towards the woods. A bullet dug a furrow into the ground behind her as she ran, and then she disappeared into the darkness of the trees as I dropped down. I reached into my pocket for fresh rounds and reloaded the gun as I planned what I would do next.

I slid onto my belly, peering beneath the frame of the car. The hard dirt beneath me sent cold tendrils through my clothing and into my flesh, like little needles. I could see under the truck as well, and waited until a pair of dirty, dark brown boots appeared. I aimed and squeezed, exhaling before I pulled the trigger. The thunder of the gun was punctuated by a scream of pain, a ragged hole appearing in the shoe, a gout of blood, then a bearded face fell into view.

A face that might have peered from the back of a speeding car, driving away from the scene of a murder.

My heart pounded, and hot anger flushed through my skin. The dwarf writhed in pain, clutching at his foot, and I fired again. The bullet caught him in the side, and he flopped over and stopped moving.

I stood and strode around the front of the car, forgetting everything in my rage. I wanted to empty every chamber into his body. Only then would I repay the man who'd killed my boss. Only then could I ease the grief and pain I'd felt since he'd been taken from me. Gone the sadness, the empty hollow in my heart, replaced by the pounding of blood in my head. Gone the good girl, replaced by a woman whose intent was murderous. The world grayed as my vision narrowed, and I wondered if my eyes were as black as Ingrid's when she worked her spells.

Something hot slammed into my side and threw me off my feet. I fell hard against a crusty snowbank, my breath knocked from my lungs. My hands shook as I reached down to my side. Damp and sticky. When I pulled them away, blood coated my fingers. The rage bled away, replaced by shame. Another mistake. Another failure. Then I laughed, the sound trailing off into a wail of anguish. Well, at least I'd put some holes in one of the bastards who killed my boss. I think even Ingy would have agreed I'd done enough.

Ingy. Jesus, Ingy. I wouldn't get a chance to say goodbye to her.

Oh god, what had I done? Yes, Mira, what did you do. You made a damn bloody mess of everything, that's what.

Another dwarf ran out of the trees, shooting as he moved. A bullet tore the ground near my face, sharp stabs of dirt and rock digging into my skin. He seemed to stagger, his head jerking back as he yelped in some sort of pain. My arms were so damned weak, but I lifted my revolver casually, languidly, and fired a single shot. Ingy said I'm ready, so I damn well would be. A hole appeared in the middle of his forehead, neat as you please, and his run turned into a staggering fall. His body hit the ground three feet from where I lay, blood pooling beneath his face. How's that for a shot? Better shot than you, Ben Templeton, even you have to agree. I giggled again; recognized the signs of shock I exhibited; giggled some more.

The rumble of an engine cut my thoughts off. Black smoke belched from the exhaust of the truck, and I caught a glimpse of a face in the cab. A third dwarf, his eyes wide and scared. He should be scared. I'm the fucking big bad wolf. You think Ingy is scary, wait until you get a load of me. He put the rig into gear with a grinding noise, and the truck lurched backwards. I turned my gun on him and pulled the trigger again and again, bullets leaving holes in the door until I'd run dry.

He'd gotten stuck, the wheels slipping on the snow-covered turf next to the road surf. While the dwarf lurched his vehicle back and forth, grinding in and out of first gear and reverse, I rolled onto my back. The pain of my wound seemed to have lessened as I fumbled in my pocket for more rounds, but I shook like a leaf in a storm. Shock. Numbing me again. I dropped several rounds and they bounced over the frozen ground before I managed to load two bullets and reseat the cylinder.

"You get down from there now!" I said. I staggered to my feet and aimed at the driver side window. A pair of hands appeared, raised over the head of a dwarf with a sour expression. He wore a red cap, and his beard was black.

"You fucking bastard," I growled. But murderous desire had left me. I didn't want to kill him. I would try and play him for information, find out who the money man was. I needed to know who had set this all up, who'd paid to have my boss killed. If I could stay alive long enough, I could get word to Ingy. Maybe find a house with a phone nearby. A telegraph office in town. Something. Give her the details.

Tell her goodbye.

More movement caught my blurring eyes, this time from the opposite side of the road. I swung the gun around and twisted my neck so I could see what was coming.

It was Hiems. No longer the Hollywood starlet, with a face made for the pictures. Her hair had grown as dark as the gap between stars, her eyes glassy black orbs set in a face lined with a spider web of white marks. She shimmered like baking pavement in summer heat, a mirage, a vision, as she floated above the ground. Her hands were raised, and a guttural voice issued from her open mouth, speaking bleak words, malignant words, words that made me drop my revolver and cover my ears, crumple to the ground once more. Ingy had shown me power. This was something more, grinding against my bones as if it would crush them to dust.

"No, no," I mumbled, curling into a ball as pressure built in my skull. "I need him; make it stop; please, make it stop." I squeezed my eyes shut.

I heard a male voice say, "Wait, please, you—" before a sickening crunch cut it off, the sound of metal crushed, glass shattering, a rising scream of pain running on for several infinite moments. It became a squeal, like an animal being slaughtered, and then abruptly cut off. The pressure faded, and I could breathe again, open my eyes.

The front of the truck had been crushed, squashed into a metal ball only a few feet in diameter, jagged pieces of metal and glass jutting in every direction. A liquid seeped from the door which hung off its hinges.

My heart skipped two beats, and I threw up onto the road. When I was done heaving, I wiped my lips with the back of my sleeve. "What did you do?" I said, though it came out more as a moan. "I needed him alive."

Hiems strode across the road, looking every inch the beautiful woman from the library, from Ben's office. "No creature will attack a season, nor any she is with. The bastard got what was coming to him. They'll all get what's coming to them."

The pain overwhelmed me, and I fell back, no longer able to hold up my head. So damned cold. I started shaking again. Someone spoke to me. Jacob? No, only pain and shock making me hallucinate. I barely felt her hands exploring my wounds, couldn't hear the words she spoke although her mouth moved. She tore something from her skirt, slid it under my shirt against my side, pressed my hand to it. Then she lifted me as though I were a doll, and eased me into the back seat of the car.

"Ingy. Ingy, I think I'm shot."

Hold on Mira, please, Jacob's voice said.

"Hush, Mirabel, it's alright. I'll get you help."

"Ingy. I love you so much, Ingy. God, you have no idea. Can't tell you. Not ever."

"You're going to be fine, Mira. Press down."

Don't die Mira, please don't die. I don't want you to end up like me

Everything grew gray and dim.

17

A Season of Witches

Hiems drove slowly as I bled to death in the back seat, only half conscious. I held the compress she'd made from the fabric of her clothing against the wound. A hole in my body to match the one in my heart. Another failure to display on the short story of my career. But I felt worse because Ingy wasn't there with me than I did because of the pain of my wound. Her absence a far greater hole in my being than the bullet had created. Or maybe shock had taken hold of me, dulling the physical pain without touching the mental.

Jacob kept talking to me, but as Jacob wasn't there either, I ignored his voice. Dying apparently made you hallucinate.

She slowed further, then turned. The car bounced hard, and I wheezed in agony as trees threw shadows over the vehicle. I wanted to raise my head and see where we were, but it took too much energy to bother. I could see the trees outside the window, pressing close around the car.

I sensed something in the forest. A watchfulness, an awareness. A *something* looked down at us from high above. The trees seemed to lean towards us, gathering around the car, and the air grew still, pressing down on me. Branches scratched against the sides of the car like fingernails scraping a chalkboard.

Ancient. Old before humans and elves settled these lands, old before the mountains rose and then fell again beneath mile-high glaciers. As old as Jack Nory, and older still. Cold like the universe, the wide, empty spaces with no suns to warm the flesh. No love, no joy, only an existence measured in endless eons. I shivered as my heart beat faster in my chest. I gulped at the air with my lungs, each breath labored.

Then the trees pulled away, sunlight returned, and we passed into an open area. The pressure relented, the ancient presence fading, and I took a long, painful breath.

"We're past the watcher, almost there," Hiems said. "Hold on, Mira."

'She's coming, Chancy,' a voice said from far away.

You leave her be, Jacob demanded. *She's not going to die.*

'He's right, it's not yet time, Mr. Sticks,' said another voice, deeper, somber.

"Who's there?" I murmured.

"It's Hiems, sweetie, Hiems," said Hiems from the front seat. "Remember?" She reached back and touched my leg, a warmth spreading from her fingers. Spoke some words in another language. The ever present cold eased and my shivering stopped. But that could be shock, the loss of blood. Me slipping away.

Templeton was wrong about her, that self-righteous prick,' the first voice said.

"Who's talking?" I said, trying to sit up. A stab of pain shot through my abdomen and I gasped loudly and fell back against the seat.

'Don't be so hasty, old friend,' the second voice said. *'She's not as weak as she seems.'*

"No one's talking, Mira," Hiems said.

The warmth of her touch spread through me, passing through the wound, easing the pain. Through my shoulders and neck, into my face. I breathed more easily, felt my muscles go slack. Felt ready to let go. My hand slipped away from the compress, and I closed my eyes.

"Stay with me, Mira," Hiems said. But I didn't want to. Too damned tired. The world didn't want me, a woman pretending to be a detective. It slapped you down if you were different. They made fun of you, then they made laws against you, then they killed you. I tried to push her hand away, but my strength faded, and I grinned at how stupid it all had been. Lost in the woods of Maine, driven around by the protegee of an old witch, leaking fluids like a busted radiator. Far from the people I loved, from Lugnut and Jacob. Far from Ingy, whom I loved above all others.

Closer now to Mr. Templeton, though.

The car stopping.

The door opening and voices talking.

Someone lifting me.

The bang of a door shutting, footsteps on wooden floors.

I smell lilacs and pot roast. How strange.

Wet cloth on my brow. Hands pulling on my clothing.

A cemetery, dark mausoleum before me, a flickering light from within. I walk inside, two shadowy forms waiting for me.

'Not yet,' said the somber voice. Something hitting my chest, sending me flying, the cemetery receding, fading, gone.

Nothing.

***

I woke in a room, a sliver of light filtering through the curtains drawn across a window. Not my room, though. My window had plain, dark curtains, not these flowered things. My window didn't keep out the orange-yellow glow of street lamps, the sounds of passing traffic, the voices of the neighbors talking to each other. Bird calls broke the silence beyond this pane of glass, along with the creak of tree branches. Uncanny sounds to a woman who had the city lodged in her soul.

I sat up, then gasped at the tightness in my side, the sharp stab of pain reminding me I'd been shot. I eased myself flat once more, taking shallow breaths to control the anguish, pressing my hand to my side. The wound had been bandaged. I also realized my clothing had been removed and beneath the warm covers I wore only my under things. I lifted my head as much as I dared and pulled back the blanket to look at the bandage. A found a cotton compress, held in place by two long strips of fabric wound around my body. I touched it lightly.

I thought about sliding my fingers under the compress to explore the bullet wound, but the door opened. More light spilled into the room and I blinked against the sudden glare of it, though the light came from little more than a few candles in the hallway beyond the door.

Hiems stood framed by the flickering light behind her. She reached back into the hall past the door, and her hand returned with a brass candle holder, the taper lit, the flame steady. "Grammy Rowan said you were awake and I should come check on you."

I opened my mouth to speak and found my throat parched, my lips cracked. "How long?" I mumbled, coughing to clear my throat. "How long was I unconscious?"

She stepped into the room and placed the candle holder on a dresser against the left wall. She pulled a small chair from beside it and placed it next to the bed, then sat. "It's been a day and a half since you were shot," she said, her eyes examining my bandaging. "You shouldn't mess with the bandage; the poultice is helping you heal."

"The Jacks?" I asked. My thoughts weren't entirely lucid, and I knew my questions were scattershot.

She gave me the tiniest of smiles. "The police took care of it. They understand it was self-defense and accepted my explanation. The Jacks won't be bothering you anymore."

I shook my head. "That's not what I meant," I said. But I couldn't string together the right question. My head remained groggy, stuffed with mental cotton, and my entire body hurt. The wound throbbed, and I imagined my body looked like one giant bruise from head to toe.

She touched my forehead with a cool hand, closing her eyes. "Fever's down at least," she said. She picked up the wet cloth and placed it over my brow once more. "You need to rest. Grammy Rowan fixed you up and you'll heal quick, but it's going to take a few more days."

I pushed her hands away from my face and thrust myself up, grunting with the effort. Something pulled in my abdomen, and my hand reflexively pressed on the bandaging. "I need to get back on the road. Get back to Baltimore."

"You'll do no such thing," she said, walking towards the door. "Didn't you get what you wanted when we put those boys down?"

The Jacks she meant. She'd killed one of them even though I'd needed him alive, but I couldn't blame her for that. Hadn't I wanted to kill them all? Hadn't a desire for vengeance taken hold of me, driven me to kill the other two? It had been that same need for murderous justice that got me shot. I put myself in danger so I could finish one of them off and opened myself up as a target. All because I needed to get revenge for the murder of a man I loved and admired.

But I had more to do. Killing them hadn't salved the pain of Ben's death. I still felt empty inside, like a gutted deer. The sharpest pain was not the one in my side, but the invisible dagger that stabbed me in the chest, drove me on to find the person or persons who'd hired the Jacks. They needed to pay.

I realized then I'd taken Hiems off the list of suspects. She'd guided me here, put herself in danger for me, and killed another being to protect me. Murdering a murderer goes a long way towards proving someone is innocent of other crimes. But that didn't necessarily absolve Rowan. And even if it did, Jack Nory had told me to come here and I'd find what I needed. Maybe Rowan had information I could use to track down the person who hid at the center of all of the bad things that had been happening. "I need to see Rowan," I said.

"Rest, Mira," Hiems said.

"No, I need to see her now."

She glared at me, her hands on her hips, and I stared back. Something passed between us; recognition, mutual respect. Maybe we acknowledged each other's humanity. Our indignities and pain. Two women measuring each other and finding the other worthy of her regard.

"I'll get her," she said, and left the room. She kept the door open this time, a promise she'd be back shortly, and she trusted me to stay put. She left the candle on the dresser, too.

There was a wardrobe and chair along with the dresser and bed in the small bedroom. I wanted to open the window and look out at the world, but I'd have to get out of the bed and walk over to it, and it had been hard enough sitting up. Those two steps felt like miles at the moment. The curtains were heavy, white drapes, the wallpaper a Victorian yellow with red and blue flowers sprinkled through it in a repeating pattern. It peeled away from one corner of the room, the color dingy in the dim light of a single candle. I closed my eyes and reached for the threads around me. I could see the house itself and the world beyond the window. A field surrounded the house, and beyond that the woods, where a thick, dark thread marked the presence I'd felt in the car. *Not a hallucination then*, I thought to myself. Very real, very old, and very powerful.

So, too, the thread of power working its way up the stairs of the house. Not dark this one, but still old and powerful, next to a young, vibrant one. The two witches climbed to the second floor slowly. Old floorboards creaked as they approached.

"You shouldn't be doing that," said a cracked voice. She sounded amused, not angry. Something pushed against my perceptions, gently but insistently, and the threads were washed away.

I opened my eyes and met those of Rowan. An old woman, stooped, leaning heavily on a cane made from a gnarled old branch, as though she'd simply picked it up off the ground. I didn't need to see her threads to feel the power radiating from her.

"You've gotten the hang of that pretty quick, ain't you," Rowan said. A smile creased the lines of her weathered face. Her features reminded me of a piece of driftwood, worn and carved by wind and tide and sand. She had the deep tan of a farmer, the teak color permanently burned into her skin from long days spent under a baking sun. She sat, sighing as she did. "Feels good to get off my feet. You get as old as me, sitting becomes much too much of a comfort." Hiems left the room, closing the door behind her with a soft click.

Rowan watched my face and waited for me to speak.

"I have questions," I said.

"Ayah, I'm sure you do," she said. "We all have questions. Where do we come from? Where are we going? What is the nature of life and death and power? Who killed Benjamin Francis Templeton?"

I nodded in agreement. Now that I'd met her, all the anger and bluster driving me forward had gone, swept away by the bullet that had taken my strength. "I thought," I began, and the words trailed off as I plucked at the blankets covering me. God, what I wouldn't give for Ingy to be here with me right now. Lend me her strength.

But I'd left her safe in Baltimore, as I'd intended. And I was still a damn fool for taking off like I did.

"You thought maybe I had something to do with it," she finished. When I gave her a brief nod, she smiled again. "Sure as hell seemed likely, what with Hiems being in Baltimore, and Jack Nory hinting as much."

"You know about Jack?" I asked.

She grinned. She had surprisingly good teeth. All the better to eat you with. "Of course. And I knew when you visited the old bastard. When you start tugging and cutting threads, some people are going to notice. More so when you're doing it to unleash death upon the world."

I sighed, and nodded. "Didn't feel I had a choice, though. Although I did bind him to other things."

She laughed, a bright sound, not at all cackling and evil. It put a smile on my face in spite of my weakness, the pain, the entire messed up situation. "Wicked clever. You outfoxed the old fox, and I can tell you right now he's not a happy demon."

"How do you know?"

She patted my hand, stopping my fingers from twitching against the covers. "I know dark folks, Mirabel Sinclair. I know all the demons that walk this world and masquerade as people. When you freed Jack Nory, I knew it, and I knew the deal he'd made. I also knew he didn't realize what you really meant, what you were searching for, the task you set yourself."

"What is it?" I asked, wanting her answer, desperate to hear it said to me. Words have weight, words have form, words have power.

She touched my cheek with her other hand, turning my face to meet my eyes. "You want to become Ben Templeton."

A sob escaped the lips I'd been biting. I wanted to nod in agreement. It wasn't enough to find his killers and take out my sadness and anger on them. Returning the golden goose would only be a start. I wanted to take up Ben's career, become the man who had taken me in and taught me so much.

"You'll fail," she said, and those two words were an anchor yanking my heart out of my chest.

"Why?" I asked, hearing the bitter taste in my voice. My fingers curled into a tight fist under her hand and I leaned back against the pillow, no longer able to look at her face.

She took my fingers in hers, lifting my hand off the bed. Her hands were rough and calloused, but I noticed her nails were neatly trimmed, painted a lovely shade of dark red. She unrolled my fingers, pressed my hand between both of hers, and a warmth passed through me. "Because you're not Ben Templeton, dear. You're not a man, you're a woman. You're everything he taught you, and everything he didn't, and that makes you other. You're doing pretty damned good all on your own despite feeling the pain of his death. You found the men who did the murder, didn't you?"

"More like they found me," I said. I took my hand back and heaved a deep breath. "I've found nothing but pain since Lucky's funeral."

"That's called life," she said. "The state of being human. Or elven, or trollish, or gnomish, don't matter which. Life is pain. You're born in pain, you grow up feeling pain, and most die in pain."

"So why bother?" I asked.

"Because in between all that pain, there's beauty that makes it all worthwhile. The smile of your mother. The cool of a lake on a hot summer day. The first time you have sex with someone you truly care about. The birth of your children. Love."

Too often in my life I'd been afflicted with shame. I thank the Catholic church for that. Rowan brought back those feelings. Old, a woman, a witch; all things the world barely tolerated in public but despised in private. She'd suffered more for her existence than I could imagine. Yet she sat next to my bed and tried to comfort me. All the stories I'd read about her? I imagined they were yellow journalism. She'd risen in power, and they'd written tales about her to frighten the world, driven her into her exile in the boondocks of Maine. No woman should be lauded in this world above the men who ran the show.

And yet she sat there trying to help me see. I pushed myself up straighter in the bed and took several long, deep breaths. Steadying myself, clearing my head. "Sorry," I said.

She laughed, and it brightened the room. "Don't apologize. You ain't the first girl I've comforted, and hopefully won't be the last."

I ran through the situation in my head, pushing aside the sadness, the anger. Focusing on the task and goals. The Jacks were dead, or at least the one who had shot Mr. Templeton. What threads were left for me to follow? I closed my eyes for a moment and pictured all the pieces of the puzzle until I found the memory of Lucky's notes. "Who is LG?" I asked out loud.

"LG?" Rowan asked. I explained the notes to her and she shrugged. "Not Lucky Gambini then?"

"No, it can't be, that wouldn't make sense. The gnomes said they were hired by an elf, and Mr. Green hinted it might be some high muck-a-muck. Lucky referred to LG several times in reference to his investigation, which led to the gnomes. I suspect the two things are related."

She took my hand and lent me her strength. "I'm not going to be able to keep you in bed, am I?" she said.

18

The Return of the Ghost

We were quite the sight, a wounded detective and a crippled old woman leaning on each other as we worked our way down the narrow staircase. I'm not sure who helped the most, but I believe she supported me more than the other way around. Her cane made hollow thumps on the creaking steps, and there were a few moments when I felt as though we teetered on the edge of falling down the rest of the flight, but we made it to the bottom. I sighed in relief.

It surprised me to learn it was only late afternoon. Heavy green curtains were pulled aside and sunlight streamed in the west-facing windows. It took my eyes a few moments to adjust. She led me down a hallway with an old desk and a grandfather clock, and doorways to either side. To the right was a dining room with a huge table and six chairs, a china cabinet in the corner. To the left a living room, a tough looking old sofa, a cabinet radio in the corner, a doily lying across it and pictures scattered over the top, a fireplace on the back wall. Everything tidy, clean, not a speck of dust to mar the gleam of the wood.

The hallway opened into a kitchen at the back of the house. The yellow, linoleum flooring was worn down to the wood in some spots. A massive, cast-iron stove dominated one wall, with a stack of wood next to it for cooking. Skillets and pots hung from hooks above the counter, and above the rear door with its flowery curtain hung a crucifix. It had been painted in bright colors down to the blood stains on his hands, feet and forehead.

Rowan noticed my eyes lingering on the corpus. "Some of my girls were raised in church and I keep their symbols to help ease their minds about the things they do. The church doesn't have much love of magic you know, or people like me. This is one way to remind them magic isn't good or evil, it's a tool like any other."

"People are evil," I said.

"Some are. You go on and sit down at the table. Those stitches should hold, but you need to be off your feet for at least one more night to let my poultice have its full effect." She led me by my elbow to the small table against the wall by the hallway entrance, and we eased ourselves into separate chairs. She rubbed her fingers after she sat, her face twisted in a grimace of pain.

"Arthritis?" I asked.

"Getting old is a bitch," she said, placing her palms down on the metal surface and smiling. "I don't recommend it."

I touched the wound hidden beneath the bathrobe and bandaging. It burned with pain, though I knew it would feel a hell of a lot worse if Rowan hadn't sewed me up and used her magic. I felt like death warmed over. "The way I'm going, I'll be taking you up on your recommendation."

We were interrupted by the screech of the screen door opening. Footsteps squeaked on the floorboard, and a soft voice said, "Grammy Rowan, is everything all right?"

"Come on in, dear. Mira and I were talking."

Hiems stepped into the kitchen, glancing at me. She placed a newspaper on the table and walked to the stove, taking a tin cup from the cupboard next to it. She poured herself some water from the kettle. There were biscuit tins on the counter, and she opened several of them and sprinkled things into the cup, then stirred it with her finger. She sat down between us and sipped from the mug, glancing back and forth.

"Who is Ingy?" Hiems said with a soft smile.

I probably blushed to the roots of my hair. I had a hazy memory of speaking her name during the blur of the car ride here. "A friend of mine."

"Don't distract her, dear," Rowan said. "She's got enough to worry about without worrying about her friends." She gave Hiems a smile that went deeper than the surface. It reminded me of the smile a parent gives their child when they are proud of them. She reached out and touched Hiems' hand. "Hiems here is my winter season. Her father was Pastor Moran, who ran Sunday services down at Calvary Baptist in Cornish. Her mother was named Grace by her adoptive family, but she was pure elf. Everyone said she cast a spell on that poor man, the way he fell in love with her. But he was only a man, and it was only the kind of spell two young, handsome people have on each other. The church frowns on such marriages. Some people do more than frown."

Hiems held her mug up. "Would you like some tea?"

"I should thank you," I said. "You saved my life."

She shrugged. "You did fine with that gun of yours. I doubt I'd gotten all of them if you hadn't been there."

I almost patted my pockets for my gun before remembering I wore a bathrobe. "Where are my clothes?"

Rowan made a clucking sound. "Your pants and shirt were ruined of course. Can't get blood stains out, and no way to sew up all the rips. Your coat is in the wardrobe in your room, where Hiems hung it. She brought in your suitcase as well, it's under the bed. I assume you brought a change or two of clothes for when you go back."

I should go back. Ingy and Lugnut would be beyond pissed at me, and Jacob would join them in righteous indignation. They had every reason to be, too. I shivered in the cold kitchen, the late November weather of Maine driving into my bones like shards of ice. I hugged myself, scrunching my shoulders together.

Rowan watched me and then turned to the empty room. "Now you stop that. I know you're angry, but she's not going to recover if you keep lowering the temperature."

Hiems read the paper, not even looking at Rowan. I followed the old woman's eyes, and ended up staring at the stove. Was she talking to her oven, chiding it for failing to warm the house? "Who are you talking to?"

She frowned at the nothing and turned back to me. "If he won't come out and show himself, then I'll tell you myself. Your friend, Jacob, is here."

"Jacob?" I said, surprised. "That's not possible. He was tied to the house."

She shook her head. "Young people never know what's possible and impossible."

And then he was there, in the room with us, his voice filling my head. And angry, so very fucking angry, and I clutched my ears as though I could shut him out. "Wait, stop, slow down Jacob," I said, struggling to hear the world beyond his thoughts.

"That's enough," Rowan said. She'd spoken softly, but her voice cut through everything, a steam train blasting through a tunnel and emerging on the other side into clear air. Jacob's ranting stilled as quickly as it had begun, and though I sensed his presence, he withheld his thoughts for the moment, waiting for permission from Rowan before he spoke again.

She nodded at the place where he floated, invisible for the moment. "That's better. You stay right there and you calm down."

Jacob gave off a sense of *sullen resentment*, but he said nothing more.

"It *was* your voice I heard," I said, remembering the car ride as I bled out. But how? "I tied him to the house."

She clucked at me again, then sighed. Her face, scowling a moment before, seemed to fall, the world sagging on old flesh, weighing her down. "He was already tied to the house, dear. Ghosts are always tied to the place they died; you know that. You picked up some new habits lately I take it. Started seeing the Great Tapestry, the threads of all things. Started playing with the root of all that is and will be."

Hiems' head came up. "That's dark magic."

Rowan clucked a third time. "No dear, not dark magic. Haven't I taught you nothing? But it's a deeper magic, older than what you've been learning, and can be more powerful if it can be controlled. There's probably not ten witches left in the world who can do that, and this young woman figured it all out on her own."

"But you're one of those ten," I said.

Hiems studied me with her pale green eyes, and I grew increasingly uncomfortable.

"You've got to be careful, Mira," Rowan said, not replying to my statement directly. She took her cane from against the wall and wrapped her fingers tightly around it, until her knuckles turned white. "When you play with the threads, you don't always get the results you want. You cut his thread and tied him to the house, but you didn't see he was already tied there. You freed him. You love him too much. Didn't want to hurt him. So, you didn't tie him tight, and it unraveled. Not like how you tied old Jack. Jacob followed you here, caught up with you right after you crossed into Maine. He's why you've been so cold."

She looked back in his direction and smiled. "It's good to have friends who care about you enough to want to help you no matter what. He hurt one of the Jacks, the second one you shot. Ghosts have remarkable ways of influencing the living."

I remembered the way the dwarf had jerked, as though in pain. Jacob could do that to someone. He must have intervened, giving me a clear shot. Her words stung, too. They did care about me, enough to want to be part of the danger my job brought. I sensed a certain self-satisfied attitude coming from Jacob. The damned ghost felt mighty smug.

"Although," Rowan continued, "it's also good to have friends who care about you so much they don't want to put you in the danger they see coming."

Chagrin swiftly replaced Jacob's smugness. I knew how he felt, though, and I tried to reach out to him. "Jacob, I'm sorry. I'm so sorry for everything." I choked at that point. I waded through the current of my emotions to pick out the right words. There weren't any, though. None could salve all the wounds I'd created. "I thought I was doing what was best for everyone, trying to keep you safe."

He knew. It tempered what remained of his anger. *I wanted to come with you*, he thought to me, and it broke my heart, the sadness in his voice, his sense of hurt pride I'd stopped him from telling on me and getting Ingrid and Lugnut involved. Prevented them from having a chance to help. Tried to prevent *him* from helping.

"I know," I said. "You're here now, and if you can forgive me, I could use your help."

He mulled it over for a while. Then his mood brightened, and he surprised me with a comment about owing me for freeing him from our drafty house.

"It's draftier because of you, you pip." A smile creased my face. The first honest-to-god, real moment of pleasure I'd had in days. It would fade quickly, but I enjoyed the warm glow of it passing through me. "Picture my arms wrapping around you. Picture me squeezing. You're a good egg, Jacob."

He seemed pleased, and I could tell by Rowan's smile she was as well. "Good, that's settled. Before you go running off, you should know you're spending the night here."

"I couldn't impose," I said, but she shook her head before I finished.

"I insist," Rowan said. "It's the least I can do for a friend of Ben's."

"How well did you know him," I asked.

"He was a local boy," Rowan said. "Did you know that?"

"I knew he was from up north, but not where he lived," I said.

"Grew up here in Damascus Mills. He was a wicked bright kid, always sticking his nose into other people's business. You know, people don't much like that around here; you keep to yourself and don't bother anyone else. Not Ben, though. He was always where he weren't supposed to be. First time he came to my door I knew he was special. You had to be to get past the Watcher. And twelve years old at the time, the boy was damned smart."

I had a hazy memory of the presence in the woods. I tried to suppress a shiver. "What is the Watcher?"

"He's a sad old thing. Some of the original owners of this land worshipped him and gave him names. Wendigo; Malsumis; Iya. Time passed, knowledge got lost, forgotten. I let him creep around my forest and keep things nice and tidy. Everyone's got to have a purpose, dear. But he's growing weaker as my magic fades, and one day he'll forget what he was, and he'll wander off to find something else to do with his old bones."

I tried to imagine that vast darkness free in the world. I shivered again at the thought of what he might do. "You were telling me about Mr. Templeton," I said, changing the subject.

"Right. When he wasn't here visiting with me, he had his nose stuck in a book at the library. He'd come here in the weekends, carrying about fifty pounds worth of books he had checked out, and he'd read every word. When he done the reading, I'd teach him the ways."

"What ways? Witch ways?"

Rowan nodded. "If he'd been a girl, he'd have stayed here and I would have given him his own season. Autumn is a nice girl and pretty as a lark, but she's numb as a fence post."

"Be nice, grammy," Hiems said. She folded the paper closed and lay it on the table. "You know how upset Augie gets."

Rowan snorted. "The girl hasn't got two brain cells to rub together. All laughter, no desire. Completely the opposite of Hiems here." Her smile radiated joy on the younger woman. "This girl wants the whole world, and studies hard to get it."

Hiems blushed, smiling shyly at Rowan. "You'll give me a swollen head, grammy," she said as she rose from the table. She got down a large pot from the hanging rack and put it on the stove. "I'll go down into the cellar and get some potatoes and corn, make us some chowder."

"Bring up a loaf of the brown bread while you're at it," Rowan said. "We'll warm it in the oven when the corn chowder's about done."

Regretful thoughts of not being able to eat any longer

"I think Jacob is jealous of the meal you're making," I said. "Can I help?"

"You can sit there and rest," said Rowan, and the steel in her eyes told me it was a firm decision.

19

Stolen Moments

I lay in my soft bed beneath the window. The curtains were drawn back, providing a good view of the field behind the house. The hour had grown late, and a waning crescent moon had risen, touching everything with fog silver tendrils of light that sparkled off the dew in the tall grass. A small group of deer grazed at the edge of the woods in the distance.

The corn chowder had been delicious; the brown bread warm and soft, melted butter running into all the crevices. We'd eaten our fill, and no one had interrupted the starving detective, who clearly hadn't eaten in a month of Sundays. Rowan even excused my after-meal burp with a grin. But when I'd mentioned it might be time to hit the road, Rowan shook her head and told me no again.

"No use you trying to leave now, anyway. The Watcher won't let anyone through after sun down, no matter what I say. He can be a stubborn one, but darkness is his realm and even I got nothing to say to him about that."

"I still need answers." I tapped my fingers on my knee, aware of an aching desire to have a smoke after a good meal.

"Come on out to the front porch with me. You can smoke out there while we talk."

She led me out to the porch, leaning on her cane with one hand and carrying the paper with the other. She moved slowly and with obvious pain. When she paused on the doorstep and started tipping to one side, I stepped close and took her elbow. Rowan gave me a small nod, cocking her head. "That's a good girl. You would have made a wonderful season. You could have been my summer, even with that dark hair of yours."

I helped ease Rowan into her rocking chair, and the old woman sat quietly, her fingers plucking out patterns in her dress. There was a wooden chair to her left, and I lowered myself into it, grimacing with the painful tightness of my stitches. I lit a cigarette and stared at the fields and woods as we watched dusk gathering up the world in its arms and pulling it down into the bosom of night.

"Pretty evening," Rowan said. "The stars will be out soon, twinkling and shining down on us. The dryads will come out, dancing through the meadow. I used to love watching them dance, when I was young. I sometimes stripped off my clothing and danced with them."

I could picture her, young and beautiful and as tall as willow, her flesh caressed by beams of silvery light as she danced with abandon in the meadows and glens. "You must have broken many hearts, Rowan."

"Only one. But he had it coming, he did. Yup." She nodded and sighed. "You said you had questions."

I took a drag and tried to piece together my thoughts. It's hard to think when you're in pain, you've lost an entire day, and you've killed two men. They may have had it coming, but it stains you somehow. I felt their blood on my fingers, sticky and warm, as though it clung to me. More of Ben's comments came to me. The things you do. The things you lose.

All his words had been true. A part of me had been lost. The part that saw the world through innocent eyes, a shiny mystery to unfold and reveal. In my story, there would be no death, no blood, only problems solved and criminals put away. Reality seemed messier.

Rowan seemed to understand my silence. She said nothing more, spread the paper out over her knees, and began to read it in the failing afternoon light. The sun had already sunk below the horizon. We sat there for a time, me lost in my thoughts, and her lost in the paper. No sounds but a few birds, the crinkling of the broadsheet in her hands, the creak of the house when the wind brushed over it.

"You should focus on each item of your investigation instead of trying to look at the whole," she said, her eyes remaining on the paper. "List them in your head, dear. You can't see the forest until you look at the trees."

Advice Ben Templeton would have given. I wondered if he learned it from Rowan. I wanted to pace while I thought, but couldn't. Instead, I tapped my foot against the boards beneath my feet, the green paint worn to gray from a lifetime of feet passing over them. Each tap another piece of the puzzle, another clue to ponder. Lucky Gambini's death. Mr. Green. The Gnomes. The golem. The golden goose at the center of everything. The notes Lucky left behind. The notes the gnomes had left behind. The elf with the strange yellow eyes. LG.

I stopped. One and the same? Maybe. "It all comes back to figuring out who LG was in Lucky's notes." I didn't really expect an answer. I'd flung the comment to the wind to help stimulate my mind.

"Lucius Gaunt?" Rowan asked, folding the paper down in her lap and looking at me.

"Who is Lucius Gaunt?" I asked.

"You said LG. It's in this article about the new trade delegation in

Baltimore. Lucius Gaunt is the diplomat in charge." She handed me the paper, the same one Hiems had brought in earlier. It was folded to highlight the article in question.

I took it from her and began scanning the text. "I remember this from a few weeks ago, The Baltimore Sun had an article about it, too."

"Well, we're always a bit behind up here," she said, sniffing. "The folks at the Portland Press Herald are slow as molasses on a cold day. Numb as fence posts, too."

The article had a New Amsterdam byline, so it must have gone out through one of the general press corps for distribution. The elves had been isolationist for more than a generation now, and everyone was interested in their new outreach, opening their first embassy in Baltimore. Now that the embassy had been staffed and trade negotiations were about to open with diplomats of the United Territories of Coventine, they were going to hold a grand opening ceremony, complete with a ball for the high rollers of Baltimore and the United Territories. I reached the final lines, and read the name she'd mention.

"The gnome we caught mentioned something about elves," I said. "What was it? The man they'd been making the weapons for is a big shot elf." I squeezed my eyes shut, ran through the sequence of events in my head. Lucky's funeral. The gnomes and their security automaton. Searching Lucky's office. Going to the Tom Tom Club to see Mr. Green. Lucky's notes. I couldn't keep all the pieces in my thoughts. Each time I grasped one, others slipped away. But it felt right. Who would be a bigger big shot of an elf than the ambassador? No one.

There are no coincidences.

It made more sense than it should. The elves were notorious in their hatred of other races. They weren't racist against other elves, so there wasn't a barrier of color like here. They simply hated anyone not of pure elvish blood. They'd have good reason to put the gnomes up to making weapons they could distribute on the street to criminal gangs and black marketers. A bunch of repressed people suddenly armed and able to fight for their rights made for good press when it happened in other places.

When it happened here? I thought of Lugnut caught up in some crack down on trolls. Then my heart skipped when I thought of Ingrid being beaten and arrested for no reason other than being black. If Lucky stumbled upon the operation, Lucius Gaunt would have had good reason to make sure he'd been removed. Ben Templeton, too.

I would have jumped up and left right then if not for Rowan's earlier warnings, plus the other questions I had. "Why did you send Hiems to Baltimore?"

"My dreams pointed to Baltimore as the place where an item I'm searching for could be found. More, we'd need the goose to trade for it. I'd had the golden goose scroll for years. Couldn't make heads or tails of it, but I take such portents seriously. I'd already planned to ask Hiems to make the trip when Ben's friend died. I sent her immediately to find the goose and locate the item. Make the deal if she were able." She paused, and her face crumpled, her voice turning husky. "Let Ben know I knew of his pain and he remained in my thoughts."

The scroll. I still needed to have the words translated. That would wait, though. "What do you need? What are you trading the goose for when and if you find it?"

"I need to get ready."

"Ready for what?"

She frowned and released her breath in a long sigh. "I'm dying, dear. I've had a long life, so I've no complaints. But I've outlived everyone I've been close with, and I'm tired. What I need is a bit more time to hand off my knowledge, and a way to protect my girls."

"You're trading the goose for something to make that happen?"

She nodded in agreement. "Once I have a shadow cloak and stolen moments, I could make us a home no one would find. I've known of shadow cloaks for centuries. The elves created them. I didn't know why one would be in Baltimore, but it makes sense now I know about the new embassy. One of the staff must own one and brought it with them."

Shadow cloaks and stolen moments. "What are they? Shadow cloaks."

She sighed and sat back. "A shadow cloak is an artifact that hides you from the world."

"And the stolen moment?"

"The cloak can hide you, but stolen moments can guide the cloak into removing you from the world entire, put you in another realm. With the two items, I can take my seasons to a safe place and pass along my knowledge. I've already found the stolen moments I needed."

"You have?"

"On the mantle." She nodded at the window showing the sitting room off the hallway. I followed her eyes and saw a stone fireplace on the far wall, several clear mason jars lined up on the mantle. In one, a green mist swirled around like a slow-moving cloud on a summer day. The mist sparkled in the light of a nearby candle.

"That's what's left of Ben's time on this world. When he died, some of it lingered in the air around his body. I sensed his death, he'd been so close to me. Pierced right through my heart." Her eyes grew shiny, and she swallowed several times before she shook her head and continued. "Well, I was able to reach out and gather some. Those are the moments stolen from him when he was murdered. All the long years he didn't get to live out."

My breath paused and a ringing rose around me. I stared at the shimmer of green, locked away behind glass. All that Ben Templeton would have lived, all the moments left to him in a life cut short, were sitting on a shelf a few feet away. I had a brief desire to march inside the house, knock the jar off the shelf, and watch with pleasure as it smashed on the floor, but I squashed the thought. There had been nothing malicious about what she'd done. She'd had a need, and it had been convenient. Rowan's words about him were respectful, even loving, like those of a doting grandparent. The pain of his death colored her world as it did mine.

"So, you need these things to create a pocket dimension?"

"Of a sort, yes, but one where the world's time has no influence. We'd be shifted out of the real world into a different one. The peoples did that with their standing stones, and I thought I could make a similar magic. It's best for us to fade away and live on as nothing but the memory they've written about us. The world doesn't want women like me."

"And the air spirit?"

She nodded. "Hiems sent one when she got to Baltimore to see if Lucky had found anything we could use. She should have gone herself; those damn things always make a mess."

I'd yawned then, and she had Hiems hustle me from the porch and help me upstairs to the bathroom, where a tub full of steaming water waited. Now I stared at the woods, watching as the dryads slipped from mossy trees into the meadow, their bodies slender and fine, ageless in their beauty. They circled each other and clasped arms, swirling around in chaotic groups that broke apart and came together time and again, dancing a pattern that had some meaning. If only I watched long enough, I would make sense of it.

Something moved closer to the house. Hiems walked from the back yard into the field. She undid the buttons of her dress and let it slip to the ground, the grass bowing to the side in worshipful respect as her nude figure strode past. She was as beautiful as the dryads, but different, carrying the weight of a woman who lived in this world, her body solid and corporeal, imperfect in her perfection. The dryads slowed as she approached, and they, too, bowed their heads to her, and then began to dance, pulling her into their circles. The laughter reached all the way to my window as I watched the distant spectacle, the world cast in misty silver from moon and star.

I watched until the moon dipped its arms below the tops of the tallest trees and the dance had slowed, the creatures breaking into smaller and smaller groups, fading into the darkness of the forest, arm in arm. I pulled the shade and slid under the covers, the springs in the old mattress squeaking in anger at the jostling until I settled into my sleeping position. Jacob's presence hovered outside the door, and though he kept his thoughts to himself, I felt like he wanted to guard over me. I smiled, as much as how that comforted me as the thought of an intangible spirit trying to stop an attacker in the middle of the night. At best, he'd wake me up. That would be enough, though, although I didn't feel any need to be on guard now.

I lay awake for a while longer. I thought of Ingy sliding into bed with me, wrapping me up in her warmth. Her strong arm across me. Comforting me. How I should be the one comforting her, protecting her. At last, with her in my thoughts, I slipped back into my dreams.

20

Train from Augusta

We stood on the porch and stared across a yard crusted with snow. Several inches had fallen sometime between the point I fell asleep and when I woke late morning, though now the sunlight was clear and bright and I remembered the crescent moon shining low in the sky the previous night. I held a cup of hot tea in my hands, and scowled. No coffee. I really would have preferred a cup of Joe, but choosing beggars and all that.

Hiems stood barefoot in the snow, and it gave me shivers to think of how cold it must be, but she seemed unbothered by the chill. She'd opened the hood of the car, and leaned over it. At least she wore coveralls, grease stains marking the worn, blue cotton.

"A bullet cracked the radiator," she said, brushing her hands off on the coveralls once more. "You're not going to driving this anywhere for a while; not until we can get it fixed."

"Can't we patch it?" I asked.

"The crack's too big, it wouldn't hold very long." She dropped the hood and it banged back into place, sending a jolt through my head.

I blew on the tea to cool it, then sipped. It tasted bitter, and I grimaced as it went down. But it warmed my insides, and I hoped it had enough caffeine to cure the rest of what ailed me. Not my wounds of course, although they ached less this morning. Whatever Rowan put into her poultice, it had done a fine job. I'd have a scar there once the bullet wound had finished healing, but at least this morning I no longer felt like a white-hot poker had been jabbed through my abdomen. Instead, I bore all pain in my heart. Behind me lay the murderers of my boss. Ahead of me lay the one who had hired them. And in between were Lugnut and Ingy and the amends I'd have to make. I think I feared their anger more than facing Lucius Gaunt. You always feel worse about the pains you've caused rather than the ones you received.

"Christ, I feel old," I said. I wondered if Mr. Templeton had mornings like this. Then I remembered how heavily he drank, and how early each day he started, and I knew he had. He carried a lifetime of scars like the one I now had, some physical, some mental. He'd be a scar in my memory as well, along with the two Jacks I'd killed. A wave of sadness drained what small amount of reserves I had and threatened to push me over the carefully constructed walls I'd built around my pain.

Hiems walked over and sat on one of the steps. She brushed a naked foot through the snow, making patterns. "What are you going to do now, Mira?"

I shook my head and reached into my pocket for a cigarette. After I'd lit it, I leaned back in my chair and looked at the blue sky, trying to come to some sort of decision. "I don't know. I'm stuck here for now, I guess. I don't suppose Rowan has a phone?"

She shook her head. "No phone. We were going to put one in last year, but it never happened. Grammy Rowan doesn't care much about being bothered with idle chat, and it's hard to find someone to lay lines past the Watcher."

"Damn it," I said.

She reached over and touched my leg. Her fingers sent a little shock of electricity through me and I twitched, which sent a flurry of new pain through my side. "I'm going to make sure you get back to Baltimore as quickly as possible," she said. "I can see you want to finish your work and find the man who caused so much misery." She rose from the porch and stepped off into the snow again. "You wait here, I'll be back shortly." She darted off through the chilly world. Her feet barely left imprints on the snow.

"Wait," I said, but she ignored me. She disappeared into the trees before I could speak again.

It seemed strange to be sitting here hundreds of miles from home on the porch of an old witch, lost in the wilds of central Maine. Everything appeared wrong, smelled wrong. Maybe it had something to do with the trees surrounding the fields, the endless forest. Baltimore breathed with heavy, hot air and bore down upon the land, crushed the life from it as it glowered over Maryland. Here, nature could exist without the weight of concrete and steel beating it into submission. No city hunkering over the world and defying it. Only the wild existed, and it felt unnatural to me. Or maybe the problem was me, the things I'd done, the deaths I'd witnessed in the last few days. I'd changed, and the Mirabel Sinclair that rose this morning didn't deserve the peaceful solitude of nature. She'd become as dirty as the city she came from.

I'd crushed out my second smoke when the sound of an engine pierced the forest. Hiems came through the snow in a rusty collection of spare parts that would only generously and with much overlooking of facts be called a truck. The front end looked like my old Model D, although badly dented and missing the right front fender. The back half was a flat, wooden bed with a small crane sticking up from it cobbled together from various pieces of scrap metal, a cable with a hook swaying from the tip. Black smoke belched from the back, and the engine didn't rumble or purr, but sputtered and coughed, lumbering its way up to the front of the house like some sick beast. The metal blade on the front scraped most of the snow out of the way of the wheels, which were clad in rattling chains. Hiems executed a three-point turn, stalling it once, and pulled to a stop in front of my car. She shut down the wheezing engine and climbed from the narrow cab.

"The main roads are better cleared," she said. "I'll drive you down to Augusta and you can catch a train to Baltimore from there." She went into the house as I rose, slowly, holding my side. I hadn't taken a step when she returned with the cardboard suitcase, my coat thrown over her arm. "My, but you're slow today," she said.

"You try moving fast after you've been shot," I said, more than a little peeved.

She laughed. "I tend to try and stay well out of the path of bullets, doll." She slid the suitcase in behind the front seat bench, then climbed back into the driver's seat.

"What about my car?" I asked, waving at it. I didn't want to abandon it here, but I didn't see that I had much choice.

"I'll see it gets repaired and I'll bring it down to Baltimore for you," she said.

I managed to work my way into the passenger seat, but before I closed the door, I turned back to the house. "What about Rowan? Shouldn't I go say goodbye or something?"

Her hand took my arm and pulled me back into the seat. "She's still abed. I think your visit tired her out. She won't wake until noon at least."

"Someone should be here when she wakes," I said.

"Someone will," she said. "Augie is down south visiting her relatives in Georgia, but Aestas is around and she'll look after Grammy Rowan until I get back. And Ver is out in the woods on a communal not far away and can be called home in a few hours. Now come on, close the door, you're letting in all the cold."

I doubted she felt the cold, not the way I did, but I closed the door. *Jacob?* I thought.

He let me know he was present.

Good, I said to him. *I wouldn't want to leave you behind.*

I sensed his amusement when he told me *never again.*

***

The Augusta train station barely qualified as one. Hiems dropped me at the curb in front of the building, with its green paint and dingy, brass light fixtures. "You be careful, Mira," she said, watching me through the open door. "Grammy Rowan will have a fit if you don't get home safely. She'll know."

I nodded. "I'm the soul of caution," I said. "Tell Rowan I said thank you."

She smiled. She had a beautiful smile, and I envied how easily it leapt to her face in spite of the dead bodies piling up around us. Would that I could so easily smile after all that had happened. She reached under the seat and pulled out a small, brown item. She handed it to me, and I took it from her, turning it over in my hands. A piece of leather wrapped around something, with a thong to tie it closed.

"Grammy Rowan told me to send that along with you," she said, nodding at the package. "There's a vial of her special brandy inside. Drink it before you sleep tonight, it will help with your healing."

I nodded my thanks, feeling awkward. She didn't speak again, but waited for me to close the truck door. Then she ground the gears and the truck lumbered away from the curb. She merged with the handful of cars, a couple of delivery trucks, and a farmer with a two-horse wagon delivering milk door to door.

I bought a ticket from a tired, middle aged woman who sat behind a grill of steel bars while Jacob drifted around the station, drinking in his freedom and chilling the locals, who shivered when he passed. She took my money and passed me the ticket through a slot, glaring at me the whole time. There were four of us all told waiting for the 2:53 train to Portland, and then on to Boston, New Amsterdam—where we'd transfer—Philadelphia, and finally Baltimore.

The train pulled in, a black steam locomotive pulling eight dark-green coach cars, and one boxy baggage car. I followed the other four passengers onto the train, making my way through the first car and into the second until I found the small roomette I'd paid for. The private room wasn't much bigger than a large closet. A small bench rested against the wall to my left, and a murphy bed could be pulled down from the wall over it. The window had blinds. I pulled the bed down, grunting with pain as the wound in my side tightened again. I hung my coat from a hook on the wall, but left the door open for now, guessing the conductor would be by soon. I sat on the edge of the bed and held the ticket in my hand so I could present it. A chill breeze swept through the opening.

"Jacob?" I said, querying the otherwise empty room.

Present.

"Thank you," I said, sighing with the relief of having him near. "And I'm so sorry for what I did to you."

Bad decision but a good result. His words carried weight, as though he wrapped solid arms around me and held me close.

"I don't deserve you."

Good people deserve good things, he said, with a chuckle.

Oh, but I no longer thought of myself as a good person. No, I couldn't lay claim to that. The train blasted its whistle before I could say anything, a banshee shriek that vibrated the window. The car shuddered, there were several fading bangs, and we began to move. I watched the world passing the window as we chugged away from

Augusta. I didn't sit up to look out, but watched the tops of trees and electrical lines pass by, the sky leaden with gray clouds.

A polite knock drew my attention to the doorway. The conductor stood there, holding out his hand. "Tickets please."

I handed my ticket to him, not bothering to rise. He punched a hole in the end of it and handed it back. He started to turn, but paused, and gave me a puzzled look. "Are you feeling alright, miss?"

I tried to smile. "I'm fine, just very tired. Could you slide the door closed for me?"

He returned the smile and nodded. "Supper starts at 4:30 if you want to join, ma'am. But otherwise, enjoy your rest." He tipped his hat, then closed the door. His footsteps receded down the hallway, and his voice passed through the thin partition as he requested "Tickets!" from other passengers.

I turned the lock on the door. The panel was flimsy and wouldn't keep out a rabbit if it wanted in, but it made me feel better. Then I pulled the blanket over me and closed my eyes, letting the rocking of the train lull me. I could sense Jacob, though, close by. Keeping an eye on me, watching the hallway, carefully examining passengers who passed by.

"You going to be a detective when you grow up, Jacob?" I asked quietly.

A damn good one, too, he said in reply.

"I bet you would, a real button man that won't take no guff," I said. "All the dames will be dizzy for you."

His thoughts swelled with pride, and he puffed up like a balloon. With him watching and the train clicking across the tracks, I relaxed. My eyes closed and the languid grasp of sleep pulled on my limbs. "No better time," I said. I reached up and dug inside my coat pockets until I found the leather pouch. When I undid the snap and rolled it open, I found a small tube of glass with a cork stopper. It was filled with dark liquid. I held it up to the window, letting the faint daylight illuminate it.

"You don't think she'd poison me, do you Jacob?" I asked. I didn't really believe it myself after all that happened.

Who knows what people are capable of, he said, which wasn't terribly reassuring.

"In for a penny." I flicked the stopper off the end of the vial, then downed the contents. The liquid had a pleasant flavor, if medicinal. Sort of like cherry liqueur. Then I wrapped the empty vial in the leather case and returned it to my coat. I reached over and pulled down the shade, which didn't completely darken the room, but dimmed it substantially. Then I lay down, pulled the blanket over me, and blinked precisely twice before I fell into a deep sleep.

21

Disembarking at Speed

Wake up, Mira

I started, then winced with pain. I sat up slowly, pressing my hand to the wound in my side. It didn't feel as bad now, though it ached like a bad tooth. "Where are we?"

South of Philadelphia, Jacob said.

I'd been asleep since we changed trains in New Amsterdam. Truth be told, I'd barely been awake then. Jacob had steered me through the crowds, guiding me from my arrival platform to the departure platform, and made sure I got to the right cabin. As soon as the conductor had come through, I'd fallen into the new bed and promptly gone to sleep again. A twelve-hour train ride from Augusta, Maine, had been reduced to a few minutes of wakefulness and a large number of blank spots. Jacob remained on guard the whole time. If not for him, I might have ended up in the Republic of Texas. I reached over and opened the blinds. Night had fallen. There wasn't much to see other than distant lights, and the black shapes of passing trees.

"Thanks for keeping watch," I said to him. I stood in the tiny space available and lifted the murphy bed out of the way.

Speaking of which, he said, which got my attention. He pictured for me a figure that had walked up and down the hallway in front of my door several times. Short, wearing a hooded cape out of style since the turn of the century. All he could see of the person's face was a long, brown beard, so presumably a man.

"Shit, the Jacks," I said, rising. I pushed the bed up to get it out of the way, and pulled my coat on.

He's coming again, Jacob said.

I pulled my revolver out of an inside pocket and checked it was loaded. Then I stood to one side of the door, pressed against the wall, and waited. The clicking of the wheels on the rails drowned out most sounds, but I thought I heard the tap of footsteps approaching my room. The noise stopped, and I held my breath, waiting for the moment he'd burst in. I left the safety on and raised my gun, planning to club him over the head. I needed information, and this asshole would be the one to provide it.

The pause stretched on. Then came a polite knock on my door. Three soft raps, then a pause. Then three more, and a soft, high-pitched voice whispering, "Miss Sinclair? May I have a word with you, please?" He knocked again.

He pulled the hood off, Jacob let me know. *I don't think it's one of them Jack fellows; it's a fake beard.*

"Please, Miss Sinclair, I need your help," the man said again.

I flipped the lock on the door and jerked it back. I held my gun, raised above my head, reached out with my free hand and pulled him into the cabin, then slid the door home again. The small figure sprawled across the floor, hitting the ground with an *oof*. As he pulled himself up by the seat, I leveled the gun at his midsection.

"Slowly," I said. "No sudden moves."

He remained on his knees, and raised shaking hands above his head. "Please don't shoot, Miss Sinclair. I'm not here to hurt you."

I waved the gun at the seat. "Sit then, and start talking."

He levered himself up and turned around until he could sit. He kept his hands visible at all times and placed them on his knees as he watched me. "I need help," he said.

There was something oddly familiar about him. Something in his eyes. "Take off that damned beard," I said, nodding at it. It had come loose when he'd fallen, and now hung askew on his jaw.

His hands trembled a little when he pulled on the beard. He raised it over his head, slipping off the two hooks holding it in place behind his ears. Then he pulled it down to his lap, holding it there, twisting it in his hands. His eyes met mine, and my jaw dropped open as I recognized him. The gnome we'd captured, and who had escaped. The one who'd built EMET.

"Bollo? Or are you Beezallel?"

"I'm Tim." His face twisted into a mask of pain, his eyes blinking rapidly. "Beezallel and Bollo are dead."

Something cold ran down the back of my neck. I understood the pain in his eyes, the loss that clung to his heart. "I'm sorry," I said, and I meant it. My own loss remained fresh in my heart; a wound no potion would ever touch. I lowered the revolver, though I held it against my leg and didn't put it down. He'd taught me a hard lesson in trusting a prisoner.

He watched the gun being lowered and nodded. "I wouldn't trust me either. Not after all that's happened since the authorities found out about our weapons."

"I was thinking more of what happened between the two of us."

He smiled thinly. "That, too."

"I'm glad you missed," I said.

His smile grew wider. "Oh, I didn't miss, Miss Sinclair. But if I'd killed you, I'd already be dead. You know the authorities would have hunted me down like a dog and strung me up by the neck. Gnome kills white woman plays well in the newspapers; they'd sell a lot of copies with that story. Very lurid."

"Is that what happened to your friends? They got caught up in the story about your weapons factory and got cut down by the authorities?"

His smile went away, although I didn't feel any pride I'd hit him where it hurt most. "They were my brothers."

Damn me and my mouth. I should have researched more about these men before I ran off to Maine like a fool. I sighed and said, "I'm sorry," again, "I didn't know. Why haven't you turned yourself in? I'm sure you'll get a fair trial. It's not like you killed anyone. They don't give folks the noose for making weapons without the proper permits."

He stared out the window, watching the night pass by as we chugged towards Baltimore. "It's not the authorities who killed them," he said. Then he went quiet, his fingers tapping a rhythm on his legs. The beard slipped to the floor and he glanced down at it as though wondering how it got there.

His silence grated on raw nerves exposed since my boss had been murdered. The anger I thought I'd put behind me when I'd killed his murderer reappeared in my thoughts. Why was he so reticent? Why couldn't he just come clean with me? Why they hell should I trust someone who tried to kill me? Twice? I squashed it quickly, reminding myself only in pulp novels did the bad guys come clean and own up to their crimes. Real life never seemed as neat and easy. What would Mr. Templeton say? Something pithy and wise about the dirt of the world and how you could never get clean, you had to work with it and mold it to your needs. You eventually became dirty yourself if you weren't careful. Something like that.

I focused on what he had said, rather than what he wouldn't say. He'd come looking for me. "How'd you find me anyway?"

He reached into a pocket, and I started to raise the gun again. "I don't have a weapon," he said. He withdrew his curled fist and held it out, opening his fingers slowly. A single brass casing from a small caliber pistol lay in the palm of his hand. "You left behind some brass when you shot my thesis." He grimaced.

I almost smiled, but it would have come out as a rigid grimace, and I didn't want to scare him too much. "I'm not going to apologize for that again," I said.

He shrugged and placed the casing on the seat next to him. "I don't expect you to. In any case, there was enough essence of you on the brass for me to turn it into a locator. I've been following you north, but didn't catch up with you until you came back. I'd gotten as far as the train station in New Amsterdam hoping for a miracle.

Focus on what he said. "Miracle?"

"Our people keep a watch on the terminals—Boston, New Amsterdam, Baltimore—watching folks come in off the ships. You know, gnomes and dwarves, any immigrants fresh off the boats looking for a new life we can help. I figured I'd run into a friend or two in my line of work and bounce them for a favor, get some forged docs and get out of the country."

I filed that detail away under *things that are very useful to know about the criminal underworld*. Maybe I could use him as a resource later. Tim's eyes kept nervously glancing at the door, and I glanced at the flimsy construction myself. "Something bothering you?"

He leaned forward a little. "I think I'm being followed," he said, his voice pitched low.

Jacob?

No one coming, he replied after a moment.

I relaxed. "Keep it together, Tim. It's just the two of us for now, having a nice, friendly chat. Why don't you tell me why you were following me?" I reached into my pocket and pulled out my cigarettes, lighting one. The smoke made his eyes water, but he didn't protest.

"I need protection," he said.

"You thought I could protect you?" I almost laughed at the notion. I'd done a piss poor job of protecting myself.

"You and Templeton," he said. He pulled another casing out of his pocket, this one larger, and placed it next to the first. "He's got a good reputation among the lower classes. But the locator I made for him doesn't seem to be working."

All emotions fled. The world dulled at the edges. Emptiness hollowed me out and left my legs weak. "He's dead," I finally managed to say.

"Oh," Tim said. He fiddled with the two casings, not meeting my eyes. "I'm sorry. I didn't know." Now he sounded like me.

I shook my head. "Nothing for you to be sorry about. Just tell me who's hunting you. Who were you working for? Was it Lucius Gaunt?"

"The elvish ambassador?" His voice sounded incredulous. Then he cocked his head and his eyes narrowed. "Well, perhaps, but I don't know. The elf never told us his name and I'm not familiar with the ambassador's appearance. But it makes sense," he began, and stopped, his head turning sharply.

"What?" I asked. My voice sounded far away, like a distant radio.

Someone, Jacob began, and his thoughts faded away, like snow melting on a hot day.

I reached for his presence and couldn't find him. The noise of the train diminished, like it moved away from me. Tim and I locked eyes, and I could see his growing big and round. "What's going on?" I asked, but no words come out. Silence encompassed me. I couldn't even hear the ringing in my ears I heard when the world quieted. Someone had dropped a magical intercession over us.

The door burst open, the wood frame splintering around the lock, all in complete silence. A hand appeared in the doorway holding a small pistol, and my body took over while my mind spent precious moments contemplating a soundless universe. I yanked Tim down with me onto the floor.

A bullet dug a groove in the wall below the window as I cracked up against the opposite seat. I tried to aim as a middle-aged man moved past the doorway, firing into my room. Splinters of wood from the floor exploded in front of my face. I thumbed the trigger, the recoil and flash at the end of the muzzle telling me I'd fired, though I heard nothing. When I cast my mind about for Jacob, I found a void where his thoughts should be, our internal conversation blocked by the same magic.

We had few options. I sat back against the wall under the window and reached above my head, opening it. I heard the faint murmur of the rails, as though the train were a million miles away, but it grew louder each second. I heard a crack from the doorway, and I fired back, the frame splintering where the slug smashed into it. My revolver made noise this time, and the ringing in my ears grew louder.

I waited for him to lean in and fire. When he did, I squeezed my trigger, my bullet dancing through his jacket and missing his body by fractions of an inch. When he pulled back, cursing, I moved. I reached for Tim, then jerked my hand away. His lifeless eyes stared back at me, blood seeping down his forehead. Shit. I leapt onto the seat, leaning out the window and reaching high to find the curled edges of the roof above. I grabbed and hauled, pulling my body out of the train, and found myself dangling from the coach car with the ground passing beneath at a fast clip. I didn't have enough strength to pull myself up, but another bullet smashed through the wall to the left of me and gave me motivation.

Two people surged through the room doorway, the middle-aged man and a woman of roughly the same age. Unassuming features, brown hair. Nothing remarkable about them. They leveled their pistols at my waist. I whistled, my tuneless notes redirecting the rush of air slamming me against the side of the train. The wind caught my legs, lifting me up away from the window. I pulled on the roof until I flipped onto my back on top of the train. Only then did I release the breeze that gave me temporary breathing room.

It took a few moments before I staggered to my feet, leaning against the harsh wind. I moved towards the rear of the train, but the man stuck his head up over the edge of the railcar. I took a quick shot, missing as he ducked down out of the way again, and then I wheeled and ran along the roof towards the engine.

I leapt over the junction between the cars and limped halfway to the next when another gunshot rang out over the thunder of the train, too loud and too close. I threw myself down like a baseball player, sliding into the gap between the cars as I rolled onto my stomach. My legs dangled over the edge, feet stabbing at air until they found the rungs of the ladder. The man dropped to his knees and crawled forward, squinting his eyes against the blast of air. He lifted his gun and fired, missing wide as I squeezed down between the two rocking cars, aiming at his big melon-shaped head.

I had a brief second to wonder what had happened to the woman, and then a hand grabbed my ankle and twisted, answering the question. My feet slid off the metal rails, and I hung for a heart-sickening moment from one arm as the woman yanked.

I managed to shove my revolver under my belt and grab with both hands. Beneath me, the woman's face shifted and twisted, as though made of clay. Her eyes were empty red orbs with no pupils.

One foot scrambled for a purchase and found it. I tugged and yanked my other foot from the woman's grip, and then smashed down as hard as I could with the heel of my shoe. The woman's nose exploded, blood shooting down over chin and clothing. She let go of me and reached up with a squeal to grab at her shattered face. With hands no longer holding on, I kicked the side of her head, and watched as she toppled off the tiny ladder and fell to the side of the train.

I peeked up over the car roof only to receive an explosion of wood in my face, tiny pinpricks of pain as a bullet gouged into the wood and shot splinters into me. He'd moved closer, so I ducked and drew my gun again. With clenched teeth I counted to five, trying to gauge how fast he moved, picturing his location on top of the car. Then I gathered my legs under me and, whistling up the wind again, I launched myself up and over the train. I took aim at his startled face as the wind lifted me above him, and squeezed the trigger.

The shot took him in the hip and he fell backwards. Hard enough to aim flying through the air, so I'd take what I got. His hand hit the roof and the gun rattled out, tumbling along the slope and falling from the train. My momentum carried me past him and I landed and rolled. Pain lanced through my side. I almost lost my own revolver as I came to a stop with my head dangling over the edge, staring at the ground racing by below.

I squirmed back around to the figure lying on the roof. His face rippled and melted, the skin running off like oil placed in water, and his eyes were the same red vision I'd seen on the woman. He gasped for air, and blood pooled beneath him.

I grabbed the lapel of his jacket and pulled his head up. "Who sent you?"

He coughed blood, and grinned through pointy, sharp, reddened teeth. I slapped his face, and asked again.

"He's coming for you," he said, and yanked himself free of my grasp. He rolled off the roof and fell out of sight.

The train whistle gave a blast. The engine entered a narrow tunnel in the middle of a vast cliff of dark rock and trees. Cut stones formed an arch around the edge of the hole, the top ones stained dark with the soot of a half century of trains passing beneath the open mouth to be swallowed and spat back out again on the other side of the mountain. There wasn't enough room between the top of the train and the roof of the tunnel for a rat, let alone a woman.

I ran.

I'd almost made it to the junction between cars when I glanced back and realized there was no more time. I threw myself to the left, whistling, trying to push away from the wall of stone approaching. The air cushioned the blow, but I smacked against the rocks and my vision went red. Pain blossomed through my body as I tumbled across rough stone, but as pain had become an obligatory part of life, I hardly noticed. I fell into darkness.

22

Petunia's Home

I floated over a cemetery. A peculiar sensation, like being touched all over, every nerve of your skin tingling and alive, the wind brushing your hair back from your face. The sky above appeared black with night, and constellations I didn't recognize wheeled overhead.

At first, I drifted high above like an airship, seeing the graves like rows of little black ants below my body. They marched along in lines across a lawn of dead grass. But soon I dipped lower until I floated close above the weathered gray stones, so near I could read the names. There was Horatio Tanner, *He Who Will Not Be Forgotten*, and Blithe Witham, *Mother and Wife*. Edward Burnham came next, his inscription worn down to the point of illegibility, and Beryl Frost, *Walking with God*.

A large mausoleum appeared in front of me as my feet skimmed across the tops of the brown grass. The door opened and in I went, landing so soft I barely discerned I was no longer airborne, my back coming to rest on a cold stone floor made of marble. I cast my gaze around and found a skeleton draped across a stone seat, while behind him a figure cloaked in black rested one hand on the back of his chair.

"What have we here, Chancy old boy," said the skeleton, leaning forward.

"It appears to be a young woman," said the man in black, his voice deep and somber.

"Is she come to pay her respects? Pay us a visit then?"

"I do not know, Mr. Sticks."

The skeleton unwound his limbs, his joints popping as he stood up. "Well, speak up, girl, there's a good lass. What are the reasons you visit our home?"

"I am Mirabel Sinclair."

"Ah, Mirabel, there's a good name. Too many girls these days being christened Faith or Hope, or—" he shivered, his bones rattling, "—Charity. Good god but I hate the name, Charity. We do not want charity, by Jesus. There's no charity in death, Mirabel Sinclair, now is there?"

"You said god and Jesus, Mr. Sticks," Chancy said. "I do hope you'll wash your mouth out when we're done here."

"Oh, be quiet, Chancy. I'm talking to the lady." He waved his fleshless hand and the tall figure receded into the shadows until I could no longer tell where shadows began and he ended. "So, Mira, what brings you to my door?"

"I am seeking a killer."

"Oh, well, yes, we have plenty of those around here. It's positively a rogue's gallery of ruffians and reprobates, anyone one of which would do you for two fingers of bourbon and a laugh. Was there perhaps one in particular tickling your fancy with a butcher's knife?"

"The one who killed Ben Templeton, and Lucky Gambini. The one called Lucius Gaunt."

Mr. Sticks laughed, his teeth clacking together. "Oh, that one. And how do you know he's the killer you seek? I mean, it's a huge wide world out there with lots of people, lots and lots of them. I sometimes think there's more living than dead, even in Baltimore, but then Chancy here dredges up a few million lost souls and, well, it's hard to argue with figures. I never had much of a head for math."

"Quite," said the shadows of Chancy.

"Everything leads to Gaunt."

The skeleton leaned forward, looming over me. "Know thyself, Mirabel Sinclair, and know you need to wake up to understand. It's not yet your time to visit us. So, go on, girl, wake up. Wake up."

Wake up.

***

I shivered as I sat up—though I could not remember exactly when I'd reclined—and rubbed the grit from the corner of my eyes. Something sharp stabbed my side, and I hissed, pressing my hand there. Pain has a remarkable way of sharpening the mind. I knew exactly where I was and what had happened. I felt warmth against my skin, and I worked my hand under my clothing. When I pulled it free, my fingers were damp and sticky. I assumed it to be blood. I'd pulled some of the stitches when I'd tumbled from the train.

I wondered how the woods of Maryland could be so dark with so many towns and cities nearby. When I was fifteen or sixteen, I would hike into Patapsco Valley along the banks of the river, following deer trails into the forest until the sun sank beneath shady green leaves and twilight began. I had a favorite spot in a clearing on a small rise where I would sit and watch the shadows grow thicker, murky gloamings melding into the night. Bright stars flickered overhead, the light of millions of suns, billions of worlds, countless Mira's sitting in their own clearings and staring up into their own eternal darkness. City lights were lost to me on those evenings, their essence absorbed and dimmed by ancient night and his companions.

Sometimes Ingy would come with me, if she wasn't busy learning magic. Those were the best nights.

I sat in a ditch at the edge of the railway, and my eyes strained to see anything beyond a foot past my nose. My head felt like two big dogs had been stuffed in my ears and were running around inside my brain barking and biting while a cat tried to claw its way out through the back of my eyes. Nothing seemed broken; everything hurt.

"Did anyone get the number of the train that hit me," I groaned. The rocky cliff which had been lit by the train passing through it was almost indiscernible from the blackness around me. A deeper pitch showed were the tunnel cut through the stone, carving a path towards Baltimore. It looked like an angry mouth. *No way I'm going that way,* I decided, picking myself up off the ground.

Concern and worry hit me.

"Jacob?" Relief flooded me. You don't realize how all alone you were until you're with someone else.

He was relieved I was awake. *I thought you'd . . . well . . .*

"Apparently my lot in life is to stay alive, but break every part of me," I said, ruefully. "I need you to help me figure out which way to go, it's dark as hades out here."

West, he suggested.

"Which way is west? I can't see and I don't have a compass."

Jacob's thoughts pulled me around until I faced across the train tracks. *Easier ground,* he thought, *you'll be less likely to walk off a cliff.*

"That would be preferred."

Do you want me to get Lugnut or Ingrid?

"No, don't drag them out here to find me. It'll only piss them off more, and they're probably planning where to bury my corpse."

He chided me.

"If you want to be helpful, go follow the train and keep an eye on my bag, make sure it ends up in lost and found so I can retrieve it later." I stood on shaky legs and took a gimpy step towards the rails, nearly stumbling to my knees when I planted my weight on the injured ankle. I sensed his hesitation, but I sent him urgent thoughts about my stuff.

Fine, he said, although he sounded miffed. His presence drifted away.

On the opposite side, the ground sloped and disappeared into the trees. I searched around the edge of the forest until I found a dead tree branch long enough for me to use as a crutch and as a way of feeling the terrain ahead. I passed into the gloomier darkness beneath the outstretched branches, feet crunching through piles of dead leaves carpeting the forest floor.

The dark had always been a friend to me in the past. Now it annoyed me, pulled on my arms with invisible hands, scratched my face. More than once I fell to my knees. Tree roots seemed happy to catch my toes, vines to hold my arms, and I constantly brushed away tangles of spider webs that caught on my cheeks and nose, ghostly tickles that made me cringe. I cursed quietly, not wanting to offend the creatures who tended this patch of wood, but unable to restrain my tongue from unleashing a torrent of abuse at the dryads here who so valued privacy they turned the forest into gloomy torture for a lost detective.

I followed the downward slope of the terrain to avoid going in circles. When my feet splashed into a narrow stream, I turned along its course, trying to stay as close as possible without soaking my shoes and socks. I managed the former, but failed the latter, and my feet were soon wet and cold. It didn't help I had to move slowly, the pain in my side reminding me not to overexert myself and rip more of the stitches.

Light blinded me. I threw my arm up over my eyes. An engine roared past nearby. A car, its headlamps flashing through the remaining thickets between where I stood and the road it passed by on. I caught a glimpse of a low bridge where the stream passed under the roadway before the taillights disappeared around a bend and I plunged into the remnants of night. I waited for my eyes to adjust again. Once I could make out nearby trees, I staggered out of the woods and up the slope of weedy grass to the edge of the road.

"Which way now," I said, looking left and right along the narrow, dirt lane. I randomly selected left and began limping along the edge, listening for cars. I noticed I could see more. The stars winked out as morning neared. The sky became pink to my rear, so I knew I headed west, which at least took me towards Baltimore, although the road wound and made it difficult to tell exactly where I was.

The sound of a putting motor reached my ears and I stepped off the road onto the grass and waited as it approached. It rounded the nearest bend, a green car I recognized, and pulled up beside me. The driver side window rolled down, and Petunia stuck her head out.

"Jesus, you look worse than Ben after that week-long bender when he got worked over by Pinky Marcel and her brothers." She opened the door and walked over, wrapping her arm around me. "Come on, you can lean on me."

We walked and limped to the passenger side and Petunia helped me slide in, easing herself out from under my arm as I settled into the worn seat.

"How'd you find me," I said after Petunia closed her door.

"Same way I know when a client is coming of course. Being quarter pixie has its uses. What happened to you?"

I sighed. "You probably already know."

"I probably do, but we've got about an hour drive to your place and nothing better to do. You can fill the time by telling me yourself."

I couldn't bear the thought of seeing the reproach in Ingy's eyes. "Can we go to your place? I can't go home, not yet. I need some time to think things over."

"Ain't you and Ingrid getting along? Maybe you should go home and talk to her first."

She kept refusing to meet my eyes. It wasn't like Petunia to turn down a request, either. "What's the matter?"

Petunia blushed. "I um . . . have company. Of the male persuasion."

"Oh damn, Petunia, I'm sorry, I don't want to intrude on you and Melvin."

"No, no, don't worry about it, toots. I should have told you right away. Anyway, you're welcome, but I don't want you to feel uncomfortable."

"It won't be."

"Are you sure?"

"Well are you two going to have sex in front of me?"

"Of course not!"

"Well then, it won't be awkward. Seriously, I can't go home. I can't face Ingy right now. Just let me lay low for a day or two and I'll get out of your hair."

She put the car in gear. "Alright, I'll let you stay. But you have to promise to tell me everything that's happened."

We drove for a few minutes, Petunia holding the steering wheel as tightly as Hiems had. Her feet barely reached the pedals, but she drove well enough. She kept glancing at me, waiting for me to say something. "Come on, spill it," Petunia said.

I spilled it. I started with meeting with Mr. Green at the club, which seemed as though it had been months ago but in reality only a few days past. I went through the whole trip to Maine, the shootout with the Jacks, the bullet wound, the meeting with Rowan and Hiems, Tim finding me, and the attack on the train. I hadn't finished spilling when we rolled into Ellicott City under the train bridge, and drove up main street. The shops were shuttered this early in the day. One small café was open, a twenty-four-hour joint where the working stiffs got their morning cup of joe, and late-nighters came to do deals over Maryland's best crab cakes. Every place in Maryland said it had the best crab cakes. Everyone had an opinion about which was true.

We drove up the winding street and through the big intersection. We passed the last of the shops, and pulled onto a narrow side street. Petunia wedged her car into a tiny spot between two buildings.

She lived in one half of a duplex, with peeling paint and a porch rotting away, columns leaning under a roof that seemed in danger of collapsing on their heads at any moment. Petunia seemed embarrassed. "It's all I can afford. Mr. Templeton was as generous as he could be, but there wasn't much money coming in."

"It's a home," I said.

"Well, it's a house. Home is where the heart is, and it's not here."

"Where's your heart then?"

She didn't respond as we walked up the front steps. When she unlocked the door, her eyes were damp and shiny. She gave a thin smile. "Not here, that's all. Come on in, doll."

The place, though sparsely furnished, had been well taken care of, the inside a complete opposite of the outside. The walls were freshly painted, the furniture decent if cheap, and everything clean and tidy with the exception of Melvin sitting in the kitchen with a cup of coffee in one hand and the newspaper in the other.

"You're out of cream, so I put the empty bottles on the porch for the milkman," he said, scratching his chest. He wore a pair of white boxers and nothing else. He was a big, burly guy with messy brown hair and not so much five o'clock shadow as midnight scruff. His shoulders and back and chest were as hairy as his face. He turned a crinkling page of the paper, oblivious to my arrival.

"Melvin, you should put some clothing on. We've got company."

He slid the chair back and stood up, his underwear sagging.

When he saw me standing there, his half-grin turned into an expression of surprise. "Oh. Ah. Hi. Mira."

"Hi Melvin."

He glanced around, and then picked up the paper, holding it with both hands in front of his waist. "So, I'll be going upstairs now. Probably time to get dressed anyway, I've gotta start getting ready for work." He sidled sideways around the two of us and ran up the stairs to the bedroom.

I started laughing, but cut it off when the pounding in my head caused me to wince.

"Jesus, you look terrible," Petunia said. "Sit down at the table; let me get my medicine box." She opened a doorway under the stairs to reveal a small bathroom, the seat cover and carpet both pale pink. From a medicine cabinet over the sink, she pulled out a white metal box with a red cross on it, and brought it over to the table.

She took a cotton ball and antiseptic, soaked the tiny piece of fluff, then wiped my forehead with it. I hissed at the sting as she cleaned my cuts. Then she applied bandages. She reached down, carefully but firmly pulling my hand away from the bloodstain marring the front of my shirt. Her face went white. "Take the shirt off," she said. When I had, she touched the bullet wound and shook her head. "Looks like it was beginning to heal when you pulled a couple of the stitches. I've seen worse, doll."

She rose and went to the kitchen cabinets, opening one of the lower ones and rummaging around. She returned with a bottle of whisky and placed it on the table with a thump. "Go on, take a couple of slugs. You're not going to like the next part."

I took a long slug, which left my eyes watering. Then a second, even longer. The booze didn't take long to hit the few remaining brain cells that were active. I hadn't eaten since Rowan's dinner, and it went straight to my head and left me swaying in my seat. She lifted my chin, examined my eyes, and nodded her approval.

Then she went to work with a needle and thread, after heating the former over a flame. The less said about that the better.

"That'll keep you for a bit." She closed the box and went over to the stove, pouring hot water from a kettle into a cup, then opened a cookie tin. She took a sprinkle of herbs from the tin and trickled it into the mug, then handed me the cup.

"Drink it all," she said.

I sniffed at the water, noting the scent of lemon and thyme, and took an experimental sip. The pain dulled, so I drank more until the cup was empty. The throbbing in my head faded, and my ankle no longer felt quite like it had been squeezed by an anaconda, although it remained swollen and bruised. It took the edge off the dagger of pain jammed into my abdomen, too.

"Thanks," I said, unable to find better words to express my sense of gratitude. I felt less pain and more exhaustion at this point. My body ran on little more than fumes and desire.

"You're going to burn yourself out, like Ben did," Petunia said, shaking her head.

"I need to know, Petunia. I need to find out who killed him and why."

"I know, sweetie. I don't want to find you at the bottom of a bottle of rum every day, though. Or, worse, at the bottom of the Patapsco River."

"What am I supposed to do?"

She took the mug over to the sink and washed it, placed it in the drying rack. When she turned, her eyes were damp with tears. "I don't know, sweetie. You find the killer. You make it right. That's your journey and you have the right to walk it. But you don't gotta always walk it alone. I'll make up a bed for you in the guest room so you can get some sleep. I got to get ready for work." She turned away before I could ask what work she still had to do what with our boss being dead and buried. But she'd keep going into the office until someone changed the locks.

A thumping on the stairs attracted both our attention. Melvin reappeared, tucking his shirt into his pants. "Gotta run, baby cakes, I'll catch you later." He gave Petunia a quick peck on the cheek and ran out the door, not sparing a glance in my direction.

Petunia shrugged when the door slammed closed. "Can I pick them, or can't I?"

23

⧼⧽

The First Apology

I limped out of Petunia's into a crisp, clear, fall day, when even Baltimore smelled fresh and hopeful. Exactly the opposite of how I felt. I had to face Ingy now. I had no illusions about how it would go.

I made my way painfully down the steep hills of Ellicott City, the suitcase Petunia had picked up from the Penn Station lost and found banging against my leg. I swung onto a single carriage trolley car when I reached the line, dropping a nickel in the slot and finding my way to a seat. I watched the passing scenery as the trolley wound its way up out of Patapsco valley, through a small forest holding hints and remembrances of the mightier wood that once stretched from the Atlantic seaboard past the Allegheny Mountains. One hoary, old tree clung to a steep cliff, its limbs gnarled and curled back on itself, the bole of its trunk lightning blasted. I closed my eyes for a moment and examined the thread of its life passing with the slowness of a river carving its way through bedrock. A single dryad tended it. I took it as a sign not everything would be destroyed and turned to ashes as my life had been.

210

The trolley took me as far as Charles Street, and I rode a bus across eastern Baltimore to Highlandtown. I noticed more police than usual on the streets, and several arrests in progress. An old dwarf with his hands cuffed behind his back glared at the officers who pressed on his head and guided him into a waiting paddy wagon. The people who watched had narrowed eyes and heavy scowls, but none moved to interfere. I wondered how much the gnome's weapons were influencing actions on the street and the police response. Baltimore tensed like a monster with its muscles bunched beneath it, ready to spring.

The house was locked and dark. When I slipped inside, I turned on lights and walked around, noting Ingy's missing coat, along with a few items from the entry room. I limped my way up the stairs one at a time, and peeked into Ingy's bedroom. She'd left her bed unmade, her dresser drawers open. Her clothing gone, as was the large steamer trunk that usually rested at the foot of her bed. All that remained was its outline on the rug.

"Shit," I said, and went downstairs. I couldn't think about this right now. If I did, I'd fall apart. No, I'd reach out to Lugnut first and try to patch things up with him. I needed food before I could face him.

A half a pot of coffee went far to revive me, and a couple slices of bread filled a yawning void I hadn't realized I'd had. I didn't have the stomach for more, though. The basic bodily urges were met, even if the emotional ones were yet to be patched up. I doubted they'd ever be.

I yanked myself out of morbid thoughts and focused on the problem at hand. Except I couldn't focus. Events replayed themselves in my mind over and over again, until I growled with frustration. Every time I turned back to the evidence and followed the trail of breadcrumbs, I'd see Lugnut limping through the tunnel. I'd see Ingrid wielding a glowing baseball bat. I'd see a dead dwarf with a hole in his head. I'd see my boss sprawled like a broken toy on the sidewalk, bleeding out. I'd see every failure of Mirabel Sinclair, a comedy of errors, flickering like a two-bit double feature in my head.

Jacob didn't help, worrying around me like a nervous child. I couldn't tell if he thought I might bolt again without him, or if he badgered me out of the kindness of his ghostly heart. He nattered at me constantly, talking to me about the case, about the trip to Maine, about being able to wander around free. At first, I hoped his voice would be the distraction I needed, but eventually it began to annoy me. Rather than say mean things to him, I fell into long, sullen silences. I snatched naps on the couch when I could, but they were restless and without relief.

Did you see all the pine trees, Jacob said. He went on about Maine again, and the train ride home. The day had grown late and I still hadn't called Lugnut.

"Yeah, I saw them," I said. "I'm glad you got to come."

Would have been funny to have Lugnut along; he hates the cold.

I almost smiled in spite of my gloom. "That he does," I said. Something tore loose and I heaved a great sigh, reached for the phone. I asked the operator to patch me to Lugnut's number and waited for him to answer, my foot tapping against the ground.

He picked up on the fifth ring. "Towsontown Motor Service, Mr. Whyte speaking. We do all automotive servicing and repairs, plus towing. How may I assist you?"

"Hey tough guy," I said, trying to sound all nonchalance while wound like a top. I twisted the phone chord in my free hand and waited for his reply.

Static filled the receiver. I started to think he might not have heard me when he said, "You're back." His voice flat, emotionless.

"Yeah, I just blew into town," I said. Damn it, stop being flippant. "I mean, I just got home. It was a lousy trip."

He grunted, but said nothing. What did I expect him to say? *Hey little witch, glad you're home, thanks for not telling us you were blowing town and leaving us to worry about you.* That seemed as likely as Ben Templeton giving up the sauce and turning to tea for liquid refreshments.

Finally, he said, "Well, okay then. Good talking to you."

"Wait!" I said. "Don't hang up. Please."

The hissing and popping of the line went on for a while, but there wasn't a click of disconnection. I listened for any sign he was there, waiting for me to say something more. When I couldn't take it anymore, I said, "I'm so sorry, Lugnut."

More silence.

"I made a terrible choice, I know that. But when Ben died, I didn't . . .I wasn't." I took a long breath and paused, trying to catch the fleeting words scattered around my brain, herd them into real sentences. The words I needed weren't cooperating. I stammered and stuttered. Some detective. I wasn't even tough enough to give a good apology.

"Well, I wanted to say I'm sorry I let you and Ingy down. I made the wrong choice. If you ever want to talk again, you know how to reach me."

Silence. I waited for what felt like hours, but it only lasted twenty or thirty seconds. I started to pull the phone away from my ear to hang up.

"I'll be over in a little while, I've got to close up the garage," he said, his voice effecting a lack of care.

I nodded as if he could see me. "Okay. I'll see you soon."

Then we did hang up, my hands shaking with relief. Jacob sent me warm, loving thoughts and told me I'd done a good job. I tried to hug him mentally, and wished like hell he'd been real enough to cling to. The thing about trying to be strong is sometimes you have to let someone else carry the weight.

When I'd recovered some control, I limped around the house. I didn't have the energy to pick up, but it wasn't in bad shape. The only mess was in Ingrid's room, and that was one place I didn't want to go. I didn't want to see the empty drawers, the unmade bed, the lack of *her* haunting the home we'd shared. Every ounce of strength I could muster would be blown away by her lack of presence. In many ways, her absence was more painful than any loss I'd suffered. I pressed my head to the cool wood of the table, and half dozed as I waited.

An hour later, he knocked on the door. He knocked again before I reached it, as slowly as I moved, all the pains weighing on me. He'd bundled in a thick, wool coat and scarf, a large fedora pulled down over his eyes. The sun had set an hour ago, and other than his size, no one would have probably noticed he was a troll.

"Come on in," I said, holding the door open. He stepped inside and I shut it behind him. I took a limping step in his direction, reaching for his coat and hat to hang them up. Instead, he grabbed me into his arms, crushing me against his chest so tightly I couldn't breathe. The bullet wound in my side shot hot pain through my body. When sparks appeared in front of my eyes, I gasped a feeble moan of protest, and he loosened his grip. I sighed with relief and with the sheer pleasure of his arms wrapped around me. Well, one down. Probably the easiest one to get through. It had only taken nearly everything I had left to give.

"I was worried about you," he said, frowning down at me. "Afraid you were dead. Or worse."

I would have smiled if not for all the pain coursing through me at the moment. "What's worse than dead, anyway?"

He grinned. "Undead," he said. "No offense to your house ghost."

None taken, Jacob said. *He's right.*

"Jacob says don't worry about it," I said.

He nodded at the invisible presence, then turned back to me.

"What you did was the height of foolishness, and if you ever do it again, I will never speak to you. You'll be dead to me, assuming you're not actually dead. And look at you!" He waved at me, his frown deepening. "You look half dead already!"

I nodded. "I deserve that, and worse. I'm sorry, Lugnut. Can you please forgive me?"

"Well," he said, and scratched his head. "I'll think about it for a bit. But I'm damned serious, Mira. You've gotten yourself into something awfully dangerous, and you're not going to leave us behind like a bunch of house pets."

Damn straight, Jacob said, agreeing with him.

Traitor, I thought to him, but sent him a smile as well. He grinned back to let me know he understood I was joshed.

"I didn't see your car outside," Lugnut said as I limped towards the sitting room. He took my elbow and helped me to a chair. I sat stiffly. I knew my face was twisted in pain, but he said nothing, and I didn't elaborate. He'd learn it all soon enough.

"It's still in Maine," I said. "I ran into some difficulties."

He crossed his arms and furrowed his brow. "I've got nothing but time to hear the whole story, little witch, so get to it. When was the last time you ate, anyway? You look like a starving wolf."

"I ate some bread earlier," I said, waving dismissively.

He frowned and shook his head. "Not good enough." Then he picked up my chair—me still in it—and carried me down to the basement. He plopped me down gently, not far from the doorway to the kitchen. "You start talking while I fix you something to eat. Food for a story."

I told him about the drive to Maine as he puttered around, opening and closing cabinets to see what I had he could work with. He dug out some spaghetti and spices, found a pot roast in the refrigerator that still had life, and the room begin to fill with the smell of food.

When I reached the meeting with Rowan, he grunted. "You shouldn't be messing around with witches," he said.

"I'm a witch," I reminded him. "So's Ingy."

"Different kind," he said, tasting the sauce bubbling on the stove. "You do magic to support your detective work. Ingy does legal spell casting for money. That one does magic because she does magic."

The distinction didn't make any sense, but I let it pass without further discussion. He was wrong, but maybe he had it right. Rowan had told me I was like her, could do something few practitioners could do. I hadn't had time to think about it then, but it nagged me now. What exactly was it I did? How?

"Well?" he said, shooting me a look. "Go on with the story."

I went on with the story. By the time I'd gotten to the train and the appearance of Tim the gnome, we were sitting at the table digging into plates overflowing with pasta. The noodles weren't much to write home about, but the sauce was the cat's meow. He had a way with spices neither Ingrid nor I could match. He'd also taken some bread and buttered it, added some garlic, and then warmed it in the oven. More food went into my belly, and more of my hunger abated. By the time I reached the end of my sorry tale, I'd been stuffed.

"So, what's the play," he said, wiping his mouth with a napkin. "What's your big plan now?"

"Gaunt. I need hard facts to prove he murdered—or was responsible for ordering the murders—of Ben and Lucky. Either he hired the Jacks, or he hired someone to hire them. There's got to be some evidence of that."

"How you going to get it?"

I tapped my fingers on the table and cocked my head. What was the best way to get information from someone? I didn't have to think about what Mr. Templeton would do, I already knew from hard experience. "If there's any evidence to be found, it's going to be located in his office."

Lugnut gave a short laugh and leaned back, lacing his thick fingers behind his head. "That man's office is a heavily guarded embassy, Mira. You're talking about the Borealian Empyrean's ambassador to the United Territories. Their first ambassador in thirty years to boot. Those bastards aren't going to let you waltz in and take what you want, even if you brought every cop in the city with you and a legitimate warrant. And we both know you're not going to have either of those things."

True. But there were other ways of getting into a locked room. "I'm going to break into the damned place and take what I need. Do you still want to be involved?"

His face broke into a grin three sizes too large for his cheeks. "Sounds like it'll be swell."

***

"Even if there are tunnels, we don't have a clue where the entrances would be," I said. I covered my mouth to stifle a burp.

Morning light filtered through the curtains, and a half pot of black coffee sat on the table. The other half weighed my stomach. Lugnut had slept on the couch rather than drive home. When I'd limped my way down to the basement from my bedroom in the morning, he'd already fixed up some pancakes. He helped me over to the little table in the corner of the kitchen and told me to tuck in as he poured the coffee.

"No syrup," he said with a shrug. "Plenty of jam though if you like."

I did like, and I'd eaten well. "You keep feeding me like this, I'm going to get fat and slow like half the cops in the city."

He grinned and tossed another hotcake onto the stack on my plate. "You're already slow, I'm just fattening you up."

When we'd finished eating, we talked. I retired to the couch, pausing for a moment as I remembered the way Ingrid used to lay on it, a book held over her head as she read. I pushed back against those thoughts. *It's a couch, nothing more*, I told myself, as if that would change the memories and make them less painful. Lugnut sat on the carpet, next to the stain that looked like Australia.

"How are we going to do this?" he asked, looking at the brick walls of the foundation.

I sighed, shaking my head. "I don't know. Like you said, this is an embassy, and there'll be guards everywhere."

Lugnut leaned back against the wall, closing his eyes. "What if we could?"

"What if we could what?"

"Waltz in the front door like we belong there. Like we did in little Italy."

"This isn't a night club, these are elves. They are smart, ruthless, and not known for merciful natures. Their Radiant Legions are the finest soldiers on earth, which is why they are picked for special duties like protecting ambassadors. These guys aren't going to fall for the same tricks." But I had a thought. "Unless . . ."

"Unless what?"

"Not a trick. An invitation."

"What, they're going to invite us in?"

I grabbed the most recent Baltimore Sun off a stack of newspapers and riffled through it until I found what I looked for. I folded the page over and handed it to Lugnut. He glanced at the headline.

"The big reception they're having? So?"

"I think I'll have a swell time, don't you?" I grinned at him.

I watched the light dawn on his face. "Oh, of course, Miss Sinclair." A beatific smile spread across his face. "You'll look wonderful all dolled up, a pretty party dress, maybe a string of pearls. The belle of the ball."

"Now I need to figure out how to get an invitation. This is a swanky event for the doers and shakers of the world, not party crashing detectives."

"Aren't you a crack researcher?" he asked. His eyes opened and swung to meet mine, and his grin grew wider. "Who better to find a way to get her hands on a copy of the invitations and make sure her name is included on the guest list? Or have I overestimated your skills, Miss Sinclair?"

It was the best plan we had. The only plan, honestly. I'd have to find someone who could provide a carbon of the guest list. Then I'd need to get a copy of the invitation and forge my own. The Undertow might be able to provide what I needed there. I smiled back at him. "Why yes, yes I am, Mr. Whyte."

I made as if to rise, and he leaned forward, pushing me back onto the couch. "Relax, you can do it later."

I almost argued with him, but remained too weak to put up a fuss. I chalked it up as much to the meal as the wounds. Lugnut's pancakes stuck to the ribs and felt like a lead belt around my waist. Hard to motivate for anything when you're that full.

"Jacob, do you want to help, too?" Lugnut asked.

Damned straight, came the immediate reply.

I grinned and lay my head on the couch. "He says yes."

"Your ghost could be pretty useful," Lugnut said.

"If they don't have magical wards to stop him from entering," I said. "I'll need to case the joint first."

"You need to rest and heal until it's time. Someone else will have to do the casing."

I frowned and shifted on the couch until I sat more or less upright. "You? What do you know about magic wards and spotting hidden security?"

"Okay, admittedly not much. But I'm not walking around with a fresh hole in my side."

I could do it, Jacob said.

"No, Jacob," I said. "If there are traps, you'd get caught, and I'd have no way of getting you out."

His mood went glum, and the room chilled.

"Stop that," I said, shivering. "I didn't mean you couldn't go along and help."

Lugnut cocked his head and gave me a considering look. "Templeton's secretary, what's her name? Petal?"

"Petunia," I said. "But I don't think she's the right choice. She's half pixie and can do lots of things, but stakeouts and infiltrations aren't really her bread and butter. She's more the typing and doing her nails type."

He frowned. "Bit restrictive, don't you think? I'm sure she can do more than that. Isn't that what the boys at the station used to tell you when you made it through the academy?"

I blew out a long, slow breath. "Yeah, you're right." Damned but if I didn't feel three inches tall. All my railing against being limited for being a woman, and I made jokes about my friends. "Sorry."

"Apologize to her when you see her. Just remember next time how you feel when such comments are aimed at you." He stood and put his hands on his hips, twisting until his back cracked. Then his eyes narrowed and a devious look crossed his face. He pointed at the stack of books Ingrid had left on the floor near the sofa. "There's only one person we know who can help."

"Who is that?" I asked, pretending I didn't understand. I didn't feel ready to face her yet.

He sat down on the sofa, squeezing in by my legs, and took one of my hands. His skin was rough, fingers calloused and chapped, warm. He didn't want to meet my eyes now, but he nodded slowly as he spoke. "You said I'm your friend. But no one's closer to you than Ingrid. You need to work things out with her. We could use her help."

Damn it. He was right. That didn't keep my heart from plummeting through the sofa and the floor below. I sighed. "Call Lucinda," I said. "She'll know how to reach Ingy."

24

Glass Half Full

The restaurant was a tidy affair tucked into the corner of Foster avenue and Bouldin street. It had once been a row house, then one of the ubiquitous bars dotting every corner of the Highlandtown neighborhood surrounding it. But when the property became vacant in the early 1920's after the previous owner had passed away, the city had sold it to Margery Mayweather for a low price and a promise to fix the place up. Margery had kept her word, and had somehow weathered her way through the depression despite everything. Low prices and good food made for a going concern, plus a willingness to serve anyone of any species or race.

She kept tulips blooming year-round in boxes along the outside wall through some sort of magic. I suspected she had elven ancestors, but she never mentioned it and no one brought it up. A side yard had been converted into a bright, cheery patio with enough seating for a dozen people. Sometimes I'd swear the sun shown on it while clouds blanketed the rest of the city. Ingrid and I'd loved the place, loved the prices, and loved the beer Margery kept on tap.

She'd learned the art of brewing from her late husband, who'd been employed at the nearby Natty Boh brewery. It became our home away from home.

I found Ingrid sitting on the patio at a table near the wrought iron fence, the small gate open to let people in. I took Ingy's location as a sign of how bad things had gone between us. On cold days, we'd normally sit inside so we could admire the decorative tin ceiling with its griffins and basilisks. Not that I needed a sign; I'd laid those markers out on my own.

I limped through the gate and stood at the table. "Thanks for coming, Ingy, I really appreciate you meeting."

Ingrid nodded without saying anything, and I decided she wouldn't provide a better invitation. I sat down as Ingy lit up a cigarette, the smoke wreathing her black hair, drifting off over the alley beyond the fence. She wore dark pants and a dark blouse instead of the usual black dress she preferred. Her long, heavy coat was slung over the back of the chair. Her air appeared one of indifference and disdain. I wondered how I would ever make this right, heal the friendship I'd damaged.

Margery trundled over, a pudgy woman with a bright red face carrying a round tray with two tall glasses on it, moisture dripping down the outside of each. "Two beers, ladies. So good to see you again, it's been a while. Bless your hearts, dears. City has been in such a state lately, it's good to have the old regulars stopping by to make things feel right." She smiled and placed the beers on the table in front of us, then trundled back into the building through the side door.

Ingrid lifted her glass and took a long pull, her throat working. When she set it down, it was a quarter empty. She wiped her mouth with the back of her hand. "Talk. You've got until I finish the beer and then I've got a man to see about a dog."

I took a small sip of my own beer, my mouth dry. Then I started.

"I know you're angry at me, and you have every right to be. I should have told you what I planned."

She shot me a blank look, which for Ingrid was the same as a sneer. "I came for Lugnut. If he hadn't asked, I'd still be a fart in the wind as far as you and I are concerned."

"I know." I stumbled through my brain which had gone blissfully silent, searching for words to carry the weight I needed, admit my faults. I'd practiced all morning, thought it over carefully. But when I most needed it, my mind came up blissfully empty. I cursed the way language skipped town and left me holding the bag.

Ingy took another long drink, leaving the glass half empty. Half full, half empty, it all depended on how you look at the world.

I tried again. "I'm not going to make you feel better, I know that," I said. "I can't make it up to you for running off like that. I had to take care of things, and I was afraid take anyone with me." I took a long breath. I would tell her my darkest secret, my biggest failure. What else could I do but bare myself? If our friendship sank, I needed to honest about why it went down. "I watched Ben die, Ingy. I was with him when he got shot. I was too slow to stop them. I failed. I couldn't let that happen to anyone else. Especially you."

The wrinkles around Ingrid's brow smoothed, and her scowl slipped. "I didn't know you'd been there. You didn't say." She stared at the mug in front of her, the fingers of her hands wrapped around it. She watched the bubbles rising inside, the droplets of water dripping down the surface of the glass.

"I held him. There wasn't a damn thing I could do. All I could do was watch him leave me, just as everyone else leaves me. He died because of me. He was right; I wasn't ready. And I decided there was no way in hell, no fucking way, I'd let happen to you what happened to Ben Templeton. Especially not after all the shit I caused at the Tom Tom Club. You could have been arrested, or killed, because I was too damned naïve and too damned white to consider anything but my own needs. So, I left, I skipped out on you both. I didn't tell you what I was doing because I was too much a coward to be honest. We would have fought, and I would have given in, and you would have been dead because of me. I already had enough blood on my hands, and I've barely held it together to get this far. It would have destroyed me to have yours on my conscience, too."

It all spilled out in a long, breathless jumble as Ingy watched people passing by and smoked her cigarette, her eyes never meeting mine. When I finished, I took a deep breath and watched Ingy polish off her beer and set the glass back down empty.

It broke my heart I'd broken hers. It killed me to think there would be no more us at all. Not even friends. Well, no reason to keep hiding my secrets. None at all. If this was the end of us, then I wanted her to know everything.

"Because I love you."

I spoke those words so softly I hardly heard them myself.

She crushed out her cigarette, and she finally looked at me. Her eyes, one blue and one brown, her face impassive, unflinching, never smiling or frowning. I could feel the anger beneath the surface, the rage Ingy contained. It had been there since the first day we met. She controlled and harnessed now, boring into me like a needle, and I let it. I knew what she wanted, so I opened myself wide to her eyes, let Ingy take what she needed. I'd give her anything to the last breath we shared. I handed her the key and let her open the door. This is me, Ingy. This is how I feel about you. God help me, I'll drive you away by showing you if I have to, because I'd rather lose you to the truth than because I'd been a coward.

"I see," she said once she'd viewed the core of me, unbarred all of me. I waited for the end to come, for her to rise and leave without another word. She hesitated, her eyes shifting away, looking out over the street, watching cars and people passing by, the tip of her tongue wetting her lips. "I know." Her voice quavered only a fraction when she spoke, but I could feel it, and my skin tingled all over with tiny pinpricks. I'd seen it in her probing gaze, but her voice gave it form and meaning. Ingy filled it power and released it. So powerful, it didn't even turn her eyes black.

One unspoken phrase. The core of her message. I. Love. You.

It lay like a wound beneath her words, had always been there, but now I heard it for the first time. I should have known. Why else would Ingy move in with me and stay all this time? Why did she take care of me so well? Why did she slip in my bed to comfort me? I'd ignored what was right before my eyes. I could tell myself what I felt wasn't real and keep myself from getting hurt if she didn't feel the same way I did. Her gaze hadn't only been to find my truth; it had been to show me hers.

"Why'd you never say anything?" I asked as Ingrid shifted uncomfortably in her seat.

"About what? What's to tell you? What could be less acceptable in the world than being a woman, being black, being a witch, and on top of all that, being in love with another woman? How many anchors can one person carry and keep treading water?" She shrugged, left it dangling, the last reason, same as mine. What if you didn't feel the same way? "Anyway, it doesn't matter."

"It does to me."

"Not the way it does to me, or you wouldn't have left."

I reached out a hand and placed it on Ingrid's, but she pulled away. "I love you," I said again, louder this time.

The hostile look came back as swiftly as turning on a light. "I'm not sure you do," she said, her voice thick. "Least, not enough."

I sat back, trying to control my reaction, still the pain in my voice. "Too much." I'd always figured I was one of those women destined to become a spinster, growing old alone with a house full of cats. Ingrid had grown far closer to me than anyone I'd ever know, and I knew I did love her, in ways that went far beyond a simple friendship. "I was afraid to tell you in case you didn't feel the same way. I'd rather be friends than lose you."

"Yet you left me behind without half a thought," she said.

I nodded, chewed on my thoughts, took a quick drink of my beer before replying. "I didn't want anyone else to get hurt. Not after losing Ben. I couldn't lose you. I'd rather die myself than see that happen. And yes, it was the wrong decision. That seems to be all I'm good at doing so far as a detective, choosing poorly."

Ingrid seemed to relax a little. She finished her beer, but didn't move to leave. "What did you do to Jacob, anyway? The poor kid was gibbering like a panicked five-year-old who had lost his mommy when you left, and then he disappeared and we couldn't find him."

Changing the subject. I went along with it. The rest we'd handle later, but she'd relented a little and I didn't want to push things. "It's a long story."

She shrugged. "I got nothing but time, Mira."

I told her everything, the way I'd told Lugnut, and Petunia before him. I'd gotten pretty good at the story by then, and figured out how to tell it without embellishing it. She ordered another beer while I spoke, and drank slowly this time, chain smoking as she listened. She only interrupted when I told her about the threads and how I could see them, influence them.

"You shouldn't be messing with the threads. Lucinda always said that's the kind of foolishness that can blow up in your face." When Margery poked her face out of the doorway, Ingy waved at our glasses to signal for a third round.

When I wound down about Lucius Gaunt and finding the evidence I needed, she stubbed out her latest cigarette. "You're moving pretty slow. You're going to need help with that."

I nodded. "Will you move back in? The house won't be the same without coming home to your jazz records every night. And your movie poster is still pasted to the basement door."

"No," Ingy said, with a definitive quality to her voice I knew meant no negotiating on the topic. Her voice softened. "You're too messed up, what with Templeton's death. I still haven't forgiven you. And I haven't . . . figured out how we do this, you know? That's no way for us to start things." Her voice dropped off again. "Assuming we ever do start things, I mean. I'm fine where I am for now. Neither of us need a relationship grounded in lies and sorrow, let alone the shit we're going to take from a world that hates people like us."

"Sure, makes sense," I said, trying to give Ingy my best smile of understanding. Inside, though, I felt an emptiness that couldn't be pushed aside. "But you're always welcome to use the Undertow anytime you like."

Ingrid tilted her head as she thought about that. "Did you pay up?"

I nodded. "High roller plan, too. Lifetime account. Come on, you helped Lucinda draw the symbol, I wouldn't have it if not for you. It's as much your portal as it is mine."

"I'll think it over."

That was the best I was going to get on the subject of our proximity. I knew I'd at least tempted Ingrid into a small concession. That made the hole in my heart a little less painful.

Margery arrived, all smiles and bustle, placing the beers on the table and taking the empty glasses. "You two girls need anything else? I've got some delicious crab cakes right now, made them myself. Best in Maryland."

"No thanks, Marge, just the tab," Ingy replied. She waited for Margery to walk back into the building. "Alright, so tell me how you're going to get the evidence you need to prove Gaunt is behind everything that's happened."

"Ever want to break into an embassy building?"

"Not that I can recall, but then most of what I've done I didn't plan to do until I did it. It wasn't on my list of things to try on for size if that's what you mean."

"I'm going to crash the reception being held in his name this Friday evening, but I need more details on the security in his office."

"What's the plan of entry?"

"The elves are very accepting of citizens of the United Territories who want to move north for religious or political reasons. They feel it gives their empire cachet when they can glorify a defector as proof of the superiority of their harmonious nature."

"You want someone to pose as an emigrant, visit the embassy, go through the rigmarole of pretending to fill out the paperwork, and report back with as many details as possible."

"Right."

"So how do they get to this asshole's office? What if the exportation office isn't near it?"

"I need someone who can look for magical wards, that's all. Assuming we can get around them, Jacob will come with me and do the rest. Once inside the walls, he should be able to find the office and lead me to it."

"And if there's no way around them?"

"I'll come up with another plan."

Ingy finished her cigarette and tossed it onto the sidewalk. She sighed, and at last she nodded. "I'll help." A small surge of joy passed through me. "But I want to get paid for my assistance."

"How much?" I asked.

She met my eyes squarely this time, and her hand snaked across the table. Electricity coursed through my hand and made my heart pitter-patter when she took my fingers in hers. She squeezed gently. "Ten percent for this job. We'll start with a contract, but I'll eventually want a full share of the business, fifty-fifty split. You can rename it the Sinclair and Wolgraf Agency. I'll let you have top billing."

I stammered for a moment, my heart beating too fast from the contact with her, my mind rebelling at the thought of renaming the agency, my subconscious thrilled at the underlying message of her proposal. But the agency had gone, along with the man. "There is no agency now," I said.

She sat back, lighting a fresh cigarette, her face breaking into a smile. "Sometimes you're a little dense, Mira. Makes me wonder why I love you so much. I told you before." She pointed the lit snipe at me, emphasizing each word as she had before. "You're the agency now."

I don't know which frightened me more. The wolfish grin which split her face, or the realization she was right.

25

The Embassy Job

"I hate this damned wig," Ingy said, shifting the long, black tresses again. She'd been fiddling with it since I'd parked the car, forcing Petunia to keep adjusting it so it sat right. This seemed to amuse Petunia more than annoy her.

"Don't play with it," Petunia said, "you'll mess up the look, hon."

Ingy scowled, but dropped her hands back to her lap and began drumming them on her legs. Then she plucked at the long, blue dress she wore, shifting in the back seat of the car. "This damn thing is too tight," she said. "Why can't I wear something I like? No woman should have to wear something this body hugging. It isn't practical."

I sighed as I turned to face her. Petunia sat beside her, a compact and makeup brush in her hands, trying to suppress a grin. She'd climbed into the back of the car to help Ingy with her finishing touches. Lugnut had work at his garage, but made us promise to keep him informed about the activities.

"You're not ditching me on this, Mira," he'd said, leaning against

230

the passenger door of Petunia's car. "You call me as soon as you're done."

I touched his hand and gave him my best *everything is going to be fine* smile. "Of course, Lugnut. I'll call you as soon as we get back to my place."

He had looked at Petunia, then at Ingrid. Ingrid blew him a raspberry. That cracked him up, and after thumping the door a couple of times, he stepped away from the car and watched us as we pulled away from the gas pumps. His arms were crossed over his chest, his face scowling as he disappeared in the distance.

We parked two blocks from the elven embassy on a narrow side street. Blank bricks walls bracketed the car. Petunia had helped Ingrid pick out her outfit, and even provided the wig. "It belonged to my aunt Malthinia, but I don't need it," she had said, shrugging.

I tried to give Ingrid a smile as she fidgeted. "You know why you have to wear the dress. You asked to help, and I need your skills to tell us what we face in the embassy. If I go in, they might remember me come Friday when I attend the reception, and that will raise a lot of questions I'd rather not answer."

She sighed dramatically, and her shoulders slumped. "Fine. But I don't have to like it, even if I agreed to this foolish plan. I don't like having to pretend I enjoy being in a room full of people who'd rather put me in chains."

Petunia opened her mouth to say something, and then closed it again. She shook her head, and went back to applying blush to Ingy's cheeks. "Sometimes we gotta do the things we do to fit in."

Ingrid's stare would have melted lead. "I don't do anything to fit in. Fuck them if they don't like who I am. They should bend for me, not the other way round."

I expected Petunia to give a nervous look, but instead she laughed. "You got more balls than I do, toots, I'll give you that. If

I could be anything but quarter pixie, I'd take the chance and run with it. I wish I had your bravery. I'd own this joint."

Ingrid sat back, and some of the tension left her face. Her scowl became more of a frown instead. "If you want to pass instead of fighting the system, that's what you should do. I'm only doing this to help the case. I hope to hell it's the last time I have to."

Petunia gave her a brief glance and shrugged. "I don't ever lie about who I am. To hell with any mooks who don't like it. It may have got me nowhere, but that's exactly where I want to be. All the best people are here." Then she snapped the compact closed and sat back against the door, admiring her handiwork. "Well, that's it then. You look good."

Top notch, Jacob added.

She did look good. Although I preferred her natural hair, the long wig worked well with her outfit, fashioned in finger waves and reaching below her shoulders. I reached over the back of the seat and placed a hand on her knee. "You're the bee's knees."

A flicker of a smile passed across her lips, there and quickly gone again. "Sure I am, sugar," she said, her voice effecting a southern drawl. "This is 1938," she began.

"Oh, no, no, no," I said, "not the speech." I groaned loudly. The line had been *This is 1848*, but she adapted it with dramatic license.

"You have no sense of honor," she went on, ignoring me. Her nose rose, face tightening, assuming a haughty manner. Her gaze could have withered a continent. "You think to place me in white ribbons and lace, put me on a pedestal as though I am an object to be worshipped. But this is not the honor upon which I live and breathe. Southern honor is no honor. No, dumpling, this is 1938, and I shall decide what is honor and is not." Not only did she sound like the actress in the movie, but I would have sworn her face took on the mannerisms of the famous character. Infamous from Ingrid's point of view. She hated that picture.

"She's ready," I said, glancing at Petunia.

"She sure is," Petunia agreed, and clapped in appreciation.

I handed Ingrid the leather clasp we'd bought at Hutzler's. She opened it, checked her documents were there, and snapped it shut again. "Turn on the radio," she said.

I twisted the knob and turned up the volume, waiting until the tubes warmed up and the hiss of static began. Then I turned the tuning knob until the needle reached the bottom of the dial where nothing but static filled the airwaves.

"Hello, world," Ingrid said. The earrings she wore picked up her voice, sent it through the intervening air, and pushed it out through the tubes on the radio. She'd enchanted the whole rig to work like a private phone line. A second after she'd finished speaking, we heard the ghostly sound of her voice coming through the radio. "Hello, world," Ingy's voice said, a ghostly reflection.

"Perfect," I said, and a moment later *perfect* crackled faintly from the radio.

"I figure this whole job will take about an hour, so sit tight, ladies. Though any amount of time with those bastards is too long if you ask me, and no you didn't, but I said it anyway."

"Be careful," I said.

Ingrid nodded, took a deep breath, and opened the door of the car. She stepped out onto the street, nearly stumbling on her heels. She graced me with her latest scowl as the door thumped shut.

Thump said the radio. As she walked away, the radio added the *click, click, click* of her heels tapping on the sidewalk.

Should I go with her? Jacob asked.

Stay put until we know what we're facing, Jacob.

It took several minutes for Ingrid to walk to the embassy doors, the three of us listening to her footsteps. She grumbled several times on the way about her shoes. "I hate these things. Damned uncomfortable forcing your feet into these torture devices. If every one of us women tossed them away for boots and flats, no one could stop us."

Petunia giggled. "The girl ain't wrong," she said.

I lit a snipe while we waited, rolling down the window to let out the smoke. The air wasn't moving, so I whistled up a little breeze to tease the smoke away, watching it swirl in circles and loops. Petunia joined me, and we made patterns in the smoke. Gray-blue airships cruised along the alley; a ponderous elephant wobbled on misty legs. Petunia laughed with delight when we turned one vaporous cloud into an image of the Natty Boh logo, the sun peering through his one open eye.

"State your business," said a man's voice over the hissing radio.

"She's there," I said, and tossed the cigarette out the window. Petunia leaned over the back of the front seat to listen, and I turned the volume up.

"I'm here to talk about immigrating to your lovely country," Ingrid said, slathering on her southern twang. "I've heard such wonderful things about how y'all keep the riff raff out, so to speak. And my views on the mixing and mingling of certain races seems to be less and less popular these days."

I held my breath, waiting for the reply. My fingers curled around Petunia's steering wheel, knuckles turning white.

"Thank you, ma'am," the male voice said, and I relaxed a little. "If you could please sign the guest book and let the receptionist know your business."

"Certainly, sugar," she said. I barely recognized her voice. Her drawl oozed with magnolia trees and cotton fields, hot summer days and cold lemonade.

"She's good," Petunia said. I nodded my agreement.

I hoped she remembered her cover name. Her footsteps sounded louder, echoing off the walls of whatever room she was in, like she walked across a floor of granite or marble.

"Name and city of residence," a new voice said, this time a woman's.

"Marcela Beaumont, Savannah, Georgia," Ingrid said.

She remembered the name I picked, Jacob said, sounding proud.

"Identification please."

The snap of the clasp on her clutch, the sound of papers rustling. "I can never find nothing in this here purse." She gave a little laugh, sounding nothing like the woman I'd grown to know and love. Why hadn't she stuck with the acting? Because she hated crowds, hated pretending to be something she was not, and hated people most of all. The trifecta of issues that would destroy any burgeoning acting career the minute she popped a nosy reporter in the face. She'd be the rage of the press for a couple of days, the actress with the nasty temper. Black actress; double whammy.

"Thank you, Miss Beaumont," the woman said. "What is your reason for visiting the Baltimore Embassy of the Borealian Empyrean today?"

"I would like very much to discuss moving to your lovely country, darling," Ingy said. "If it's not too much trouble."

"And what reasons would you have for wanting to migrate to the Borealian Empyrean?"

"Well," she said, her voice dropping almost to a whisper, "I've heard such wonderful things about the many freedoms one can enjoy there under the hospitality of you darling elves, and away from all these—and I'll try to put this delicately—violent non-humans."

The woman interrupted with a brief snort of laughter, as though agreeing with her description, before Ingy continued "There is also the matter of persecution of my own people simply due to the color of our skin. I hear y'all don't discriminate against people. I want to live someplace where I will be shown the respect I am due."

"Miss—"

"—And you see, I'm also a pagan, and pagan persecution is becoming anathema for a southern woman these days. You have no idea the hatred one faces when they wish to dance naked by the light of the full moon. As god is my witness, I must be free."

I thought she went a bit overboard. *Less is more*, Ben would have said.

"Yes, that's fine, Miss Beaumont, you can stop now," the woman said. Her voice had grown flat and icy cold. "Down the hall, second door on the right. I'll notify them you're coming. You'll fill out a form, and they'll process your application."

"And I can move to the north?" Ingrid asked, sounding sincerely happy at the prospect of joining a nation of xenophobic isolationists whose racism made the United Territories look positively progressive.

"It takes a few months to make a determination," the woman said. She sounded disinterested now, clearly done with the woman in front of her.

"Oh sugar, thank you. You are the kindest, sweetest elf I do believe I have ever met."

"Sure, whatever," the woman said, dismissing her. "Next please."

More footsteps over the radio. Ingrid muttered, "Snotty racist bitch," but said no more. A door knob rattled, hinges squeaked, and then the door thumped again.

"Miss Beauregard?" another male asked.

"The last name's Beaumont, sugar. Don't wear it out."

A pause; the sound of a chair moving. Then the wet smack of lips. I hoped it was her hand he was kissing, and only suffered the tiniest pang of jealousy. "Charmed to make your acquaintance," he said.

"Oh, you flatter me, you dear man," Ingrid said, and gave that high-pitched laugh again. "But who told you I was coming?"

"The receptionist," he said, sounding confused. "Here's a clipboard with some forms for you to fill out. Please don't skip any of the answers, and if you have any questions it will be my absolute pleasure to answer them for you."

"Why thank you, darling," Ingrid said. I could almost see the smile plastered on her face.

Footsteps, a chair squeaking against the floor, the rustling of clothing. Then the sound of a pen on paper as Ingrid began filling out the forms she had been given. I knew she did more than that, though. She had several spells prepared and muttered them under her breath. They enhanced her perceptions and allow her to see magical traps and barriers, any wards cast upon the embassy. They couldn't have much, though, we'd all agreed. They'd only opened the building a few weeks ago, and truly useful magical wards could take months to set in place. The sooner we went in, the better our chances.

We waited a long forty minutes, the hand on my watch seeming to pause as though time stood still. I tapped my fingers against the car door and smoked nervously, worried about the time. If this ran too long, if they noticed her spell casting . . . I didn't want to think of what might happen then. Oh, there would be hell to pay, although I suspected Ingrid would be dishing a good deal of it out. I'd have to ask her to teach me how she called up her baseball bat.

Her footsteps came through the radio again, and she said, "Here you go, sugar."

"Thank you, Miss Beaumont," he replied.

Her voice dropped lower, and I pictured her leaning over the desk he sat behind. "Tell me handsome, are all the elves in the Empyrean as attractive as you are?"

He coughed and his voice rose two octaves when he spoke. "Only the lucky ones, doll. Say, I'm due to rotate back north in another month. When your application is approved, why don't you swing by the city of Münchensteig. Take my card."

She laughed. "Well I do hope I get to see you again, you dear, sweet elf." She apparently didn't give him any time to reply, her clicking heels coming hard on her words. The echoing footsteps were soon replaced by the sounds of cars, the voices of people chattering, and the whiney of horses. A few minutes later and she came around the corner. She slid into the back seat and yanked the wig off. The haughty expression faded, and she became Ingy again. Maybe a touch angrier than usual. Downright murderous in fact.

"All the black hearts in Hades, I need a smoke," she said. I handed her my pack and waited for her to light one and take a drag. "Don't you ever ask me to do anything like that again."

"I didn't plan on it."

"Don't argue with me."

"You did swell," Petunia said, patting her on the knee.

Ingrid grimaced and shook her head. She wrapped her arms tightly around her chest and sat back stiffly against the seat. "The first floor is somewhat secure. Not enough to detect subtle spells like the ones I used, but enough to pick up spooks, spirits, sylphs, any sort of natural familiar or conjured minion. But most of the wards are loose and spotty. Shitty work, those elves. They've got at least another month before the entire first floor is enchanted to the point I couldn't walk in there three days after charming a busted seam on my dress but they'd come running because it tripped the sense spells. Everything above is clean. Little sign they'll get around to the rest of the floors anytime soon."

Is that good or bad, Jacob asked me.

Good and bad, I told him. "Jacob wants to know how we're going to get him in if they can detect him."

"Thought about that," Ingy said. "Let's go back to your place, though. I need a long, hot bath to wash off the filth of those bastards. Then I'll explain."

"Right." I started the car and put it in gear, ignoring the short, sharp pain of her calling the home we had shared mine, not ours.

26

A Wake of Vultures

The mirror reflected a stranger. The woman seemed classy, with cheek bones accentuated by makeup, her dark hair sleek and pulled back with a silver hair band. The black, silk dress flattered her figure, but remained demure enough to be respectable, and swept down her legs to mid-calf. A wide belt wrapped around the waist, fastened with fabric buttons of matching color on the right side. One could say elegant and sophisticated, words I didn't feel comfortable using when describing myself. I pinched my cheeks to make sure it was me in the mirror.

Petunia had once again picked out the dress and applied the makeup. She'd also insisted on flats instead of heels, bless her heart. I hadn't needed the reminder, but appreciated she thought of it. "If you've gotta run, toots, there is no way you're going to do it in a pair of heels," she said, with the sort of cool logic that made sense when you were about to invade a fancy ball full of high rollers, sneak past the best guards in the world, break into a racist diplomat's office, and try to find evidence linking him to the murder of two ex-cops. Nothing easier.

I walked down the stairs, disconnected from my body, the unreality of the evening growing with each eight-inch riser I descended. When I reached bottom, I turned and walked into the dining room where Lugnut, Ingy and Petunia waited. Each of them checked me over carefully, professionally.

"Not bad, little witch," Lugnut said, crossing his arms. "I'd hardly recognize you." He wore his best pinstripe suit tonight, along with a slick fedora, playing the role of my driver.

Petunia silently stared at me for several long heartbeats, her eyes sweeping up and down with a critical look, until I could no longer take the heat of her gaze. "What?"

"You forgot your purse," she said, smiling.

"Shit, I left it upstairs on my bed."

"I'll get it for you," Lugnut said, patting me on the shoulder. "Sit down and have a drink. You look pale."

Petunia rose and went to the basement door. "I've got to use the powder room," she said, glancing back and forth between Ingy and I. She paused longer than she needed, which made it obvious she wanted to give us room to talk, then headed downstairs.

I sat down across from Ingy, grabbed a wine glass, and poured myself some red from the bottle on the table. I drank half in one swallow, wiping my lips with the napkin Ingrid handed me.

"Is this how you felt all dressed up the other day when you went into the embassy?" I asked her.

"Stomach churning, like you're about to throw up and can't find a place to vomit?"

"Yes."

"Yeah, pretty much," Ingy said. "Although I didn't have to face a whole bunch of big shot Baltimore mucky mucks. I only had to put on a face I didn't want to so I could impress a bunch of racists who pretend they'd want black folks to move there only because it annoys the people here so much. They'd as soon see me six feet under."

"Thanks, you're a big help."

"Anytime." She rose and walked around the table, holding a pair of pearl earrings in her hand." Pull your hair back." She carefully inserted the earrings into the holes in my lobes and fastened the tiny clasps on the back. She'd wanted me to wear the same earrings she had, and I'd agreed. They'd know if things went south, though they wouldn't be able to do much to help. The touch of her fingers against my ears and neck sent shivers through me, but I was too wound to do more than let her finish and return to her seat.

"Are you sure there's only the one magical barrier on the first floor—" I began.

"—I am, don't worry," Ingy said, soothing me. "We've been over this a dozen times. The barrier is the only magical ward they have in place. They have lots of regular guards, though, and you'll have to figure out how to get by those on your own. Well, with Jacob's help."

I wanted to talk about us, the Mira and Ingy show, an ongoing radio serial of two people in love dancing around each other. Now seemed as good a time as any. But nervousness kept my mouth clamped shut, and throat dry. I'd just about screwed up the courage to say something when Lugnut came down with my bag and handed it over.

"You got your ID and the invitation?" he asked.

I nodded and pulled them from the purse to show him. Both forged of course. They'd let me nap all day after I'd spent a long night working on the documents. The Undertow served its purpose, and gave me a detailed image I could work with. Petunia's boyfriend, Melvin, got hold of the invitation list through his contacts at city hall. The ID said I was Mrs. Mildred Statton, the much younger wife of cement factory owner Henry Statton. In truth, Henry Statton had left town, the real Mildred with him. I didn't think they'd have any way of checking, though, and I was as near a match in age and looks to her as anyone else I could choose. Rich men always seemed to want a younger woman on their arms. Maybe she really loved him; maybe she was a gold digger. I hoped he made her happy, whichever the case.

A fake Baltimore ID had been easy. I'd made my first when I was only ten. The invitation, though, was a work of art. On heavily embossed paper, written in near Gothic print with swirls and curly Q's, and all the ostentatious trappings required. It carried a seal of the Borealian Empyrean, enchanted by Ingy so deviously it would present to the eye as an official marker but trip none of the wards. The copy would be indistinguishable from an original.

Lugnut looked at it over my shoulder. "You two have skills."

"We do indeed," Ingrid said.

"Come on, time to go," Lugnut said. "You want to arrive late but not too late." He nabbed my coat off the hook by the door and held it out for me to slip into.

My dress had a single pocket, cleverly concealed by the hem. I slipped my hand into it and checked Mr. Templeton's medallion remained where I'd placed it. I hoped it would keep me grounded and focused on the task at hand. I didn't want to lose my cool like I had with the Jacks.

You ready, Jacob?

Another reason to carry it. I'd tied Jacob's thread to the medallion, hiding him from the magical detection. Exactly the kind of spell their rickety wards wouldn't detect. Once we were past the first floor, he'd be free to roam.

Right as rain, if a bit crowded, he replied.

Crowded? A strange way to put it, but I guessed it meant uncomfortable. I suspected he feared he'd be tied to it forever, the way he'd been tied to the house. He didn't want to give up the freedom he'd found. "You'll be out soon enough. You're a pip for doing this."

I know, he replied, and tried to send me some cheerful thoughts. *But this thing is chock full of Templeton.*

"He owned it a long time. Some of him was bound to rub off on it."

He said nothing else, and I pulled my hand out of my pocket. "Alright," I said to the other three. I walked to the door where Lugnut stood. "Where did you guys get all the fancy duds, anyway?" I asked as he held it open for me.

"You ain't the only girl's got skills, toots," Petunia said, a smile lighting up her face. "I got friends at every department store in the city and they helped me get what I need. But you need to be careful, I gotta return them when you're done. You break 'em, you bought 'em."

I nodded my thanks and took a deep breath. "Alright, let's go," I said. Lugnut opened the door for me and we headed out into the dark, cold night.

We dropped Petunia and Ingy off at a diner two blocks away to wait for Lugnut to return. Lugnut drove me on to the front door of the embassy. An elf in a red uniform waited on the curb, and he stepped up to the car and opened the door for me. He was handsome and young, with dark, wavy hair and the ethereally beautiful face they all seemed to have. I was certain he had a gun underneath his blazer, below the emblem of the Borealian Empyrean on his left breast pocket.

"Ma'am," he said, taking my hand and helping me out. I turned away before his gaze could meet my face. Nervous, more than out of a concern he'd make me. He probably had never met Mildred. The car pulled away from the curb, but I didn't risk a look as Lugnut left. I wanted to play it cool, act like an aloof, rich snob.

I walked the red carpet, my heart beating a tango inside my chest. An attractive, older couple stood in front of me in beautiful clothing, his teeth impossibly white, her cleavage deep enough to rival the Grand Canyon, both sets of physical accoutrements high-lighted as if they were the most important features of these two. They chattered on with each other about inconsequential things like the cost of the symphony, the rude service she'd received at the country club from the black staff, and the nearness of the Block, with its seedy clubs.

"I swear, Gerald," she said, tugging at his left arm, "you need to get on those police people and have them do something about it."

He patted her elbow with his right hand. "I've told you, dear, I don't have much pull in that direction. They tolerate these *people* and I'll never understand why."

She sniffed and lifted her nose, as though she smelled something bad. "Those people don't deserve our decency and respect. They're little more than soulless animals."

I struggled to remain impassive and keep myself from interject-ing into their conversation. Nothing I said would be polite, and the last thing I needed would be a scene. That would nix any chance I had of pulling this off. I stood behind them and stewed and hated every inch of their primped and preened selves. They dished out hate, so I guess we were even.

When it was their turn, the man named Gerald handed his invi-tation to one of the two guards, and they stepped through the door without waiting for a response. I pulled mine from my purse, and stepped forward. Another elf, this one dressed in a tuxedo, greeted me without a smile and took the invitation from my hand. I started to step through the door without waiting, but his left hand hooked my elbow.

I glared at him. "What is the problem?"

He smiled, sickly sweet, and said, "Please let me check the list be-fore you enter, madam."

I sniffed, trying to sound like an obnoxious and bigoted wife. "Well I've never been so insulted," I said. My mind, though, swirled through a complex series of events, none of which ended well if my name didn't appear on the list. Or, to be more precise, if Mrs. Statton's name didn't appear on it.

His fingers ran down a piece of paper held to a clipboard, the text tiny and barely legible. It stopped moving and he tapped the paper, his face frowning. I tensed to leap down the steps and beat feet towards the diner. This was such a stupid plan. It had been my plan of course.

His face broke into a stiff smile. "My apologies, Mrs. Statton," he said, opening the door for me. "Please enjoy the rest of your evening."

I didn't reply, but sniffed again and turned towards the door. Haughty, not humble, Mira. I had to keep reminding myself of that. Every encounter I wanted to step aside, defer, try to please the other person. I couldn't afford to be Mira the sidekick tonight. Nor Mira the detective. I had to be Mrs. Statton, with money and power and the attitude that went with those luxuries. I stepped into the lobby and followed the ropes to another pair of guards.

"Bags on the counter," one said. I stepped up, placing my clutch on the granite topped desk and waited, hoping my sweat wasn't visible. The guards opened my clutch and glanced through it, then handed it back. Gerald and his dear wife appeared positively ready to kill as they walked away from their own search. Then, the guards finished with me. Their attention slipped away like water off a duck as they turned to the next attendee. Two check points down. Only a dozen more things could go wrong.

Everyone queued at the elevators, but I walked past them and approached a guard who stood beyond. A big, a broad elf with a puffy red face, tugging at the collar of his tux. His black eyes swiveled to me as I did my best to sashay in his direction. I barely glanced at him as I tried to ooze sex appeal. Not my natural habit and I didn't know how anyone managed to get through their day swinging their hips that much. Only mollified by knowing Ingy had had to put up with a hell of a lot worse when she entered the embassy. Not only having to use her sex appeal to cover her intent, but having to act cheerful in a place where they'd happily pack her off to the north in a tiny crate and stick her in chains if they'd caught her.

"The elevators are over there," he said, pointing back the way I'd come.

"I need a powder room; now in fact, not later."

He grimaced. "First door on your left. Make it snappy." I felt his eyes on me as I walked to the ladies' room. *That's right, asshole, keep staring at my ass.* I longed to put a knee to his crotch.

The bathroom looked empty. I took a deep breath when the door closed behind me and glanced at the watch I wore. Not my usual one, but a fancy gold number Petunia provided. There were thirty seconds remaining. The window was high over the sinks. I kicked off my flats and carefully stepped up onto the mahogany counter, hoping it would hold my weight and I wouldn't slip off. I stretched up, struggling to reach the clasp holding the window closed.

Ten seconds. I pushed the window open, a tickle of outside air cooling my skin. I prayed they didn't have anyone watching the alley behind the restroom.

"Now." I waited, and several more seconds passed. Now? Anytime now. The seconds ticked away and I feared the worst. I pursed my lips to whistle a greeting when a small, black bundle flew through the window and thumped on the floor. I shut the window again, locked it. I almost fell off the sink in my haste to get down. The dark cloth loosened easily, revealing my gun and a leg strap. I hitched up my dress and wrapped the twin belts around my thigh, tightening and syncing them. It wouldn't be easy to get to, and I'd walk a little bowlegged, but at least I had some protection.

A knock at the door startled me, and I jammed the cloth in a nearby trash can.

"Ma'am?"

"Just a moment," I replied, turning on the faucet in front of me and smoothing the dress down. I wet my hands and pretended to wash them, then dried them with a hand towel. I took two deep breaths to slow my heart rate, and then opened the door, smiling at the big elf.

"The powder room is filthy," I said, eyes squinched in mock disgust. I moved past him without looking at him directly. "You should have someone clean it before another important person is forced to endure the incompetence of your staff." I kept a languid pace, feeling his glare on the back of my neck as I slid into line for the elevators. I refused to look acknowledge him further, and moved into one of the cars with the crowd.

The ride to the twelfth floor went quickly, my body crammed into the elevator with the well-heeled, well dressed swells of Baltimore society. The jewelry worn by the women staggered the mind, from a ring with a diamond the size of my fingernail, to necklaces with pearls like grapes. One woman wore a silver hair band like mine, but studded with sapphires that caught the light and sparkled bright blue, like glittering stars on a frosty winter's evening. Noise grew as we rose, a low buzz of voices and orchestral music.

When the elevator came to a stop and the doors opened, the music swelled. The eleventh and twelfth floors of the building were merged into one, the elevators opening into a grand, two-story foyer with a massive glass chandelier hanging over the open space below. The lower floor was marble, and in the center of the room the white and gray stone had been inlaid with a circle representing the seal of the Borealian Empyrean, a red eagle with its head turned and wings spread wide, holding arrows in one claw and a torch in the other. Might and reason, war and peace, two halves of a whole. Truth be told, they paid the second half little concern, preferring the might part. But talking of peace made for good propaganda.

The crowd swept me from the landing and we flowed down the wide stairway into the lower room. They began to break up into clumps, heading different directions. Some towards a large bar at the far right of the room, and others towards one or more clumps of folks who were chatting. I caught sight of the mayor and his wife talking with several dour looking elves who wore sashes over their white uniforms. His cheeks and nose were flushed either from drink or the heat in the room. With so many people crowded together it was warm, although grand double doors leading to a balcony over-looking the city were thrown open to let in the cool November evening.

In between the bodies of humans and elves flitted the servers. Each of them a fairy, dressed in gossamer red gowns that flowed around their bodies like smoke, their tiny wings beating as they swirled through the mass of people with trays full of hors d'oeuvres and drinks. It took two of them to carry each tray. When one beat past my ears, the buzz of her wings against the air momentarily drowned out the music. She wore a tiny, jeweled collar.

Slaves.

It nauseated me and I waved them away when they paused in front of me to offer me refreshments. I probably looked like a surly rich woman. Useful for my cover and a behavior I found appalling. I checked my anger with a reminder we couldn't claim ethical superi-ority. We'd banned slavery, but not bigotry and segregation.

I sauntered over to the bar and, when the bartender came over, ordered a glass of chardonnay. I slipped my hand in my pocket as I waited for the glass. I felt for the strings binding Jacob to the medal-lion and tugged on them until his thread unraveled.

About time, he said, a little peevishly.

Sorry. I had to wait for the right moment. Can you start scouting for Gaunt's office? Remember to stay above the first floor.

Will do, he said. His presence faded as he drifted through the crowded ball room.

I took small sips of my wine, wanting to keep a clear head, and walked towards the stairway. As I climbed, the sound of the small orchestra in the corner of the room faded out, leaving the drone of voices. A sudden staccato of drums broke over the buzz, followed by a short blast of marshal notes from the trumpet players. A voice rang out.

"Ladies and gentlemen, I give you now his excellency, Lord of the Northern Province and Chancellor of Sylfe Edhil, the Borealian Empyrean's diplomat to the United Territories of Coventine, Lucius Gaunt."

Applause rose and I watched the man who killed my boss stalk his way to the front of the room, shaking hands with the bigshots and movers, the captains of industry, the political sycophants, and other mercenaries of Baltimore. Black hair had been slicked back tight to his scalp, and his eyes were the gold color of an elm tree in Autumn, rimming his dark pupils.

The raptor had arrived to greet the vultures.

27

Water Safe

This had been the elf talking to the gnomes, I knew it for true now. He wore a high-collared, black suit and a blood-red diplomatic sash indicating his rank. A podium had been brought out and placed in front of the double doors opened to the outside, as he faced the attendees. His smile resembled a wolf's, ready to eat the flock of sheep quivering before his dripping fangs.

"Friends, honored guests, and officials of the city of Baltimore and the United Territories of Coventine. Thank you for the welcome. I greet you in humble friendship." He paused, bringing his hands up and pressing them together. "Truly the best of people stand here tonight."

More applause. My hand trembled with rage, a hatred so deep I almost broke the wine glass I held as I squeezed. I closed my eyes and counted to ten, trying to steady myself. The cold weight of gun steel rubbed against my thigh. I wanted to pull it out and put a bullet right between those piss-colored eyes.

While the applause echoed around the room, Jacob returned. He radiated pleasure. *I think I found his office. Pretty sure. Mostly. Top of the landing, down the hall to the right where those two guards are standing. Biggest office in the building, and there's a wall full of books. Huge desk. Seems important. Oh, and his name is on a plaque on the door.*

I almost laughed out loud. He'd held the last piece of info to keep me guessing. Cheeky ghost. I finished climbing the steps. He moved along beside me. Everyone smiled, laughed, applauded Gaunt's speech. I urged my cheeks to pull my lips into the expected sign of pleasure, and applauded with the rest of them. I eased closer to the hallway, my gaze focused on Gaunt, letting my peripherals guide me into position. I left the wine glass sitting on a table next to the balcony rail.

Alright, go ahead, I told Jacob. *Give someone's liver a squeeze.*

Someone grunted, then groaned, and a glass shattered. A man slumped to the floor with a gasp of pain. A woman knelt next to him, her voice lost in another round of rising applause. Nothing like having a ghost reach into you and pummel your kidneys to bring you to your knees. The guard flanking the hall nearest to the injured man moved towards them, and then the other followed. I had an opening. I slipped quickly down the hallway while attention focused on either the podium or the prone figure. The room sound of throngs in rapturous adulation of their host covered any noise I made.

I glanced back to see the guard returning to his post. My stomach lurched into my throat and sweat trickled down my sides, but he watched the crowd below on the main floor and never glanced my way. I made it around a corner, exhaling slowly when I realized I'd been holding my breath.

Jacob's distraction had been enough. It took a lot out of him, but he really could jab someone's kidneys when he pressed, the same way he could steal a hair ribbon. Hard enough to put a man on his knees it turned out. I owed him for saving me from the last Jack I'd killed.

I reached into my pocket and rubbed Mr. Templeton's medallion for luck. In the dim light of the hallway, the green verdigris of its surface almost seemed to glow. "Full of Templeton," I murmured.

The doorway at the end of hall belonged to Gaunt. I approached it, placing the chain of the medallion around my neck, my fingers rubbing the surface. I ran magic through my hands and passed them over the door without touching it. I sensed no traps or spells. I pulled the picks from my hair where they'd been hidden beneath the edge of my hairband. Picking the lock took me all of thirty seconds. I slipped inside the room and closed the door behind me.

A small sliver of city light slipped through the curtains, illuminating a strip of plush, green carpet and providing enough light to see. A banker's lamp rested on a huge desk near the windows. I flipped the switch. I took white gloves from my clutch and slipped them on, then sat in the large, leather chair. There were three drawers in each side, and I worked my way down the right and then left, being careful to leave things as I found them.

The bottom left drawer contained files, and I rifled through them. Time flowed too fast as I gave each document a brief glance and moved to the next until I found my first piece of evidence. Receipts from Beezallel, Bollo and Tim documenting purchases totaling hundreds of thousands of dollars. Magical affirmations were spelled into the ink, legally binding purchaser and payee. Solid proof of a connection, although what had been bought wasn't detailed. I folded the papers and slipped them into my pocket.

"Jacob, check all the bookcases and walls. See if there's a safe."

He sent an affirmation, and his chilly breeze swept around the room as I continued to go through paperwork, the minutia of a diplomat with work as diverse as expected. Everything from ribbon cutting ceremonies to plans for creating a commission to explore purchasing mineral rights from the United Territories. Requests for asylum to the Empyrean to consider. But nothing about the goose, and nothing linking him to Ben or Lucky or the Jacks beyond the gnome's receipts. Circumstantial at best; he wouldn't even break a sweat.

"Not enough," I murmured. I fingered the medallion, examined the threads of the world inside the office. and had a momentary feeling of being watched, the hairs on the back of my neck standing up. I turned in that direction, looking at a bookcase filled with volumes. Books of legal code it appeared. I walked over, my hand reaching out to stroke fingertips across the spine of each. I stopped when I felt a tingle as my hand passed the thread of one.

"The Rise and Fall of the Dwarven Empire," I read, my eyes tracing the gilded letters down the back of the book. I stared at the threads attached to the book. The letter D seemed to shift as I watched. I tugged and pushed at the book until it depressed with an audible click. A large portion of bookcase to my right swung open silently, and I stared at a six-foot-tall metal door with a handle and a spinning lock, black with white numerals on it.

"Shit."

A Welter Water safe. Small banks used them as vaults. They were made by gnomes, steel composite with black runes swimming across the metal, dancing in slow swirls and circles, making it appear the surface rippled like the surface of a lake. I could feel the magic emanating from the face of the vault, passing over me like the summer sun on pavement. When I touched the dial a current ran through me, setting my skin alive.

"Jacob, get over here."

His chill grew close, and I shivered as my back cooled with his proximity even as my front baked in the warm magic of the safe.

What's up, boss?

"I need to crack this safe, but if we get the combination wrong, it'll trip the safeties and it'll flood the room, drowning me. I don't have any of the tools I need to drill it open, although that would probably trip the wards anyway. I don't even have my scope so I can listen for the clicks. Probably wouldn't hear them even if I did."

Jacob suggested an exit and regrouping.

"No, it's now or never; we won't get another chance like this. If we leave, there won't be another opportunity to break in here before they've beefed up the wards."

But what if we fail? he asked. I could feel his worry growing, a sense of frustration.

"There's always a risk of failure, Jacob. But we need to know the truth."

So, what do we do?

I stared at the metal beast and ran through a dozen scenarios in my head, each less appealing than the previous. Each ending in my death and the evidence destroyed. The death part, of course, being the worst part. I chewed my bottom lip and wished I could light a cigarette.

Shame I can't punch it in the kidneys, Jacob said, his emotions now rueful.

"Yeah, it'd be great if you could pass through it and knock it out." The more I thought about that, the more it tickled at the edge of possibility. I focused on what Jacob could accomplish. "You can't affect it. But what if you stuck your head in where the lock is?"

His chill moved past me and I shivered, wrapping my arms around my body for warmth. Jacob could see the internal mechanism, but there was nothing he could do. *I can't make the parts move.*

"Yeah, but you can see the tumblers, right?"

Sure.

"So, you can see when they fall into alignment?"

Oh, he said.

"Smart ghost you are. Stick your head in there while I turn the knob, and tell me when each one falls into place. Oh, and Jacob? Remember: if we get this wrong, I'll be the one haunting you."

He snickered his understanding and told me to begin.

I placed my fingers on the dial, the zing of electricity flowing through me again. Gritting my teeth, I turned it clockwise, one number of the one hundred number dial at a time, each number another click. I went slowly, leaving a pause in between each click for Jacob to notify me, all too aware time passed quickly. The longer we stayed in the room, the more likely someone would find me. Fifty passed, and still he stayed quiet, then sixty, then sixty-three, sixty-four—

—Stop!

"Damn it, don't yell at me," I said. His shout had almost caused me to jerk, spinning the dial further. I shook myself to clear my head.

Sorry.

"Forget about it. Sorry I snapped at you. Let's move on to the next one."

I turned counter-clockwise this time, passing quickly back past sixty-four before slowing again. We had counted back down to thirty-three when Jacob signaled me to stop. Then clockwise again, and at eighty-two he said stop again.

The safe made a noise like a click and a sigh combined. Air stirred my hair, and the symbols stopped moving. I wrapped my hands around the metal handle and let my breath out slowly. "Here goes nothing."

The handle turned silently until it pointed at the ground. I closed my eyes, waiting for an explosion of water. When none came, I pulled on the heavy door and it swung open with the hushed swish of well-oiled hinges.

Beyond the door was a small room filled with drawers. There were five rows on each of the three walls, and there were five drawers per row. Twenty-five per wall, seventy-five total, and each of them were featureless except for shiny silver handles to pull them open.

"Random or methodic?"

Best guess

Top row right. I opened the drawer. Paperwork filled the space, some of it old and yellowed, the paper stiff and brittle like parchment. I thumbed through it and moved on, repeating the process again and again, scanning pages quickly and hoping I didn't miss anything.

Drawer nine was empty except for a piece of black cloth which shimmered and rippled, a darker darkness twisting and skimming beneath its surface, as though it contained anti-light, a primal night. I pulled it out and examined it, my eyes trying to follow the patterns in the silky material, slipping off each time I thought I'd begun to grasp it. This had to be the shadow cloak Rowan had wanted. I owed her for saving my life and helping me heal. I fastened it around my neck with its black, metal clasp and returned to the search

When I reached the thirteenth drawer, I found receipts with signatures. Some items were coded, the signatures obscured by magical wards. But I recognized those codes. They were identical to the ones the gnomes had used. I stuffed them into my pocket along with the other documents. Beneath the receipts were multiple sheets detailing a contract. I glanced through it, struggling to understand what I read. The words swam in my vision. The document oozed magic, the letters shiny gold and shimmering. I suspected they'd used manticore ink. Ingy would have known for certain. I could feel the bonds of the contract even though it wasn't mine, the link created between the signers. But I couldn't read it. I couldn't tell who signed it.

I closed my eyes and found the threads. I focused on the document in my hands. Two red lines, twined together, racing off into the world to join with others, one far distant, one no more than a hundred feet away. Gaunt, and who? I sent my mind racing along the line, following its path to the edge of Baltimore, faster, the world blurring as it passed by, trees and road and people gone as soon as they arrived. Time, time, I had no time for this.

The end approached and I slammed to a halt. A car raced along a concrete road, the face behind the steering wheel familiar. A smile crept over her features, and her eyes focused on mine.

"What did grammy Rowan tell you about following the threads? Tsk, tsk, that's some wicked dangerous magic. I'll see you soon, Mira."

Ben's Fjord. Hiems behind the wheel, heading towards Baltimore. She waved at me, and a hard push slammed into my head, shoving my mind away. The world blurred again.

I snapped into my body, gasping for breath. "That can't be," I said. "She saved my life. Why would she save me if she was involved in all this?"

"Why else, but to cover her tracks," said a male voice from the office behind me. "Now if you'd please come out here and join me, Mrs. Statton, we have a great deal to talk about."

28

Escaping the Raptor

Lucius Gaunt stood in the center of the office, smiling. The gun he pointed at me looked small, but as lethal as any other. I stuffed the contract in the pocket with the other documents before I turned around. I lifted my hands in front of my body, and stepped out of the safe room, stopping once I'd cleared the metal doors. Maybe I could bluff my way out of this. Small chance given I'd been caught red handed inside his safe.

"I'm so sorry, ambassador. This is embarrassing, but I seem to have gotten lost. My husband, Henry—"

"—is visiting the Holy Prussian Empire with the real Mrs. Statton," he said, interrupting me. "You are not her, and I should know. Mrs. Statton is a very good friend of mine. She's quite supportive of reducing the influence of the soulless on society and admires what my country has done in that direction. She plays a magnificent game of Bridge, too. The question is, who are you and why are you in my office? I'd like to know before I kill you."

Ingy, Lugnut and Petunia were listening. I only hoped they didn't

258

do anything Mira level of foolish and try to rush to the embassy. I had to handle this somehow. But I shook with the desire to pull my gun out of its strap on my leg and put a bullet through his thin skull, watch his gray matter spray across the room in a cloud of red blood. I knew I would be dead the moment I reached, but anger burned inside me, screaming for release.

"You killed Ben Templeton," I said. "You killed his friend, Lucky Gambini. And I'm going to see that you are tried, convicted and put on death row for your crimes."

"Ah, now I know who you are," he said, his smile widening. "You're the girl who was with him. The pathetic one who almost got trampled by a gnome's toy, and who let her boss get shot. I would have taken care of you sooner if I'd thought you were worth worrying about. Well, I suppose he didn't have many choices. It's hard to get good help these days."

I seethed with rage, and with the deep shame of agreeing with him. Yes, Mira Sinclair, the pathetic one. It fit. "You were working with the gnomes—"

"—I work with many people, some better and some much, much worse than you could ever imagine, girl. My business is wide and varied and I have my hand in many pots. But you wouldn't be here, skulking around my office and breaking into my vault, if you had any evidence. You have no proof of any wrong doing on my part, and we both know it. In the meantime, you have been caught breaking into an embassy, falsifying documents, and carrying a concealed weapon."

"The name is Mirabel Sinclair, not girl," I said. Not much as far as defiance went, but I worked with what I had. "I have documents tying you to the weapons manufacturing of the gnomes. And I will testify in court I witnessed you working with them in person."

He nodded his head. "You've got sand, I'll give you that. Miss Sinclair then. Would you be so kind as to remove the weapon you have?

Slowly of course, I get quite nervous around weapons." He chuckled and waved his gun.

"What weapon?" I asked, trying to sound confused. I wasn't the actress Ingy was, though.

He sighed and shook his head. "Disappointing. Your boss, Mr. Templeton, would have simply complied and not lied about it." He pointed his gun at my thighs. "You were able to find a way to smuggle a weapon into the place, and it's currently strapped to your leg."

My mind raced through the possibilities, but nothing come up. Instead of humiliating Gaunt, I appeared to be the one who would now be put on display as a criminal, tried and convicted, and likely executed.

The cloak drew my frayed attention, the patterns in the fabric once again trying to form recognizable symbols that never coalesced in my mind. "What do you use a shadow cloak for?" I said, more to myself than to Lucius Gaunt. I fingered the material. It slid against my skin like silk

"You don't need to know, Miss Sinclair. But it's worth a magical goose."

"The golden goose isn't yours; it belongs to the gnomes. Maybe it belongs to no one. Why do you need it, Gaunt?"

He waved the gun towards a large chair against one wall. "Sit down and you can tell me, assuming you do more than dress up for fancy parties. Certainly, we can chat like civilized individuals before I remove your life. I'm so tired of talking to the stuck-up rich assholes of Baltimore. These people are even more pretentious than we are."

I sat where he indicated, pulling the cloak into my lap. "You need the gold so you can pay for the weapons. But what are you doing with the weapons?"

"Look around you, Sinclair. All you see out those windows are the pain and suffering of thousands of beings whose lives are miserable. Cut short by humans who only care about their own greed and money. This building is filled with the rich, the powerful, and did you see anything but human wealth in there? A war is coming, a war they started and which the other races will most certainly end. Wars need financing, though."

Not convincing. It didn't jibe with what I know of the Empyrean, and therefore not likely to be the right answer. He shared a fiction, his monologue to explain all, and most people would accept it at face value. It was a lie. "No, that's not it. Not all of it, anyway. There's more to it."

"Yes? Well then, why don't you enlighten me, please?"

"You're arming dwarves and gnomes and trolls to get them to attack humans. When they do, humans will fight back. And everyone, even those who are tolerant, will support a crackdown, or at least not resist very much. You're starting a race war, one which you'll support from the north. You'll bring the Empyrean closer to the United Territories, and you'll gain control of lucrative trade deals your nation might otherwise not receive because you're slavers, and nobody really likes you at all, even if they are bigots."

He smiled. "Well, I'll have to revise my disappointment to almost respect. You might be smarter than I'd assumed."

"So, why'd you kill him?"

He stared at me with those yellow eyes, and smiled. "The truth?"

"Sure. What have you got to lose?"

"Nothing from the likes of you," he said. "Obviously I killed him because he knew too much about what was happening. I couldn't afford to have him stumbling around, getting involved in my little projects."

"You hired the Jacks to kill Mr. Gambini and Mr. Templeton."

He shrugged. "The witch gave me a good contact, one that wouldn't be tied to me or my country."

The witch. I flinched at the word, and remembered what I'd seen. "Hiems you mean."

Gaunt nodded. "Attractive girl. Too bad her blood is corrupt. Half human, half elf, nothing but a soulless half breed. But if she can bring me the goose, I'll give her that shadow cloak in exchange. Fair trade. I'll take care of her later and get my property back."

Half-breed; corrupt blood; her kind. I'd gone well beyond anger and fear now and drove righteous indignation into my voice. "You disgust me."

He snorted. "Be disgusted. You're white, you've got all the advantages in this country. You can afford it. Now imagine how a negro feels. A dwarf. A troll. Elves are going to end all that nonsense and we'll do a better job of keeping the peace when it's over. Nothing for you to worry about, Miss Sinclair. This is far beyond your level."

I *could* imagine. That's all I could do though. The advantage of being a woman perhaps, dealing with sexist men like Halley. The advantage of having friends who were trolls, quarter pixie. Of being in love with a black woman. It didn't take much at all to stretch, and though I might get things wrong, they remained my friends. For that I was thankful. I hardly deserved them.

What do you want me to do? Jacob asked, his voice cutting through my pity party. *Should I punch his kidneys?*

I need a distraction, I told him, and turned my attention back to Gaunt.

"Whatever you thought, it doesn't matter now," he said, pointing the gun at my head. "I can't have you spouting off to the press with your wild accusations and insane conspiracies. You won't be able to prove anything, but it wouldn't serve my needs to have the police or the F.B.M. poking around in my business. It's going to be hard enough to replace the gnomes."

"You won't kill me; you'd bring everyone running."

"Even if they could hear me through the sound proof barriers on this room, all they would see is the Ambassador to the Borealian Empyrean killing an intruder. Goodbye, Miss Sinclair."

The lightbulb exploded, and the room plunged into darkness. I threw myself to the right a split second before his gun flashed, the sound deafening, the bullet tearing into the fabric of the chair I'd been sitting in. I rolled, trying to tug the hem of my dress up so I could draw my gun as Gaunt shot twice more. The tang of gunpowder choked the air.

Good job, Jacob, I thought as I crawled across the floor, grasping the cloak in one hand. The thick carpet silenced my movements. My eyes began to adjust to the darkness.

"There are guards in the hallway, Miss Sinclair. There's nowhere for you to run."

I ignored him, sliding around the big desk and pulling my gun out of the holster on my thigh. I spared the cloak a glance, the swirling pattern of dark upon dark drawing my eyes to it. Even in the near blackness of the room I could see the pattern, the anti-darkness forming and reforming, endless shapes and figures. Something pulled at my neck, and I frowned. I gripped the medallion and looked at it, the green glow now bright and vibrant.

It tugged towards the cloak.

Crowded. So much of Templeton in here. Moments of his life. Moments stolen from him when he died, clutching his medallion in his hand. Son of a bitch. He'd put a part of himself in here, just like Rowan had put some in a jar on her mantle. My heart stopped.

The cloak shone like sunlight as I touched the medallion to it. The symbols moved faster and faster, breaking apart and reforming, and then my heart skipped a beat as the pattern became firmament, glorious, sparkling in iridescent colors to leap like glittering gems into the air, revolving around me like a solar system.

"What are you doing?" Gaunt said, the report of his gun sounding again. The bullet thudded into the desk that shielded me, and his weapon clicked as he cycled through empty chambers, cursing.

With my hand holding the medallion, I pulled the cloak around my shoulders.

The words from the scroll rose into my thoughts. Why didn't I ever have it translated? Lugnut would have done it for me if I'd thought to ask. But I'd recognized the words *shadow* and *stolen*. Shadow cloaks. Stolen moments. I could see the medallion in my hand, the cloak Saint Brendan wore across his back, so similar to this one. I rubbed Ben's medallion and closed my eyes against the brightness of a growing light.

I heard Gaunt's footsteps moving towards the door. "Guards!" he yelled.

They were too slow. My mind exploded in pain, like a dagger had been thrust through my skull, and the room expanded. The walls and floor and ceiling moved away from me in sparkling shards of color, racing towards an empty horizon.

I tried to scream, but when I opened my mouth the only sound that came was a whimpering, "Oh," and then darkness stole over my eyes.

29

The End of All Things

An infinitely long moment passed before I could see again. Existence became darkness, and there was nothing around me. Nothing to smell or feel or taste. Not even myself. The disembodied sensation seemed to last for eternity, and I fought growing panic as the universe stretched on and on forever. I wondered if this was what death felt like, an eternal nothing leading from nothing to nothing, a timeless void breaking a mind with its inescapabilty. I'd often felt sad for Jacob and his never-ending existence as a ghost, but this? This seemed worse. Nothing could match the realization the end would be endless nothing.

After a time stretching from the start of existence to the end of all things and the cosmic whimper of a universe's death, I perceived grayness. A fog swept around me; clouds came and went without noise or sensation. No wind pushed the mist. It moved and rolled in a silent parade of shifting shapes, began to form objects, only to break apart again.

A sound grew, a murmur of voices, muffled as though through

passing through a vast salty sea. I could not pick out words, though I strained to hear what they said. I had a notion they were talking about me.

Then feeling returned, my skin tingling with pinpricks of sensation. I curled my fingers and felt the palms of my hands, began to feel I no longer floated but rested on a hard, cold surface, like stone. I pressed my fingers against it, and whimpered with relief as solid reality returned. The world, and the shifting gray clouds of everything that formed nothing, became a dark room. My body lay twisted on a cold marble floor reflecting a wan, flickering light. The voices rose, climbing through thresholds of muted dimness to register as two people, speaking nearby.

"Do you think she'll wake soon?"

"Perhaps she will, Mr. Sticks. I still maintain she—"

"—She looks so peaceful, like a child—"

"—will not be capable enough to face what comes next."

The first voice crackled with laughter. "Nonsense, Chancy my good man. Well, not man perhaps, but you catch the drift I'm sure. She is a child, a waif, a creature of the day and night, two halves of a whole, yin and yang, ah . . . well . . . all that rot. But she was the only one who completed the riddle and made the trip. She didn't even need a trolley car."

I pushed against the floor and managed to rise to my knees.

"Ah, she wakens, Chancy!"

"I can see her, Mr. Sticks, I'm well aware."

"Always the glass half full with you."

I sat up, pressing my back against a cool wall next to me and took in my surroundings. Once more I found myself at the mausoleum I'd dreamed of, complete with the skeleton on the throne. He leaned forward, one elbow resting on an arm carved from stone, his hand pressed to his chin and cheek. His bones were dingy white marred with black spots, and on his skull rested a top hat that leaned at a precarious angle.

To his right stood the shadow man, his face visible, the rest of him merging with the darkness behind the throne, so only small parts of him were in sight at any given moment. His face severe, long, drawn down into a perpetual frown. His eyes narrowed beneath thick, wild black eyebrows shot through with strands of silver.

"Where am I?" I asked. I realized the cloak remained wrapped around my shoulders, and I yanked it off, balling it up in my lap. Beneath, I was dressed for detective work, the ball gown and leg strap replaced with workaday skirt, blouse, shoulder holster and trenchcoat. "What happened?"

"Welcome, Mirabel Sinclair," replied Mr. Sticks. "You are in our home, and we are pleased to have you visit us."

"Where is this place?"

"The end of all things," said Chancy. He stepped out of the shadows, dressed in black from neck to toe, resting his hand on the back of the great stone throne. "We wondered when you would arrive."

"What do you mean?"

"I must say, it's been a difficult time for us," he continued, ignoring the question. "Portents of danger and so forth, the ramblings of old babushka women in the market place as they read palms and stroked their crystals. But one ignores such things at one's own peril—"

"—Oh, would you stop babbling," Mr. Sticks interrupted. "She's obviously at her wits end, poor girl." He began laughing again. "She came to The End without her wits, her wit's end! How delightful!"

"I believe—" Chancy began.

"—You do—" Mr. Sticks said.

"—yes, I do," Chancy said. "Please stop interrupting me, Mr. Sticks."

"Bah, you're never any fun," said Mr. Sticks. "I don't know why I spend so much time with you."

"Because no one else will," said Chancy, "and because this is my crypt and I allow you the privilege of staying here."

The skeleton waved his hand in the air. "Oh, fiddle sticks, old man. Details, shmetails. The important thing is she's here now. Welcome, welcome. Are you tired? Hungry? Would you like a drink?"

I shook my head. "I need to get back and stop Hiems." Ingy, Lugnut and Petunia would be going crazy with worry, too. I prayed they would stay put. Wouldn't come after me.

The skeleton stood, his bones cracking as he stretched. "I'm as stiff as a board, Chancy. Sitting here waiting makes my bones ache."

"Quite," said the man in black, receding into the shadows.

"Send me back," I pleaded. "I know what I need to do now."

"Oh look, Chancy, she *knows*. Oh, isn't that precious. She is filled with the light of truth and knowledge."

Chancy stepped out in front of the throne. He was tall, far taller than anyone I knew with the exception of Lugnut and Mr. Green. His eyes were blue, sparkling with an inner light. "You know very little, Miss Sinclair. You have been led by the nose, allowed to fumble around like some messy child. You have equally been led to your conclusions by those with a vested interest in finding something of real value to their causes."

"The goose," I said.

"Perhaps. Or maybe power. Or revenge. Isn't that what you seek, revenge?"

Mr. Sticks bent over, tipping his oversized hat with his hand. "Oh, my dear friend, but you are scaring our visitor. Perhaps it is time she was getting on with her job."

"My job is to find the killer of Ben Templeton."

He leaned towards me, his empty eye sockets growing larger until his face became the only thing I could see. The scent of the crypt flowed from his breath, old moldy clothing and rotting flesh mingled with the musky odor of earth and decay.

"Your job is to find the golden goose. You were hired, you signed a binding magical contract, you spent the money, and you can no more quit the work than you could shoot your friends in the back. That is not your nature, it's his." He pointed behind him at Chancy.

"Sticks and stones, Mr. Sticks," said Chancy, looking aggrieved.

Mr. Sticks whipped around. "Tell me it's not true and I'll show you a dead parrot who can talk in Cantonese."

"It's not germane to our discussions—"

"—although it would be a neat trick, now that I think of it. I'll have to find me a parrot. Do we have any language dictionaries around here? Oh, never mind, I can teach it pig Latin."

"Enough!" I struggled to my feet, leaning against the wall for support. "If the goose is here, tell me where it is so I can get back to my city. My friends are in danger."

Chancy looked on me with sad eyes, his expression no longer stern and angry, but appearing as though he felt sympathy. It didn't feel like an improvement.

"You have the shadow of a doubt. You have a stolen moment. They will lead you to the goose. What you won't find is the peace you seek, Mirabel Sinclair. Even when you do find the murderer, there will be no peace."

"Just tell me which way."

He took my arm and strength flowed into me, my head clearing. His cold fingers gripped like a vice, and he pulled me away from the wall and guided me to an arched opening leading into the same cemetery I'd floated across in my dream. The gray headstones were worn and stained, some of them cocked sideways or lying on the ground.

"You are now on the border with dead Baltimore and living Baltimore. Follow Mr. Templeton's trinket. Wrap your hand around it and hold onto it tightly, it will show you the way through Baltimore's ghosts." He gave me a push, enough for me to take a few stumbling steps through the stone arch. "You will of course have to make your way through the trials before you find the treasure. Fail them, and you'll remain with us forever."

I turned to look back at him and found a blank wall, the archway gone. I placed my hands on it, feeling the rough surface of the stone.

"Well I guess there's no going back," I said, my voice muffled.

I picked my way through the gravestones until I reached a rusty iron fence covered with ivy that ringed the grave yard. I followed it to a gate falling off its hinges, and stepped into the dark night beyond.

My feet slapped against concrete, and I looked down on a sidewalk stretching left and right. The walkway bordered a street, and across the road stood a line of two-story row homes, with broken windows and boarded up doors. There were no cars and no people, no birds or rats. A few trees lined the walkway, devoid of leaves, gnarled branches reaching out into the foggy darkness to grope their way skyward.

The world had been cast in sepia tones, as though my eyes could only see it through a dirty diner window. There were tall poles spaced at regular intervals topped with the curving shape of sodium arc lamps, their glow wan, creating shadows instead of light.

My fingers wrapped around the metal surface of the medallion, and it pulled, the trinket quivering against my flesh. I took it from my pocket and curled my fist around it, holding my hand away from my body. I turned to the right, following the impetus of its desire.

"Lay on, McDuff."

The sound of my footsteps echoed off the derelict buildings around me, muffled, like listening through a blanket. I walked to the first cross street and glanced left and right, saw the same blighted buildings stretched to the limits of my vision. The medallion led forward without turning, so I continued.

Every block looked the same, and for a while I wondered if I were making any progress at all. Only when the road began to rise along a shallow incline did the repetitiveness fade, and I noticed features I recognized. A corner bar with broken panes of frosted glass on either side of the doorway. A home with a blue door, the paint peeling in long, ragged strips. A wrought iron fence, rusted and collapsing, framing a small patch of dead grass beside an alley next to a restaurant I'd often frequently. It was Canton, and I walked up Hudson Street, heading into Highlandtown on the east side of Baltimore. Not my Baltimore, though. There would be no Emery spreading its leaves in front of my door; no Ingy listening to Jazz music in the basement. This Baltimore was dead.

A breeze stirred against my cheek and tugged at my hair. I tasted mold and must in the breath of the city as it exhaled slowly. It crouched around me, its broad shoulders supporting the weight of concrete and brick, a sleeping giant that stirred as I trod upon its surface. It opened its one good eye to peer down at me through the gloaming laying over this place, the dark ass end of all things. Far above me, the half-awake face of the monstrous creature looked down, and I stared back at the red glow.

Natty Boh.

A tremor passed through the ground like a small earthquake, and I stood for a moment until it passed. It knew I'd come, waited for me. But the medallion urged me on towards it. I strode up the hill, the baleful color of hell spreading around me as I grew closer to the beast.

In the growing light, I could see faint figures now. Spectral floating forms moved along the sidewalk; wraith-like cars drifted down the street; phantom horses trotted in front of ghostly wagons. The crowd of phantoms grew heavier and thicker, and I tried to avoid stepping through them, unsure what I would feel, if the results would be the same as feeling when Jacob passed through you, the cold nearness of the dead leaving your flesh twitching.

I crested the hill and reached a large intersection. The activity of the ghosts converged near the hulking shape of the old National Brewery building, which rose eight stories to tower over the road. Figures went in and out of double doors opened to reveal a blackness that seemed absolute, no light escaping from the room beyond the entrance. Over the building, the eye continued to look across dead Baltimore.

Looking for me.

The medallion pulled me towards the dark doorway. "Figures," I mumbled. I approached it cautiously, watching the wraiths as they floated in and out of the building. I saw no way to avoid them in their tight bunches. I pondered the situation for a few minutes, and then pulled the cloak around my body and stepped into the moving line.

One of the figures brushed against me, its elbow pushing into my side as we jostled through the opening. "Sorry," I muttered, but the ghostly person didn't respond. I shuffled along and reached out, letting my hand touch the back of a shape in front of me, feeling solid contact. Another bumped me from behind, so I moved again, tucking my arms under the cloak and keeping them close to my body. I shifted with the line, feeling clumsy in comparison with the floating creatures.

The blackness inside engulfed me, and it blinded me. I stumbled along, swept into the building by the shuffle of specters around me. But the darkness dissipated like the passing of a cloud that had covered the sun. I could see a huge open area that made up the main floor of the long closed-brewery.

They were everywhere. Wraithlike figures passed by, some jarring my side, a swirl of bodies flowing around the room. Like watching a thick mist rolling in off the harbor, drifting between the long lines of brick houses, pulsing with the wind off the sea. The room itself seemed devoid of furniture. There were bits of trash and decay strewn around the floor, but nothing substantial.

The medallion yanked on my fist, lifting it towards the ceiling. I searched for a stairway to climb. Further into the chamber, I found a doorway, shimmering as thousands of ghosts passed between me and it. It appeared big enough to drive a truck through, and the specters near the doorway weren't as mobile. A crowd of them stood and stared at the dark area beyond. Something drew their attention.

I thrust my way through the crowd of ghosts and worked forward until near the front where I could see clearly. Past the doorway was another room, smaller than the one I stood in. Nothing seemed worthy of their rapt interest, so I angled through the last of the phantoms.

I smelled lavender. The fragrance caught my attention and I paused, taking a few small breaths through my nose, savoring the thick aroma. It reminded me of spring . . .

. . . the trees outside the convent blush with fresh green leaves, beneath which the purple flowers spread across the small garden the nuns maintain. I sit under the trees for hours, reading books with Ingy, enjoying our first warm days of the year, winter quickly forgotten. Dinner time pulls us reluctantly away, but before I retired to my bed for the evening, I walk alone under the branches once more, reaching out to touch the lavender blossoms, the smell of them clinging to me as I slide under the sheets. Summer is for exploring the city beyond the stone walls around the garden, immersing ourselves in the streets and the people. But spring is all about the lavender.

I stood in front of the doorway. I'd been standing there for a while I realized, a long while. I shook my head to clear my thoughts, took a step, exhaled deeply. When I inhaled again, I caught the scent of cranberries, and remembered . . .

. . . Thanksgivings at the convent, rows of girls in clean blouses and

black skirts sitting at long tables, heads bowed in prayer, the meal spread over white tablecloths. Someone always donates some turkeys to the orphanage, and the Sisters add stuffing and mashed potatoes, cornbread and peas, bought with the meager money they received from the church and private donors. But it is the canned cranberries I love the most, though Ingrid thinks real ones are better. I take a spoonful of sauce and place it on top of a piece of turkey, spreading it like jam over the meat so I can eat them both together . . .

"Damn it," I swore. I'd stopped again, and a great deal of time had passed while my mind drifted. My stomach rumbled and my throat felt parched. None of the ghosts nearest the entryway had moved, either, though some in the back came and went.

Now came the scent of freshly cut grass, and I recalled . . .

. . . hot summer days at Patterson Park, walking across the fields, taking a short cut to the library where I find a book, a mystery perhaps, and sit in the cool, comforting dark of a corner and read until it's time for the library to close. I check the book out and walk home, a first real home shared with Ingy, cutting across the grass, some of the blades clinging to my shoes. The sun sets in the west, the muggy air surrounds me, the breeze blows languid kisses against my sweaty skin. I hear the rumble of thunder in the distance, the sun blotted by dark clouds, and I hurry to get home before the rain begins, a cooler wind sweeping through the city streets as it approaches. I can't wait to see Ingy and bask in her presence, now that I've realized what I feel for her . . .

I gasped and nearly collapsed to my knees, tears rolling down my cheeks. My hunger had become a ravenous beast, my limbs weak. It had been hours—days perhaps—I'd stood here remembering the past, and I'd made no progress towards the doorway, though the medallion insisted I go forward. I tried not to breath, fighting the urge to suck in another lungful of air. I knew another smell would trigger a memory; another span of hours would be lost in the cage of the past. I couldn't hold it for long and I contemplated stepping away, but doing that would be to admit defeat.

The memory of the rain storm rang in the back of my thoughts, the breeze rolling before the heavy clouds unleashed their torrents. With the breath I had left in my lungs I whistled, the shrill sound biting through the closed space of the building. The city listened, and the city exhaled, and its breath surged up the street, swirled through the open doorway and across the great chamber. The wind swept across my body, my hair whipping into my face. It blew through the smaller entry before me. Dust stirred from the floor, black powder rising and racing around the room in circles.

The ghosts around me began to move.

My heart pounded and a ringing grew in my ears. I fell to my knees and gave up the game, unable to go any longer. I sucked in a huge lungful of air as the breeze slackened, died. No memory came, no thought took me away on a boundless journey of minutes and hours and days, lost in memories of falling in love with those places and people nearest my heart. I whistled again, soft this time, the wind of this Baltimore now slow and gentle, enough to keep the air flowing past, flowing into the room ahead. To keep the smells at bay, push them aside.

Then I rose to my feet and walked through the door.

30

The Watcher

The next room was not as high or large as the brewing floor, but seemed bigger with no ghosts crowding around me. To my left were multiple large doors leading to loading docks for the trucks and wagons that would have hauled away the beer for the thirsty citizens of the city. To my immediate right was a closed door. Saint Brendan guided me right and I stepped towards the dark gray rectangle, rubbing my thumb across the rough surface of the medallion as I mouthed words of detection. The door remained a plain, gray door. I opened it to find a stairwell beyond climbing towards the top of the building.

I withdrew my gun from the shoulder holster, wondered for a moment if it would work in this place. I shrugged and began to climb. I tried to ignore my pangs of hunger and thirst as I took the steps. I covered the corners as Ben had taught me, trying to focus through the empty rumbling in my stomach, or the way my hands shook from lack of food, lack of water, lack of rest. My boots rang dully on each step as I wound my way up six, seven, eight floors and reached the top landing.

Another gray door stood to my left, but that crafty bastard, Brendan, pointed towards a ladder which led up through a trap door. I tucked the gun and the medallion away. I pulled myself up the rungs, pausing at the top to catch my breath. The ankle ached again, and my gunshot wound throbbed in my side. Then I heaved against the trap door, inching it open until it fell to the side with an echoing clatter. I hoisted myself onto the roof and lay there, panting.

Something stirred. A cold shiver ran down my back. Metal strained, wood cracked, and something crunched, like the sound of chicken bones being snapped. I lifted my head until I could peer across the roof.

Natty Boh of dead Baltimore waited for me, a giant as big as the sign in living Baltimore. He sat with his legs crossed in front of him, his eye high above the roof and casting its fiendish light across the city. A puckered mound of scar tissue covered the hole where his second eye would have been. His hair was a thick, black mat; his moustache long and tangled; his chin covered in stubble. One hand held a bone and he lifted it to his mouth, bit down, the limb of some long dead creature splintering and cracking open. He smacked his lips as he sucked the marrow from it, then tossed it aside. He reached for another from the jumbled pile lying near him.

"S'good, bones good, but mo fresh is better," he said, the rumble of his voice shaking my body and the roof beneath me. "I hear mo fresh, I smell mo fresh. Talk to me, mo fresh, mo fresh, and tell me who you are."

"I am no one," I said, pulling the cloak tightly around my body.

"Am No One, mo fresh, but smells like someone." He felt around the roof, his fingers stirring through bones and rubble. "Tired of the dead, mo fresh, want fresh. Come, No One, let me taste."

The shadows shifted behind him. A line of specters, deep and wide, stretched back into the dark of the gloom, standing still as Natty reached towards them. His hand wrapped around one, lifting it, and he swung it hard. Its ghostly head dashed against the side of the building with a sickening crunch real enough to make my stomach clench.

He lifted the figure to his mouth and I caught a brief glimpse of it. Female in shape, its head a misshapen lump on its body, the front of its dress speckled with blood. I squeezed my eyes shut as he shoved it into his mouth and tried to ignore the sounds as the giant ate. My empty stomach roiled and churned. I tasted bile.

"Mo dead is good, s'good. No One is fresh, is better, s'good. No One should come out, mo fresh." He spoke in between the sounds of chewing and smacking, and I heard a wet thump on the roof in front of me. I pried open my eyes and peeked. The remnants of the ghost were almost solid now. A chunk of torso and bits of limbs, white bones jutting from the holes, blood oozing from each wound.

"Mo dead," Natty said, and he grabbed another figure, a man this time. Everything solidified. The ghosts became real. As the giant lifted him, I could see the trench coat and fedora, the five o'clock shadow on a square jaw, the outline of his nose, the crow's feet.

"Ben!" I rose to my feet, the cloak falling to the ground. The red eye of the giant swung towards me, casting me in crimson.

"There No One, you are. Mo better for me." He reached for me and I dodged, spinning around as the fingers brushed against my clothing. I swung around the trap door, putting myself out of reach of his grasping hand. He leaned forward, placed his free hand on the roof and pushed himself upright. He held onto Ben in his right hand as he stood, the roof groaning in protest under his weight.

"Pretty little No One, I see mo sweet flesh," he said, stepping forward. I moved back, sliding my feet over the loose, brown rocks which covered the surface of the roof until my ankles were pressed against the small lip of the wall running along the outside. Behind me, an eighty-foot drop; in front of me, a twenty-foot giant. Scylla and Charybdis.

He stepped forward and stumbled as his foot crashed through the open trap door. His out thrust hand smashed against the roof, close enough to knock me off my feet. I tumbled against the edge, the lip digging into my waist, my breath trapped in my throat and lungs as I stared down the dizzy fall to the street below. The dead floated in and out of the building in their miasmic pattern. The gun dug into my waist painfully, and I rolled away a moment before his hand slapped down on the spot I'd vacated.

I came up on my knees, drew my revolver, and aimed center mass. He reached again and I fired, the sound of the report tinny and echoing, the flash of the muzzle drowning out the wash of his red eye for an instance. A small hole appeared in his chest, but on he came. This time I moved too slow, his scabby fingers grabbing the bottom of my jacket.

He yanked me off my feet, and I dangled fifteen feet over the roof. I lifted my arms above my head, the sleeves turning inside out as I slipped free and fell with a hard crack. Fire shot through my left ankle. I screamed as I fell to my back. The bullet wound flared in pain as well. All my myriad injuries and insults swept through me. I screamed again, my voice dying as it left my lungs. I managed to keep a grip on the revolver as scrambled towards the corner of the roof, my elbows and heels pushing me along, tiny rocks digging into my skin through my pants.

He tugged his leg free from the hole, sending a shower of roof material down into the stairwell. He took one lumbering step towards me and bent over, reaching to grab again. The red eye swam in my vision until it was my world entire. His fingers wrapped around my body and squeezed. My lungs emptied of breath, and my bones creaked as pressure grew. He pulled me towards his open mouth.

I lifted my arm and aimed, put the final shot I'd ever take through the great red orb of Natty Boh's one good eye. Here's looking at you, Natty.

A gush of blood and fluid poured from the wound. The monster bellowed, letting go of me as he clapped a hand over the ruin of his eye. I crashed onto the roof once more. He staggered, his screams drowning out the possibility of any other sound, until his foot stepped into the hole again. Then he tumbled, his arms going up, the ghostly body of Ben Templeton sent flying. The giant smashed down onto his back. The roof gave up the fight, steel beams snapping like twigs under the weight of his fall. A massive hole appeared around him, and his body fell through the gap into the space below. Dust rose out of the yawning chasm, and the building shuddered.

My eyes followed the arc of Ben as he sailed across the roof and hit the lip, his legs slipping over the eight-story abyss. One ghostly hand caught the edge of the building and he held on, swinging off the side of the brewery.

I scrambled, dragging my leg behind my, biting my lip against the pain. Fresh blood trickled down my side. His fingers slid, the tips slipping to the edge of the brick and I leapt towards him awkwardly, reaching out. Stretching. His hand lost its grip. I caught him around the wrist, hanging off the roof myself. I splayed my legs wide, my knees pressed against the inside of the low lip, but I lacked the strength to pull him up.

"Mr. Templeton, please, you need to grab me with your other hand. You can climb."

The face met mine, revealing a glint of blue in those ghostly irises, his lip curling in a smile I remembered well. "I told Chancy and Sticks you'd come. It's good to see you, Mira. How's the case going?"

"Please, Mr. Templeton, pull yourself up to me. I can't hold you." Even as a ghost, he weighed too much. My body slid, the pebbles beneath my knees crunching as I tried to widen my stance. My waist slipped a half inch, then another, putting me closer to my tipping point and the long tumble to the hard pavement below.

"I read all the signs and portents. Knew this is how it would end." He lifted his free hand, but didn't grab mine. He tipped his fedora back and looked down, then into my eyes. "You were always my rock, did you know that? Best thing I ever did in my life was help you. You've hung on to me too damned long, Mira; it's time to finish the mystery and catch the killer. Not like Nancy Drew, though. Like I taught you. Let me go."

Tears wet my cheeks and I shook my head, gulping at the air as I strained. "No, no, Ben . . . please . . . grab me, I can help, I can save you this time. I won't let you go . . . I won't."

"You're a good kid. The one thing I was ever good at was seeing the truth of someone. I could tell good from bad. You've been ready a long time. It was me who wasn't ready. It's just that, well, I love you, like a daughter. You and Lucky and Petunia were the closest thing to a family I ever had. Then someone took Lucky from me. I couldn't lose you, too."

"Please, Ben." Sweat slicked my palms and my grip faded. "Give me your other hand."

"I don't need saving, kiddo. I'll be watching you; all you do is whistle up a wind like Petunia taught you. Hell, she learned it from me. Let me go, Mira."

I slipped again; my balance changed. I knew I would fall. I squeezed my eyes shut, and whispered, "I'm sorry." But, before I could let go, his hand slipped free.

"Nothing to be sorry about, kiddo."

I kept my eyes shut, couldn't watch the fall, holding back a scream of anger and terror by biting my tongue. I waited until enough time had passed, but heard no sound of a body slapping wetly against unyielding concrete. When I opened my eyes, he had vanished, along with the rest of the ghostly figures. Dead Baltimore had become dead again. As dead as my boss had been when my hands caught his cold, ghostly wrist. The dead are always with us, but not really there.

I pushed myself carefully onto the roof. The pains returned, and I hissed as I rolled onto my back. "I have to finish." I said to the empty city, wiping away the tears. I set my jaw and slowly stood. Everything hurt equally bad.

I stared into the dark maw of the hole, and my mouth fell open in surprise. The body of the giant had gone with the ghosts, except for the debris left in the wake of his collapse. A small object sat on the rubble where he should have been, glowing with silver magic.

"Son of a bitch."

31

The Cavalry Arrives

The goose sparkled with an inner light. From above, it seemed real, as though it would begin to walk and talk at any moment, though it glowed with strong magic. I lay down on my belly, twisting my way carefully over the lip until my legs dangled free. I paused to grit my teeth, then slid down a sloping piece of roof onto the landing below the hole. I hit the floor with a brief cry when pain shot through my ankle. I lay for a moment, panting, waiting for the electric jolt of agony to fade, then turned onto my belly and crawled to the artifact.

Closer, I could see the outside shell was an illusion. The form came from a filigree of delicate metal, a latticework shaped in the image of a goose. White gold for the feathers, yellow gold for the beak and feet. Two black opals comprised the eyes. Even without the magic powering it, it was worth a fortune as a piece of art. You could have auctioned it for millions. But the magic made it so much more than a piece of bric-a-brac. Beneath the metalwork was a shiny blob of quicksilver producing the white glow. On its surface, above the eyes, swam strange symbols, unreadable to me. Gnomish perhaps, another language I didn't know. How little I knew, how much a case turned on lucky guesses and chances of fate. The help of others, living and dead. Lugnut. Petunia.

Ingy.

"No one can do it alone," I said to myself. No one could protect everyone else, either. But Ben had tried every bit as hard to protect me as I'd tried to protect Ingy since he'd left us. Age doesn't always bring wisdom.

I sat upright, stretching my damaged leg in front of me. I held the medallion over the goose, dangling from the end of its chain. My eyes closed. I dredged up incantations from muscle memory, hidden words engraved in my soul, verses I'd not learned but knew. I felt the tangled skeins of dead Baltimore around me, threads winding around and through each other, and I followed them, my mind racing along paths and angles, plucking and pulling.

The goose had no thread, a dark blot in the vast gray web of connections. No spooks or grindy in this Undertow, nothing but pulsing beats of magic traveling along the lines, cells firing in a giant, dead brain. There were no hidden traps, no security of any kind beyond the giant who had protected it, the memories holding it, the dead world surrounding it. I stopped speaking, and my vision returned to the end of all things.

"Hello beautiful," I said, picking up the artifact. Beneath it, crushed into the dusty debris, lay a single, fat, golden egg.

"Holy hell." I picked the egg up. I thought it would weigh more than it did. Heavier than a normal large egg, but less weight than my revolver. I brushed the dust off its surface and slipped it into a pocket.

The goose didn't weigh much, but it was bulky. I laid it on my lap, tucked the medallion away, and holstered the revolver. I ran my hands over the filigree surface of the goose, feeling the ridges, staring at the light from the silvery fluid beneath. The liquid seemed to glow brighter, and I squeezed my eyes shut, the piercing light filtering through my eyelids with a red haze. There came a familiar twist and pull, as though I were visiting the Undertow. My stomach tied in knots, and then the light faded again.

I opened my eyes, blinking, an after image of the goose clouding my vision and fading slowly. I caught a whiff of the ocean mingled with the scent of gasoline and manure, heard the murmur of engines, the punctuation of a horn blaring, a horse whiney. As my eyes adjusted, I looked out over the bright lights of living Baltimore from the roof of the brewery. The roof had been made whole again, and my body bathed once more in the red glow from his one great eye as the Natty Boh sign loomed above me, casting its inanimate gaze over the city. I wore the party gown, my gun strapped to my leg, but the goose remained in my lap, as beautiful as when I'd first seen it.

Then I cried. I hugged that hunk of magic metal and sobbed until my breath came in wracking hitches. It had been long overdue, I knew that. I'd held back too long all the grief of Ben's death, the sadness over Ingrid moving out, my agony over every wrong choice I'd made. Like a hard rain, a good cry cleared things right out, at least briefly, though it didn't solve a single one of my problems. Ingrid I'd at least ironed some of the wrinkles out. But Hiems was still on her way. Ben was still dead. Lucius Gaunt still ran free.

Jacob arrived in a flurry of wind and plunging temperatures. His thoughts were a tangled jumble of imagery running on in a long stream.

"Whoa, slow down Jacob. I'm fine." I considered for a moment. "Well, not fine, but I'm okay at least. How'd you find me?"

He suggested he had his own way of checking threads. When I'd disappeared from Gaunt's office along with my thread, he'd assumed the worst. I'd been killed. He'd gone to find Ingy, Lugnut and Petunia, and the four of them had been deciding what to do next.

"You spoke to them?"

He paused, and radiated chagrin. *I could have talked to anyone if I'd wanted too, but it seemed more trouble than it was worth. The living are usually annoying.*

"You and I are going to have a talk about things later."

Why'd you take a powder?

"I figured out the puzzle. It led to the end of all things"

He got quiet, and if not for the temperature, I'd have thought he'd left. *You met them.*

Not a question; a statement. "Yeah, I met Chancy and Mr. Sticks." I didn't tell him I met Ben, too, and Natty Boh. We didn't have time for details. We could do that later, if we survived. I was a broken shell of a woman, wounded and hurting. Hiems was close to Baltimore. I could see it when I checked the threads. "You need to go get the others. Hiems is on her way here and she'll want the cloak. We can't give it to her."

Coming here? Jacob asked. *I thought she was a friend?*

"There's no time to explain, just go get them, please. Hurry!"

He floated for a few ticks. Then his resolve hardened and he went, a tiny cyclone of debris stirred into a lazy circle as he raced away. I lay on the roof and closed my eyes, gritting my teeth at the throbbing pain pulsing through my ankle, my abdomen. I let the city talk to me. The cars on the street, distant voices shouting, the buzz of an engine as an airship cruised over the harbor. The scent of a bakery, and the cotton candy aroma from the sugar refinery on the harbor. Baltimore had a language all its all, and its lifeless counterpart could never compare, even if it had ghost wagons and giant guardians. "Natty Boh was an evil, marrow eating giant watching over a dead city. Christ, Mira, will you ever handle a weirder case?"

When my body began to shiver, I sat up. I tugged off my flats, releasing a fraction of the pressure from the swollen ankle. Rubbing it didn't help the pain, and there was nothing to do but bear it. I rolled onto my knees and struggled to stand.

Fresh fire shot through my ankle and I almost fell, which sent another dagger through my side. I held myself upright through the sheer power of gritted teeth, most of my weight on the right ankle. I slowly bent to pick up the artifact, hand pressed against the bullet wound. In the dark shadows beside it lay the cloak, bundled in a ball. I took the soft fabric, wrapped it around the goose, and tied the ends around my neck to make a sling for it. On a whim, I checked my pocket. Among the matt of folded papers, I felt the shape of the egg. It had come to real Baltimore as well. Then, grimacing, I limped and hopped over to trap door. I had to move some boards pressed against it, but once the door opened, I sighed with relief to see the stairs leading down into the gloom. "Only a ladder and eight flights of stairs until I can get to the bottom."

The ladder taxed me, but those eight flights took forever. I had to stop and rest at each landing. The ankle wouldn't support any amount of weight, and I leaned heavily on the banister as I hopped down on the opposite foot. The goose thumped against my back painfully with each step. Sweat dripped off me by the time I reached the bottom. The dress had acquired a lot of stains, and a tear along the bottom hem. Damn it. Now I'd have to pay Petunia for it. I had little left from the down payment Mr. Green had provided, but the golden egg bounced heavy in my dress pocket. Hopefully we'd get enough out of it to pay off the tab for this case.

At the bottom, I held the rail and sank onto the second to last step, my leg out in front of me. I rested the ankle, biting my lip against my need to groan in pain. Jacob should have returned by now, but the room remained a steady, if autumnal, temperature. I needed the cavalry. At this rate, it would be an hour before I got to the nearest phone box and convinced dispatch to send someone to deal with the crazy woman spouting off about elven diplomats and gnomes and magic geese and nasty old witches. Young witches. Whatever. I wouldn't have believed it, and I'd lived through it.

With a groan, I stood and forced myself to hop to the door. I opened into the loading dock area, more light spilling through broken windows. Beyond lay the chamber of the brewing room, the city's pale, orange glow showing it empty but for some trash and debris. It seemed like a long way across the main floor to reach the exit, with nothing to brace my weight. I'd have to hop again. Maybe I'd try crawling. I leaned against the doorway to the loading dock, steeling myself for the journey.

I'd taken one shaky hop, teeth gritted, when the front door crashed open. Lugnut tumbled into the room, falling to the ground in a heap as the door slammed against the wall. A thick, metal chain tinkled across the floor, broken where it had snapped under the force of the blow from his shoulder. Ingrid followed a few steps behind him. She held the glowing baseball bat in her hands, and her eyes were black mirrors.

"Mira!" Lugnut cried, scrambling to his feet as I slumped to the floor. Honestly, I was just so damned relieved I wouldn't have to carry myself further. I even laughed a little as I sat. He raced to my side and slid to his knees, wrapping me in his arms.

"Okay, okay, ease up!" I said, as he squeezed fresh pains into me. "I'm not dead yet. Just back from there in fact."

"Are you okay?"

I nodded. "Just my wounds acting up. But I killed the giant, so it was a square deal."

"Giant?" Lugnut asked.

"Natty Boh," I said.

"Natty Boh?" Lugnut asked.

"Natty Boh the giant," I said.

"Natty Boh is a giant?"

"Yes, Natty Boh is a giant."

"Natty Boh, the beer mascot, is a giant?"

"A giant who eats the dead at the end of all things, yes."

"Natty Boh is a—"

"—It's a long-damned story," I said. "I'll tell it all when this is over. Where's Petunia?"

"She's waiting down the street with the car," he said. "I told her to stay put. Didn't want her to get hurt. She almost wouldn't listen to me."

I understood that. I patted him on the arm. "You're a good egg, Lugnut. But in the future, let her decide, okay?"

Ingrid stood over me, the heat of her anger a bonfire. Oh, how beautiful when she was angry. Beautiful and terrifying. "Where's Gaunt?" she said, her voice unrecognizable, the sound of an animal about to spring on its prey.

I shook my head. "Not here. I left him back in his office when I escaped. Bastard caught me trying to find evidence. I must have missed a hidden alarm in his office. But he's not the only one we need to watch for. This was all set up by Hiems."

"Hiems?" Lugnut asked. "I thought she saved your life."

"She did," I said, "but I'm pretty sure she did it to cover her own tracks and get me to get her the shadow cloak. She's the one who told Gaunt about the Jacks. She's been working with him all along."

The click of a gun being cocked drew our attention to the doorway. "I knew you weren't as dumb as you seemed," said Hiems, framed by the street lights outside.

32

Blowdown in the Brewery

Ingy took several brisk steps in her direction, lifting her bat. Hiems waved a hand at her, speaking one word of power. Ingy froze, her face contorted in a mask of rage, the bat quivering in her hand. "Stay there," Hiems said, and walked past her, patting her cheek.

"Does Rowan know everything you've done, Hiems?" I asked. I pushed myself away from Lugnut and stood on my own, trying to appear tougher than I felt.

Hiems shook her head. "Grammy Rowan told you the truth. Well, her truth at least."

"You're working with Lucius Gaunt, a man who would as soon bury you in a shallow grave as give you the time of day," I said. Trying to goad her. Trying to cut into her perfect smile and steady hand.

"Lucius doesn't matter," Hiems said. "He was a means to an end and it was expedient to work with him up until this point."

"You had part of what the other needed," I said, taking a hopping step towards her, but keeping my hands up to appear nonthreatening. "You had a scroll pointing to the location of the goose, and he

290

had the shadow cloak Rowan had asked for. You helped him contact the Jacks, and he used them to commit murder. You killed the Jacks when you feared I'd uncover the whole plan." I left off she had used me. I had enough damning me already without the need to admit that last out loud.

"Nothing but the truth now, is that what we're doing here, Mira?" she asked.

"You're a powerful witch," I said. "Why didn't you go take the shadow cloak from him? Why'd you hire humans?"

Her smile dropped and her eyes narrowed. "He may be a waste of air, but Lucius and his country aren't entirely stupid. They'd have detected me before I got through the doorway, what with my—how do they put it—tainted blood."

"So, you double crossed Gaunt," I said. "The irony is neither of you knew the shadow cloak opened the way to the goose. You should have trusted each other and worked together."

She laughed. Hiems' voice when I first met her had been light and airy, a breathy sound tickling the ear. It sounded deeper now, a knife to cut through the heart, make someone love and loathe her at the same moment. "He double crossed me first. He made sure Lucky Gambini had an unfortunate accident after I hired him to find the goose for me. Then he killed your boss. He's really the man you're after, not me."

I kept my voice under control, my words flat and even. Ticking them off like reading a grocery list. "You hired Lucky to do the dirty work, and Gaunt used the Jacks to kill him when he discovered his little weapons factory. You knew Lucky's death would pull Ben in and you'd get a free run at the cloak and the goose again, so you sent Mr. Green to hire us so Ben wouldn't know you were involved. But Gaunt had him killed, too."

"Almost got you as well," she said, grinning.

"Almost," I said in agreement, but didn't return the smile. "When

I came to Maine, you made me wait for you in the library lobby while you went in and out of the back room. You called the Jacks on one of those trips, figuring you'd cover your tracks. You killed the last one to give me a reason to trust you. I was another chance to get the goose so you could trade it for the cloak without dirtying your hands. Then you loaded me up like a bullet in a gun and aimed me when you gave Rowan the paper, folded nice as you please to Gaunt's name."

She shrugged. "You fell for it."

I nodded. "Yeah, I did. Then you sent some grims to kill me on the train ride."

She shook her head. "No, that was Lucius. Trying to kill those damned gnomes, cover up his own incompetence. I needed you to get back to Baltimore. You were primed and ready to get the goose for me. Lucius unintentionally gave you all the motivation you needed. All I had to do was point you the right direction." She pointed her finger like a gun. "Bang."

I took another limping step towards Hiems, and she cocked her head as she watched. "You're a mess, doll. Is your bullet wound still giving you pain?"

"I've had worse," I said, with a bravery that didn't match how the pain that coursed through my body.

"Good, I wouldn't want you to die until you've had a chance to see the results. After all, you were an integral part of it." She tilted her head again, her eyes sliding up and down me. I shivered under her gaze. "Yes, you would have made a fine season, Mira. Grammy Rowan was right about that. It's almost a shame to have to kill you and your friends."

"What I really want to know," I said, cocking my head, "is why."

She walked in a slow circle around us, moving away from the door. "Rowan wanted to hide us away from the world. Like the tribes did when their lands were stolen, moving their entire existence someplace else, living outside of time. But she never asked what any of the rest of us wanted. That isn't a life. I'm not going to hide who I am, or what I am. I'm not going to let the bigots and racists win and send us fleeing into exile. You want what I want, too, I can tell. All of you. Haven't you been pushed around enough by those who think you less than they? Who call you half-breed, piano movers, soulless?" She paused and nodded at me. "Tell you that you're nothing but a woman?"

I nodded. "Yes. But I wouldn't murder to make it happen. I wouldn't help an elf start a war that will kill a lot of innocent people."

"Innocent?" she asked. She laughed then, a sound that broke into a half sob of anguish at the end. "No one is innocent if they tolerate a system that oppresses people. They might not be enslaving us anymore, but they sure as hell aren't doing us any favors, either. Everyone is complicit. Everyone is guilty."

"This is not the way," I said, shaking my head. I would have told her what the right way was if I'd known it. But I couldn't see the way forward any more clearly than she could. It probably wasn't my place to say anyway, only my place to help us get there when folks found out. I only knew killing people to prove the rightness of her point wasn't the path leading to the result she sought. The opposite in fact. It would hurt the people we loved most.

"It's my way," she said. "I'll follow it until it's done. Now that you've brought me the cloak, I don't need to give Lucius the goose. The cloak alone would have allowed me to break free of Rowan and go my own way. Now the goose will give me all the cash I need to bring others over to my side. You can join me, too, or you can die."

I opened my mouth to speak, but Hiems fired her pistol before I could. I flinched, waiting for the blossom of pain through my flesh, the trickle of blood to begin, but I felt nothing. Instead Lugnut fell backward, his body doubling over as he collapsed to the floor.

I reached to draw my own revolver, but Hiems aimed the muzzle at me again. "No, no, you won't need your weapon. Besides, that won't keep your friend down for long, I only winged him. Pull your gun out slowly, keep your finger off the trigger and toss it aside."

I got this, Jacob said.

"The revolver," Hiems repeated.

"Mira, don't," Lugnut said in a low voice.

"I have to." I carefully hitched my dress and pulled the gun from its holster, holding the handle with two fingers and my thumb, letting it dangle. When Hiems nodded to the left, I tossed it over there, watching it slide across the floor and smack up against a wall.

A flurry of dust rose around Hiems, a cyclone engulfed her. The temperature went sub-arctic as Jacob tried to attack her, knock her down, squeeze her organs. Debris spit from the cloud, pelting me, and I covered my face to protect my eyes. I moved in the direction I'd thrown my gun, staggering, falling to my knees in pain and crawling. If I could get to it, I could end this, put a bullet in the woman who'd taken so much from me already. Stop her from taking more.

But she proved too strong for Jacob. Her voice cut through the wind, deep and clear, one simple word ringing in the air like a bell. The swirling cloud around her froze, particles suspended in the air, and Hiems stepped clear of it, brushing off her dress with her free hand. The gun came around and aimed at my skull. "You don't need to crawl for me. Join me."

Slowly I stood, gritting my teeth against all the pains running through my body. I brushed my hair back from my face, and turned my eyes on hers. "I don't crawl for anyone."

"Good. Now where's the goose?" Hiems said.

"It's here."

"Show me."

I unslung the cloak from my shoulders and held it loosely in my hands, feeling the weight of the goose tugging on the fabric. Before I could toss it, Lugnut rose and stepped forward, moving towards Hiems with raised fists.

"Bullets can't kill me," he growled when she pointed the gun towards him.

She pulled the trigger and the gun howled. Smoke and fire belched from the muzzle, and Lugnut dropped to his knees with a scream of pain. Dark red blood leaked from around his fingers, which he held clamped down on his leg.

She sneered at him, and for the first time her beautiful face became twisted and ugly. "Did you really think the seventh daughter of a seventh daughter, the niece of an elven lord, a witch of the dark deep, a disciple of Rowan and one of her seasons would come unprepared? I've kept a close eye on sweet Mira and her friends; I knew who'd she sacrifice."

It stung more than I cared to admit. She knew right where to twist the knife. My fear of putting the ones I loved in danger, of losing them because of my choices. But she'd picked the wrong word. They weren't sacrifices. I'd never do that to anyone. I'd sacrifice myself first.

Lugnut launched himself from the floor and rushed at Hiems, limping on his blood-stained leg. She casually raised her free hand. The door slammed open and a wind caught him, lifting him high overhead, his body a piece of straw in a gale. He crashed into a wall, the sound a sickening crunch, and fell to the floor not far from where I'd thrown my gun, lifeless.

She turned back to me, the evil face gone, smoothed away. A consummate actress. The movie starlet smiled at me once more. "Toss me the cloak and the goose."

I complied. The cloak fell next to the witch, who bent over and shook it out until the goose fell with a clatter to floor. Then she wrapped the shadow cloak around her shoulders and tied it off at her neck.

"Thank you, Mira," she said. She even smiled sweetly, the bitch.

"What now? The blood of a virgin?" Ingrid had spoken. She walked towards Hiems, stalking her. Ingrid's eyes were made from the night sky, her pupils filling the white spaces until nothing remained of them. No moon or stars or galaxies, an empty void.

"You've got some skills I see," Hiems said, turning the gun towards Ingrid. "Not many folks could get out of a binding so quickly." She lifted the muzzle and pulled the trigger.

Nothing happened.

She squeezed again, but the gun remained silent in her hands. She snorted in disgust and tossed it aside. "I'll grant you've got talent, girl. But you're no season."

"No," Ingy said. "But I sure will enjoy killing one." She raised her hand as Hiems did the same, locking eyes. The lights outside began to flicker and I could feel the tangle of forces wrapped around the brewery, flowing between the two women as they faced each other. The glass in one of the windows shattered, shards exploding outward. A rain pelted in on a driving wind and howled through the structure.

I went for my gun again, falling to the ground and scrambling on my knees.

"You're weak, girl," Hiems said. She drifted closer to Ingrid now, her feet not moving. The gap between them shrank, the space growing smaller without either woman having to take a step forward. Ingrid's brow furrowed, and she lifted both arms outward as Hiems closed the distance.

Hiems gun was closer and I grabbed it. I whistled at the wind, guiding it against her. Her dress whipped around her like a dervish. Hiems laughed through clenched teeth, waggling a finger at me. Her spell threw me against a wall, my head cracking against the wood.

"Wait your turn," she said, and bore down on Ingy, who leaned back, her body shaking. Her eyes had lost their black sheen and her face twisted with the effort she made.

Ingy. My Ingy. I couldn't lose her, too.

I aimed at Hiems and squeezed the trigger, but nothing happened. I checked the mag, found it half loaded, thumbed the safety off and on, pulled the trigger again. Nothing. Whatever Ingy had done, it protected Hiems as well. I glanced around, desperate to think of something, anything to help. Anything to save Ingy at the very least, even if I'd to lose my own life.

My eyes fell upon the goose, lying on its side on the floor. I crawled to it, and beneath the delicate lace of metal found the gnomish lettering, engraved on the silver jacket below. Above its eyes a symbol, three curling slashes joined at the center. Like Tim's construct, with the word EMET on its forehead, the bullet obliterating the letters and the magical creature falling to pieces in front of me.

"Hiems!" I screamed, pointing the gun at the goose's face.

The witch spared me a glance, and her eyes widened. "Wait—"

I interrupted the rest of her sentence by pulling the trigger. Hot lead ripped through the delicate, lattice frame of the goose. Fragments of metal tore into my hand, but the pain barely registered over all the rest. The headless body of the ancient artifact skittered across the floor in a shower of sparks, smoke rising from it. The two eyes rolled in opposite directions until they stopped and began to steam, melting into small obsidian puddles. They steamed as they evaporated.

"You stupid girl!" Hiems released Ingy, who fell to the floor coughing. She moved but didn't move, one moment standing over Ingy, the next grabbing my throat, as though she existed in both places and neither. Her hand was tipped with ragged red fingernails like claws, her face slashed with white lines. She opened her mouth and a green mist came out, wrapping its tendrils around my head, constricting me, choking me. I gagged and found the air gone, sparks flickering at the edge of my vision as my eyes began to roll into the back of my head.

"Run," I choked out to Ingy, barely a whisper. "Ingrid . . . go . . ." The world dimmed, and through the dark cloud the mausoleum appeared, faintly at first, but growing steadily and inexorably firmer and more real as living Baltimore faded. The door opened, and in the gloaming beyond I could see Mr. Sticks on the throne, Chancy's gaunt face gazing over the skeleton's shoulder as they waited for my arrival.

"What now, Mira?" Mr. Sticks asked. "You missed us? So soon to return to our charming companionship?"

"I do believe she is dying, Mr. Sticks," Chancy said, stepping out of the shadows as he watched me. "Perhaps she was not ready after all."

"The thing's not decided yet," Mr. Sticks said. "Watch this next bit; it's a doozy."

A crash and a cry of rage, of pain. The hand released me, and I fell to my knees, coughing as Hiems wheeled again. The mausoleum faded, and I heard the last murmur of Mr. Stick's voice as it disappeared, a faint echo across a wide gulf. I thought he said, "Batter up!"

Lugnut stood behind Hiems, wielding Ingy's baseball bat. His right pants leg had soaked black with blood as he swung again. Hiems right arm lay limp at her side, and I thought the elbow was cocked crookedly. She raised her left hand, and the bat stopped inches from the side of her skull, quivering with the force he'd put behind the swing. Lugnut's muscles strained to move the weapon, his face contorted in anger.

"You pitiful thing," Hiems said, "you don't know I'm trying to free your people from persecution." She flicked her fingers. Lugnut rose, accelerating towards the ceiling.

Lugnut released the bat and grabbed something at his waist. "Mira, catch!" he screamed, tossing a black object at me a moment before his head hit the roof high above with a crack. He fell, his body as limp as a ragdoll, and crashed into a stack of rotting pallets with the sound of splintering wood.

The object bounced and skittered across the floor. I scrambled for it and wrapped my fingers around the comforting weight of my revolver. I relished the heft of it as it molded to my hand. I turned in a circle on my knees, my left hand scrapping the dust and dirt into a ring around me, and then pointed the gun at Hiems. I pulled the trigger and received a click in return, though I could see the cylinder was loaded.

Hiems tossed her head back and laughed. The wind faded and the rain slackened. "All your steel can't stop me. Go ahead, pull the trigger on another misfire. If you won't join me, I'll rip you apart, tear your soul asunder, never to rejoin. You'll be less than a ghost; you'll be nothing, not even dead. You will be no one."

No one. I'd already been no one, had felt like no one all my life. *No one is ever ready*, Mr. Templeton had said to me when this all started. Natty Boh called me no one. Something in me hardened, molten steel at last cooling and reaching its final form. I found words, dredged them up from somewhere deep inside. Things I needed to say, to tell the world that so used and abused us.

"I went to the End of All Things. I traveled through dead Baltimore. I killed Natty Boh, the giant who guards the city and devours its ghosts. I have met the Watcher and survived his attention, and I was taught by Baltimore's greatest detective, who was like a father to me. I have been shot, beat, burned, cut, and scarred forever. Yes, I *am* No One, mo fresh."

I grabbed the threads, the skein of the world, traced the one touching the bullet, the silver-jacketed and symbol-marked round that would click into place beneath the hammer when I pulled the trigger. I hooked the line of it, cast it out, tied it to Hiems' dark red line with a pretty little knot, like a ribbon around a Christmas package.

I aimed and squeezed the trigger.

The sound of the gun echoed through the room, my hand rocking back with the kick, fire and smoke belching from the barrel. The bullet took her in the heart, the .38 caliber slug ripping through her.

Hiems eyes shot open, staring down at the hole in the front of her dress, growing quickly dark with blood. Her hands slapped over it as though to hold back the flow. "What did you do?" Her voice sounded so small, so afraid. A child's voice. Her eyes met mine, afraid, lost. I almost felt a moment's pity until I remembered all she'd done.

"What I had to do."

She began to shudder, faster and faster, a wail escaping from her lips as she tossed her head back and spread her arms wide. Louder the voice grew, and I covered my ears with my hands. Glass shattered, the remaining glass in the windows of the brewery blowing out as her scream climbed through resonant frequencies to rattle the very foundations of the building. Then it stopped, cut off like a siren in mid-wail. She pitched forward onto her face and went still.

Legs appeared at the corner of my vision, sheathed in a long black dress. I glanced up through watering eyes and Ingy stared back at me. She had dark patches beneath her eyes, and her hand shook as she squatted and touched my shoulder.

"Are you going to live?" she asked.

There were more pains to add to the litany of injuries I'd suffered. I mentally assessed my condition and decided that yes, I'd probably live, more's the pity. I shrugged my reluctant acceptance of the cruelty of the universe and nodded to let Ingy know I'd survive. "Is it over?"

"It's over," Ingy said. "She's dead."

Then she hugged me, so hard it would have squeezed water from a stone. I clung to her for as long as she would have me, and longer still. Lord, I needed it.

33

Aftermath

"Lugnut?" I didn't look in his direction once we'd separated again. I didn't really want to know for sure. Not knowing he were dead or alive provided a small comfort.

"Probably," Ingy said. Her voice sounded cold, flat. As empty as I felt.

"It was my fault."

"Stop it," Ingy said.

I tried to see her through eyes filled with tears. "I can't stop. Everything that happened here is because I wasn't good enough. I wasn't ready."

I could see her own eyes were red, on the verge of her own tears, but she held them back through the sheer force of her will. "You didn't kill them, she did. Every dead body is a paragraph in her story, this whole mess the final chapter in her book. She's the criminal. You're the detective. We solved the case, found the treasure, and stopped the criminals. We did that, not Ben Templeton. You've been ready for a long time, Mira. We all have. He knew it." *I love you* lay unspoken, unsaid, hidden beneath the words.

I shook my head, and Ingy took my face in her hands, stopping me. She stared at me for what seemed like an eternity, her eyes boring into mine, opening herself to me. Her love washed over me and I gasped with the force of it, the way all trouble and pain melted from me under its spell. Then she kissed me, hard and deep and fierce. The world stopped. Everything paused to take a breath. Heat flushed my cheeks as pleasure flowed through me. I savored the taste of her warm lips against mine.

"Finally," Ingrid said when she pulled away. "I've wanted that too long. We're not going to leave you, you know. Not everyone is going to abandon you. Trust us enough to not leave us." She hugged me again, wrapping her arms around me tightly until the perfection of the moment drained away. Only then did she release the pressure and shift away slightly, as though embarrassed at her outpouring of emotions. "You're ready for anything."

"You think so?" I asked. The flush of her need and love lingered on me, pushing my doubt far away. A reflexive question, nothing more. The training of Catholic guilt is hard to overcome.

"Yes. You don't think Ben Templeton watched people die in his lifetime? You don't realize he thought he wasn't good enough either? Everyone is wracked with worry all the time, guilt. We were both raised Catholic, so we maybe more than most even. But we keep going on. He held you back because he knew death is inescapable and he didn't want you facing the pain of it like he did, just like you tried to shield Lugnut and me from it. He knew you were ready. He wasn't ready to let you go."

His words, spoken by another I loved. "I miss you."

Ingy turned away. I caught the flash of a smile. "I miss you, too. I'm going to go check on Lugs."

Sorry, Jacob said. *I couldn't stop Hiems.*

I sent him a mental kiss on the forehead. "You did swell, Jacob. You slowed her down and bought us a little more time to stop her."

Ingrid yelled over to me, "He's alive." She turned back to the limp body in front of her. "Lugnut? Come on, wake up, wake up." She shook his shoulder, and he stirred, but didn't speak. Ingrid tugged the hem of her dress until she tore off a long, ragged strip of cloth. She grabbed small pieces of shattered pallets from around them and wrapped the cloth around his leg above the wound, tying it tightly to the sticks, and then twisted them to tighten it further. He gave a moan of pain, but never spoke.

"Help will be here soon," Ingrid said. As if to confirm her comment, sirens sounded in the far distance. She gave me a brief nod. "I called that officer, Bronchowski, you said was a friend of Templeton's before we rushed here."

I remembered holding Ben as he slipped away in my arms, the sirens sounding distant like they did now. So much pain and misery brought on by so few. I turned my thoughts to Gaunt. Thoughts of bringing him to justice brought me back to the present, rooted me in the now, the living. This couldn't all be put on Hiems. She'd done the wrong things, but for the right reasons. Gaunt did the wrong things for the worst of reasons. She wanted to save the world, free it from bigotry, she just didn't know the right way.

Neither did I. But I could at least stop Gaunt.

Flashing lights swept up to the curb and spilled garish gleams into the old brewery. People swarmed the building and we had no more time for thinking or crying or grieving, no time for reflecting on what remained undone and unfinished. Only time to answer questions and try to direct the doctors so they could save the life of a friend.

***

Two hours later, I sat on the back bumper of an ambulance, bandaged from head to toe. I felt tired, a bone-weary sensation where every muscle ached and my brain had trouble cogitating the correct responses to simple questions, like *where do you live*, and *how many fingers am I holding up*. Bronchowski, who'd been the first to arrive, sat next to me.

I was glad it had been him and not some other cop. The officers were livid. For a few tense minutes, I thought we were heading towards a public hanging without courtesy of a trial. A troll, a black woman, an injured white woman, *and* a dead body? It did *not* sit well with the bigots who made up the bulk of Baltimore's men in blue. Their hostile faces and clenched fists told me in one brief glance we were on a precipice. But Bronchowski got the worst assholes to go outside to direct traffic and keep away the gadflies. The ones he trusted most stayed to gather evidence and take statements. Crisis averted; the tension slowly drained from the scene.

He took mine personally, scribbling furiously in his notepad. "One more time, please."

I sighed and tried not to glare at him as he held his chewed up pencil poised over his notepad. The conversation had already gone on for well over an hour, and he seemed incredulous. Lugnut had been carted away in an ambulance and Ingrid had gone with him, along with two officers Bronchowski personally assigned. As much for their own safety, I thought, as to keep an eye on the potential suspects. Petunia had followed them in her car, though not before delivering my smokes to me and hugging me for a very long time. That left me the unenviable task of cleaning up the mess left behind, and a dead body to explain.

I ran through the sequence of events again, consciously slowing myself so I could keep the details consistent. I didn't tell him everything, not by a Baltimore mile, which felt considerably longer these days. I left off little things, like breaking into a diplomat's office and cracking his safe. Nothing changed the overall narrative, although I suspected he suspected I held back. He gave me that, like he had before. Good man.

"And this woman is?"

"Her name is Hiems. She's one of the witches I met in Maine. I guess she was working for the elvish diplomat, but I don't know much else." That wasn't entirely true either. I could have added, *and one of the coven of the seasons, a seventh daughter of a seventh daughter, and she found a worthy goal, and then couldn't find a way to make it a reality without losing a part of herself. Something I'm beginning to understand all too well.* "I'd heard there might be something going on at the brewery involving her, so we came to snoop around. Then the shooting began."

Bronchowski face pinched with worry. "Can you prove the ambassador was involved with the illegal weapons?"

I reached into the pocket of my dress and pulled out the folded papers. "It's all detailed here, his contracts with them, and with her. If you have your staff witch review them, he'll confirm they are magically binding and entirely genuine. They should match the documents Mr. Templeton found at the warehouse."

He took them from me and slid them into a large envelope he'd brought for evidence. "And somehow you managed to walk away from all this unharmed."

I tried to chuckle, but it turned into a cough. "Hardly. My ankle is a mess, my hand looks like I played with a porcupine, and my head has been rung so many times I'm beginning to feel like church bells live in my brain. Assorted cuts, scrapes, bruises, a gunshot wound that's still healing. Not to mention a dead boss, who was a good man and deserved better. I'm far from undamaged goods, officer. I don't suppose you have some aspirin?"

He smiled sadly. "He was a good man. Best I've known. Wait here; I'll go see if I can find some for you."

He walked through the throng of cops and officials in their

snazzy suits and fedoras, leaving me alone with my thoughts. I pulled out my pack of smokes, lit up a cigarette and took a deep drag. A scrap of newspaper drifted by on the breeze. I reached for it and scanned the headline. Yesterday's news.

Bronchowski arched his eyebrows when he returned and nodded at the paper. "Anything interesting?"

"Just making sure I'm not dead."

He seemed confused, but tossed me a bottle of aspirin. I opened it, tipped two into the palm of my hand, then jammed them into my mouth. I ground them up with my teeth.

"Don't you want some water with those?"

"No, better this way. Gives my teeth something to do besides yell at me they haven't been brushed in a month of Sundays."

He took the notebook off the bumper where he had left it and scanned his writing. "Alright, well, that's probably enough for now. Can you come down to the station day after tomorrow to talk about this some more? I'll give you a day to rest up. Some of this stuff . . ." His voice trailed off. "Well, chief's not going to be too happy about it. You'd be doing me a favor. We can talk about the agency, too. Since you plan to keep it going, you're going to need a license. I can help with that."

"Alright. But you're buying me lunch. I never get interrogated on an empty stomach." Right now, I doubted I'd ever feel like eating again. Too many pains, mental and physical, to feel hungry.

"You're on. Meet me at Lucille's at noon. Over in Little Italy?"

"I know the place."

He stood and paused in front of me. "It's all going to be fine, Mira. I'll see you soon. We'll finish getting this straightened out."

"Fine, right, sure," I said as he walked away. Then the doctors came, two men even younger than me, interns assigned to ambulance duty. The helped me into a stretcher, and they took me off to the hospital to get patched up with my friends.

***

I found Ingrid sitting on a bench in the waiting area, her eyes closed, when they released me. They'd wanted to keep me overnight, but I'd declined, rather forcefully. She propped one eyelid open when I approached and then closed it again.

"He'll live," she said.

"Thank God."

"You can thank God, but I won't. He might lose his leg. If she'd shot him anyplace vital, he'd be dead now. And if Bronchowski hadn't interceded, they wouldn't have brought him to the hospital at all. They would have stuffed him into a prison cell until he bled out, the bastards."

"He shouldn't have been shot," I said. "That's on me."

Ingy grunted and sat up straighter. "Sit down for a minute." When I had, she took my hand in hers. "We offered to help you. You tried to refuse and we forced you to include us. If you hadn't, you might not have pulled this off, and I would have lost you. So, don't blame yourself, Mira, when we all got what we deserved."

I toyed with the arm of the chair, not replying. The phrase *I would have lost you* kept replaying in my thoughts. It felt good to be wanted. To have a place in someone's heart. Ingy wouldn't stop staring at me, though, so I nodded. "Alright, fair enough. But we can't keep ending up in hospitals. I can't keep remembering . . ." The words trailed off as I struggled to put my thoughts into language. "Ingy, how do I do it?"

"Do what?"

"How do I get over pain and grief, all the shit life wants to bury me in? One case, and I'm already broken."

Ingrid stared at me for a long time before she spoke. She chewed on her thoughts for a while as though surprised by the question. "You don't. You carry it with you, always. Some things in life you aren't meant to get over. Some things you learn to live with. They're like a rock tied around your neck, but you get used to them. Sometimes carrying all that weight makes you stronger. Sometimes it breaks you. You need to trust you have others in your life who'll be there for you when you crack. And you be there for them."

We sat in silence while the hands of the clock on the wall ticked past the seconds. I didn't want to believe what she said, but deep down I knew she was right. I'd done the best I could, and the whole case had teetered on failure numerous times, but we succeeded. I got what I wanted—some of it at least—and had to learn to live with the outcome. I nodded. "Okay."

She glanced around, saw we were alone, leaned in and kissed me. Briefly this time, barely north of chaste. Still, it sent delicious shivers through me, although I felt guilty I could enjoy anything right now. "Good," she said.

"Shit," I said.

"What?"

"I destroyed the goose. Hiems was the bag man, and she's dead. I used most of the down payment for the Undertow account. We won't get any more pay for this job."

"So, what? You're broke again?"

I grinned. "Not entirely." I double checked no one was near, then pulled the egg out of the dress pocket and showed her.

"Holy hell, is that—"

"—Not so loud."

"Is it?" She covered the egg with her hand, glancing around wildly.

"Damn straight. I think we'll come out ahead. We can at least pay off some bills."

"And pay off your contract witch, too."

I kissed her. "Damn straight."

"Thank you."

"For what? Helping you get your ass kicked by some bitch of a witch?"

"No." She gnawed her lip as though not sure if she should say anything else. After a long pause, she continued. "For being my," she began, and paused again. "Friend. I'm not easy to get along with."

I shrugged. "Cacti are less prickly than you."

"Naturally."

"Will you move back in?" My heart ached to hear her say yes.

Ingy looked away and shook her head. "It's better if I don't, not yet. Neither of us are in the right frame of mind. Too many emotional hits the past week. Not a good place to start a relationship. But eventually I might. Give it some time, this is new to me. Okay?"

"Love?" I asked very quietly, feeling a shiver pass through me.

She nodded and leaned closer, pressing her shoulder against mine, and that felt like enough for now. A promise perhaps of a future where she did move in with me again. A hope for something more than uncomfortable and awkward moments like these.

We sat in silence for a while until it grew too quiet, and then began planning.

"So, should we get new letterhead for the Sinclair and Wolgraf agency?" I asked.

"Why don't you leave it as the Templeton Agency? When your customers ask, tell them you're his adopted daughter."

"Brilliant."

"Shiny."

"Golden."

"Eggs."

"Goose."

"Explode."

"Death."

Ingy grinned. "You win. I'm going back in; you can visit him when I'm done." She walked down the hall and left me sitting in the waiting room. Thinking about the agency kept my mind from thinking about all the other things too painful to think about.

34

December's Goodbye

We drove in silence to Grubby's diner, me at the wheel, Ingy riding shotgun, Petunia and Melvin in back. All of us quiet as the city rolled by. No one seemed inclined to break the mood holding our tongues in check. We watched the scenery out the windows on as pretty a winter day as you could ask for. Some of the remaining leaves left on the trees were almost colorful, and a light snow had left everything sparkling. For one day, Baltimore put on its finery and joined us in celebrating one of its own. The best it ever produced.

The news had, at last, turned to fresh stories, though the affair with the gnomes, the weapons, and the Empyrean had dominated the papers for almost a month. Lucius had left to return north shortly after I disappeared from his office, leaving the mayor and other dignitaries outraged. When the papers carried the story of his involvement with the illegal weapons factory, they'd suddenly gotten very quiet about the whole affair. I wondered how many of them had been providing Lucius financial support for his little scheme, or tacitly encouraging it. By the time the F.B.M. and other agencies raided the embassy, it had been cleaned out. They had nothing to prove anyone else from Baltimore had been connected, so they got away from it, and the city began moving on. The Solstice and Christmas holidays were upon us, New Year's close behind. People wanted to forget their troubles, for at least a little while.

We'd done well enough with the egg, too. I'd sold it for almost half a grand. That paid off the rent on the office for the next year, the dress I'd ruined, repairs to the car, and some other incidentals including Ingy's bill, which she'd handed to me with a smile. We had money in the bank, which might have been a first for the Templeton agency.

Grubby had gotten here before us and peered around the edge of the front door as we parked in front of the diner. His run-down diner wasn't far from the cemetery where Ben was buried. The dirt parking lot was empty but for a dented old pickup parked beside the building, which Grubby had bought to replace the wagon and horses he'd used to pick up his supplies. Its silver sides reflected the sunlight, but were in need of a good polish in places. The windows hadn't been cleaned in years. He'd had two signs painted special for his place. The big one on the roof said *Grubby's* in a stylized swirling script. Over the entry, a smaller sign proclaimed "Baltimore's Best Chicken Steak" in bold red letters, in between two crude drawings. The one on the left represented a chicken, though a rather scrawny, ill-bred fellow with yellow eyes. On the right, a steak with arms and legs and a leering face in no way would entice a patron into purchasing said item from the menu. It could, however, induce nightmares of what might happen when your dinner rises and strikes back at you for attempted steak slaughter.

Ben had loved this place.

"Come on in and warmup," Grubby muttered, holding the door open for us. When we were inside, he locked it, turning the sign around to show the place was closed. "Just us today. Don't need anyone else bothering us."

"It was kind of you to give us the place for the afternoon, Grubby," I said.

We'd all decided, and Grubby had immediately said yes when I called. We'd missed the wake after Ben's funeral because we'd been so focused on the case. Now we wanted to remember the man who, in many ways, had brought us all together. Inspired us. Died trying to protect us and the city he loved. Maybe I was finally ready to grieve for him. Say goodbye at least. It certainly felt different than his funeral, when all I'd been was hollow, an emptiness to be filled with anger and vengeance. We needed a clean start. Maybe this would be it.

"Anything for Ben," he replied, and waved us over to one of the booths, upon which he had spread a clean white tablecloth and had placed a couple of candles in brass holders. "Good man. Good cop. Kept sending people here even as times got tough. I'd probably never have stayed open this long if not for him, not with the way the economy has been. One man billboard."

He trundled off to the kitchen. When he opened the door, we caught a whiff of food. He soon returned with a rolling cart laden by several large platters, each with a lid he proudly removed. He had a roast turkey, complete with stuffing, sweet potatoes, corn on the cob and cranberry sauce. The jellied kind from a can, not the real stuff, which pleased me. On a lower shelf of the cart there were several bottles of sparkling cider along with glasses. He served up a plate to each of us, and filled our glasses. My stomach gave a rumble. It felt like months since I'd eaten a big meal. Perhaps today I could stomach more than a few bites.

"To Ben Templeton," Grubby said, lifting his glass.

"Here, here," we all said.

"And Lugnut," added Ingy.

"Lucky," replied Petunia.

"Jacob," I chimed in. I felt Jacob's amused appreciation of the irony of toasting him along with the other injured and deceased.

Melvin looked around. "I'm sorry, should I name someone? Ah, to, Edgar Allen Poe, who passed away too young. May the ravens not, you know . . . eat your face."

After a silent pause pregnant with wide stares and open mouths, everyone laughed. Melvin's face turned pinkish, but then he smiled and joined the laughter. We drank our toasts and tucked into the food. I ate with passion, as though it were my last meal. Certainly, my first big meal in some time, and I fed the need, not standing on delicate ceremony. I tucked a napkin into the front of my dress and heaped food onto my plate. Ingy and Melvin followed suit, and Grubby smiled in pleasure. Petunia took smaller portions, but clearly enjoyed the repast as much as the rest of us, cleaning her plate off carefully. Twice.

When everyone sat back contentedly, Grubby whisked the plates away to the kitchen and returned with a tall, dark bottle. "Best booze I got. Two hunnert year old scotch from the family distillery in Scotland." He poured a finger measure in a stack of shot glasses he carried in his other hand. Then we each took a glass and tossed back the shot. The liquor flowed smooth down my throat, leaving only a slight after burn. I waited for the bad taste and heartburn, the cough and watery eyes, the usual results I'd get when Ben had offered me a shot. When it didn't come, I squinted at the bottle.

"Ben always bought the cheap stuff," I said.

"You going to buy the good stuff?" asked Ingy.

"If we ever get any work. I think most folks came for Ben Templeton."

Ingrid nodded at me, her face serious. "People will come for you. The way your name got plastered all over the papers for busting up

Gaunt's weapons factory? Former police officer and private detective, Mirabel Sinclair. They'll come."

"They should have included your names as well," I said. "I kept telling the reporter."

"Like they'd any give credit to a black woman or a troll," she said. "But they gave credit to you, a woman. Small miracle, but it's a start. Trust me, they're going to start wanting my name in their papers soon enough. I'll damn well make sure of it."

Petunia nodded. "Mr. Templeton would be very proud if you girls kept the agency going. He always said you'd replace him one day."

I hesitated before speaking. I didn't deserve these people in my life, or their respect. Their love. I hoped they understood what I'd be asking of them, because I certainly did. It wouldn't be pretty. It would sometimes be dangerous. Our lives would be at risk. But they wouldn't have come here if they didn't. They wouldn't be encouraging me to continue and asking to be a part. I had to trust they knew what they were doing.

I did trust them. Loved them. Believed in my heart they wanted me in their lives. "I'll need all your help, if you're willing. Someone has got to keep me out of trouble."

"I can manage the office," Petunia said, "and hide the booze from you."

"I know a lot about Baltimore history, so could help out in my free time," Melvin added, his voice trailing off at the end. "I know a few folks at city hall, too. Might prove useful."

Everyone needs a ghost on their side, Jacob said.

"You've got me if you've got the moola," Ingy said. "Witch consulting don't come cheap, and mama needs a new pair of boots."

"Alright, you've all got jobs. Or contracts," I added, glancing at Ingy with a smile. "Anyone want to drive out to Towsontown and roust Lugnut for a while? He's getting around better on those crutches now, we can try and cheer him up."

"A one-legged troll, how droll," Ingrid said. "Sounds like fun."

"'Tomorrow is," I began, then glanced around hoping Grubby had a calendar. "Shit, what day is it?"

"Thursday," Grubby said as he cleaned up the remains of the meal.

"Everyone take the rest of the week off. We'll start work on Monday."

We helped Grubby clean up. Least we could do for his spectacular meal. Then I led them out into the cold December air. January was right around the corner. The shadow of the cathedral cast itself across the road to the north, made long by the low winter sun. It beckoned.

I touched Ingy's hand and nodded at the cemetery. Then I gave her my keys. "Go on, warm the car up. I'll be right back."

She glanced towards the towers of Saint Brendan's and she once more climbed into my thoughts as she seemed to do. "You need company?"

I squeezed her hand and released it. "Not this time. This is something I should do on my own. I won't be long. But thanks for offering."

"Anytime, Sinclair." She grinned that crooked, beautiful grin before piling into the car.

I walked up the street, pulling my coat around myself to fight back the wintry chill, and headed for the cemetery to say a proper goodbye to Benjamin Francis Templeton, who was like a father to me.

END

Acknowledgements

Any book is the sum of more than a single writer's efforts, despite what you may have heard. Even those who self-publish. There are the people closest to us who provide emotional support, the beta readers who endure our terrible early drafts and help us improve the narrative, and those who help us construct the final product.

First, my wife Jennifer. Not only did she read the first version of what would become *Shadow of a Doubt*, but she read a ton of my other writing as well, much of it of dubious quality. Without her encouragement, love, and support, I wouldn't be the writer I'd dreamed of being since I wrote my first story at eight years old. Thank you for everything, my darling otter. I love you enough to have married you twice, and twice more if you'll have me. Qa 'pla!

To Jules, Sydney, and all the many other beta readers who helped guide me, thank you for your advice, your comments, your ability to help me see the flaws and improve the work. Critiques are a hard process to go through, but that's true for many authors. I'm glad I've been able to lean on you for my critiques, and count you among my friends.

To Kaetlyn Considine, Kisa Whipkey, and Maria Tureaud, thank you for the editing advice you each provided. Each of you brought something new to the table as I struggled to decide if I wanted to keep querying the novel or go the self-publishing route. Thanks as well to John Adamus for his marketing advice, and especially the night so long ago when he helped me take my original crappy query and make it something glorious. It didn't attract an agent, John, but it's light years better and I use it as my blurb.

To my Viable Paradise classmates, the instructors, and alumni, who have kept me sane and writing the past four years. Your encouragement and support were everything I needed to take my efforts to the next level and make writing more than a dream. Your stories inspire me as well. I will never forget what you returned to me: the belief that I am and always will be a writer.

Thank you as well to James at Bookfly Covers for his work on the stellar cover. It went above and beyond what I expected. It's wonderful to watch other artistic professionals take a vague idea and come up with something entirely relevant and beautiful. Making the title look a little like the famous Domino Sugar sign that graces Baltimore's Inner harbor was genius.

And last but far from least, thank you to SFWA for all you do to support creatives and their work, even those who are self-publishing, and particularly POC and other marginalized communities of writers. I'm proud to be a member and love that those of us creating speculative fiction have such a strong, empathetic advocate for our careers.

This book was always meant as a one-off. I'm aware I left more dangling plot threads than there are fish in the sea. There's a possibility I may return to Mira's world to tell more stories. Nine years is a long time to have your head in a particular novel, and there's so much more I want to write. But, it's a world I wouldn't mind visiting from time to time. If you feel the same way, let me know.

About the Author

Jeff Reynolds is an author from Maryland who works for Johns Hopkins University Applied Physics Lab, home of New Horizons, Parker Solar Probe, and the Dragonfly mission to explore Titan. He's only a software licensing analyst, though, and doesn't do any of the cool stuff, like building space probes or meeting Brian Mays.

Besides graduating from Viable Paradise writers' workshop as well as the Stonecoast writers' conference, Jeff holds a Bachelor of Science degree in Simulation and Digital Entertainment from the University of Baltimore. This makes him one of the 29% of graduates who do not actually use their degree for work, although it did make him a fabulous panelist on Video Game Nostalgia during Worldcon 2019.

Jeff lives with his amazing wife, Jennifer, and a dog named Cooper, who did the voice over for Doug in the Pixar movie UP (at least in the human's heads) and who worships at the altar of Ball. All cats living in the household shall remain nameless, because calling on them opens a gateway to purr-gatory.

His short stories have appeared in a variety of venues, including: Clarkesworld, Escape Pod, Daily Science Fiction, Apparition Literary Magazine, and Andromeda Spaceways Magazine, most of which you can access for the low price of free. In addition, his story, *Fishing Over the Bones of the Dragon*, is included as part of the excellent Common Bonds Anthology of Aromantic Speculative Fiction, which you can pick up at the usual suspects.

He plans to grow up to be a librarian. All the coolest people are librarians.

You can learn more about Jeff or leave a comment by visiting his website:

https://www.trollbreath.com
or
https://www.jefferyreynolds.com

www.ingramcontent.com/pod-product-compliance
Lightning Source LLC
Chambersburg PA
CBHW072048190726
48294CB00005B/1459